Also by Allan Mallinson

**A CLOSE RUN THING
THE NIZAM'S DAUGHTERS*
A REGIMENTAL AFFAIR
A CALL TO ARMS
THE SABRE'S EDGE
RUMOURS OF WAR
COMPANY OF SPEARS**

*Published outside the UK under the title HONORABLE COMPANY

AN ACT OF COURAGE

ALLAN MALLINSON

BANTAM BOOKS

LONDON • TORONTO • SYDNEY • AUCKLAND • JOHANNESBURG

AN ACT OF COURAGE
A BANTAM BOOK : 0553817884
9780553817881

Originally published in Great Britain by Bantam Press,
a division of Transworld Publishers

PRINTING HISTORY
Bantam Press edition published 2005
Bantam edition published 2006

1 3 5 7 9 10 8 6 4 2

Set in Times New Roman
by Falcon Oast Graphic Art Ltd

Bantam Books are published by Transworld Publishers,
61–63 Uxbridge Road, London W5 5SA,
a division of The Random House Group Ltd,
in Australia by Random House Australia (Pty) Ltd,
20 Alfred Street, Milsons Point, Sydney, NSW 2061, Australia,
in New Zealand by Random House New Zealand Ltd,
18 Poland Road, Glenfield, Auckland 10, New Zealand
and in South Africa by Random House (Pty) Ltd,
Isle of Houghton, Corner of Boundary Road & Carse O'Gowrie,
Houghton 2198, South Africa.

Printed and bound in Great Britain by
Cox & Wyman Ltd, Reading, Berkshire.

Papers used by Transworld Publishers are natural, recyclable products
made from wood grown in sustainable forests. The manufacturing processes
conform to the environmental regulations of the country of origin.

To
Duggie
Lieutenant-Colonel C. R. D. Gray
Skinner's Horse
1909–2004
The Ultimate Cavalryman

The Siege of Badajos. Reproduction of contemporary map.

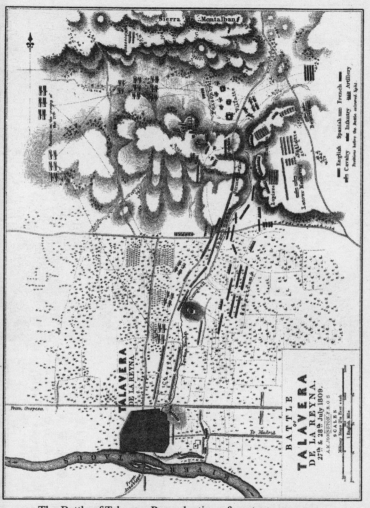

The Battle of Talavera. Reproduction of contemporary map.

FOREWORD

The cuts in the British infantry announced last year will change the face of soldiering for ever. Regiments whose names the Duke of Wellington would have seen each day in the 'morning states' during the long years of the Peninsular War and Waterloo will disappear – the Royal Scots, Green Howards, Cheshires, Royal Welch Fusiliers, Black Watch, to name but a few. No longer will a man – commissioned or enlisted – join a tight-knit band of six hundred brothers, his county regiment, and stay with them throughout his service as they move as a body from post to post. Instead an infantryman will go from one battalion to another within a large 'regional' unit – what is known as 'trickle posting'. It is, of course, a judgement as to what effect these cuts will have – how continuing commitments and new contingencies will be met by fewer battalions – and what effect the enormous change in regimental organization will have on recruiting, retention and cohesion, the three areas in which the county regiments have been so strong. However, from the long perspective of military history – which is the perspective of my tales – it appears there is but one unvarying lesson of war: there is never enough infantry. Vide Iraq.

This, I believe, is the first *lesson* of war because the man himself is the first *weapon* of war – all too easily forgotten in an age of beguiling and expensive technology. The man and the regiment are inextricably linked: trust and cohesion in battle come from soldiers living and training together, long term, and acquiring a sense that they are part of something bigger than just the collection of individuals who answer the roll call on a particular day. It was never planned thus. Ironically, the regimental system, which the historian Sir John Keegan has called 'an accidental act of genius', grew out of the eighteenth century's penny-pinching arrangements for raising more troops.

In the period of which I write, the danger in not keeping infantrymen together in the battalions in which they train is well illustrated by a letter from one of the Duke of Wellington's generals after the Battle of Talavera (where, in *An Act of Courage*, we shall find Matthew Hervey in the thick of things once more). Complaining of the poor performance of a 'detachment battalion', one in which the men were cobbled together from half a dozen different regiments, the general observes, 'They have no *esprit de corps* for their interior economy among them, though they will fight. They are careless of all else, and the officers do not look to their temporary field-officers and superiors under whom they are placed, as in an established regiment. I see much of their indiscipline.'

So the new 'mobility' of infantrymen, as they change from one battalion to another, was not unknown in Wellington's day. In Wellington's army, too, the *officers* – both infantry and cavalry – would often move from one regiment to another as vacancies occurred, since that was what promotion by purchase required. The duke himself served in half a dozen regiments on his way to becoming lieutenant-colonel of the 33rd Foot, which was renamed The Duke of Wellington's Regiment in his honour (and which is now also to be disbanded).

However, an examination of the annual Army Lists during the years of the Peninsular War (1808–1814), which record the name and seniority of every officer, shows a high degree of stability. Fortunately for the cohesion of the fighting battalions, officers seemed happy enough to stay with their regiments, accepting that promotion would be slow or might not come at all. Perhaps this was because many officers had little real appetite for promotion: there was, after all, no great financial advantage to it (indeed, it usually required capital outlay). Perhaps they did not see the army as a 'career', and therefore did not have a strong commitment to the profession of arms, content instead to be in agreeable, gentlemanlike company, doing their bit to defeat Bonaparte until their share of the family fortune permitted them to retire to an equally agreeable sporting life as a country gentleman. As a rule they brought neither great intellect nor address to the regiment. But they did bring absolute physical courage. As many an old soldier would say later, 'The NCOs showed us how to fight, and the officers how to die.'

There were, of course, exceptions to the 'brave amateur' rule. There were aristocrats who regarded generalship as a natural extension of their rank in life, and who applied themselves to it as diligently and effectively as they would to any undertaking touching on their fortune and honour. The Duke of Wellington is the pre-eminent exemplar. There were others of humbler birth driven – as today – by some intense professional instinct or hunger for promotion. Without money or influence, theirs was a precarious and frequently disappointing quest, especially during the long period of retrenchment after the Napoleonic Wars. Matthew Hervey is one such man, and in this latest volume we see him struggling with his ghosts and the desire for advancement – and also with the consequences of being an ambitious, capable, but relatively junior officer in a rapidly atrophying organization.

One may speculate on what might have become of Hervey, and others like him, had not Bonaparte occasioned the expansion of His Majesty's land forces and the Royal Navy in the first place. The young Master Hervey was in the classical remove at Shrewsbury when His Majesty's government saw the opportunity to carry the war to the French on the Continent instead of just at sea and in the colonies. He would otherwise perhaps have followed his brother to Oxford (where their father had been), and taken Holy Orders as they had. Would he have enjoyed making sermons? Who knows: one of Hervey's contemporaries in the Peninsula, Ensign George Gleig, who left Oxford to join the 85th (Buckinghamshire Volunteers), was afterwards ordained and some years later became chaplain-general. But, to begin with at least, Hervey, like Gleig, was one of those of whom Dr Johnson wrote: 'Every man thinks meanly of himself for never having been to sea nor having been a soldier.'

And Hervey is nothing if not a thinking man – a thinking soldier. But he is also a son of the country parsonage, and alumnus of the old, if provincial, public school. His is a Tory view of history, and an instinctive Tory perspective of the future. Life does not leave him untouched, however; quite the opposite. Mine are tales of regimental soldiering, but the exposure of this moral, principled, if somewhat naïve, son of the minor English gentry to the reality of war, life and the march of time is the theme of this series.

All my arrangements preparatory to the attack on Badajoz are in train, and I believe are getting on well; some of the troops have marched for the Alentejo, and others will follow soon; and I intend to go myself the last, as I know that my removal from one part of the country to the other will be the signal for the enemy that the part to which I am going is to be the scene of active operations ... Pray let us have plenty of horses for cavalry and artillery, and the reinforcements for our infantry, as early as you can. If we should succeed at Badajoz, I propose to push our success early in the year as far as I can.

Viscount Wellington of Talavera
to the Prime Minister,
19 February 1812

CHAPTER ONE

HONOURED IN THE BREACH

Badajoz, 10 p.m., 6 April 1812

'*Tout va bien!*'

The forlorn hope, clambering in pitch darkness over fallen masonry in the dry ditch, could hear the sentries calling to each other on the walls above.

Then a shot rang out.

'*Alarme! Alarme!*'

A single shot: the game was up. Some movement had betrayed them, perhaps, or the clank of a scabbard – and an alert sentry.

'*Aux armes!*'

The storming party had known it would come, but a few minutes more and they could have gained the top of the rubble.

A blazing carcass arched over the ramparts, lighting up the breach as if full moon – seconds only, but enough to give the French their mark. They opened a furious musketry. Artillery soon followed. Lead and grape cut down the struggling infantry before a man could reach the razor-sharp blades of the *chevaux de frise*, which the defenders had dragged to the rupture when the siege guns ceased firing at last light.

Cornet Matthew Hervey, standing dismounted with the

17

rest of His Majesty's 6th Light Dragoons on the high ground half a mile east of the great border fortress of Badajoz, took a firmer hold on Jessye's reins. It had been four years to the day since he had taken an outside seat on the *Red Rover* for the Sixth's depot at Canterbury. Two weeks before that, he had sat in the upper remove of Shrewsbury School, the master still hopeful that Hervey would follow his brother to Oxford and thence take Holy Orders, as their father before them. But the army had claimed him. It had from his earliest days; above all, the cavalry. In large measure it was Daniel Coates's doing, 'the shepherd of Salisbury Plain', sometime trumpeter to General Tarleton and adopted master-at-arms and rough-rider to the younger son of the Horningsham parsonage. Thus armed with a cradle-knowledge of his 'profession', the seventeen-year-old Cornet Hervey had sailed with the Sixth to Portugal in the summer of 1808 – only to limp home with them via Corunna six months later.

What a learning that had been. When the Sixth went back to Portugal, but three months after Corunna, he felt himself the complete troop-officer. He feared nothing, not the enemy, nor the Sixth's own dragoons, nor his own fitness for the rank. And the three years of advance and withdrawal which had followed – offensive and defensive, siege and counter-siege – had confirmed him in his own estimation. He had remained a cornet, however, for although there had been deaths among the lieutenants, the consequent free promotions had not reached down as far as him (and he could not afford to buy his promotion in another regiment even if he had wanted to). They no longer sported in the mess with the old toast, 'To a short war, and a bloody one!'

There would be bloody war tonight; that was certain. He had seen sieges enough in those three years to know that this one at Badajoz would be a sight harder than the others. He knew how strong were the defences. Badajoz was the guardian of the road to Madrid; when it had been in allied hands it had been a sure guardian of the road to Lisbon. Three summers ago, the Sixth, with the rest of Sir Arthur Wellesley's army, had marched into Badajoz after the bruising victory at Talavera, and there they had stayed a full three months. And then, forced to abandon the fortress because the Spanish could not, or would not, support them, they had crossed into Portugal. A year of covering had followed, like the wary boxer: Lord Wellington, as by this time Sir Arthur Wellesley had become, could do little more than land the occasional blow – but stinging blows, so that the French began to weaken. However, like the wounded pug fighting on with all the instinct of years at the booth, it was a *slow* weakening, and never so certain that Wellington dare drop his guard or over-reach himself. So that, eventually, every man in the army knew there would be no knockout blow, just a fight until the French at last quit the country, and while the other allies forced the same on France's eastern borders.

But this siege was not their first attempt to dislodge the French from the great guardian of the Madrid high road: twice, the year before, Badajoz had held out against Wellington's men. And in the depths of a freezing January just past, Ciudad Rodrigo, a fortress almost as strong, had claimed a thousand dead and wounded before the Union flag was hoisted above its castle. No, Badajoz would not fall tonight without a heavy butcher's bill. The Sixth would not pay, of course. There was no job for the cavalry on a night like this. Tonight it was an affair of the bayonet.

Hervey knew what the men with the bayonets were saying, too: if the defenders of Ciudad Rodrigo had been put to the sword, in the old way, the French here at Badajoz would not be resisting, for Wellington's engineers and gunners had made a practicable breach. The mood in the ranks of red was not in favour of quarter; certainly not if the French continued to put up a fight. Those were the 'rules of war'.

But above all Hervey feared for the Spanish, the civil

population of the city. He did not suppose the people of Badajoz were any more or less disposed to the French than they were elsewhere. True, they had had the French in their town for a year and more, but that did not make them *afrancesado*. Yet somehow that was what the men with the bayonets thought.

He started. A great fiery flash lit the Trinidad bastion, and a second later came a terrible roar. Jessye squealed. Hervey put his left hand to her muzzle and shortened the reins as he peered at the distant fortress walls. There was smoke now to mix with the mist coming off the Guadiana river. He shivered. Poor infantry: there was no glory in this. Weeks of sodden cold in the trenches, then consigned to oblivion in the dark of the night. Some of them would get through the breach, perhaps, if fortune favoured them and their blood boiled hot enough. And then what?

'Poor bastards, sir!'

'Yes, Serjeant Armstrong. Poor bastards.'

At that range, in the pitch darkness, they did not actually see the limbs and the guts scattered like ash from a volcano for a hundred yards about the breach, but they knew well enough what a mine did. The defenders had lost no time, evidently, counter-tunnelling under the breach.

'By God, sir, them French is putting up a fight and a half,' said Armstrong, shaking his head in disbelief. 'I wish I were down there!'

That one mine might mean another was of no consequence to either of them.

'So do I, Serjeant Armstrong; so do I.'

The whole front was now musketry. Hervey had no idea what were the plans for the assault – how many breaches or escalades, or where – but he had watched the assaulting divisions assembling late that afternoon: four of them, no small affair. If they all succeeded in breaking into the fortress there would be a desperate fight inside unless the French struck their colours at once. He did not see how the defenders could make any sortie now, with so many troops at the walls, yet that was why the Sixth and the other regiments of cavalry were here. Only three weeks ago the French had poured out and driven off the working parties in the parallels below where they stood now. Humiliating it had been. They had filled in the trenches and carried off the picks and shovels (the French commander had offered a bounty for every entrenching tool). But there was no chance of that tonight; not with musketry and cannonading so intense.

'Hot work for our friends, Hervey.' The voice was assured, the glow of the cigar familiar and comfortable.

'Indeed, Sir Edward. I was just thinking that our chances of action seem small.'

Serjeant Armstrong retired a respectful distance.

Captain Sir Edward Lankester lowered his voice but a fraction. 'You imagine the real reason we are posted thus, Hervey?'

'I imagine as we are ordered, Sir Edward. I cannot suppose our arms will be needed in the breaches.'

Sir Edward kept silent for a moment. 'What do you imagine will happen when the army is *through* the breaches?'

Hervey sighed: cruel necessity. 'I should not wish to be a Frenchman.'

'Ay. You cannot contest a practicable breach and then expect quarter. There'll be precious little of it. It was not that of which I was minded, though. What of the Spanish?'

Hervey grimaced. When Ciudad Rodrigo had fallen, it had been three hours and more before the officers got their men back in hand. The riot and destruction had been prodigious, just as the looting and despoiling on the retreat to Corunna – and a good many Spaniards abused along the way.

They stood silent the while, trying to make out the progress of the storming from the powder flashes, the rattle of small arms and the explosive roar of the field pieces. There seemed a deal too much of all three to suggest the breaches and escalades were being carried – not with the bayonet, at any rate. There *should* have been a great display of fireworks and then a full-throated roar as the storming parties went to it with cold steel – and a *feu de joie,* perhaps, as they took the place. But a fire-fight like this spelled trouble. It meant the infantry could not gain a footing on the walls. And they couldn't keep up an assault for ever: some time soon they would be exhausted, all forward momentum lost. Then the defenders would have carried the day, again – or, rather, the night.

That was how it had been the last time at Badajoz, and the first time too, by all accounts. Not that he had seen for himself any of it; only heard the course of things, and then what the survivors had told them in the dejected days that followed. A man did not like to have his friends cut down, but if the result was victory he could bear it. To be thrown off the walls of Badajoz *and* taunted by the French was not to be borne. The men with the bayonets were certain of one thing: the French could not have defied them if the Spaniards had not been helping them. A fortress standing against two assaults by Nosey's men – what else could be the explanation?

The walls of Jericho – that was what Cornet Hervey was minded of, detached from the bloody business of the breach. How had the walls of Jericho fallen to Joshua's trumpets? It was allegory, surely, as his brother suggested? In a thousand years they would speak of the walls of Badajoz falling to Lord Wellington's bugles (he fervently prayed). Had the Israelites undermined the walls of Jericho, as he supposed the engineers had here? And did Lord Wellington do at Badajoz as Joshua had at Jericho? Did he send spies into the city? Joshua's spies had found the Canaanites terrified of his army after its victories on the other side of the Jordan. A terrified people – perhaps the sound of the trumpets alone induced them to surrender? But Joshua's spies had nearly been captured; they would not have escaped without the help of Rahab. Was there a Rahab in Badajoz to harbour Lord Wellington's spies? Hervey smiled. Rahab the prostitute: there would be Rahabs aplenty in Badajoz, and they would take in men right enough *after* the place had fallen.

He shivered again. If there were prayers to be said for any tonight but the poor devils with bayonets, it should be that Badajoz did not meet the fate of Jericho: *And they utterly destroyed all that was in the city, both man and woman, young and old*. Except that Joshua saved Rahab the prostitute alive, and her father's household, and *all that she had*. Could he hope that Lord Wellington's orders would save the Rahabs in Badajoz when blood was running hot among his redcoats? Could he even hope that Wellington's orders would save the *Susannas*, for virtue had not always been sufficient protection against the heated blood of the best-regulated men in this campaign. Exactly as at Jericho.

Indeed he could hope, for after Badajoz there was Madrid to relieve, and the fortress at Burgos. Lord Wellington would brook no check to progress, unlike the Israelites after Jericho: the Lord God of Israel, angered with the looting of the city, had punished Joshua at the siege of Ai. Lord Wellington would not want such a punishment; Lord Wellington was an upright man, and he would waste not a day in his zeal to eject the French from Spain (word was that he had not spent a day but at his duty since coming to the Peninsula). He would not contemplate a defeat at Ai; there must be no riot in Badajoz, no regiments incapable through drink of continuing the advance. He had given strict orders to that effect. Who would dare defy them?

'By God, sir, they'll be hotted up after this!' said Serjeant Armstrong, a furious musketry now the length of the walls.

Hervey woke to the grim truth before them. 'Let's hope their blood's boiling this minute, Serjeant Armstrong, for those walls will not be theirs without it.'

Armstrong knew it better than most. He had been in the trenches that afternoon, volunteering for the working parties taking grenades forward. 'Never saw men writing their wills like that, sir,' he had told him afterwards. 'They were giving me letters and all sort o' things to send for 'em. But by hell they'll go to it tonight! Never seen men as hotted up. And them without a drop inside 'em yet!'

Hervey hoped for their sakes they had rum inside them now. It fired the belly and dulled the pain. 'It *is* the very devil to stand and watch. I don't think I ever had more feeling for a red coat.' But too many of Serjeant Armstrong's letters would be read by widows, or mothers bereft of a son, he reckoned. It was beginning to look as if the third attempt on Badajoz would go the same as the other two, for all the infantry's ardour.

Another mine exploded, a galleried one, big and deep, so that the earth trembled even where the Sixth stood.

'Jesus!' gasped a dragoon.

'As you were!' growled the serjeant-major.

He disapproved of profanities, especially in the face of the enemy. But in truth, he only silenced the cursing; he did not stop it. In the next hour there were a dozen more earth-shaking explosions, so that there could not have been a man in the Sixth who did not curse with his teeth clenched, thankful, deep down at least, to be standing-to his horse rather than in the breaches below them.

At eleven o'clock a galloper came, almost taking the videttes by surprise. 'Sixth Light Dragoons?'

'Ay, sir.'

'Lord George Irvine, please.'

Hervey heard the exchange well enough: the videttes were but fifty yards in front, and the galloper shouted (no doubt he was deafened if he came from the trenches).

'This way, sir.'

They peered to see who he was, for they might then have some idea what he brought.

'Here!' called the adjutant, as galloper and guide approached the line.

'Lord George?' called the galloper again as he slid from the saddle. If he was deafened by the explosions, he was equally blinded by the flashes.

'Yes, Pontefract, before you!' Lieutenant-Colonel Lord George Irvine had the advantage of an orderly with a torch.

Lieutenant the Earl of Pontefract threw his cloak back over his shoulders and saluted as another orderly took his reins. 'Good evening, Colonel. Sir Stapleton Cotton's compliments, and would you have one squadron dismount and come up to the trenches in support of General Picton's division at once.'

Hervey's ears pricked, as did everyone's that heard. The orders were precise, yet their purpose unclear. What kind of support did 'the Fighting Third' Division have want of?

'Sir Stapleton suggests you may stand down the remainder until dawn.'

That settled one thing at least, thought Hervey: Wellington must be sure there could be no sortie.

'Very well, Pontefract,' replied Lord George Irvine resolutely. 'Is there a guide?'

'I will take them to the rendezvous myself, Colonel.'

Lord George Irvine did not hesitate: unless there were good reason otherwise, First Squadron would do duty, its captain being the senior. 'Sir Edward?'

'Colonel!'

'One to three, then.'

'Very good, Colonel. Sar'nt-major?'

'Sir!'

'Squadron will dismount, every third man horse-holder.'

It was not a very practised drill. However, the ranks numbered off in threes at stand-to morning and evening, so there should be no untoward confusion now, even in the dark.

Private Jewitt, Hervey's groom, took Jessye's reins from him. 'Will you take my carbine, sir?'

'No, just my pistols I think, Jewitt.' Hervey had no more idea than the next man what their duties would be, but if they were going to scramble into a breach or attempt an escalade, he would be better unencumbered. It was the first time they had been called forward in a siege. He had to be ready for anything.

CHAPTER TWO
PRISONER OF WAR

Badajoz, 20 December 1826

Hervey pulled his cloak about his shoulders. It was more than the damp cold of his quarters – *prison* quarters – that troubled him. The remembrance of that night at Badajoz, though fifteen years gone, was enough to chill the blood of any Christian, let alone one now confined within the very walls they had breached that day. And if he could no longer hear the screams (at first of the men in the breaches, and then of the wretched Spanish civilians), he could picture the night well enough. The night *and* the days that followed. In everything he had seen since, even in India, nothing quite had the power to make him shiver, and boil, as did the name Badajoz.

But when he had passed through those walls on that infernal night, it had at least been his choosing. Or rather, he had followed orders willingly. This time he had done so anything but willingly. His *ruse de guerre* had almost come off, but when discovered, he had seen no alternative but to surrender his sword. Fearing the very worst, he had even contrived to set down the circumstances in writing – for the benefit of the one person to whom he felt true obligation to justify himself *post mortem*. It had not been easy, for that person had neither knowledge of the soldier's art nor of the world in general.

Badajoz,
Spain,
19th December 1826

My dearest Georgiana,

If by mischance I am not able to return to you ever, I must trust to this letter to give the fairest account of the circumstances, for it may not be expedient to those in authority to have the truth out at once, and perhaps for good reason since affairs of state are never straightforward.

I was sent to Portugal to assist with the making of plans in case a British army was sent here to the aid of the young princess who would be the new Queen (she is but your age) and her father Dom Pedro who wishes to abdicate in her favour and of the new 'Constitution', which is a covenant giving certain rights to the people which they had not previously enjoyed. You may read that some in England are opposed to such an intervention, for they believe that the young Queen's uncle, Dom Miguel, should be Regent, certain as they are that his principles of upholding the old order of things are in the best interests of the country. Those who would overthrow the Queen in favour of Dom Miguel have gathered about them officers in the army who with whole regiments now take up arms against the Queen, and in this they are assisted by Spain and, perhaps, by France.

When our little party began its work, at the beginning of the month, it was at once plain to me that our colonel was of too cautious a view, and I determined to go to the frontier with Spain. In this I was supported by His Majesty's envoy in Lisbon. Upon arriving in Elvas, a great fortress which stands only a few miles from the equally great Spanish fortress of Badajoz, across the Guadiana river, I learned that the Miguelite forces had made attacks into Portugal from Spain, where they had been given arms and provisions, and that an attack at Elvas was imminent. Although the fortress at Elvas is a great one, no fortress will stand if it does not have sufficient men to repel an attacker.

So it was that I found the defences at Elvas, with few men, although good, especially the general who is called Dom Mateo de Braganza. He and I devised a scheme which we supposed might trick the Miguelites into believing that English troops had already come to Portugal, for the Miguelites would not then have the nerves to continue their attack. However, by a stroke of misfortune, the ruse was discovered, and in circumstances which allowed but one means of escape for the loyal Portuguese, which was that I myself should surrender to the Miguelite commander, thereby gaining the time for the safe withdrawal of the loyal troops (which, as I write, I must believe was accomplished).

I was then conducted to the fortress at Badajoz, where I am now held prisoner, though in comfortable quarters, and here await my fate. It is a consolation to me to know that my actions may have so disconcerted the Miguelites that, if His Majesty does send troops here, they will find a part of Portugal at least in loyal hands, a part which is of the first importance in defending the country, lying as it does on the direct route from Madrid to Lisbon.

It is a great comfort to me, too, that I have a daughter with the spirit of her mother, who will understand now why I act as I did, in spite of what she may hear to the contrary. My only regret is that it has parted me from she who is dearest, and from your loving aunt, my sister, and all your people.

Your ever loving father.

Hervey had woken early, his second reveille as a prisoner of war. The first morning, he had sprung from his bed, the daylight streaming through the high, barred window, rebuking him for sleeping beyond the customary dawn stand-to. There had been no Private Johnson to wake him, and the body, left to its own, took liberties, not caring for the customs of the service, for field practice. Weary, it had wanted only repose, and perhaps, too, the mind had craved oblivion. But this morning he had woken before first light, and now the awful truth – that it did not matter whether he stood-to or not – bore in on him like a great weight, like his big black charger at Waterloo, stone dead, pinning him in the mud so that he lay like a stunned bird while the French went from man to man despatching the wounded.

He cursed, and sat up. *No*, he had not lain still under the dead weight of his charger; he had fought his way free. He cursed because he was losing his resolution. He was angry again – with his captors, and even more with Colonel Norris. If Norris had not been so cautious it would never have come to this. Above all he was angry with himself. But it was no good his fighting himself, and he could not fight Colonel Norris. He had to fight the Spaniards, or the Miguelites, or both – whoever it was that incarcerated him here. He might not be able to fight in the usual way, but there were others. It was unthinkable that he remained passive, simply waiting for rescue or release. That way lay ruin to his self-esteem. And he was in trouble enough with Lisbon, likely as not.

Any pretext for a fight would do, just something to show resistance (show to *himself*, to begin with). His Prayer Book, for instance: he could not claim that he needed it, but he saw no reason why he should not have it back. How long could it take the authorities here to establish that Cranmer spelled no danger? What else was he supposed to read, for the books in his room were hardly diverting? Why should he test his Spanish? In any case, it had been too long. There was a Greek New Testament, but that would only exercise rather than engage him. The usual Articles of War required that the personal possessions of an officer were not to be denied him insofar as they did not aid him in escape; he would therefore demand his Prayer Book at once. They would have to give it to him, and he would be the victor.

The trouble was (he saw well enough) that the Spaniards were embarrassed by his capture. No Spanish officer had so far spoken directly to him, perhaps so as to be able to deny all knowledge of his nationality. The Miguelites, too, were treating their unexpected and unwelcome prisoner with a degree of circumspection. He was a Portuguese – a Miguelite – prisoner, but Badajoz was, after all, a *Spanish* fortress.

It was at least a comfortable confining, however, as he had conceded in Georgiana's letter. That he could neither sleep nor eat well (even his sleep beyond first light yesterday had been fitful) was not the fault of his jailers. If *only* he could stop thinking of Colonel Norris and the prospect of that officer's delight in the news of his capture, for Norris would, no doubt, see it as a vindication of his own prudent proposal to stand only as far east as the lines of Torres Vedras. No doubt, too, Norris would be reminding the chargé d'affaires in Lisbon of the grave embarrassment to His Majesty's ministers. Would Lisbon know, yet, of his capture? How could they not? For hadn't his last words to Dom Mateo de Braganza, as he surrendered his sword to the Miguelite general, been that he should inform the legation? He wished now they had been otherwise, but in that crucial moment his words had been instinctive, the duty of an officer to report the situation to his superior. Only now did he think in terms of his own best interests. But would not Dom Mateo, a brigadier-general, act on his own cognizance? Perhaps, in the security of the fortress of Elvas once more, Dom Mateo had judged it best *not* to alert Lisbon, sure in the knowledge that he could effect an escape soon enough. Corporal Wainwright might have acted on his own initiative, too. But his coverman had no access to the telegraph or a courier (was the telegraph even working yet?), and Wainwright would be strongly averse to galloping to Lisbon when his principal was captive in Badajoz, especially if Dom Mateo advised against it.

But early release, he had to conclude, did not look likely. The Spaniards might wish that he were not incarcerated at Badajoz, but that was not the same as wanting him let free with a story to tell in Lisbon, especially at such a difficult time in the affairs of their two countries. Certainly the Miguelites would have no wish to antagonize His Majesty's ministers at the very moment parliament debated intervention. Opinion was divided in Britain: Whigs for Pedro, the infant-queen and the constitution; Tories for Miguel and the old order. This was no time to stir John Bull when he might otherwise be content to doze.

A manservant brought hot water, and breakfast, which Hervey tackled dutifully rather than with relish. Later he heard the bolt on his door being drawn again, and then a knock – a fine point of courtesy, he noted wryly. He turned, half rising, saw the same benevolent features of the day before, and of the day before that, and rested easy. Only the physician. But today he was unaccompanied, no guard to defend him against assault by the prisoner. What was to be gained in overpowering such a man, however, even if he had the inclination to? The physician carried no sword, and Hervey did not suppose a pistol was usual about his person either. He rose and acknowledged the bow. They spoke in French again.

'Good morning, monsieur. May I enquire of your condition today?'

Hervey was mindful of the civilities, however hard it

went with him. 'Well enough, monsieur. But I should be much the better were my few necessaries returned to me.'

'Oh? And what are these, monsieur?'

'Merely the contents of my valise, the appurtenances of the toilet and such like. And a book. They were taken from me when I arrived.'

The physician frowned. 'I am but the medical officer, monsieur. However, I will relay your request to the proper authority. It seems a perfectly reasonable one.'

Hervey wondered if the physician knew who that authority might be – Spanish or Miguelite? 'I am obliged, monsieur.'

The physician inclined his head by return. 'Now, monsieur, if you are in the same good health as yesterday, and have no further complaints that touch on it, I shall not detain you further. I am asked to give you this.'

Hervey took the envelope. The seal was already broken.

'I enquired as to the broken seal, monsieur, and was informed that since the letter is from Elvas the authorities were obliged to search its contents for warlike sentiments. It is, I regret to say, an ignoble state of affairs to which we are come. I do not profess to understand it. Your country and mine have been worthy allies in the past.'

Hervey scarcely heard the regrets, intent as he was on learning what constituted the correspondence. The physician saw, and took his leave. Hervey opened the letter as soon as the door was closed, looked at once for the signature – Dom Mateo's – then began to read.

18th December 1826

My dear friend,

The Nation will soon have cause to honour your name, for so gallant an action as yours this day will not long

33

*remain unextolled. But for the mean time it must
perforce be so until I myself have exhausted every
prospect of securing your release.*

Hervey quickened. The English was as apposite and
elegant as when the writer spoke it, an unusual accomplishment, in his experience, no matter how fluent a man in
speech not native to him. And it brought a great measure of
relief in the assurance that Lisbon would not yet know of his
predicament. He read on.

*Your friends, I may assure you, are all well and safe,
and your design admirably accomplished.*

This latter surprised him – not the fact of the success, but
that the censor had not thought it proper to excise. Perhaps
the phrasing was equivocal, as no doubt the author intended.
But three days ago, when their *ruse de guerre* had been
tumbled, he had bought time for the little brigade to run for
safety in the fortress at Elvas by his solitary walk, captive,
to the enemy's lines. He had had no idea since whether they
had made that sanctuary or not, and it cheered him greatly,
now, to learn that they had. The reference to 'friends' he
took to mean Corporal Wainwright, and for that, too, he was
greatly relieved.

*I beg you would reply with indications of your own
condition.*

Hervey wondered if he would be permitted to, or whether
'the authorities' would oblige Dom Mateo only with their
own assurances. But allowing him to receive such a missive
in the first place, and from the very man who stood astride
their advance on Lisbon, was promising. He read on. There
were more felicities but little of real consequence. He knew

34

Dom Mateo not so very well, but enough to know that he was capable of checking his instinct, and that the words would be measured. Dom Mateo's intention in this subterfuge would have been, first, to communicate his own advantageous situation in Elvas, then the safety of the admirable Wainwright, and finally that he himself regarded the incarceration of his friend as a matter for local resolution – hence the reference to 'every prospect of securing your release'.

How Hervey prayed that it would be so! It was not merely the thought of Colonel Norris's delight in his predicament; if the news reached Lisbon it would then reach London, and he had seen enough in his eighteen years' service to know that bold tactics that were not successful were never admitted as bold, only reckless. He called the guard, outside, and asked in Spanish if he might be allowed writing paper and a pen.

It was an hour before his door reopened. Hervey was surprised to see the physician returned.

'Monsieur, the authorities have consented to the return of your necessaries.' The physician placed a valise on the table. 'And to writing paper and ink.'

The guard placed these on the table, and three steel pens.

Hervey searched at once for his Prayer Book; the other items could be easily replaced.

'And I have brought you this,' continued the physician, giving him a small but new-looking volume. 'I should not apologize for bringing you Holy Scripture, monsieur, but I wish there had been something more in English in our library.'

Hervey was unsure as to which library the physician referred, but he was grateful enough. He wondered, indeed, if the 'authorities', Spanish or Portuguese, found it expedient to use this medical man as go-between.

'Monsieur, you are very kind. The letter you brought me is from Elvas. I would write by way of acknowledgement and assurance that I am well treated. I believe the authorities could have no objection?'

The physician shook his head slightly, sufficient to indicate his own agreement with Hervey's proposition. 'I will represent that to the authorities, monsieur.'

Hervey took careful note of the physician's choice of words. The anonymity of 'authorities', repeated, was too convenient to be mere chance; there was evasion here. The physician had told him that the Spaniards had made much on his arrival at Badajoz of not being able to take him at his word: he might be a mercenary, an adventurer, a renegade – and of any nationality. There were formalities to go through to establish his credentials. That, at least, was what they had claimed.

The physician appeared to hesitate. 'Monsieur, I have it on good authority . . . that is to say, I *believe* that if you were to give your parole, the authorities would conduct you without delay to England.'

Hervey did not doubt it. He had expected as much, though perhaps not quite so soon. If he gave his parole he would be taken to Madrid, likely as not, and there given over to the British ambassador, who would arrange for his transport northwards into France, to the consul in Bordeaux, perhaps, and thence to England by claret boat – a long journey, with plenty of opportunity to contemplate his situation, an age in which to imagine the opprobrium awaiting him at the Horse Guards, the Duke of York incandescent. And there would be no opportunity to redeem himself in arms against the Miguelistas if a British army were sent to Portugal, for those would be the terms of parole. No, it was insupportable.

'You are very good, monsieur,' he replied, and with a trace of a smile. 'But I am not at liberty to give my parole.'

The physician looked pained. Hervey could not imagine why.

'Then I wish you good day, monsieur,' said the physician, with (thought Hervey) the merest touch of sadness. 'When you have written your letter please give it to the guard, unsealed. He will know what to do.'

Hervey bowed. 'I am obliged, monsieur.'

The physician hesitated again. 'Monsieur, my name is Sanchez.'

Hervey bowed again. 'Doctor Sanchez.'

How might a man escape Badajoz? Not by force of arms, reckoned Hervey. When he contemplated that night in April 1812, three whole divisions of the most determined men hurling themselves against the walls of this place, any such thought was absurd. It had taken three sieges and the lives of more men than the army could rightly spare to break in to Badajoz. The Duke of Wellington had not had Joshua's spies, and in the end it had all been done in the old way – with brave men's breasts. There was nothing new under the sun: a soldier appropriated the methods of his forebears, adapting them as circumstances and means changed, but if science and ruses failed, there was but one way left to fight! Joshua had been lucky. His spies had almost been discovered. Only Rahab the prostitute had saved them, hiding them in her house. And what luck there had been in that, *for her house was upon the town wall, and she dwelt upon the wall*. Could there be such a woman in Badajoz, to let him down by a cord through the window, as Rahab had let down Joshua's men? Even if there was, how would he find her? Joshua's spies had entered the city before the siege, to speak with whom they pleased. How might *he* meet with anyone but his jailers?

No; it was for Dom Mateo to find a Rahab. All he, Hervey, could do was communicate with him, so that when the time came they would be of the same mind. He might of course take every opportunity for exercise, for then he could spy things out, but he must have a care not to shackle himself thereby, perhaps unwitting, by any local parole, as Joshua had with the men of Gibeon. He must judge it finely. One thing was certain, however: he *must* escape this place. There could be no question of exchange, or even of unconditional release if it meant the Spaniards handing him over formally to the authorities in Lisbon. That way lay humiliation, and military oblivion thereafter. How long did he have? Days rather than weeks, for sure. Did Dom Mateo comprehend this too?

He opened his Prayer Book, turning routinely to the psalms appointed for the twentieth day, as had been his practice all those years ago. Psalm 102, *Domine exaudi*: it spoke his supplication perfectly, if only he had the faith. *Hear my prayer, O Lord: and let my crying come unto thee. Hide not thy face from me in the time of my trouble: incline thine ear unto me when I call; O hear me, and that right soon . . .*

How aptly did God speak to him! What sound principle it had been all those years ago to read the psalms, day by day, as long as darkness or the enemy permitted. It had been a sustaining regimen, not mere duty, and even now, after all the late years of indifference, it could sustain (and, he imagined ruefully, it could keep him from trouble in the first place).

But *Domine exaudi* did not comfort: it spoke of his days 'consumed away like smoke', his heart 'smitten down and withered like grass: so that I forget to eat my bread'; he was 'become like a pelican in the wilderness: and like an owl that is in the desert'; his 'enemies revile me all the day long'. The words rebuked him as if from his father's pulpit: *out of the heaven did the Lord behold the earth; That he might hear the mournings of such as are in captivity . . .*

He closed the book, very decidedly. In Badajoz there could be no mournings, only the resolve to escape – and quickly.

CHAPTER THREE
PLANTING THE STANDARD

Belem, Lisbon, 23 December 1826

Three days later, the frigate *Pyramus*, thirty-six guns, dropped anchor in the Tagus, as so many of His Britannic Majesty's ships had during the late war with Bonaparte, and hands began swinging out her boats. Smoke from the royal salute hung about her gun deck still as Lieutenant-General Sir William Henry Clinton MP, commanding the expeditionary force to His Most Faithful Majesty's Kingdom of Portugal, descended from the quarterdeck to the gangway on the port side and thence to the barge which would take him and his staff ashore.

Sir William, lately deputy to the Duke of Wellington at the Board of Ordnance, had no very great experience of campaigning, but his reputation was for a sure and steady hand. He picked his way carefully into the barge. The swell was not heavy, but Sir William was fifty-seven years old, and although but the same age as the duke, evidently by his appearance he was not nearly so active. He settled in the stern, where a bosun's mate placed a blanket and a light paulin over his legs, pulled down his cocked hat, turned up the collar of his greatcoat, and set his gaze at the shore. It was his first sight of the city, although he had served briefly in Spain under the duke. As a young captain he had seen a little action (and much discomfort) in Flanders under the Duke of York, and as a colonel he had been aide-de-camp at the Horse Guards when the Duke had been appointed commander-in-chief. He had briefly been governor of Madeira, and as a major-general had seen a little service in Sicily, but since the end of the French war his time had been taken up with parliamentary duties. However, Lord Bathurst, Secretary of State for War and the Colonies, was of a mind that these credentials were apt enough for an intervention essentially diplomatic in its nature. Besides, he would have good brigadiers.

The barge made easy progress to the shore three cables distant, past the Moorish Torre de Belem, which old Peninsular hands had told Sir William to observe closely, with its statue of Our Lady of Safe Homecoming to bless the nation's navigators and merchantmen. Sir William gave it a passing look, but his thoughts were more engaged by the audience he would have with the regent, and the warning that Lord Bathurst had given him just before he set out. Sir William liked clarity in affairs of all kind, and he was feeling the want of it now, for Bathurst had revealed strong disquiet over the purpose of the Foreign Secretary, Mr Canning, in sending five thousand men to Portugal. He reached inside his cloak and took out the tattered copy of *Hansard*, which had been his constant reference during the passage. He had been in the House of Commons when Mr Canning had read the message from His Majesty, and he had thought he had understood it plainly – before Lord Bathurst had sown the present doubt in his mind: His Majesty, said *Hansard*, had acquainted both the House of Lords and Commons that he had received an earnest application from the princess regent of Portugal, claiming, in virtue of the ancient obligations of alliance and amity subsisting between His Majesty and the Crown of Portugal, His Majesty's aid against hostile aggression from Spain.

Sir William well recollected the acclamation in the Commons. There was a sentiment for Portugal stronger than for most places. Doubtless the fortified wine of Porto had much to do with it, but the sentiment went beyond commerce and taste. Portugal had been as good an ally as any in the late war with Bonaparte, and superior to most. Her soldiers had fought as well as His Majesty's own (and in truth, on occasion, better). There was a fellow feeling for this country, and he was most conscious of it.

He took up *Hansard* again. It recounted that His Majesty had informed both houses of his exertions, in conjunction with the King of France, to prevent aggression, and of the repeated assurances of His Catholic Majesty neither to commit, nor to allow to be committed, any aggression against Portugal from Spanish territory. But His Britannic Majesty had learned that, notwithstanding these assurances, hostile inroads into the territory of Portugal had been concerted in Spain, and executed under the eyes of the Spanish authorities by Portuguese regiments which had deserted into Spain, and which the Spanish government had repeatedly and solemnly engaged to disarm and disperse . . .

The Tagus spray was giving *Hansard* a salty soaking, but still Sir William sought to assure himself of the King's mind, and the government's intentions. He read that His Majesty had left no effort unexhausted to awaken the Spanish government to the dangerous consequences of this apparent connivance, and that His Majesty made his communication to parliament with the full and entire confidence that both houses would afford him support in maintaining the faith of treaties, and in securing against foreign hostility the safety and independence of the kingdom of Portugal, 'the oldest ally of Great Britain'.

They had been fine words when Sir William had first heard them, and they were fine, yet, on the page. As a dutiful member of the House of Commons, and deputy to

42

a member of the cabinet (which rank the appointment of Master General of the Ordnance carried), Sir William had voted without hesitation in favour of the King's proposal, as had the overwhelming majority of members, laying aside for the time being any party prejudice for or against Pedro or Miguel. And the Foreign Secretary's own eloquence in the matter had been so affecting: Mr Canning might not enjoy the trust or affection of many, even in his own party, but his words had been received uncommonly well that day (and faithfully recorded in *Hansard*).

If into that war this country shall be compelled to enter, we shall enter into it, with a sincere and anxious desire to mitigate rather than exasperate, and to mingle only in the conflict of arms, not in the more fatal conflict of opinions. But I much fear that this country (however earnestly she may endeavour to avoid it) could not, in such case, avoid seeing ranked under her banners all the restless and dissatisfied of any nation with which she might come in conflict. It is the contemplation of this new power, in any future war, which excites my most anxious apprehension. It is one thing to have a giant's strength, but it would be another to use it like a giant. The consequence of letting loose the passions at present chained and confined, would be to produce a scene of desolation which no man can contemplate without horror.

Sir William pondered deeply on those words – 'a sincere and anxious desire to mitigate rather than exasperate, and to mingle only in the conflict of arms, not in the more fatal conflict of opinions'. That had been the import, as he understood it, of the King's message. Yet Mr Canning seemed to believe that a force of intervention could not avoid the enmity of faction. Sir William read over the lines once more. Who, precisely, were 'the restless and dissatisfied of any nation'? His orders from the Horse Guards were one thing, but what the Foreign Secretary had in mind might be quite another. Sir William shook his head. But at least, it seemed to him, Canning had nailed his colours to the mast in his grandisonant final flourish: if it came to 'a scene of desolation', and he, General Clinton, was hauled before parliament to give account for the wages of ambiguity, he would at least be able to point to the magnificent purpose of the intervention:

> Let us fly to the aid of Portugal, by whomsoever attacked; because it is our duty to do so: and let us cease our interference where that duty ends. We go to Portugal, not to rule, not to dictate, not to prescribe constitutions – but to defend and to preserve the independence of an ally. We go to plant the standard of England on the well-known heights of Lisbon. Where that standard is planted, foreign dominion shall not come.

What, indeed, could be plainer than that? Sir William recalled, too, the Duke of Wellington's words to him, that 'the expedition ought to bring the Spanish king to a sense of what is due to himself and his own dignity'. Sir William smiled at the characteristic terms in which the duke had added, 'our business is to drive out the enemy, Clinton; nothing else!'

If only Lord Bathurst had not said that Portuguese deserters combined with disaffected citizens were the likelier enemy than the Spanish! What should be his position, therefore, if *Portuguese* forces – the Miguelites – invaded from across the border with Spain, but without Spanish troops?

It was, Sir William considered, a deuced tricky state of affairs into which he was come. It did his temper, and his dyspepsy, no good whatever. He only hoped that people here in Lisbon saw things clearly.

'Damn it, gentlemen! Can you not keep the water from inside the barge?' he barked suddenly, as more Tagus spray fell in his lap.

The midshipman touched his hat to his choleric passenger. They were, thank God, done with pulling, anyway. 'Boat your oars!'

He brought the barge smoothly alongside the landing, stood up and held out a hand. Lieutenant-General Sir William Clinton, the advance party in person of England's first expedition to the Continent in a dozen years, was about to make his own first-footing on Portuguese soil.

Ill tempered though he may be, the symbolism of the outstretched hand was not lost on Sir William. There was one thing of which he was certain – that a British army in the Peninsula must never be out of contact with the Royal Navy. That would be his first and settled principle. Then, if there came that 'scene of desolation which no man can contemplate without horror', he would at least be able to evacuate his force with honour. He wanted nothing of the retreat to Corunna.

A guard of honour from the Guarda Real da Polícia presented arms, the late-morning sun picking out the gold lace and the red facings of the blue uniforms. An official from the court bid Sir William formal welcome, presented Mr Forbes, chargé d'affaires at the British legation, and then conducted him briskly to the carriages and escort of light dragoons. It was all very practised, observed Sir William, *comme il faut* yet matter-of-fact, and entirely without sign of the exigency which caused him to be here.

The cortège set off without further ceremony, the court official, the chargé and Sir William in the first carriage, the military staff in the two following. The drive to the Palácio Cor de Rosa would be but a mile, although a frustrating mile, for Sir William had hoped for a confidential word with the chargé. The diplomatic usages did not permit of it, however, so he had to content himself with the official's polite enquiries about the passage from England and his previous acquaintance with the country, and with looking out of the windows and making appreciative remarks, pretending to as much ease as he could.

When the Palácio Cor de Rosa came into view, he expressed delight with its faded pink façade, though in truth he thought it a pleasing rather than a magnificent aspect, judging it to be a house the size of Kensington Palace, a place to take tea rather than to receive ambassadors. The official explained that, for the present, the regent considered it better to be at a certain remove from the city.

There was more splendid ceremony, however, for another guard of honour awaited his inspection in the forecourt. Halberdiers of the Archeiro do Guarda Real, not long returned from self-imposed exile in Brazil, resplendent in scarlet coats, blue velvet and gold and silver lace, stood to distinctly grand attention. Sir William removed his hat and bowed, for these were gentlemen-at-arms. Then the lord chamberlain conducted him to an ante-room, its mirrors and gilding as fine as any he had seen, and here at last, with the officials of the court withdrawn, he was able to speak with the chargé d'affaires.

'Where is Colonel Norris?' he asked as the door was closed, taking a pillbox from his pocket and swallowing a dose of calomel. 'I had imagined he would be here. Indeed, I expected he would be at the landing.'

The chargé d'affaires spoke quietly, though they were alone except for a footman. 'It was his intention to be here, Sir William, but to be frank I wished first to have words with you privately. I confess Colonel Norris and I do not see eye to eye in respect of how the army is to be used. And since I have no expertise in these matters I felt I must talk directly with you.'

'Indeed, sir?' Sir William wondered at the presumption, and his dyspepsy made it plain.

Mr Forbes was not dismayed. 'There is scarce time to rehearse the disagreements before the audience with the regent, Sir William. We shall have opportunity when we drive to the legation. For the audience itself, I have taken it upon myself to suggest that it would be better to conduct matters in our respective languages rather than in French.'

Sir William nodded. 'I am obliged, Mr Forbes.'

'And though the regent will undoubtedly press you as to intentions, I think it better to defer to the pending discussions with the minister for war.'

'I am happy to follow your lead in this respect.'

'And if I may add, perhaps you might reassure Her Highness as to the size of your force?'

'Indeed I shall. The number is in excess of five thousand, of mixed arms, including two battalions of Guards. They will arrive in a few days. And there will remain a presence of one ship-of-the-line and two frigates for as long as may be.'

Mr Forbes nodded appreciatively.

When they left the palace, an hour later, the chargé d'affaires was more at ease. 'I thought the princess regent pressed you hard on your discretion in the employment of your force, Sir William. I compliment you on your evasion. These are early days, and it is as well that the insurgents do not know what to expect. I am afraid I would not give a farthing for the privacy of anything divulged in that place at present.'

'Well, Mr Forbes,' replied Sir William, taking another calomel pill, 'I should *myself* prefer a more certain understanding of the limitation. You will have seen the princess regent's look of satisfaction when I informed her that my orders were to co-operate with her forces in order to drive out the enemy. I imagine she believes there is an enemy to be driven from the capital.'

'It may come to that, Sir William, yes. But the minister for war, Senhor Saldanha, will be much more pressing in his questions, I assure you.'

'He may press me all he likes, Forbes, but he is unlikely to learn more than the regent.' He made to pocket the pillbox again, thought better of it, and took another calomel. 'But tell me now, what are these misgivings of yours concerning Colonel Norris? I am acquainted with his work from his previous appointment, and I know him as a most diligent and scientific officer.'

The chargé raised his hands. 'Sir William, I have no grounds for complaint in that regard, I assure you. Put very simply – and I repeat that I am all too unread in these matters – Colonel Norris's opinion is that the lines of Torres Vedras should be the limit of intervention. He wishes to restore the lines to what they were during the time of the Duke of Wellington's occupation.'

Sir William's brow furrowed. 'There is prudence in that, is there not? It was the duke's opinion that, since the whole of Portugal is border with Spain, the country is indefensible, yet if Lisbon is held then the country is unconquered. Lisbon was saved by those lines, I rather think.'

The chargé knew it was presumption, indeed, to bandy strategy with a lieutenant-general, and he wondered at Sir William's forbearance. Yet he was determined to understand why his own opinion was so ill found. Not just *his* opinion, but that of one of Colonel Norris's own staff, who, he understood, was possessed of wide experience and enjoyed the confidence of the Duke of Wellington himself. 'You see, Sir William, if the Miguelites are allowed to run free up to the lines of Torres Vedras, they may gather such . . . *momentum* that it might provoke an uprising in Lisbon. In which case, fighting front and rear, a force might be overwhelmed, defeated ... *destroyed* even. Especially since, in those circumstances, and given the orders under which the force is sent here, resistance might in fact be beyond your remit.'

Sir William did not reply at once, recognizing in this otherwise insignificant-looking envoy a man with a firm grasp of the principles of strategy. He chose his next words very carefully. 'Mr Forbes, have you represented these views to London?'

'I have.'

'Did you propose any alternative?'

'In very general terms, yes. In truth, Sir William, I cannot own to these designs being mine, only the sentiment of unease which underlies them. Colonel Norris has upon his staff a Major Hervey' – he did not see the slight change in Sir William's countenance, and if he had, he would not have been able to determine what it portended – 'a very enterprising officer who has made a personal reconnaissance of the frontier at Elvas, and has consulted with the Portuguese authorities there. He is of the firm opinion that a *forward* deployment of British troops would be the most expedient from every point of view.'

Sir William took a deep breath, thumped at his stomach two or three times, and took out the pillbox again. 'Except, Mr Forbes, from the point of view of withdrawal in the event of serious reverse!'

The chargé looked anxious at the mention of failure.

'Oh, I do not mean a reverse to our *own* men, but to the regent's forces.'

Still the chargé said nothing.

'It is a contingency that must be considered, Forbes.'

'Yes, of course, Sir William. And I confess I do not know what Major Hervey's thoughts on that are, though I imagine he weighed them carefully.'

'I don't doubt it, Forbes. Indeed, I *know* he has,' Sir William huffed. 'We are well acquainted with Major

Hervey's estimate and plan. I believe I have three copies of it, by the courtesy of his friends at the Horse Guards, Mr Canning's own office and the Duke of Wellington himself.' He did not say that this latter had come to the duke by way of Lady Katherine Greville.

'Ah yes,' replied Forbes, somewhat abashed. But he was determined to press his case, not least since Sir William now appeared to him to be uncommonly open to debate. Indeed, he found it curious to meet with such equanimity in a lieutenant-general when a mere colonel had been so intransigent. 'Sir William, since the end of last month there have been Miguelite incursions the length of the country. By all accounts even Oporto has been harried, and there are so-called juntas of regency in the name of "King" Miguel. These Miguelites are not so many, however, or else they would by now have been showing themselves this side of the Tagus. And their Spanish seconds have neither the stomach nor the means for a true fight. But let them advance without check to Torres Vedras, and nine parts of the country will be theirs. All they need then do, as I indicated before, is sit where Marshal Masséna once did.' He held up a hand to stay Sir William's point. 'Yes, well do I know that Masséna had to raise the siege and quit the country before long. But then, he could not expect a rising in Lisbon. With a Miguelite army camped in front of the lines, and another marching on them from Lisbon, what, then, would be the purpose of the forts? They might protect His Majesty's regiments, and such of the regent's as might be induced to follow, but they would not be defending Lisbon. And from the state of the forts as I have seen them, I would not wager short odds on their protecting the occupants either. Nor is there any prospect of adequate repair, for there is not the money, even if there were the time.'

Sir William looked thoughtful. 'I know what we heard

at the regent's just now, but what is your own intelligence?'

In truth, the chargé's intelligence was little, but it was inevitably more recent than anything London might provide. 'I received a communication from the ambassador in Madrid this very morning. He has been obliged to withdraw from the court in Madrid, which is not a gesture of a power disposed to be friendly. And he appeared not to know that a British force was being sent here, so we may suppose the Spanish court does not either. We may suppose, therefore, that the Spaniards will give the Miguelistas no less succour than hitherto.'

Sir William looked disappointed. 'Then we shall proceed blind in respect of their true intentions, unless the minister – Senhor Saldanha? – is better served with intelligence than the court. But as to Torres Vedras—'

The carriage swung into the courtyard of the chargé's residence, interrupting Sir William in the delivery of his judgement. It pulled up sharp, footmen opened the doors, and the two men stepped down.

As they did so, Colonel Norris appeared from inside the residence. Hatless, he bowed. 'Good day, Sir William,' he said briskly.

Sir William bowed by return. 'Good day, Norris.'

The chargé thought the reply a shade curt, but he was unused to the company of military men, so not disposed to think much of it. 'You are come very much apropos, Colonel Norris,' he said as they went inside. 'We were speaking of Torres Vedras.'

Colonel Norris quickened. 'Indeed? I am just come from the ministry. We were discussing the same.'

Sir William turned, to see his staff alighting. 'Colonel Ash, join us if you please.'

A green-jacketed colonel stepped forward. 'General!' He nodded to Colonel Norris, not so much a greeting of recognition as acknowledgement.

'I think we will have this out here, now, before we go to the ministry.'

'Very good, General.' Colonel Ash looked at the chargé.

'My library; this way, Sir William.'

The chargé led them to the room from which he conducted the business of the legation. It was not large, but it faced south and there was a fire burning.

'Perhaps we may sit at this table?' He called for coffee.

Sir William was not obliged by ceremony any longer. As soon as they were seated, he began. 'Colonel Norris, I have what I believe are your preliminary recommendations.' He held up a manuscript copy. 'Do you have anything to add before we address them?'

'No, Sir William, other than that I now have the detailed estimates for the restoration of the forts.'

Sir William held Colonel Norris's gaze.

'The first estimates were in my judgement too imprecise. We have been calculating them afresh these past three weeks, else I would have sent them to London.'

'Very well, and what is the precise cost?'

'In sterling, six hundred and fourteen thousand.'

Sir William blinked.

'And two hundred and twenty thousand for their equipping and provisioning.'

Sir William looked at the chargé, who said nothing. 'By my understanding that is three times their original cost, Norris.'

'Yes, Sir William, but the lines are in poor repair.'

'And the Portuguese are able to find such a sum?'

'I do not know, Sir William. The ministry has yet to present the estimates to the Cortes.'

Sir William looked at the chargé again.

This was Mr Forbes's area of expertise, and he at last felt confident in expressing his opinion. 'I know the figure to be beyond the country's immediate means, and that it does not include any element of compensation to those whose industry and livelihood would be interrupted. I am told that the regent would look to a subsidy from England.'

Sir William was puzzled. 'Then the authorities *are* of the opinion that the lines should be put into proper repair?'

The chargé did not hesitate. 'I did not say that, Sir William. The war minister's opinion, Senhor Saldanha's, is that if it were a condition of intervention on our part then he would agree to it and seek to raise the money – principally, as I said, by requesting a subsidy from London, but also in loans, although I have to say that I do not imagine credit will be easy to come by, in the circumstances.'

'I believe I am correct in stating that any substantial subsidy would not be voted by parliament,' said Sir William, shaking his head in a way that suggested the notion was pre-posterous. Then he turned to Colonel Norris again, and fixed him very intently.

Norris looked uncomfortable.

'What would be the consequence of occupying the lines as found?'

'I . . . that is . . . it would not serve, Sir William, for the defences are not in any condition to stand.'

'And if the money *were* forthcoming, how long would the works take?'

'Three to four months, Sir William.'

Lieutenant-General Sir William Clinton, beetle-browed, lowered his voice. 'You may suppose that if His Majesty's ministers send troops as promptly as they do now, His Majesty's ministers are of the opinion that invasion is imminent.'

Colonel Norris now looked distinctly uncomfortable.

'What is your alternative design?'

'Alternative? I do not have one, Sir William. My initial appreciation of the situation determined me upon the best course, which is the restoration of the lines of Torres Vedras.'

Sir William slammed his hand on the table. 'Damn it, man! There's neither the money nor the time to restore the lines! Have you no other thoughts on the matter?'

Colonel Norris was stunned. He opened his mouth, but he could only splutter.

'Ash, give me that paper of Hervey's!' barked Sir William.

What was left of the colour in Norris's face drained away. 'Major Hervey? What has he to do with it?'

Sir William ignored the protest. He all but threw the manuscript across the table. 'See, here: it was you who forwarded it to London, I imagine?'

Design for the Employment of British Troops
in the Defence of the Portuguese Regency against
Invasion

Object *to repel invasion by land by those Portuguese*
forces disloyal to the Regency, and their Spanish abet-
tors.

Information *It is known from the assemblage of the*
Portuguese elements that there exists the threat of
invasion in the north of the country, into Tras os
Montes, and in the south from Huelva into Algarve.
These however would not threaten the capital
immediately. This latter is likeliest from south of the
Serra da Estrela and along the valley of the Tagus, or
through the passes of the Alentejo, having crossed the
frontier at Portalegre, Elvas or Ardila, each of which
places is fortified.

Intention *A general reserve be constituted from which*

troops may be sent to Tras os Montes or Algarve. The
line Portalegre– Elvas–Ardila be re-inforced by infantry
and cavalry of the Ordenanza. A mobile division be
formed at Lisbon or Torres Vedras, three brigades, light,
two Portuguese one British, and cavalry brigade mixed.
This division ready to march to frontier once it is known
where the enemy intends his main advance. Portuguese
Telegraph Corps to establish line from Torres Vedras to
Elvas, and thence to Portalegre and Ardila. Cavalry
to establish despatch routes in case of failure of
telegraph.

M.P. Hervey
Bt-Major
Lisbon, 26 October 1826

Colonel Norris turned the pages of the memorandum, and its detailed annexes, with increasing alarm – and anger. It was familiar enough, but no more welcome than on the first occasion he had seen it. 'No, Sir William, I did *not* send this to London. I considered it, as I would a submission from a subordinate, and dismissed it as unfeasible. I am greatly dismayed that Major Hervey should have sent this to London without my leave. Indeed, I regard it as—'

Sir William turned to the chargé, as though he did not hear. 'Mr Forbes, I should like to go at once to meet Senhor Saldanha.' He rose and walked from the room without a word.

CHAPTER FOUR
REPUTATIONS

Badajoz, the same day

Hervey sat down again as the door closed. It had been three days since he had given Dr Sanchez his letter for Dom Mateo, and there had been no acknowledgement from Elvas. Sanchez had assured him he need not worry: the 'authorities' had no objection to a reasonable correspondence. Indeed, they believed it would help secure his prompt release – on the proper terms. It was just that the couriers were slow; and, no doubt, the censor too. But to Hervey there could *be* no terms. He could no more give his parole than he could turn and run in the face of the foe. It was unthinkable to promise not to bear arms against the King's enemies merely to gain one's release, prompt or otherwise. Parole was for dilettanti, not for 'professional' officers. And, as if to rub salt into the wound, although he did not truly imagine they intended it, by the terms of the parole which the 'authorities' had now placed before him, he was to quit the country by means of a merchantman from Corunna.

No place was calculated to stir memories of ignominy like Corunna. In all that had passed since, in his heights and in his depths, Corunna still had the power to shock him, to sadden him, to make him anger faster than most everything else. He had watched the heroes of his boyhood, His

Majesty's redcoats, behave with every perversion the Mutiny Act could name during that retreat to the sea. He had watched as officers turned their back on duty; he had seen the cruellest destruction of the noblest of animals; he had witnessed craven merchant captains abandon their ships and their human cargoes; and at Plymouth, when they had finally been delivered from the nightmare, he had seen the horror in the faces of his fellow countrymen as they beheld the condition of the nation's soldiers. He had been but seventeen, and he had wondered if there could be any recovery from such a calamity – in his own regiment not least.

The recovery had been more rapid than anyone had supposed possible. In part this was due to Major Joseph Edmonds – or Captain Edmonds, as first he was when they came back from Corunna – whose unremitting exertions drove every man to the greatest effort. The best of the non-commissioned officers, too, had shown energy and enterprise of a high order, and the troop-officers themselves – denied leave even to *request* leave of absence by Edmonds – had achieved much by their mere attendance at parades. But it was the prompt appointment of a new commanding officer, and the nature of that officer, which turned endeavour into spectacular success.

Hervey could picture it still, as if it had been two, not eighteen, years past. Lieutenant-Colonel Lord George Irvine, second son of the Marquess of Tain, arrived at the Sixth's Canterbury depot the fortnight following their own arrival, and it was at once evident that the new commanding officer was intent on gathering up the reins without delay. Instead of a stately progress from London by a Tain chariot, he arrived in a high tandem cocking cart covered in the mud of the Brighton road, for he meant business, and the earliest start to it. Hervey recalled Edmonds's surprise as Lord

George jumped from the box, in front of the officers' house, and began brushing the mud from his hat.

Edmonds knew him by sight (and reputation) right enough, which was as well since Lord George's plain clothes gave little clue to his rank. 'Good morning, my lord,' he said, saluting. 'Edmonds, senior captain. We did not expect you so soon, else I should have turned out the quarter-guard.'

Lord George Irvine smiled as he took off his travelling coat. 'It is of no matter. And "Colonel" will serve well enough.'

Edmonds took the outstretched hand. 'Indeed, we had an express only this morning from Lord Sussex saying you were appointed to command. My congratulations, Colonel. I am sorry you will not find the regiment in hale condition.'

'That is why I am come so soon. Tell me of it.'

'You will want to retire first, Colonel. Will you come inside?'

Lord George Irvine, invigorated by the drive, was impervious to the cold of the early February morning. 'I think I will take a turn of the camp, if you please, Edmonds.'

Edmonds smiled to himself appreciatively. 'By all means.'

They struck off towards the horse lines.

'I have the scrip for your majority, by the way.'

Edmonds guarded his relief. The promotion by death-vacancy was his by right and custom, but these were difficult times and there was no knowing what the Horse Guards might direct. Money might yet speak. He had advanced free the last time, when two captains had been appointed major on the raising of five new regiments, and before that to lieutenant when the Flanders fevers had laid low so many. A third time was fortune indeed.

'I am gratified, Colonel.'

'No, Edmonds, not "gratified": you are *rewarded*, if all I hear is true.'

Major Edmonds allowed himself a moment of happy contemplation. Margaret would be as relieved as he at the improvement in their situation: it was no easy thing raising two daughters and keeping an establishment on captain's pay and two modest annuities. It was a pity the three of them had quit the depot for Norfolk when the regiment sailed for Portugal, for he had seen so little of them in the decade of war with Bonaparte, and news by letter would be flat . . .

And then he remembered there were others who would benefit from his free promotion. 'Lennox will be obliged, as senior lieutenant, Colonel. He is nicely fitted for a troop.'

'Capital.'

Two dragoons approached, throwing up sharp salutes as they passed.

'I would speak with them, Edmonds, if you please.'

'Crampton, Hardy!'

The two men spun about and stood at attention.

'Your troop, Edmonds, I presume?'

'No, Colonel: D.'

'Indeed?' Lord George Irvine marked his major's recognition of dragoons other than his own.

'Both chosen-men; distinguished themselves in Portugal.' Edmonds eyed them directly. 'Your new commanding officer, gentlemen.'

'Sir!'

Lord George Irvine looked them up and down, carefully. 'The patching is well executed, I must say. There's more of it than serge, though.'

'We've had to scour the county for cloth to patch with,' said Edmonds. 'I've had promised an issue of cloaks by the end of the month, but coats and breeches there's no sign of.'

It had been a point of some pride in the Sixth, even among those officers not usually given to administrative detail, that the regiment was able to patch itself into a passable state so quickly. For years after, Edmonds was as much revered for his address with interior economy as he was for the way he handled a squadron. But even Edmonds had not been able to restore the regiment's spirits entirely, for something of their pride had gone, as it had, indeed, in the army as a whole. The retreat to Corunna had cost them dear, and the storm-tossed passage through Biscay had taken a heavy toll as well, so that all the army could do on landing in England was lick its wounds and hide from public gaze in the tatters of their regimentals. They would not be fit to send back to the Peninsula in six months, perhaps a year. Not even the cavalry, for their horses were but maggot-ridden meat on the cliffs of Corunna.

'Which of you is Crampton?' asked Lord George.

'I am, Colonel.'

'Do you have a cloak?'

'No, Colonel. Lost it at Corunna.'

'And you, Hardy?'

'Lost mine an' all, Colonel. We was in the same boat, an' it tipped over.'

Lord George shook his head. 'And your sabre and carbine?'

'Managed to hang on to both, Colonel.'

'Good man. And you, Crampton?'

'The same, Colonel. I think we all of us 'ad us carbines clipped on us belts. That were the orders, Colonel.'

Lord George turned to his major. 'Your orders, Edmonds?'

'I'm afraid so, Colonel. I had assumed command the day before.'

Lord George knew the unhappy circumstances well enough; Colonel Reynell's death by his own hand was remarked throughout the service. He turned back to the dragoons. 'What else did you manage to save? Not much, I imagine.'

'Nothing, Colonel, not even us small-pack things,' answered Crampton for them both.

'Half the regiment will say the same,' added Edmonds. 'We didn't save a single trooper, burned every piece of leather, and we brought off only a few of the chargers. The paymaster has sent in a return, and we can draw from the imprest account until the losses are adjusted. But we've had few remounts so far. I've ridden as far as Lewes, buying.'

'Mm. Thank you, gentlemen,' said Lord George, turning about and touching the peak of his hat as they saluted. 'Tell me of the captains, Edmonds.'

Edmonds took him by way of the empty manège to ensure a little privacy and freedom from salutes. 'You may know that Rawlings advanced to major, and has gone onto half pay.'

'Yes, and Sussex believes he will remain thus for a year at least. He is really quite ill. I know him a little: he will fight to get back on the Active List, but his doctor is adamant on the matter.'

Edmonds nodded, doubly grateful for the information, for even though Rawlings was senior, it confirmed him in the regimental (as opposed to the second) majority. 'Twentyman has D. He bought-in a year ago from the Tenth. Very steady, he was, in Spain. Lennox shall have my troop, C. He will have a good lieutenant and quartermaster, which he will need. He is inclined to upset when things go wrong.'

Lord George made a mental note. 'A *Richmond* Lennox is he?'

'Old General William's younger son.'

'Very well.'

'The best by a good many lengths is Sir Edward Lankester. He has A. I had a mind he would transfer to half pay when we came back: he's not long come into his estate, but he says he will stay until Bonaparte is in a cage.'

'We may all say "Amen" to that. His brother is *Ivo* Lankester, I imagine?'

'I can't say I know, Colonel.'

'Cornet in the Royals. No matter. Who else?'

Edmonds cleared his throat. 'E Troop is Underwood, who is sound, in a plodding sort of way, and F is Moore, who intends exchanging with an Indiaman. And there is Joynson, who formed the depot troop when we sailed. Since we are to re-form eight-troops-strong, he will have the seventh, and one of the captains from the Unposted List will return. Who, I don't know.'

'Joynson, I imagine, is . . . at home in a depot?'

'At his worst he's an old woman. At his best there's no officer with a better facility for administration. The depot will be found correct to the last penny and nail.'

'A most useful facility,' declared Lord George Irvine, with perhaps more a note of determination than conviction. 'And the others?'

'The veterinary surgeon is, I'd hazard, the best in the service: John Knight.'

'Ah, indeed, *Knight*. We are fortunate to be sure. Lord Paget spoke of him for Woodbridge, as I recall. I should be loath to lose him, even to there.'

'He was the difference of a dozen remounts a month in Spain.'

Rounding the corner of a half-empty Dutch barn, they came on A Troop's hutted horse lines. Fresh whitewash did not entirely disguise their rackety condition.

'How many shall we see here?'

'A Troop is remounted, the only one complete – fifty-five. We contracted with a good man in Arundel as a matter of priority, but Lankester paid twice the price.'

Lord George nodded. '*Fifty-five*: not strong. You didn't lose many in Spain, though? Until having to shoot them all, I mean.'

'Twenty-seven.'

'And men?'

'We lost thirty-one, dead or invalide. But we've lost that number since. Five were dead of fever by the time we landed at Plymouth, and twenty-odd coming on here. I'm surprised it wasn't more – filthy weather, ill clad, no shelter, poor rations. A dozen are absent without leave. They might return; they weren't bad hats.'

Lord George shook his head; the story was not confined to the Sixth. 'What is the sabre strength, then?'

'At muster, and with local sick, we are four hundred and forty-six today.'

Lord George raised his eyebrows. The establishment for eight troops was twice that number.

They opened the door and went inside. At this time of a morning, between watering and second feed, the stables were quiet, with one dragoon on duty. The only sound was of teeth grinding hay, the odd chain running through its ring, and the occasional shift of a foot. Lord George took a deep breath: an officer who knew his job could smell the condition of a stable.

'We did not speak of him: there is a surgeon at duty?'

'Yes, and fair he is too,' replied Edmonds, eyeing the straw in the first stall for signs of parsimony or excess. 'But the paymaster is a drunk, and I've begun proceedings against him.'

Lord George sighed. 'There's never a good moment to be deficient of a paymaster, but now of all times . . .' He paused to look into each stall as they made their way to the other end.

'Indeed not, but I've put one of the lieutenants to do duty meanwhile – Hirsch.'

Lord George frowned. 'Hirsch? A very *Jewey* name.'

'Yes. His father is one of Rothschild's men. A deuced handy officer is young Hirsch, and uncommonly good on the flute.'

'Well, there would have been scant specie in Flanders had

63

it not been for Rothschild's arrangements, that is certain, though doubtless he made a good rate on it. Let us pray that Mr Hirsch has his tribe's facility with money.' He stopped to study one of the troopers, a dun mare. 'She looks a very good sort. My compliments to you and Lankester, though we wouldn't have bought her twelve months ago, not that colour.'

Edmonds tilted his head. 'I confess I gave the colour not a deal of thought, Colonel.'

Lord George smiled ruefully. 'I fear there are many who still would, Edmonds. I don't believe the scale of the enterprise is as yet understood by one half of the army.'

To Edmonds, who had thought of nothing but the calamity of Corunna, and its aftermath, the notion was astonishing. 'Even going as we have, it will be six months before we can call ourselves ready.'

'We don't *have* that long,' said Lord George, emphatically.

Edmonds said nothing. It would take as long as it took; and so far, six months was the best that anyone could imagine.

Lord George stood contemplating the dun mare a while before resuming the inspection. 'What of the adjutant?' he asked, giving the busy tail in the next stall a wide berth.

'Tipping? In the daily administration of the regiment he is not at all bad, though I think he is deficient in true zeal. If we are to take to the field again I believe you might find him wanting.'

Lord George held up a hand. 'I am by no means dismayed by that. I intend bringing a man from the Royals as soon as may be.'

Edmonds nodded. 'Tipping may be glad to sell out. I presume he may exchange with your man?'

'That might be arranged, yes. I would not hear of any

64

turn-out, mind, but I should be obliged to have my own man.'

'Of course, Colonel.' Edmonds knew he would do the same. It was fortunate they did not have to shift a crack man.

The duty dragoon came out of the feed room, saw Edmonds, and the stranger, and drew his arms to his side. 'Morning, Cap'n Edmonds, sir.'

'Good morning, Johnson. All sound after exercise?'

'One o'm's got t'gripes – dry soort.'

Lord George looked puzzled. 'What was that, Edmonds?' he whispered as best he could.

'One of the horses has dry colic, Colonel. This is Johnson, who was in my troop until last year. He comes from the infernal regions.'

'Indeed?'

Johnson advanced, halted after a fashion, and stood awkwardly, feet together but the rest of the body at ease. His uniform was patched even more than Crampton's and Hardy's, and he was wearing a short smock.

Lord George was clearly intrigued. 'What has been the treatment, Johnson?'

Before Johnson could answer, Edmonds thought to avoid any misunderstanding; he knew his man only too well. 'Johnson, your commanding officer.'

Johnson shifted his weight slightly, which passed as a bracing-up. 'Mr Knight gev 'im a clyster, Colonel, an' stuck 'is 'and up 'er an' pulled out all t'mard 'e could. Like rock, it were.'

Lord George nodded, confident he had understood the import, if not every word. 'Very well. And you, Private Johnson: what were you able to come away with from Corunna?'

'Nowt at all, Colonel.' Johnson sounded surprised. 'We 'ad a few things we'd found on t'way – a bit o' silver an' that – but t'infantry'd got all t'best.'

Edmonds sighed. 'Johnson, I believe the colonel meant what of your own *equipment*.'

'Oh, nowt, Colonel. Just me sword an' carbine, an' what ah stood up in.'

'And have you received any money?'

'I've 'ad all me pay, Colonel. An' ten pounds for us lost things – me razor an' that. But they 'aven't taken for me diffies yet.'

Lord George looked at Edmonds, who turned to Johnson again.

'Johnson, I cannot believe you have not been told at least five times: there will be no stoppages for deficiencies arising from the exigencies of Corunna.'

'No, ah knows that, sir. But t'quartermaster says 'e's not just gooin to write-off ev'rythin'.'

Lord George Irvine, impressed by this evidence of zealous interior economy, was nevertheless puzzled by the method. How were the quartermasters going to determine what were legitimate field losses and what were not? 'How so, Johnson?'

'We 'ad a full kit check just before we went t'harbour, Colonel.'

'Ah, I see.'

'What did you lose between then and here?' asked Edmonds, as intrigued now as was the commanding officer.

'Me spurs, sir.'

'Careless, that.'

'Ah bloody well threw 'em away, sir; after we'd shot all t'orses!'

Edmonds wished he'd never asked. He'd felt like doing the same after shooting his own.

Lord George spoke to recover the situation (he hoped). 'You have a good remount?'

Johnson's face lit up. 'Ah do, Colonel. This is 'er 'ere.' He indicated a bay mare, about fifteen hands two.

Lord George took a closer look. 'I'd have her myself, Johnson.'

'Ay, Colonel. She's a good'n.'

'Well then,' said Lord George, turning. 'Let us continue. Thank you, Johnson, for your candour.'

'Ay, all right, Colonel.' Johnson put his feet together, braced himself vigorously, and passably well, and saluted.

As they walked away, Edmonds saw a smile on Lord George's face.

'I have seen no lack of spirit so far.'

'I think that is a fair representation of the regiment as a whole, Colonel, though Johnson, I must say, is singular.'

'I am sorry to hear it! By the way, the regiment salutes with the hand when hatless, or was that just Private Johnson?'

'It does.'

'Good. Where do we go now?'

'The other troop lines, Colonel.'

Lord George halted. 'No, I think that if the horses are of the same stamp there is no need. I think I would see the stores.'

'Very well. But I fear they are misnamed, for there's barely an item within.'

'Well, I may speak to the storekeeper, I suppose,' Lord George replied, smiling still, appreciative of his major's drollness. 'Now, tell me what I should know of the subalterns.'

Edmonds made a sort of face. What to say? 'I imagine they are no better or worse than elsewhere. One or two of them have the makings. Martyn, Lankester's lieutenant, is capable. So is Darrington, the Duke of Sheffield's son, but he has bid for a troop in the Fifteenth. And Conway knows what he's about. The cornets have capability; very pleasing some of them. Hervey has a commendation from Robert Long. He galloped for him at Corunna.'

'And what of the quartermasters?'

'The serjeant-major's time is up; he'll have his discharge. He's done all he can, and that well, but there's not a commission for him. He'll go to the yeomanry.'

'There is a suitable replacement, I trust?'

'Senior quartermaster is Lincoln, D Troop. They don't come better.'

Lord George looked content. 'Then what would you have me decide for the rest?'

Edmonds shook his head. 'Nothing. In that respect the last three months have decided things. But as you perceive, there are no horses, and there's a want of dragoons. We must get back into the saddle; that is all.'

Lord George took mental note again. He considered himself fortunate indeed to have a second in command of such vigour and address. The regiment had bottom – he knew so by its reputation and from what he had seen and heard in one hour this morning – but it would require a prodigious investment, not a little of which would have to be his own. He intended losing no time in its restoration.

For his part, Joseph Edmonds considered himself and the regiment fortunate to have a new executive officer with such credentials and – from what he could judge in one hour – manifest decency. Colonel Reynell he had held in high regard, as much for his humanity as his aptitude. His handling of the regiment at Benavente had been masterly, but to Edmonds's mind there had always been something other-worldly in Reynell. He thought it his undoing, in fact. Reynell had pulled the regiment through to Corunna with but a handful of delinquencies when others could count theirs in dozens. The orders to destroy the horses had been grievous – no one doubted it – but they had been Sir John Moore's, and in the grim logic of that wretched campaign they made sense. Why, therefore, had Reynell had to put a pistol to his head? What was the dishonour awaiting him?

None; none at all. Indeed, he might have expected some recognition, for there was clamour enough for heads, and the Horse Guards would want *some* heroes to parade. They were where they were, however, and they had the Marquess of Tain's younger son, with the reputation as the coolest head in Flanders, and known to be on the best of terms with the Duke of York. He, Joseph Edmonds, could not – *must* not – fret that Lord George Irvine was a dozen years his junior.

'Will you dine in mess this evening, Colonel?'

Lord George halted. 'Indeed I shall, if you will dine too.'

'But of course, Colonel!'

Lord George smiled. 'Edmonds, before I left Lord Sussex's I had formed an opinion that your experience in this regiment was unrivalled. And at my club I met a man who said there had not been a better troop-leader in Spain.'

Edmonds's brow furrowed. 'Who—'

Lord George half frowned. 'You would not have me divulge a club confidence?'

Edmonds had no acquaintance with the clubs of which Lord George Irvine was an habitué. He shook his head, annoyed with himself. 'No, Colonel, indeed not.'

Lord George smiled. 'Forgive me, Edmonds. It should be no secret. It was Paget himself.'

'Paget?' There could be no greater accolade than from the commander of Moore's cavalry. 'I—'

'No modesty, Edmonds. He said your handling of the troop at Sahagun was exemplary, and afterwards, at Corunna, the regiment.'

In truth, Edmonds intended no modesty, only surprise that anyone took note of anything unless it were done by somebody's son. 'I am obliged, Colonel.' He even thought he might relay it to Margaret.

It was not the new lieutenant-colonel's easy manner and air

of capability at mess on the first evening that impressed itself on the young Cornet Hervey so much as his activity in the weeks that followed, and above all his address to the officers six weeks after his arriving. At mess that first evening, when Lord George had spoken a few words to the officers informally before dinner, there had at once arisen a universal sense of satisfaction in having a commanding officer who might secure for them their proper prestige. But none of them had imagined the practical use to which Lord George would put his standing. When, but one and a half months after first driving through the gates of their Canterbury depot, he called them together again, no one but Edmonds had the remotest inkling of the announcement he would make.

'Gentlemen, I have news that will stir your hearts!' Lord George began, smiling as if he were going to declare that Bonaparte himself was clapped in irons in the regimental jail. 'The government is to send a second expedition to Portugal.'

This was scarcely surprising news, but it caused exactly the hubbub he had calculated. He would now raise it by degrees. 'And the general commanding shall be Sir Arthur Wellesley!'

There was cheering. None of them knew Wellesley, save that he had a good reputation from India, and Denmark, and of course Vimiero, the battle they had missed; but there had to be *some* bravado (and there were precious few other names). Joseph Edmonds permitted himself a sigh before resolving that he could not – *must* not – fret that Lieutenant-General Sir Arthur Wellesley was but his own age.

Lord George held up a hand. The room was hushed. 'And, gentlemen, I am delighted to be able to tell you that the Sixth shall accompany the force to Lisbon without delay!'

Silence: the whole room was stunned. And then came the whoops, and more cheering. Only two weeks ago, the notion of their going back to Portugal would have been impossible. No one would have laid a guinea at 100–1 that by this day the regiment would be remounted and up to sabre strength – and warned for active duty. What might not money and influence achieve, even in these times! The colonel's zeal, they had all seen for themselves; exactly how much money he had laid out, they could only guess. And they did so with much admiration.

'Who shall command the cavalry, Colonel?'

'Not Paget,' whispered Cornet Laming to Hervey. He had come down from London that afternoon, but too late to tattle before they were assembled, which vexed him somewhat, for although he had beaten Hervey to the troop by but a month, he enjoyed the superiority it gave him.

'Do you know who, Laming?' whispered Hervey in obliging awe, but incurring a frown from the adjutant.

Lord George finished his studied sip of wine. 'Sir Stapleton Cotton, I believe.'

When they were dismissed, Laming was able to relay his intelligence fully. 'Paget has eloped with Wellesley's sister-in-law! Run off with her in a whiskey from clean under his brother's nose!'

Hervey hardly knew what to say. Lord Paget had seemed so ... *complete* a soldier that he could scarce imagine him in any other guise.

'A damned fool, they say in Brooks's – throwing away his chance of command thus. But you must concede, Hervey, with what cavalry style did he do it!'

'London must indeed be scandalized,' said Hervey, dryly, though he must picture it only, for he had yet to visit.

'Hah! That is not the half of it. The Duke of York is resigned. There's a fearful scandal about his mistress selling promotions.'

Hervey shook his head. He knew little of affairs, though

he knew that the Duke of York was held in some regard for his efforts in respect of the soldier's welfare. But a mistress selling promotions? Was that how so many men of evident incapability obtained their advancement? He sickened at the thought. The commander-in-chief with feet of clay: it did not serve.

Hervey retired to his quarters as soon as he could. As picket-officer of the day before, he had been up half the night, but, also, he knew he must order his accounts quickly now that Lord George had put them on notice for Portugal. There would be the devil of an extra expense equipping himself, for his losses at Corunna had been more than he had first supposed, and his uniform had seen such hard service that he knew he must replace the better part of it. The regimental tailor had come down from London the month before, and then again a fortnight ago, and the account would be due rendering at the month's end. He looked at the list, dolefully:

Pelisse	£32	5s	0d
Undress	19	0s	0d
Full-dress jacket	25	0s	0d
Undress	15	0s	0d
Dress pantaloons	7	18s	6d
Dress vest	13	0s	0d
Undress	3	18s	0d
Greatcoat	12	12s	0d
	£128	13s	6d

To this he would have to add, perhaps, another seven pounds for a Tarleton helmet. His boots would serve, but for other necessaries he calculated he would need to lay aside a further ten. He had already paid fifty pounds for a second charger, and its appointments.

He had no idea what government would finally allow to make good his losses; there was much speculation, none of it optimistic. His year's pay did not amount to a hundred and twenty pounds, and he had laid out four hundred on commissioning. His father allowed him three hundred a year; how, he had no idea, for the living of Horningsham was a poor one by any standard. The proceeds of the Mameluke he had taken from the French general at Benavente had been mortgaged to Messrs Greenwood and Cox, the regimental agents, in the interest of Etoile du Soir – 'Stella'. The mare had been, perhaps, a prodigal buy, but Hervey reckoned she had saved General Craufurd's brigade two hours' marching when he had galloped after them with Sir John Moore's order for the recall, such was her speed and handiness. Jessye would have done as well if she had not stood quarantined in England; but not his others. Two hundred guineas to save the Light Brigade two hours' marching! He smiled wryly: if he had taken up a subscription from the ranks that night he would have had ten times the sum. And then to be parted with her for a few dollars at Corunna . . .

No, all *that* he must put down to experience. Heavy outlay on blood was best left to the blades who wore aiglets. His priority must be to replace his camp stores – tent, bedding, canteens and all the rest. He had come away from Corunna with next to nothing, not much more than Private Sykes could carry, and what he himself had stood up in at the end of the day's galloping for Colonel Long (which was in truth not very much). He dare not ask his father for a farthing more, and he had no other expectations. At least his living expenses would be reduced once they were in the field. And this time there would surely be prize money? Greenwood and Cox were very obliging, of that there was no doubt, but for how much must he prevail on them for

Portugal, and with what security? What of his bills here-abouts, too?

He resolved to take the subaltern's course. He closed the book and pushed it to one side. He would honour all his debts – that went without saying – but it would have to be when fortune allowed. He had the King's business to be about, after all. He opened his journal and picked up a pen.

It is a fine thing to be in a well-found regiment when so much without is uncertain, and well to know the men on whom one must depend, and to know them true rather than by mere reputation. I have seen enough in my short months in His Majesty's service to know the nature of some men, and I think it our greatest good fortune to be so strong set-up a corps. I have heard some of the old Indiamen speak of Sir Arthur Wellesley, and they say he is the man to beat the French, but there are many among my fellows who deride him for a placeman. We shall have ample of opportunity to judge it however, since Lord George has by his exertions got us with his army. God grant that this time we may be set fairly to the task, for it would never serve to make such a retreat as Corunna again.

CHAPTER FIVE
GHOSTLY COUNSEL

The British Legation, Lisbon, Christmas Day, 1826

If Cornet Laming had once complained of 'the mummery of a Catholic Lent' at Lisbon, the Feast of the Nativity could not offend him now, for the clanging joy of the city on Christmas morning was only what the streets of London might be hearing on its own midwinter holyday.

'Colonel Laming, sir?'

He stopped mid-stride at the gates of the British legation, and turned to see a smart-looking NCO of the regiment that for so many years had been his own – as astonished to see him there as he was that the man should recognize him. 'Yes?'

'Sir, it's Corporal Wainwright, sir,' said the NCO, saluting. 'Major Hervey's coverman.'

Laming half smiled. 'Indeed! Do you seek me out? How *is* Major Hervey?'

'He's in trouble, sir,' replied Wainwright, lowering his voice. 'I came here to tell, sir, but I don't know who.'

'Trouble? What sort of trouble?' Laming glanced about. There was no one within earshot, but it was perishing cold, and the street was no place to hear of it. 'Come inside.'

Wainwright removed his shako as they entered the legation, a fine *palácio* not many minutes' walk from where

Hervey was meant to be lodged at Reeves's Hotel in the Rua do Prior. Laming removed his forage cap after announcing himself to a footman, who showed them to a small ante-room.

'How do you know me, Corporal?'

'Major Hervey spoke of you, sir, and you came to the barracks at Hounslow once.'

Laming's brow furrowed. 'Are you the man who carried Major Hervey to that ship at Rangoon?'

'Sir, yes, sir.'

'Very well,' said Laming, thoughtful. This was the man who had saved both Hervey's life and his rein-arm, and by holding a pistol to an army surgeon. Laming was at once disposed to hear him carefully. 'Tell me what is Major Hervey's "trouble".'

'Sir, the Spaniards have got him prisoner. He's in Badajoz.'

Laming's aspect changed in an instant. He scowled like an affronted hawk. 'How? When? What's to do?'

'Sir, it's a bit of a long story, but—'

'Sit you down, Corporal,' said Laming, and warmly, man to man, throwing his cloak roughly over a damask settee and settling in a big armchair. 'But first, tell me: who else knows this?'

'Well, sir, those at Elvas know, the general – the Portuguese general, I mean. And Dona Delgado and her father; they're old friends of Major Hervey's, sir. I went to them straight away.'

'Delgado? *Baron* Delgado, is he?'

'Sir; you know him, sir?'

'Many years ago.' Laming began to think he ought to let Wainwright give a chronological account, but he needed to know one thing more. 'Who has sent you here, from Elvas to Lisbon, I mean?'

'The general, sir. Well, he said as I could go.'

Laming frowned. 'Corporal, I know from Major Hervey what sort of a man you are, but—'

'No, sir. I mean that when it started to look like they weren't going to be able to get Major Hervey out of Badajoz I said that we had to tell somebody in Lisbon – the colonel or somebody. The general didn't want to because he says that it wouldn't go well for Major Hervey if it got out.'

Laming huffed. 'And no doubt it would go very ill for the general too!'

'No, sir, he's not like that. He's offered to exchange with Major Hervey, but the Spaniards won't have it.'

'I bow to your good opinion, Corporal. So why have you not told the colonel yet? Which colonel, by the way?'

'Colonel Norris, sir. He's in charge of the mission here, the special mission, I mean, the one from England. There are three other majors too.'

'Then why have you not told him? He is Major Hervey's commanding officer, is he not? Yours too!'

'Sir. But as I thought of it, coming to Lisbon from Elvas, I don't think Major Hervey would want it. You see, he and the colonel had their differences about what should be done if troops come from England. The colonel wanted just to go as far as Torres Vedras, sir, but Major Hervey wanted to have men up near the border.'

Laming raised an eyebrow, and sighed. He had heard it all before: Hervey and his certainty. 'Major Hervey is ever of the opinion that between himself and the commander-in-chief there is but dead wood!'

'Sir?'

Laming shook his head. 'No matter. Are you aware of any good reason for Major Hervey's contrary opinion to that of a superior officer, Corporal? No – that is unfair. Proceed.'

'Well, sir, as I said, I went to tell Major Hervey's friends at Belem, the Delgados, and then came here, thinking as I might try to find Major Cope. He's the Rifles major who gets on with Major Hervey, but he's not here still, and neither are the others. And I don't think Colonel Norris is either. So I was just wondering how I could get the message to Mr Forbes, sir. He's the envoy here, and he seems to take Major Hervey's side.'

Laming raised an eyebrow. 'You are remarkably well informed, Wainwright!'

Wainwright was not in the slightest abashed. 'I am Major Hervey's covering corporal, sir. I couldn't do my job right if I didn't know. That's what Major Hervey says, sir. He tells me everything. At least, everything he can, sir.'

'Admirable,' said Laming, sounding not altogether convinced. 'Well, I think we may have resolved your difficulty in bringing the matter before the envoy, since that is very plainly what I myself am able to do. But there is now a British general here, and we must inform him.'

Wainwright looked uneasy. 'Would that be wise, sir?'

Laming's head rocked back. 'You are *very* sure of yourself, Corporal!'

Wainwright said nothing.

'But then, as I recall, you did aim a pistol at one of your own officers in Rangoon.'

'Sir, that was because he would have sawn off Major Hervey's arm if I hadn't. That's why I took the major to the ship, sir. The surgeon there was able to save it!' Wainwright was now sitting at attention.

Laming held up a hand. 'Hold hard, Corporal! I am by no means of a contrary mind to yours, but this is hardly something that the general is *not* going to hear of, one way or another. And it would be a deuced fine thing if he did so and then found out he might have had it from his own men earlier.'

'Sir.'

'Sit easy, man. Now tell me, why did you go to Baron Delgado?'

'Because *he* wanted Major Hervey to go to Elvas in the first place, sir. His brother is a bishop there, and both of them are strong for the regent. And Dona Delgado, sir – she's his daughter – she speaks English and went with him; the first time, I mean. And then Major Hervey came back here and wrote a report for Colonel Norris, but then later there was word from Baron Delgado that the Miguelites were going to attack Elvas, and so Major Hervey went there again.'

'Without Colonel Norris's permission, I imagine?'

'I'm not rightly sure, sir, but I would think so, yes.'

Laming sighed. 'Dona Delgado – is her name Isabella, do you know?'

'Sir.'

Laming nodded, slowly. 'When the regiment was in Portugal,' he began, as if explaining to a fellow officer, 'during the war, that is, we rescued Baron Delgado and his family and brought them to Lisbon. We were going into the lines at Torres Vedras, and the baron had an estate at Santarem, on what would have been the French side. He was an officer in the militia, too, I think. What did they say to you when you told them of Major Hervey?'

'Sir, Dona Delgado said to come here and speak to Mr Forbes while she went to see a friend of theirs in the government, and then to come back to Belem, where they live, so as to work out what to do next. Sir.'

Laming looked long at Wainwright, trying to judge the affair properly, for here, indeed, was an NCO of uncommon percipience. 'Dona Delgado – she speaks English well?'

'Sir. She was married to an Englishman here, a consul.'

Laming nodded again. As he recalled, when first the Sixth's subalterns had paid court to Isabella Delgado, she had spoken a *sort* of English – very formal, learned from books. They had all got on so much better in French, with the baron especially. 'What do you imagine Dona Delgado will say to this friend in the government?'

'I don't rightly know, sir, but I know that she won't say that Major Hervey is in Badajoz. She said that right plainly, sir.'

'Very well. When I have concluded business here we will go to Belem, and on the way you may tell me exactly how it came about that Major Hervey was made prisoner. Is there anything else I ought to know at present?'

Wainwright thought for a moment. 'No, sir.' He stood up.

Laming remained seated, mulling over things one more time before committing himself to his interview with the chargé. 'One more matter, Corporal Wainwright; sit down.' He waited, then forced himself to the question. 'Do you know who is Lady Katherine Greville?'

Wainwright shifted only a fraction, but it was enough to alert Laming to the awkwardness – as if he needed alerting. 'Sir.'

'She is here in Lisbon, is she not?'

Wainwright rested easy again, for the question was matter of fact. He shook his head. 'Sir. Her ladyship *was* here, sir, up unto a fortnight ago, but then she went to Madeira, as was always her intention, she said.'

Laming could only wonder again at Wainwright's easy confidence. He did not like exposing so much to a corporal, but Wainwright's attentiveness and discretion gave him confidence to pursue his line of questions. 'Did she have dealings with the legation, do you know?'

'Sir. She used to go there a lot.'

'And Colonel Norris – were they acquainted?'

Wainwright shifted again. 'Sir. Lady Katherine tried to get him to see things Major Hervey's way.'

'*Did* she indeed. How very fortunate is Major Hervey with his female supporters.'

'Sir?'

'Nothing.' Laming rose. 'Wait here. I shan't be long.'

* * *

At Badajoz, Hervey's defiant anger had again given way to guilty introspection. He had woken early; and alone in his 'cell' (as he thought of it, for good furniture and fine hangings could not disguise a locked door), the failures and pain of the decade and more since Waterloo, the high-water mark of his uncomplicated subaltern's life, were displacing any recollection of the good he had done since, or of his short-lived marital bliss, or of his occasional joy since Henrietta's passing.

The midday bells of the fortress-city, pealing exuberantly for *Natividade*, drew his thoughts to that other cell, at Toulouse, when the war with Bonaparte seemed at last finished. There he had lain on a simple bed, his leg bandaged, the wound sutured, and in a place not unlike this – stone walls, a certain solid austerity. The nun sent to tend him, Sister Maria de Chantonnay, a Carmelite and a Bourbon remnant, one of the few of either order to escape Bonaparte's persecution, had nursed him back to fitness for the saddle, and in the course of it, though he had not realized it at the time, nursed his mind too. For in five years' continual campaigning in the Peninsula he had never slept out of reach of sabre and pistol; and, he had later come to recognize, such a sleep eroded the Christian man's sensibility. Sister Maria had spoken of her *aubade*, her prayer of joy on waking. At the time, it had seemed to him a charming thing, perfectly suited to her calling, but nothing more (his long catechism in his father's church, and at Shrewsbury, had stamped on him a somewhat 'upright' habit in his devotions).

The *aubade*, which he had never forgotten, had of late years touched him deep, perhaps because of the manner of its expression – everyday, unselfconscious – but also because (as only later he came fully to understand) it was the most perfect vocal expression of her calling, the waking wife's embrace of her husband: 'Oh my God, it is to praise you that I arise. I unite myself to all the praise and adoration offered you by your son Jesus on his arising, and I abandon myself to you with all my heart.' Once, he had known that exultation himself, with Henrietta; but not since. Since then, he felt nothing at all on waking. Sometimes he had found a certain pleasure, in the arms of his bibi – and, he would freely admit, with Lady Katherine Greville – but it was never so deep, and never frequent enough. More often he felt only black despair. After Henrietta's death, the despair had continued day and night, week in, week out, month after month. And but for the grace of God and the love of his sister, and the fellowship of the Sixth, it might have been year after year. Henrietta was a dimmer memory now, but a memory nevertheless, and a memory that often rebuked him. How he envied Sister Maria. Her vows had been liberating, while his own – or rather, his chosen way – had brought him to this.

He shook his head. *That* was too easy; he could not blame obligation to the army. He had re-read his letter to Georgiana (several times), and the pride in it was all too evident – and the conceit. He had brought himself to his situation now through ambition unchecked by the usual decencies – the *dastur*, as they had it in India: the observances, the customs of the service – and through an arrogant presumption of his own superior judgement in all things touching on his profession. Nor indeed was it 'just' the sin of pride that accounted for his dispirits: he stood in unequivocal contradiction of Scripture, through a liaison with another man's wife. And that adultery was doubly to be condemned, since he had very patently *used* Lady Katherine Greville. True, she had used him; but that did not diminish his sin.

He shook his head again: *and there is no health in us*. The words of the Prayer Book had a way of laying bare the soul. Indeed, they raged at him: *if there be any of you, who by this means cannot quiet his own conscience herein, but requireth further comfort or counsel, let him come to me, or to some other discreet and learned Minister of God's Word, and open his grief; that by the ministry of God's holy Word he may receive the benefit of absolution, together with ghostly counsel and advice.*

He had never had so unquiet a conscience as now, but there was no minister with ghostly counsel or advice for him here in Badajoz. For now, he must take his own counsel. There were comfortable words in his Prayer Book. They had seen him through dark and dangerous times before. They asked him the questions that a 'discreet and learned Minister of God's Word' would ask. Was he in love and charity with his neighbour? He could not claim it. He even deceived and neglected his sister, and by extension therefore his daughter. Did he, truly and earnestly, intend to lead a new life? Yes; but if he was to follow the commandments of God, and walk from henceforth in his holy ways, he must walk henceforth from Lady Katherine Greville.

He needed no ghostly counsel to tell him this. Perhaps, then, this cell was not entirely a defeat? Perhaps, as at Toulouse, the introspection it imposed was a blessing. One way or another he would have to amend his life; of that he was certain.

But how did he first escape his manmade chains, for he could not lead a new life shackled thus? He looked at the tray on the table in front of him. It was so much better than he had had in the days before. Steam came from the coffee pot, the bread was warm, there were eggs, oranges too. This was his own Christmas feast, and it must be the physician's doing. In Dr Sanchez there was indeed some curious sort of affinity, and Hervey began to wonder if in him lay his best chance of escape. What other was there? At every visit, Sanchez pressed on him the option of parole: all he had to do was give his word not to take up arms in Portugal again.

They probably did not expect him to keep it anyway. The general he had taken prisoner all those years ago at Benavente had given his parole at Dartmoor and returned to France, only to appear before the regiment again at Waterloo. Hervey shook his head. That might serve for Frenchmen – or a Spaniard, no doubt – but it was no option for him. An Englishman did not break his parole.

What made the physician so keen to press him for it? Hervey pondered something Sanchez had said the day before, something about the obligations of old allies. Might it be that he was himself antipathetic to the Miguelite cause? He was a physician of the town, after all, not an army man, nor even a government official. He was obviously trusted by the authorities, but being a medical man he might not have been obliged to declare any opinion. Hervey fancied there was, too, a certain something in the man's air that suggested a partiality to a red coat – more than the merely humane. But when would that partiality be ripe enough to gather? And how would he know?

Colonel Laming, having presented his card at the legation, and having no immediate duties requiring him to return to General Clinton's headquarters, took a *coche* to Belem. He had changed his mind about taking Corporal Wainwright with him, instructing him instead to continue searching for the Rifles major, but to reveal nothing to Colonel Norris, and then to report to the headquarters that evening – in the hope, simply, that the news at Belem would be good.

Finding a conveyance on Christmas morning had not been easy, and progress had then been even slower. The streets were full of people on their way to or from church, or to the family celebrations of the festival, and every carriage in the city seemed to be abroad, nose-to-tail and driving at the snail's pace. The cacophony of agitated pedestrians, hawkers, vendors, iron wheels and church bells had made the transaction with the one coachman he found for hire all but impossible, for Laming pronounced Belem as it was written – 'Balem', Bethlehem – whereas the coachman knew it only as 'Beleim', so that even as they drove, Laming was uncertain that they were actually bound for the Delgados. There ought to be a star to guide them, he told himself drily. However, once they were free of the narrower streets of the city, and he caught glimpses of the Tagus and the docks to his left, he became less anxious. He knew he would recognize the house once he was close, for he and the other cornets had been frequent callers, shooting with the barão, enjoying his cellar and table, squiring his daughter and her cousins. Agreeable days' furlough they had been, the French at a safe arm's-length beyond the lines of Torres Vedras, and Sir Arthur Wellesley content that his officers should have a little recreation, especially if it disposed the people of Lisbon to have confidence in the army and its commander.

Two and a half hours after leaving the legation, he reached the Rua Vieira Portuense, where the white house with its porticoed doors was at once familiar. He saw that the courtyard was all activity, as he might have expected on this day, but instead of the carriage there setting down visitors, servants were carrying portmanteaux to the boot, and others were stowing blankets inside. Two brindle pointers stood close by, their tails wagging as one, spaniels were running free, and an old *perdeguerra* lay in the sun in a corner, watching the bustle with a wistful look as if he imagined there would be sport today, and he long past it. There had always been dogs at Belem, just as in the best of houses in England. Laming warmed to the recollection of his days here.

A footman opened the door of the *coche* and unfolded the step. Laming replaced his bicorn as he stepped down, straightening the sash of his frockcoat and pulling at his gloves to have them taut for the salute. Even so, he was not quite ready when Isabella came out of the house in travelling cloak and hat. A glove button came away in his hand as he pulled too urgently, disconcerting him for the moment.

'Senhor?'

Laming brought his right hand sharply to the point of his hat, awkwardly conscious of its unfastened glove. 'Dona Delgado?'

'Yes? Are you come with news of Major Hervey?'

He was surprised, despite what Wainwright had told him, that she assumed the connection. 'No, ma'am. I have only just learned of his situation, and came here at once, believing you perhaps to have intelligence . . . from the government. I am Colonel Laming, of General Clinton's staff, the general commanding the army of assistance. We have met before, ma'am. Major Hervey and I were officers in the same regiment.'

Isabella smiled, politely rather than full. 'Indeed? That is very agreeable, Colonel Laming. Forgive my not recalling it. It was some years ago.'

Laming had removed his hat. His thick brown hair belied the passing of so much time, and to his mind those years were now rapidly falling away, for it did not appear to him that Isabella Delgado herself had greatly changed. There was the raven hair, the big, dark eyes – like pools of port-wine, the cornets used to say – the proud set of the head, the figure for a fine gown, which not even the travelling cloak disguised. 'And we were many, too,' he added quickly, for his own sake as well as hers. 'Forgive me, ma'am, you are evidently to take a drive. Do you have news?'

Isabella shook her head. 'None. I am travelling to Elvas directly, therefore. My uncle is bishop there, and he will have ways of communicating with Badajoz, I feel sure.' She looked at her carriage and then back at the house. 'You had better come inside, Colonel. Perhaps, too, I may present you to my father?'

'It would be a pleasure to make his acquaintance again, ma'am. Have you time to speak of the situation at Elvas before you must leave? I am in the dark respecting everything, and I fear there may be some here who will view Major Hervey's actions unfavourably.'

Isabella nodded. 'I understand perfectly, Colonel. And I will tell you all I know in that regard, although I am uncertain what is to be done. It is Colonel Norris who will view Major Hervey's actions unfavourably, is it not?'

'It is, ma'am.'

Isabella began walking back to the house. 'Are you acquainted with Lady Katherine Greville, Colonel?'

Laming braced himself to the reply, and what he imagined would follow. 'Very slightly, ma'am.'

Isabella acknowledged the footmen as they held open the doors of the house. 'In that case it will be the easier to explain, I believe. Come,' she said, forcing a smile. 'Let us resume our conversation after you meet my father.'

In Badajoz, Hervey was now convinced that Dr Sanchez was his man, though he could not entirely fathom why. When he had picked up the coffee pot and poured the black liquid into the big china basin, and found it strong, not merely bitter as in the days before, he was sure it was not just a good man's courtesy. He had thought the same when he tried the bread, for it was not coarse or black as hitherto. And the eggs – they were a true comfort (Daniel Coates had always told him to fill his pockets with hard-boiled eggs).

His spirits began to rise again with the certainty that Sanchez would be the agent of his escape, so that as he put a knife to one of the oranges, he was able to smile at last in happy recollection of his cornet days. He took the fruit for granted now, but when he had first come to the Peninsula he had never seen one but on a canvas. His dragoons had positively babbled at the first sight of oranges on a tree, as if they were explorers in unknown parts. And the oranges before him now were sweet; they were not always so. Those at Corunna had been sharp – he fancied he could taste the bite even after so many years. But never had a fruit been more welcome than on that day when they had come out of the icy mountains of Galicia, with Corunna's temperate plain below them like some vision of the promised land, with sea and salvation beyond.

Salvation it had indeed been, but their respite had not been long. Lord George Irvine had wanted his new regiment to return to the Spanish fray as soon as may be, and he had allowed no obstacle to stand in his way. Those in the regiment who had wished too loud for ease were transferred elsewhere – but kindly, for the most part, and quietly. A few, but only a few, of the officers had gone; and none of the cornets (Laming had told Hervey he would call out any who sent in their papers); the adjutant had transferred to the militia, the regimental serjeant-major left the colours altogether, and a couple of quartermasters did likewise. The consequent promotions and transfers had been welcome: new brooms were rarely liked, but they invariably swept clean. He recalled it well, the exhilaration of not quite knowing what would come next, yet confident it would be better, the pride in being ready before any other regiment to go back to the Peninsula, and having a commanding officer with the influence at the Horse Guards to arrange it all. The Sixth were a veteran corps, that second time in Lisbon, and they intended that all in the city would know it.

CHAPTER SIX

FIRST FLUSH

Belem, Lisbon, April 1809

Hervey tugged at the sheepskin to check it was secure. If he were to play his part in impressing the population of this capital of England's oldest ally, as Lord George Irvine intended, he wanted to be sure of his seat. It was good to be reunited with Jessye again; he felt it keenly. She had gained her pratique at last after the prolonged quarantine: farcy, that ulcerating virus, which could spread through a stables in a day, had struck in one of the Sixth's layerages just before they had sailed for Portugal the first time. It had seemed to him nothing short of disastrous, but in truth the outbreak had served Jessye well, for he knew that if she had gone to Portugal she would by now be just whitening bones on a Corunna cliff – and he, Hervey, would have had to put the ball in her brains. The thought was not to be borne.

Jessye was by no means of a common stamp, though she had but a fraction of the blood which the blades favoured. Laming's Fin was a full hand higher, sleek and leggy, a beauty in a shabraque. Jessye's dam was from the Welsh mountains, a pony. Jessye's legs were shorter, with a good deal more bone. She looked perfectly made for a bat-horse, or a covert hack (as his fellow cornets taunted), a horse fit to ride to the meet so long as there was a decent hunter to change to for the chase itself. But the ponies of the Welsh mountains had an ancient and fiery lineage, back to the part-barbs of Andalusia; Jessye had both a turn of speed *and* endurance. She was honest, always; she was a good doer; she did not fret when turned out in foul weather; she had bottom. Hervey would not exchange her for a dozen Fins.

Cornet Laming affected to raise an eyebrow. 'With pains or perils, for his courser called; Well-mouthed, well-managed, whom himself did dress; With daily care, and mounted with success; His aid in arms, his ornament in peace.'

Hervey frowned. 'Laming, you are a very poor judge of horseflesh, if a considerable scholar. I would have you consider *multum in parvo*! Where is your wisdom from, anyway? I recall it, faintly.'

Cornet Laming continued in the studiously airy manner of the older hand (if only of a month). 'Virgil. Or rather, Dryden.'

'Ah yes,' said Hervey, matter of fact, as he tightened Jessye's girth-strap. 'Not a very faithful translation, though. Or so said my tutor.'

'But apt, and well sounding nevertheless.'

'Indeed. But in the matter of horses, Laming, I can't but think of the country we saw to Corunna, and I don't suppose we shall have much better this time. I'll wager the first Mameluke I take that your Fin will be cast before Jessye is.'

'I am perfectly happy to accept. A thro-bred will outrun a cocktail when it comes to long points.'

Hervey smiled. 'Then I will remind you again, Laming: handsome is as handsome does.'

The regiment stood in better stables than any in Portugal, being billeted in the royal mews at Belem. The ceilings were high, the stalls wide, the grilles and columns were painted white, with generous gilding. Hervey imagined that it gave Laming, and his fellow cornets, too ornamental a view of the requirements of a charger, and he shook his head in despair, if with some irony. Heaven knew they had had a hard enough lesson not three months earlier at Corunna.

Two of Hervey's fellow cornets now came into A's lines – from one of the new troops, H. They stood silent for the moment, and, Hervey fancied, with something of a superior air. He braced himself: if one of them so much as made remark about his mare, other than honest praise, he would chastise him roundly.

'Wheell now,' ventured one of them, a Galway squireen whose manners and pugnacity had endeared him to no one from the first day he reported for duty a month before. 'We're off to the city to see what the ladies there offer. Are ye inclined to come with us? We'll be back in time for fothering.'

Laming answered for the cornets of A Troop, and coolly. 'In the Sixth we say "evening stables", Daly. And we have not time to be calling upon ladies in Lisbon; there's drill to be about. We are not come back here for amusement.'

'The divil with that, Laming! I'll not give up my recreation for a damned Frenchman.'

'Nor me,' said the second H cornet, in an accent not unlike a Leadenhall street-vendor. 'I'll have *my* sport while there's chance. That's what we al'as say in Piccadilly!'

Hervey groaned, though inaudibly. He was about to second his fellow cornet's opinion when Daly seemed suddenly to tire of the exchange.

'Come then, Quilley m'lad. Let's leave these *professional* officers to their own enjoyment. They'd be dull company for the senhoritas in any case.'

Hervey was a little inclined to make some riposte, but Laming merely gave them a look of such hearty disapproval that he thought it must rupture their communication permanently.

The two H cornets left without a word.

'I cannot conceive of any exigency when men of that character might be thought worthy to join a regiment such as this,' said Laming, having watched the two quit the lines in as brash a manner as they had spoken.

'Nor *any* regiment indeed.'

Laming sighed. 'True. I would not trust them with commissary work, even. Daly might have made a passing officer had he been introduced to any decent society ten years ago, but Quilley is an abomination. You know what was his business before he came to us? Billiard marker!'

Hervey looked incredulous. 'What?'

'Billiard marker – in White's Club. His father is steward there, or some such. Seems he managed to be of assistance to a member of parliament over a matter of debts at the tables, and got his boy a commission in return.'

'How have you learned this?'

'Last night, at mess with the Coldstream. It's infamous. We shall be the very laughing-stock of the army. I can't think why Lord George tolerates it.'

'I should be less inclined to call it infamy if Quilley showed the slightest address about his duties here.'

'You may as well look skywards for a pig, Hervey.'

Hervey finished lengthening Jessye's stirrups as his groom brought a pot and paintbrush. 'Martyn said last night that their troop-leader will place them in arrest before the month is out.'

Laming shook his head. 'The devil of a thing it must be for Warde to come in from the Tenth and find his two cornets as ill as those. Deuced embarrassment it is. I wonder what Lord Sussex had of it?'

'A letter of nomination, I suppose; that's all. It was the same for me: I saw no one. I can't imagine the colonel has course to see every man before he accepts him.'

Indeed, so rapid had been the Sixth's reconstitution, driven as it was by Lord George Irvine's determination to have the regiment ready to return at once to Portugal, it was a wonder the regimental agents had been able to handle the commissions at all.

'Perhaps so,' said Laming, frowning the while. 'Well, Warde will have his work cut out with those two in his troop, and I fear he'll have little help from Daddy Joynson as squadron leader.'

Hervey raised an eyebrow, signifying agreement, if regretfully, then nodded to his groom.

Private Sykes began painting Jessye's hooves with an oily paste.

Laming looked inquisitive. 'What does he do there, Hervey?'

'Marshmallow ointment. It will keep her feet from cracking.'

'I did not know that. Singular!' (Cornet Laming, though he might banter in judging a horse, was ever ready to give Hervey his due for an evident greater knowledge of equine husbandry.) 'But why has John Knight not prescribed it?'

Hervey smiled. 'He has. He instructed the quartermasters yesterday.'

'Mm. You are as *courant* with your intelligence as I am, and perhaps more worthily.' Laming continued to frown. 'But no matter. Do I suppose you have heard anything of our movements?'

'We march east these Saturday seven days.'

Laming cocked an ear. 'Really? How on earth have you heard—'

'A fellow with whom I was at school, on Sir Arthur Wellesley's staff.'

'Really?'

Hervey smiled, admitting the tease.

'Mm. Well, *I* have heard that Wellesley will not set foot outside Lisbon until Beresford has whipped the Portuguese into shape. And how long do you suppose *that* will take?'

Lord George Irvine rose as his major and senior captain entered. 'Gentlemen, take a dish of wine and sit ye down. We have a deal to speak of, and you shall not leave until I am content, and certain that you are too.'

The commanding officer's quarters occupied the better part of a wing of the palace at Belem, although half of it was the domain of the regimental staff, the orderly room. Lord George's servant, who had followed him to the Sixth from the Royals, served them glasses of Madeira and then took silent leave.

'Well, gentlemen, I will make no bones about it: I have been pressing the regiment's case with Stapleton Cotton, and I believe we shall have it. We may have green horses, and a deal too many green dragoons, but I believe the surest remedy is to plunge them into the thick of things without delay. I see no merit in drilling here when the rest of the army is on the march. It would be vexing in the extreme to the Corunna ranks, and doubtless we should drill to the wrong tunes. I've a mind that Wellesley doesn't intend the cavalry to go at it in the old manner. To begin with, he doesn't have enough to hurl about the battlefield knee-to-knee. This is damnable country, as you know better than do I. Patrols, scouts, videttes – that's what Wellesley will want, not lines of sabres.'

Joseph Edmonds and Sir Edward Lankester sipped their Madeira and nodded just perceptibly.

'And that sort of work, given officers with a good eye and a cool head, is best learned at first hand.'

Edmonds listened with especial care. Nothing so far since Lord George Irvine had assumed command disposed him to think anything other but good of his new colonel. It was not easy, however – the exercise of command by a man a dozen years his junior, and who, although he was well shot over, had seen nothing like his service. Edmonds was on his guard, therefore, half expecting (though not hoping – *indeed* not hoping) some betrayal of weakness of character or judgement. Yet he still saw none to speak of, even after three months' intense study. The lieutenant-colonel's passionate determination to get the Sixth back to the Peninsula might have appeared in other men as mere pursuit of ambition, for personal glory; but in Lord George Irvine it appeared wholly as the impulse of an instinctive soldier and a patriotic Tory. Edmonds could have no objection on either count.

Nor, indeed, would Sir Edward Lankester. He had succeeded to his father's baronetcy not two years before, his temperament as a soldier was effortless accomplishment, and his inclinations were as Tory as those of his major and commanding officer. Without question he agreed with Lord George's opinion that lessons were better learned hard and soon.

'Very well, gentlemen. Let me now tell you what is in the mind of our commander-in-chief.'

It was said without the slightest condescension or self-delight, Edmonds was certain. Nor was it self-delusion: they all knew very well by now that Lord George Irvine was a coming man, and that he enjoyed the confidence, in the widest sense, of Sir Arthur Wellesley. This of itself changed the character of the regiment somewhat, for to have a lieutenant-colonel of such evident quality and influence both increased the respect in which they were held by other regiments and multiplied the prestige of every man, for the meanest dragoon was no longer a mere legionary in this army of fifty thousand, but a man with connection (only once removed) to the commander-in-chief himself. What that profited a man was another matter, but without doubt it felt better to be in a regiment commanded by the likes of Lord George Irvine than in one whose lieutenant-colonel was of no account outside.

Edmonds knew exactly the value of such a connection. They would be made privy to Sir Arthur Wellesley's intentions, not merely to his instructions. That was a pearl of rare price to cavalry, for it was in the nature of war that events could only be dictated (if at all) *before* contact was made with the enemy. It was then that the cavalry – the commander-in-chief's eyes and ears – was of incomparable worth. Since, too, the commander-in-chief could not communicate rapidly with his cavalry when they were dispersed, much depended on the judgement of the individual cavalryman – on his *coup d'oeil*, as the theorists had it.

Without knowing what was in the mind of a general, forming a right judgement was a hit-and-miss affair – if, Edmonds reflected ruefully, there *was* anything in the mind of the general (he was certain there was nothing in 'Black Jack' Slade's). Thank God that man was left behind in England – never to see service again, he prayed (not active service at any rate)! Edmonds could curse long at the very thought of Slade and the system that permitted such a knave to advance. But so it was, and there was little point in fretting about it. If Wellesley could keep the Slades out of the Peninsula then he for one would be inclined to think favourably of the commander-in-chief. And if Wellesley were to bring Paget here then he would entirely revise his opinion of him! Stapleton Cotton was no Slade – he had seen enough of Cotton to be certain of that – but he was no Paget either, and with so few cavalry at his disposal, Wellesley required a commander of genius. Edmonds was by no means certain that these general officers were universally apt.

'Edmonds?'

'Colonel?'

Lord George Irvine smiled. 'You were in another place, I think.'

Edmonds glanced at his glass; it was all but full still.

'I'm sorry, Colonel. I truly was in another place.'

'Well, I may tell you that Wellesley intends to eject the French from the north of the country. He is determined to have them out of Oporto by May's end.'

Sir Edward scarcely batted an eyelid, but Edmonds was at once on the edge of his seat. 'I'm astonished. I heard that he would first drive east at Lapisse or Victor; their armies threaten Lisbon more directly than does Soult's.'

Lord George Irvine inclined his head. 'And that would have been your counsel would it, Joseph?'

'By no means. If we move quickly, Lapisse and Victor can be of no assistance to Soult on the Douro, and they wouldn't be able to take Lisbon without a deal of preparation.' Edmonds glanced again at the map on the wall. 'And if Soult's driven from Oporto, then he'll have no option but to continue north, and away from any prospect of their assisting him. The Spanish ought then to be able to tie him down in Galicia. We would then have *two* armies to contend with instead of three, for if we were to drive at Lapisse or Victor directly, Soult would hare down from the Douro to be at our flanks.'

'Then we not only understand the commander-in-chief's intention, gentlemen, we approve it!' Lord George Irvine knew as well as the next colonel that executing orders that were heartily disapproved of went hard with a thinking officer. 'Cotton shall take a brigade north to make contact with the Portuguese already watching the Douro – ourselves, the Fourteenth and the Sixteenth, and the Third Germans – while Wellesley brings up the army. He'll keep a division here for the defence of Lisbon in case there's any move by Lapisse or Victor, and Beresford shall take one of his Portuguese brigades of infantry and another of cavalry to stand astride Soult's route of withdrawal east, which should drive him north into Galicia. Exactly as you prescribe, Edmonds.'

Edmonds nodded, the merest confirmation – no sign of self-satisfaction.

Sir Edward Lankester, his face impassive, enjoying the comfort of a good chair and passable Madeira (though by no means fretful for the want of comfort when circumstances demanded), recrossed his legs. 'Who shall do – how shall we call it? – the *éclairage*, Colonel?'

Lord George Irvine smiled. '*You* shall, Sir Edward. You will scout for Cotton's brigade – a day ahead, if may be.'

Sir Edward's face remained impassive. 'Very well. Then the sooner we begin, the better.'

'Just so, Sir Edward, just so. Shall you be ready two days hence?'

'I trust I shall, Colonel. If I am given the requisite mules.'

Edmonds addressed the proviso. 'A shipload arrived this morning from Algiers. I believe we may have a hundred of them.'

'You shall have fifty in that case, Sir Edward. Enough to carry your hard feed, but it shall have to be green fodder unless I get more.'

'That should not be too great a problem at this time of year, Colonel, although cutting it will take up a part of the day better spent.'

Lord George Irvine looked pleased nevertheless. He knew full well what the difficulties would be, but they were not such as to jeopardize the mission, and in that case there was no profit in parading them. Sir Edward Lankester understood this, evidently: an officer in command of a regiment had worries enough without those of a squadron being added to them. Yet he had known many a captain who could not feel his ease until he had acquainted his superior with every hazard and contingency in consequence of an order. Sir Edward's was a prudent habit, too, for when he *did* express a concern, he could be certain that he, Lord George, would hear him the better. 'You are well found, Sir Edward. I think your officers will enjoy the sport.'

'I am certain of it, Colonel.'

Lord George nodded, then looked at Edmonds again – and with the suggestion of pain. 'What are we to do with Fourth Squadron?'

'With respect, Colonel, were I you, I should be inclined to order H Troop to march under your command, and close-by at that. Warde would understand. Joynson might then manage his own troop well enough without the worry of a full squadron – if you keep him rear.'

Lord George smiled. 'So you may keep an eye on them, Edmonds?'

'That would be one of the advantages of such a course.'

'Very well. What say you, Sir Edward?'

A Troop captain lowered his glass. 'I have known Edwin Warde these dozen years and more, Colonel. Given time he will come to a right method.'

Lord George inclined his head.

'If you press me to say more, Colonel, I would only add what I imagine is known to you already, that Daly and Quilley are a disgrace to the service no less than to the regiment.'

Lord George's eyebrows rose. 'It is insupportable that we should have to speak of such men. Two more reprobate officers it would be difficult to contemplate. They've not the slightest conception of duty – and nor, I might add, do I see any prospect of driving them to it. I shall order them in arrest at the next flagrant offence and take measures to cashier them.'

Even Edmonds was taken aback by the resolution. He was minded to rehearse some redeeming virtue, some mitigating circumstance (they were but cornets, after all); but in truth there was none – certainly not charm. 'A turn-up before the off may be no bad thing. There's none that dare swerve too much after such a warning.'

Sir Edward took another sip of his Madeira, as if disdaining mention of two men he would not have passed the time of day with had they not been gazetted to his regiment. 'I hope we may reward the active sorts, Colonel, as well as punish the villains. I am of the opinion that more should have been made of the exemplars of their rank when we returned from Corunna. We had not a single merit promotion given us.'

Lord George nodded. 'You're right, of course, Sir Edward. And it must pain doubly when the mess sees so ill an outcome of influence as Mr Quilley. I'll press the matter on Sir Stapleton Cotton when I see him next.' He smiled wryly. 'I have no doubt that you are thinking of laurels ahead for A Troop?'

Sir Edward kept his countenance, for he was in perfect earnest. 'I am, Colonel.'

On the morning two days following, First Squadron paraded as usual, but Sir Edward Lankester had confided to only three men, the evening before, to what purpose other than routine was the muster. He was obliged, naturally, to inform B Troop's captain, Jesmond, what was afoot, and he had told his own lieutenant, Martyn, and Quartermaster Watten. Jesmond he had also authorized to inform *his* lieutenant and quartermaster. He had no great expectation of the intention remaining in confidence to those five, however, for even if not a word was spoken of it the mere amendment to routine would signify something. And so when First Squadron paraded, in marching order, no one supposed it was for inspection only, especially since the quartermasters had given orders for the baggage to be assembled under guard in one of the courtyards.

Sir Edward had received his orders in writing the afternoon previous. They bore the lieutenant-colonel's signature, but he knew the words had been crafted in Sir Arthur

Wellesley's headquarters, and in that case very probably by the commander-in-chief himself. He did not know Sir Arthur except by reputation, but he read in those three succinct sentences what he imagined was the essence of the man – and *everything* of his intention:

Belem
30th April 1809

To the Officer Commanding No. 1 Squadron

You are to march in advance of the Army via Caldas da Reinha, Leiria, Coimbra and Aveiro to Oporto, to form a junction with the Portuguese forces there operating against Marshal Soult and to ascertain the dispositions, strength and intentions of the enemy, especially in their extent south of the Douro river. You are to take whatever opportunity is presented that will serve for the destruction of the enemy by the main force that follows, or, failing that, and in concert as necessary with General Beresford to the east, to drive the enemy northwards into Galicia in order that General La Romana's Spaniards may effect that destruction. On no account are you to follow in Spain without express approval of the Commander-in-Chief, with whom you are to remain in communication through the QMG Department's couriers until the remainder of the Regiment closes on the Douro, whence you will revert to communicate to me.

Signed
Irvine
Lieut Col 6th Light Dragoons

Sir Edward understood that he might at best have a

week's march on the rest of Sir Arthur Wellesley's force, and a day or so only on the rest of Cotton's brigade. The distance to the Douro was a hundred and fifty miles, over indifferent roads and with horses not yet fully up to service. He could risk no more than thirty miles in the day if he was to have a squadron even half capable at the end of it. But he could at least pick his best men and horses and take them in advance of the rest of the squadron to make the initial junction, for the Portuguese would already know a deal of what he was required to discover, and he could then simply direct his efforts towards confirming their information rather than discovering it anew. He therefore placed B Troop's captain in command of the squadron, leaving Martyn in charge of A Troop, and left Belem as soon as muster was over with the remaining officers, a servant apiece, a serjeant, a dozen corporals and dragoons, and a farrier.

Hervey could scarcely contain his zeal as the chosen band set out. Jessye was in hale condition. The other officers may have scorned her to begin with, and they continued with the tease occasionally now, but in those weeks on the Sussex Downs, when Joseph Edmonds had had the officers out for 'saddle-talk', they had come to recognize a handy charger and march-horse combined. He had not the slightest doubt that he would win his wager: Fin would be cast before Jessye, and the first fine sabre would be the prize.

His second charger, Loyalist, was of an altogether different stamp, a starling gelding, a racer who had run head-up once too often. But he had got him for a good price and had re-bitted him. Laming had watched his early attempts with disbelief: 'Hervey, there are three kinds of fool. There's the fool, there's the damned fool, and there's him as hunts in a snaffle!'

But the merest contact of rein and martingale had by degrees brought Loyalist's head down, and Hervey could only wonder at what thin bar that passed for a bit – as well as mutton fists – had hardened the animal's mouth in the first place. Instead he had bought a round snaffle, jointed, and sewed a length of sheepskin to the noseband so that the gelding had to drop his head to see front. A few days' schooling soon implanted the association of soft bit and forward vision in Loyalist's head, but embarkation had interrupted their training, so that the regulation double bridle was as yet unknown to him. But Hervey had reckoned Loyalist would need the curb nothing likc as much as his fellow cornet thought. 'Laming, half the troop goes with just the snaffle, for they have the curb chain so loose!'

It would have taken a full three weeks more of riding school, however, before Hervey could count Loyalist a sound battle-charger, and this early march north was no occasion for schooling. The horse was a fine sight on parade at least, and promised to be finer still when his summer coat was through. Indeed, with Jessye and Loyalist, Hervey considered himself passably well provided for. He had a march-horse that would serve him true as a battle-charger, and one that had the makings, as well as being fleet enough even to do galloper duty. He needed a little better luck than he had had with Stella; that was all.

Luck seemed to favour him. When they went into billets on the third night, Hervey was more pleased with his *écurie* than he had supposed likely. After stables, and a stew of fish at a modest but clean *albergaria*, he took up his journal enthusiastically.

3rd May

Estarreja, 3 leagues north of Aveiro

Today we marched from Coimbra, not very fast, for

there were many patrols of cavalry that wished to interrogate us, and we them, a distance of 15 leagues, and here have made a proper junction with the Portuguese corps of observation. E.L. is all activity, forever enquiring of his map or the Portuguese guide, and tonight called for me to interrogate some French deserters, who were in mean condition and knew little, though that little they were content enough to surrender. Soult has outposts to the south of the Douro, that much is certain, but is not otherwise perhaps in too great strength. These men said that there are numerous ferries by which the troops cross the river, and so it may be concluded that Soult would be able to transport his corps in a little time to meet a threat from the south. By the same token he is able to evacuate those men to the safety of the north side if he chooses. There are not many bridges, and those considerably upstream of Oporto. E.L. declares that we will begin tomorrow to make a reconnaissance of the line of outposts and ascertain too the bridges, though he believes this latter will likely as not prove too exacting for so small a number, unless the Portuguese attend.

L lost shoe just before we arrived, which we did not see because Sykes was leading him. Farrier Dilkes will fit new this evening after same for E.L.'s second charger. Have ridden L a very good part of way these last days, and he does capitally well, carrying his head much more steady and answering now very promptly to the leg. J never tires and does well on short rations.

Not so much green fodder as expected on account of bad weather of late. Rain has stopped, I am glad to record. It had become v. heavy indeed by this mid-day. E.L. says the days to come will be all scouting, and that we must expect contact with the French at any moment. Everyone says it is a fine thing that we are come back

to turn the tables on Marshal Soult. I for one want
nothing more than to pay them back for the humiliation
of the retreat to Corunna and the destruction of our
horses.

CHAPTER SEVEN
SPEARPOINT

Oporto, nine days later, 12 May 1809

Sir Edward Lankester rubbed the plaster from his eye as a heavy-footed dragoon upstairs dislodged more of the ceiling of the dilapidated *pousada* that served as the squadron's mess-headquarters. They were so close to the country's second city, now, that the final hours were beginning to drag by.

'Mr Hervey, I would have you go at once with an escort to meet with one of Sir Arthur Wellesley's observing officers. He has a mind to take a look at the river.'

They had closed to the Douro, as instructed, and they had done so promptly, but Sir Edward's tone betrayed nothing of the demands of a week spent in the saddle, the last two days entirely within cannonading distance of the enemy. The squadron – or rather, his hand-picked detachment – had been the point of the spear, so to speak, since crossing the Mondego. Meanwhile, the shaft of the spear – Sir Arthur Wellesley's main body – had been marching steadily north behind them. Two days ago, the squadron reunited, the point of the spear had had its first brush in earnest with the French cavalry; and yesterday the shaft had seen a sharp action on the Vouga, eight leagues south of Oporto. It had been a botched affair, though, Sir Edward told his officers:

Wellesley had been heard railing against several unfortunates who had failed to bring their men up on the French in the right place. But the spear was close now. Porto stood waiting, Sir Edward had written in his despatch; it would not do to keep them waiting long. However, Soult's cavalry had been able to slip away in the dark, he told his officers, ruefully, 'like rats scuttling off as the water rises'. Or depending on the point of view, he added, like practised cavalry in a line of surveillance. It was always touch and go what others thought of men who did not stand and fight.

Hervey felt his head nod, even in the fraction of time between Sir Edward's giving him the order and his acknowledging it. He was dog tired. All he wanted to do was take advantage of the *pousada*'s shelter for an hour or so's sleep. Just an hour; that would be enough – a dry hour, though, not another soaking. By God he had had his share of drenchings this week gone!

He shook himself, hoping his troop-leader had not noticed. 'Where is the observing officer now, Sir Edward?'

'He is gone to Villa Nova. He'll meet B Troop's picket there, but I want *you* to conduct him forward.'

It made sense. Hervey had ridden to Villa Nova, on the south side of the Douro opposite Oporto, at first light.

'No, the observing officer can wait a little longer,' said Sir Edward suddenly, turning his head to the door. 'Bancroft!'

His dragoon-servant came at once. 'Sir Edward?'

'The coffee, Bancroft, ready or no.' He looked back at Hervey. 'You have need of the bean as much as do I.'

Private Bancroft stood a moment, with a look that questioned the order. He was a fastidious servant, until a year ago a footman to the late Sir John Lankester. He had exchanged livery for regimentals with a will when the new baronet had asked for volunteers, for he might otherwise have been balloted into the militia and that would have been all the inconvenience of the regulars without one quarter of the status (though admittedly one tenth of the danger). Bancroft was of the unflinching opinion that coffee, whatever else its properties, must be hot.

Sir Edward saw, and understood. 'There's a good fellow,' he added, in a softer voice, and with just something of the supplicatory, so that Bancroft felt obliged, indeed almost content, to fetch the half-made sustainer.

Hervey took careful note of the exchange. Sir Edward's way with men intrigued him. Whereas Joseph Edmonds was all commanding – brusque, active, hungry for the fight – Sir Edward Lankester frequently appeared as if he were engaged in some private interest or other; although as soon as he perceived the enemy to be at hand he could become as much a fighting cock as any of them. The curious thing, observed Hervey, was that the dragoons seemed equally to trust both men. With Edmonds, there was in that trust a touch of admiration; with Sir Edward, it was affection. In the terrible retreat to Corunna, Edmonds had cajoled his troop into virtue; Sir Edward had flattered his. But the outcome had been the same: their dragoons would do anything for them. Both troops had embarked in good order, and with fewer losses than the others. Hervey wondered if some sort of synthesis were possible, or whether the essentials of the one style militated against those of the other. He knew – it was an axiom of the service, indeed – that leading men was a natural business: a leader was born. He himself had been born into that society which made of its sons the stuff of command (Sparta, he reckoned, could have had no quarrel with Shrewsbury School, nor Salisbury Plain in winter). There was a mask to command, however. That much he had divined from Daniel Coates, listening to the tales of America and Holland. But perhaps, in truth, the mask was a technique for greater ranks than cornet – although Quilley and Daly would profit by one, he was sure.

'Hervey,' began Sir Edward, sitting down in a rickety old carver and pulling the spurs from his heel-boxes. 'What thoughts do you have of events?'

Hervey had come to recognize the deliberate ellipsis in his troop-leader's manner of speaking. It did not appear studied, or affected, neither did it mark any vagueness of thought. Rather, it seemed the means of encouragement, like the good rough-rider letting out the rope inch by inch, so that the young horse did not take fright – or advantage – at the sudden discovery of the freedom to do what it liked. But Hervey would not think over-carefully of his response, this time trying to imagine *which* 'event' Sir Edward considered proper for a cornet to speak of. He answered frankly. 'I am astonished by the audacity of the advance to Oporto after so short a time. Our movements are so much bolder than before.'

Sir Edward nodded, thoughtfully. In the saddle his fine features could look severe, so intense as to seem almost cruel, yet at other times he looked like a contented man surveying his acres from astride his favourite hunter. This morning, off-parade, at leisure almost, he wanted only spectacles to complete the resemblance to a bookish squire. 'Do you consider there is a chance we will pay for such audacity in the way we did before?'

'You mean as we had to retreat to Corunna, Sir Edward?'

Sir Edward inclined his head.

Hervey thought a little. 'We have the sea as our left flank, we do not advance deep into the country, we advance against an enemy who cannot be rapidly reinforced, the Portuguese are more reliable allies than were the Spanish, and it is May not December.'

Sir Edward quickened. Hervey's reply was not only succinct, it was almost complete. 'Admirable. Anything else? Anything to our disadvantage?'

Hervey thought a little more. 'They say the infantry is not as good as Sir John Moore's, perhaps?'

'They do. There are too many second battalions, for sure, and very green. Do you believe our general will be able to shape them as Moore did?'

Hervey was doubly intrigued. This was a rare exchange indeed, a captain asking a cornet his opinion of the commander-in-chief, and he wondered to what it tended. 'Sir John Moore had many months in England to shape his, Sir Edward. I understand Sir Arthur Wellesley has not had that advantage.'

'Do you consider that he possesses other advantages over Moore?'

Hervey's brow furrowed. These were deep waters indeed for a cornet, and in truth he knew little of either man. But he knew that if Sir John Moore had not been killed in his hour of victory they would not be having this conversation now, for, by all accounts, Moore would have been hauled before parliament to answer for the retreat. 'Truly, I cannot say, Sir Edward. Only that I recall as much praise for Sir John Moore when first we landed in Portugal as now there is for Sir Arthur Wellesley.'

Sir Edward nodded. 'You are wise to be acquainted with that, Hervey. The fact is that Moore was incomparably the better soldier, but I believe Wellesley will prove much the greater commander-in-chief.' He leaned back and began buffing a spur on his breeches. 'This business here in the Peninsula: it is not so much the fighting a man must do – we may suppose there are generals enough who could do that tolerably well; recollect Hope at Corunna when Moore was shot – it is dealing with the politicos, and the allies. Wellesley will handle London right enough, and his brother will guard his back there, and he's not fool enough to trust the allies – Spanish *or* Portuguese for that matter – so that he ends up hazarding things as Moore did. We'll not see brilliance, as we did with Moore, but I believe we may trust to consummate skill in so far as strategy is concerned. That, and sure administration. It will just take so much longer with Wellesley, that is all.'

'I do not believe I have been able to contemplate that, Sir Edward.'

'Indeed not. Of course not. But you must contemplate the long point we're beginning. It will be no bolting Reynard and running him fast to the kill. Believe me, Hervey, these French marshals will show us more foxery than you'd see in a dozen seasons in Leicestershire!'

Hervey thought he was beginning to grasp the import, but he was troubled. Did Sir Edward have concerns that one of his cornets – he – might not have the stomach (or the horse, so to speak) for the long point? 'I did not think we would see England for a year, at least, Sir Edward.'

'A year? Mm.' It was not unreasonable of his cornet to speak of a year: His Majesty's armies did not campaign abroad much longer, as a rule. But Sir Edward shook his head. 'I will speak plainly. You have done well these past days, as I observed you did in Spain. It would not do if you weren't to gain some . . . responsibility in this war. Both you and the service would be ill served. You are but eighteen: you may imagine that I do not have this interview with every cornet.'

Hervey, warmed as if he had just swallowed fine brandy, nodded. 'Thank you, Sir Edward.'

'No need to thank me, Hervey. I'm giving you nothing but counsel, and that is my duty. In any case, you may not like what follows. You must know that you can have no advancement in a cavalry regiment unless you are prepared for a very considerable outlay. In the infantry it would be different: there is much more free promotion.'

Hervey knew precisely what he meant. More officers were killed in the infantry.

'And there is more opportunity for distinction there, and consequently for merit promotion.'

Again, Hervey perfectly understood. If one survived in the ranks of red, and stood in the right place, there was the chance that a senior officer might notice.

'I consider that you should buy into the infantry, Hervey. You would have a company in no time. This war will last very much longer than a year – *five* years more, I'd wager. You might even have a major's brevet at the end of it.'

Hervey felt his stomach tighten. Was his troop-leader saying that he was not cut out for the regiment? Was he trying to warn him off, kindly? But if he were, why now? Why not in England when the prospect of campaigning had been remote?

Sir Edward saw the dismay. 'The fact is, Hervey, you will scarce have opportunity for distinction in the cavalry. Ours, in the end, is a business unobserved. Not the *charge*, but that is an infrequent sort of affair, believe me. You saw for yourself in Spain. And if you are bent on long service, as I perceive you are, then you shall have to seek your advantage wheresoever it may be.'

Hervey felt reassured: Sir Edward appeared genuinely solicitous. And he had come to trust that whatever appeared to be the case with Sir Edward was indeed the case. He did not like the advice, but he could not resent it. 'Sir Edward, I thank you for your good opinion of me, but I have no thought other than to advance in the Sixth. I already feel it as a family.'

Private Bancroft came with the half-made coffee. Hervey now saw that its purpose was to sustain the interview rather than anything else.

Sir Edward took his cup, and a sip, then pulled a face and set the cup aside, sharing Bancroft's opinion on lukewarm coffee now that its original purpose was passing. 'That is as it should be, Hervey. As long as you're content with its price, that's all. And when you speak of family, have a care: let me remind you that to become too close to any man in our business is folly when you must send him to his death next day.'

Hervey marked very carefully what his troop-leader was saying, wondering if he displayed some tendency in this direction. He was not aware of any. Indeed, he had rather feared that the opposite had been true during the retreat to Corunna, for he had been zealous in his duty as he saw it (not least over the matter of Serjeant Ellis). 'I shall endeavour always to maintain a proper distance, sir.'

'Mm.'

There was a long pause. Hervey tried his coffee again, thinking to show appreciation.

'What do you think of Armstrong?'

Hervey at once assumed that he *must* be guilty of the offence of which Sir Edward had just spoken. Nevertheless he would give his opinion plainly. 'I think of him very well indeed, sir.'

'Good. How long will it take before he is ready for serjeant?'

Hervey brightened; evidently he was *not* guilty in this regard. On the contrary: it appeared that Sir Edward valued his opinion, though he scarcely imagined his troop-leader had need of it. He contemplated the exemplars of serjeant's rank in the regiment, quickly dismissing Ellis as wholly aberrant. Armstrong certainly looked the part – the authority that came with the indeterminate age of the non-commissioned officer, the voice that commanded attention, the way of moving, purposeful, confident; and that something extra, an understanding of what it was the officers were about, so that he stood not in opposition ever, while being entirely true to himself. Armstrong, for all his rough-hewn qualities, was 'regimental', as Daniel Coates called it, an attribute defying precise definition in a handy volume, if at all. Hervey was sure of it: 'I venture to say, Sir Edward, that were he required to act in that rank today he would do so very creditably.'

'You think him worthy of promotion over the heads of his seniors?'

That was a different question. It called for a judgement in more things than simple quality. 'I have not the wherewithal to give a safe opinion on that, Sir Edward.'

'Mm. Then you are indeed a shrewd officer. Well, I would have Armstrong given every chance to display himself. He has not the seniority to advance otherwise than by some act of distinction.'

Hervey made no reply.

Sir Edward began polishing the silvered spurs again, breathing on them then buffing on his overalls. After a while he stopped and looked at Hervey directly, as if he were turning over another matter of promotion. 'I do not know how Wellesley fights,' he said, with the air of a man who considered it right that he should know.

Again, Hervey was surprised more by the sharing of a confidence than by its substance. It was generally supposed that Sir Arthur Wellesley knew the business of fighting and would make his intentions clear enough. He remained respectfully silent.

'Wellesley's got up here quickly, no doubt of it. I'd feared we would delay on the Mondego a good many weeks. But by all accounts his opinion of cavalry is not great. He may yet favour the cautious way, whatever intelligence we are able to bring him.'

Sir Edward paused, as if to weigh again his surmise.

Hervey inclined his head, expecting some conclusion, some course of action which followed from the estimate.

Instead, Sir Edward leaned forward, pushed the spurs back into the heel-boxes, and stood up.

Hervey rose at once.

'Have a mind of it then, Hervey!' Sir Edward said it almost absently as he picked up his Tarleton and stepped briskly for the door.

CHAPTER EIGHT
THE CHANCE TO DISPLAY

Later

It did not take him long to be ready for the task of escorting one of Sir Arthur Wellesley's observing officers. Sir Edward Lankester's last order to the squadron had been to off-saddle but remain booted: there were no French this side of the Douro any longer, they were assured, and the Portuguese dragoons had a vidette line on commanding ground between the river and the assembling army. In any alarm the squadron could be stood-to in but a few minutes. Hervey had saddled Jessye in no time, and by his own hand.

Not that he knew exactly how close was the main body behind them. For the past three days he had watched as the Portuguese cavalry danced about Soult's, and all the while Sir Arthur Wellesley's redcoats had been marching up from the Mondego. Recalling the stumbling, dispirited retreat to Corunna, he had imagined their pace would be slow; he had quite forgotten how fast the infantry could march when it was *towards* the enemy. However, he knew where the contact points were, and that was what mattered.

He watched as the escort of six dragoons mustered under Corporal Armstrong. They were tired, if not quite so tired as he was. They fumbled a bit, taking longer with straps and buckles, but it did not look too bad. Armstrong was as a rule unsparing with his tongue, but now he encouraged rather than cajoled. He knew the dragoons, and he knew if they were 'laking'. It did not profit an NCO to bark if there could be no response. He would bark loud enough when the last bit of spare effort was required, effort a man did not know he possessed until squeezed from him by his corporal.

Hervey smiled to himself. He was content – *very* content. He had recognized in Armstrong a special man, a man he might trust entirely, rely on to the ultimate degree, just as Daniel Coates had told him he would, although the old dragoon had warned that it might take many a year to find such a man. It was Sir Edward's opinion, too, that Armstrong was special, which made Hervey doubly content.

But still the talk of transferring to the infantry troubled him. Why had Sir Edward even broached the subject of selling out and buying into another regiment? Was that really to be the only way of advancement in this war? He knew it had been the way already for some – for Sir Arthur Wellesley himself in his early years (there was no secret to it). But now that the army was so decisively, indeed *desperately*, engaged with Bonaparte, the old way could not stand too long? Hervey shook his head. Truly, it was mystifying what Sir Edward had intended. Had he, when he spoke of Armstrong, been saying the same again, indeed – that promotion would not come without some particular act of courage? Hervey trusted he would have sufficiency of *that* quality (he had never even imagined the want of it). Was he supposed to seek out the opportunity rather than wait for it to be presented? Was that what Sir Edward meant? He began wondering if Joseph Edmonds would have been quite so elliptical in his advice. He imagined not. But there again, said the cognoscenti, Captain Sir Edward Lankester knew his way in that world, as did Lieutenant-Colonel Lord George Irvine; Major Joseph Edmonds did not.

Hervey shook his head. What a repugnant business it was! How different from Edmonds's injunction when first he had joined his troop at the Canterbury depot: 'Do not trouble to impress me, Mr Hervey; it is they you must inspire,' he had said, pointing to the dragoons at skill-at-arms on the square. Hervey hoped now that he would continue to try to do so, not least because they were all tired and the man they were about to escort would form his impression of the regiment by what his little command did this morning. Their charge was no ordinary staff officer; he was an observing officer, one of the men whom Sir Arthur Wellesley relied on for intelligence of a certain kind, that which not even the most vigorous scouting by cavalry could provide. As a rule, such officers did not wear uniform, since their business was behind the enemy's lines. 'Spy' was a word not infrequently used of them, if loosely – and, moreover, dangerously, for by the usages of war a spy might be shot out-of-hand, whereas by those same usages a man in his country's uniform enjoyed the protection of his captors. Hervey quickened at the thought.

Lieutenant-Colonel Shaw was a hard-looking man, in his forties, Hervey reckoned. There was a pronounced powder-burn on his right cheek, and his upper front teeth were missing. Yet there was nothing of the bruiser in his manner, which was more schoolmasterly than soldier. Hervey had already begun to note how different officers in other regiments could seem. It was not just that they were un-familiar, they were formed in another way. Some, he knew, would have been formed in half a dozen regiments, but he thought he was beginning to discern a certain stamp; and not merely between Foot and Horse, Guards and Line. Colonel Shaw could not have been in the Sixth; *that*, he was sure. It was not appearance alone, although he did wear uniform of sorts, which Hervey imagined was on account of his working within the allied lines of communication. No, it was not the 'uniform': there was something about him that did not suggest an acquaintance with dragoons.

In fact, it was not possible to determine Colonel Shaw's regiment even by close inspection of his dress, for he did not wear any distinguishing sign. His coat was a curious affair, dark blue, the buttons half-ball horn, its cut nodding to the military but which might otherwise be that of any man of quality. He wore buff breeches, and butcher-boots, not hessians. Only his headdress was decidedly military, a plumeless bicorn with black cockade. Even his horse furniture was of civilian pattern, so that if he were to remove his hat he could pass for a private gentleman – which was, Hervey concluded, the intention. But hat in place, there was just sufficient mark of the man of rank to draw a salute and, more importantly, *laissez-aller* from Sir Arthur Wellesley's men. But Colonel Shaw wanted now to pass through Portuguese lines, and for that, someone had judged it prudent to have an unequivocally military escort.

'Mr Hervey, my compliments to your captain: an exemplary smart body of men!'

'Thank you, sir,' replied Hervey, nodding to Armstrong and the others to take note. Compared with muster at the depot they looked in rag shape, but for field conditions he fancied they were indeed a cut above the usual standard.

'What are your orders?'

'I am at your disposal, sir.'

'That is understood. Very well, I wish to take a look at the Douro.' Colonel Shaw paused, fixing Hervey, hawklike, as if to gauge his reaction. 'A *close* look.'

Hervey nodded. 'Very well, Colonel.'

'As close as may be.'

'I understand, sir.'

'I am in your hands, Hervey, but from my map it appears there might be an opportunity to approach the river from

Villa Nova . . . *here*.' He indicated the point on his map.

Hervey saw, then glanced at his own. 'There's a picket half a mile short of there, sir – Portuguese, I mean – on the high road, but I have been no further forward. We might have a guide from them.'

'Capital, Mr Hervey,' said Colonel Shaw briskly, folding his map and taking off his reading-glasses. 'Let us hasten thither.'

It took them but a half-hour to reach the outskirts of Villa Nova. Even as they trotted, Colonel Shaw made notes, constantly searching the country, slowing occasionally to study something or other through a compact telescope. As they eased to the walk a hundred yards short of the picket, Hervey could only marvel at how composed Shaw looked for a man intending to slip behind the French lines at the first opportunity.

'Upon my word, Mr Hervey!' The observing officer pulled up suddenly and began peering through his telescope again at the middle distance.

Hervey reined sharply to the halt, wondering what had alerted him.

'You see that bird yonder,' said the colonel, with a distinct edge to his voice. 'What do you say it is?'

Hervey, not a little taken aback, lifted his spyglass, wondering what the bird portended. 'A hen-harrier perhaps, Colonel?' he tried, after a not entirely perfunctory study.

'An understandable conclusion, Hervey,' said Shaw, keeping the glass to his eye. 'The colour is much the same; but observe its tail closer. How is it in shape?'

Hervey frowned, though his Tarleton concealed it if his voice did not. 'Colonel, I think we ought—'

'Yes, yes, Mr Hervey. I know we have business to be about, but you may see a river any day. You will not see a black-winged kite again once you have left these parts.'

Hervey's frown faded. If Colonel Shaw wanted to watch birds rather than the French then that was his business. He raised his telescope again. 'I observe that the tail is spread and slightly forked.'

'Just so. Whereas the hen-harrier's is . . . ?'

Hervey thought for a moment. 'Long and straight?'

'Exactly. But observe also what it does. A bird reveals its identity above all by its habit, Mr Hervey.' Shaw's telescope seemed positively fixed to his right eye. His mare stood obligingly still, as if used to episodes of intense study. 'See how it flies, very much active, like the owl, and how it twists its tail. The harrier is altogether more measured in its move-ment: a few leisurely beats of the wing as it flies low – far lower than the kite – and then it glides, the tip of the wing raised. Quite unmistakable.'

Hervey saw what was Colonel Shaw's game, and found himself rather more happily drawn in: a *rara avis*, evidently, the observing officer – like his black-winged kite. He imagined he might learn a lot from such a man, even if a good deal of it by riddles. 'Yes, I see, Colonel.'

'The observation of birds, Hervey, of all the kingdoms of the natural world, is really most apt for our purposes. Observing is a skill to be acquired, and its practice in the kingdom of birds is an exemplary thing. I commend it highly.'

Hervey nodded. 'Yes, Colonel.'

'Indeed, a capital scheme would be to have your dragoons observe what birds there may be in a place, and to note their appearance and habit, and to report what they observe. It will test their powers admirably.'

Hervey was intrigued, but not sure such a scheme would find favour, least of all with dragoons, though he recognized the method's merit well enough. 'I shall commend it to my captain, sir.'

At length, Colonel Shaw lowered his telescope. 'Well,

well, well: a black-winged kite, the first I ever saw. I shall take it as a propitious omen. Well, well!'

Hervey gathered up his reins. 'Walk on, Colonel?'

'Yes, Mr Hervey. We may now go about the King's business once more, but with a blither spirit for certain!' Colonel Shaw smiled contentedly, the gap in his teeth most pronounced.

Hervey smiled to himself. Was it in the nature of observing officers to appear . . . abstracted, or was it the nature of the work that made Colonel Shaw appear so? Whatever it may be, and despite the colonel's manifest seniority and experience, he resolved to have a special care if they did close with the French – even if only the width of the Douro.

The few hundred inhabitants of Villa Nova, caught in the fear-laden interval between the withdrawal of an occupying army and the arrival of the liberators, had done as generations before them, seeking refuge behind doors and shutters, and begging protection of the Almighty through the intercessions of the Blessed Virgin and numerous patron saints. They feared the fire of enemy and friend alike, and knew how rapacious a liberator could be in the heated blood of battle. The French had been proper enough occupiers, for the most part paying for rather than taking, and so sudden had been their departure early that morning that they had left without the customary depredations. That was fortunate indeed, but soon would follow their fellow countrymen, and allies; and those citizens of this quiet and unfashionable suburb on the wrong side of the Douro who had not already hidden their valuables now did so. Wives and daughters sought further refuge in cellars or eaves, smearing their clothes, hair and faces with anything that smelled foul – even with excrement – so as to render themselves repulsive to the most determined raptor (it could be a heavy price that a husband or father paid for the ejection of the invader –

ironic that liberation bore its cost). Now, the narrow, cobbled streets, running steep and straight to the wide Douro, were peopled only by cats, and scabbed dogs which dug among the refuse of the fleeing army, scavengers which might have found meatier fare had the army decided to contest the streets rather than give them up to a few cavalry patrols.

Hervey's men dismounted and advanced warily nevertheless, two dragoons at point with carbines ready. Hervey himself scanned the buildings on either side of the street for an open window, to hail someone with his few words of Portuguese and Spanish; but he saw none.

Colonel Shaw glanced about even more, like an owl, surprising Hervey by the sudden change from languor. His eyes kept returning to a large building on a promontory to the right. 'The convent of Serra, Mr Hervey. It should afford us a clear prospect of the far bank.' He did not consult his map. The country was imprinted on his mind.

'Do we take a look there, sir?'

Colonel Shaw shook his head the merest fraction, enough to convey that he was most decided on it. 'It is very evidently apt for its purpose: the artillery shall have it. I want to get to the water's edge.'

Hervey was puzzled. If Colonel Shaw wished to slip undetected across the Douro in broad daylight then he could scarcely be choosing a less promising place, for the heights on the southern side of the river were matched by those on the north; what could be seen from the Serra convent could as easily be seen from the other side.

Or so it seemed. But when they came to the water's edge, they found a wild place of reeds and rushes, unlike the wharves of the far bank. Five minutes' searching with their telescopes found no sign of the French on the heights opposite.

'They conceal themselves skilfully, sir,' said Hervey, sounding surprised.

'It is curious indeed,' replied Shaw, in a lowered voice, so that the Douro's gentle lapping made Hervey strain to hear him.

It was not the colonel's voice he heard next but Armstrong's. 'Boat, sir,' he whispered almost, gesturing over his shoulder with his thumb. 'Hidden, I mean. Not very big, mind. Two or three men at most. But it'd serve.'

Colonel Shaw's ears pricked. 'Has it oars?'

'Ay, sir, a pair on 'em.'

'Careless of Soult, that; *very*,' he declared, standing tall now among the reeds, hat off, telescope to his eye once more. 'Tut, tut; even more careless to leave boats on his *own* side in such a place. See, Hervey: by that place with the red and white flag yonder.'

Hervey picked up the reference point with his spyglass, searching left and right until he realized that what he had first taken for a wharf was in fact several barges of the type that, until war interrupted the trade, brought barrels of the region's wine down the Douro to English merchantmen anchored in the estuary. This morning they lay empty, and the possibilities were at once apparent.

Colonel Shaw shook his head as he tutted, taking a second look with his telescope. 'Why in the name of heaven did he not have them towed to the river mouth if he hadn't the stomach to fire them?'

Hervey assumed the question was rhetorical. He certainly had no opinion to offer. He was more occupied with what the colonel intended next. Would he take the boat, and cross? He himself thought they should send word to the engineers that there were strong and ready pontoons with which to improvise a bridge: the one stone bridge, from what he could make of it, was now a work of many days' restoration, even weeks. Perhaps first, though, the infantry might be able to use the boats to get across? Except that the boats were on the wrong side.

Colonel Shaw snapped shut his telescope and reached inside his coat. He took out an oilskin package no bigger than a fist, unwrapped a vellum notebook, squatted with his left leg under him to rest the book on a foreleg, and began writing in a small, neat hand.

> *To Colonel George Murray for immediate attn Sir AW.*
> *Convent of Serra affords commanding battery.*
> *Opportunity presents for immediate crossing under*
> *cover of guns. Company of light troops may be ferried*
> *as one. French not at all active.*

He tore out the page, folded it and slipped it inside a waxed envelope. 'Mr Hervey, may I rely on one of your men to take this with all speed to Sir Arthur Wellesley's headquarters? Do you know how it is to be found?'

'Yes, sir.' Hervey checked the impulse to add 'of course'. It was every cavalry officer's duty to know how may be found the superior headquarters. 'I shall take it myself.'

'No, Mr Hervey. I would have you stay with me. Your corporal here, perhaps.'

But Hervey preferred that Armstrong remained with him, not least for Sir Edward Lankester's purpose: some opportunity for distinction. There was none to be had galloping, unless with the victory despatch (and that, he knew, was a privilege that would never fall to any of them). 'I have a lance-corporal who will do it capitally, sir.'

'A *lance*-corporal? Great heavens, Mr Hervey, but you have a very high opinion of your men! Yours is the decision, however. I would speak with him, though.'

'Of course.' Hervey turned to Armstrong. 'Collins, please, Corporal.'

* * *

125

Armstrong and two dragoons steadied the skiff as Hervey and then Colonel Shaw clambered in.

'There's room for me an' all, sir.'

Hervey saw there was, just. He glanced at the colonel, taking up the oars as if he were back once more on the river at Shrewsbury.

'No, Mr Hervey. Two are sufficient to my purpose. There will soon be enough for *all* your men to do, please God.'

Armstrong pulled a face. *He* had found the skiff after all.

But another voice intruded, agitated, pleading. '*Senhor, senhor, se faz favor!*'

Armstrong swung his carbine round.

The voice became frantic. 'Plees, long leef king!'

Armstrong grabbed hold of a dapper little man with oiled hair and mustachios.

'Plees, my sheep, my sheep!'

Colonel Shaw turned and gabbled so fast that Hervey could make out but two or three words.

The dapper little man replied, less frightened now, though Hervey could still catch barely a word. There were a few more exchanges, and then Colonel Shaw turned back to him.

'Mr Hervey, give this fellow five dollars. I have promised him ten more if we don't return his boat in good fettle. Have your corporal mark that, if you will.'

Hervey looked at Armstrong.

'I've five dollars, sir, but it'll have to be a chitty for the ten!'

Hervey grimaced: the conditional tense would have been more agreeable to hear at that moment. Then he smiled wryly. 'Be sure not to sell Jessye too quickly, Corporal!'

Colonel Shaw turned again and nodded, obliged, to the owner of the skiff, then back to Hervey. 'Interesting fellow: a barber. He was supposed to leave his boat on the other side, where his shop is, but he lives here and so hid it

126

instead. Our good fortune indeed. Oh, and he says there's a snatching current a quarter of the way across. To make yon barges we need to strike fifty yards upstream to begin with. Rather longer exposed, but there's nought to do about it.' He slapped the sides of the skiff. 'Pull away then, Mr Hervey!'

Hervey dug in the oars carefully, wanting to see how his boat handled, before rowing with any strength. The skiff was wide enough to be stable without needing the oars to balance it, but he might still pitch them out if he 'caught a crab' in the barber's snatching current.

Only now, as they left the cover of the reeds, did he wonder if he exceeded his orders. He frowned: what did it matter? There was probably a *tirailleur* drawing a bead on them this very moment! And even if they weren't sniped off the water, why did the colonel not imagine they would be helped ashore by French hands? He frowned again: happy alternatives indeed – shot, captured or cashiered! But he hoped nevertheless that he himself would have seized the opportunity even if Colonel Shaw had not been there. Could a man be faulted very greatly for advancing on the enemy, even if by unconventional means? 'A cavalry soldier if properly mounted should never fall into the hands of the enemy' – that was what Joseph Edmonds said. But he wasn't mounted, properly or improperly. He wondered ruefully if he might plead history in mitigation, that a dragoon had first been a foot soldier whose horse took him from place to place . . .

He felt the snatch mid-stroke. The bow swung downstream before he could correct with the right oar, and he struggled for a few seconds to use it as a rudder so that he could push back with the left and then take up the stroke again across the current.

Colonel Shaw sat impassive, telescope to his eye. 'You may let us down a hundred yards, Hervey,' he said by and by.

Hervey was glad of it. The water was slackening but it taxed him hard enough. He expected shots at any moment, yet Colonel Shaw looked for all the world as if he were taking a pleasant turn about an ornamental lake.

'Fifty yards to run, Hervey, no more.' Colonel Shaw lowered his telescope: they were under the heights now, and at this range the naked eye was better to detect movement at the water's edge.

Hervey glanced over his shoulder to look for his landing. He saw the four barges, high in the water, a useful gap between the middle two, just wide enough if he boated the oars. He kept glancing every two or three strokes, the current now so weak that he was barely having to correct. Five yards out, he swung the oars inboard and turned to fend off the barges as the skiff ran in. When they touched the staithe he realized he would have done better to turn and run the skiff in stern first, but it was too late now. He would have to inch forward himself and try to get a hand to what might pass for a mooring.

A face appeared above them, then another, and then two more. '*Boa tarde, senhores*.'

To Hervey, the Portuguese sounded ominously laconic. He could not catch what followed.

'You were left behind, eh, senhores?'

A pistol appeared, then another three, the faces now gleeful.

Hervey, balancing precariously, with one hand grasping a piece of rope just above the waterline, reached for his own pistol.

But Colonel Shaw had more than the measure of the situation. 'Good morning to you too, gentlemen. But we are not the last of the French; we are the first of the English!'

The glee turned at once to delight. '*Sim, senhores?* You are very welcome to our city!'

Helping hands stretched out to the skiff.

Colonel Shaw began the instant his foot touched the top of the wharf: 'Where are the French? In what strength? What do they do? How many cannon? Where is Soult?'

His interlocutors were uncertain on all points. There were many French, they explained, but for some days now they had not been able to speak as freely with them as before. A week ago there had been ten thousand; that much was known because of the requisitions of food and fuel. Of guns they knew nothing. One of them, who supplied the head-quarters with wine, said the French were afraid of being caught between the English and General Silveira's Portuguese marching from the south-east, cutting off their withdrawal into Spain. There was even talk, he said, of a landing by the English north of the city, for they knew the Royal Navy commanded the entire coast; most of the French cavalry had been sent there to watch.

Colonel Shaw translated it all for Hervey's benefit (at any moment a French bullet could strike him dead, in which case it would fall to a cornet of light dragoons to take this valuable intelligence to Sir Arthur Wellesley). 'You see, Hervey, Soult's in all likelihood so panical, a rousing assault here would bolt him!' He turned again and fired off more questions.

The answers sounded very certain.

'I asked why there are no sentries. They say there are, but downstream, nearer the bridge. And we would have been taken for French: there've been officers crossing by boat since the bridge was destroyed.'

Colonel Shaw turned once more, this time with less of an enquiry in his voice.

Suddenly agitated, the men began gabbling among themselves, until the supplier of wine spoke up for them, and stern-faced. '*Sim, senhor*. We will take the boats across. We will gather twenty men more – half an hour, that is all – and then we will take the boats to Senhor Sir Wellesley!'

Colonel Shaw merely smiled, and nodded.

The men smiled too as their confidence swelled.

It was an anxious half-hour for the two of them, crouched waiting in one of the barges. Colonel Shaw explained what he intended. He wanted the barges to cross to the south side as soon as the men returned, for although the French would see, and stand-to-arms, and they would lose surprise, he couldn't wait on this side until the infantry were ready to cross, risking discovery by a French patrol. He told Hervey he wanted *him* to take charge of the boats, while *he* slipped into the city to discover Soult's intentions. 'And, Mr Hervey, I shall commend you in very decided terms to Sir Arthur Wellesley. You *and* your dragoons.'

It was as much as any cornet could wish to hear, and with Sir Edward Lankester's words of but a few hours before, it promised certain advancement. This, indeed, was the fortune of war; and he had never expected to be favoured by it, let alone so soon. Daniel Coates used to speak of the bullet's brute chance: was there such a thing as a lucky soldier, a man whom fortune naturally favoured? Was that why they had found the boat hidden in the reeds? Perhaps that was Colonel Shaw's luck, though, not theirs. Such a man, who devilled behind the enemy's lines, needed it in the largest measure. But lucky they had been, as well, to be his escort. Hervey smiled: such notions were absurd – but they were agreeable. 'We are honoured, Colonel.'

When the men returned, it was with nearer fifty than twenty, and all of them armed.

'Well, Mr Hervey,' said Colonel Shaw, allowing himself to look gratified. 'Here is your command. You will never have another like it!'

Hervey could not know it, but his luck was greater than he supposed. As the Porto boatmen and the other willing hands began paddling the barges across the still-silent Douro, the commander-in-chief himself stood watching from the terrace-heights of the Serra convent. He said not a word, while about him artillerymen manhandled four six-pounders and a howitzer into position, and below and a little further upstream, taking the greatest care to conceal themselves from any sharp-eyed sentry on the heights opposite, men of the 3rd (East Kent) Regiment – the Buffs – were assembling in the narrow streets. It had been the work of but an hour; the work *and* good fortune, for Corporal Collins had ridden straight into Sir Arthur Wellesley and his staff not a mile from Villa Nova. Later, Collins would recount how the commander-in-chief had at once seen the possibilities in Colonel Shaw's despatch, sending gallopers to the advance guard, and how the horse artillery had come careering past them not twenty minutes later, gunners hanging on to the limbers for dear life; and then the Buffs, double-marching, sweating like pigs but grinning ear to ear, knowing they would be first at the enemy.

Corporal Armstrong stood at attention before the Buffs' commanding officer. The colonel was red in the face and short of breath, as every one of his men, but he was concerned for one thing only. '*Four* boats, you say, Corporal?'

'Yes, sir. They're coming across now.'

'Very well. Is there any view of the far bank to be had from this side?'

'There are no houses near where the barges'll come, sir, and it's very reedy. I think it would be better to take a look from upstairs here, sir.'

But the houses were strongly barred, and in any case the colonel was certain of his instructions: Sir Arthur Wellesley wanted him to cross the river straight away and establish a strongpoint so that they could ferry the entire army over as they arrived. The French would be sure to launch the most ferocious counter-attacks as soon as they realized what was happening, and everything would depend on how strongly the Buffs could lodge themselves.

The colonel turned to his leading company commander. 'You shall just have to choose your ground when you're over. Make sure you mark your positions for the gunners. And take off your jackets: it's just possible the French'll be confused if they don't see red.'

'Very good, sir.' The captain turned about. 'Jackets off, serjeant-major. Company will advance.' He nodded to Armstrong. 'Lead on, Corporal!'

As the Buffs began filing to the river's edge, Hervey and his little command began making headway. He would willingly have taken up pole or paddle, but the boatmen would have none of it; the river was theirs. Instead, he stood in the bows of the leading barge, searching the opposite bank. He wondered how long they would have to wait for Sir Arthur Wellesley's men to come up. He had no idea where they had bivouacked that night, how near they might be, or even how long it would take Corporal Collins to reach the contact point. He reckoned they would have to wait until nightfall, at least. Oughtn't he to have gathered some willing citizens of Porto to make barricades and defend the quay where they would land? But that must have occurred to Colonel Shaw; perhaps he judged that it would surrender all surprise? Perhaps, though, in slipping into the city, the colonel intended raising such a party? He wished he had asked. Did he have the authority to act on his own initiative? Or had Colonel Shaw supposed that it was sufficient merely to instruct a cornet to do something, with no need of elaboration as to what he might *not* do? These things were knotty. In any case, his first priority was to get the barges to the south side; he could always slip back across in the skiff . . . He turned and scanned the enemy bank with his telescope. It was as deserted as when he had first crossed.

The barges plied effortlessly. The steersmen knew the river well, the crews bent hard to the oars or put their shoulders to the poles, and the snatching current did not trouble them. Hervey, his telescope now trained on the south bank, spotted Armstrong at the waterside, with men either side of him – local men, he supposed. Perhaps he should take them across at once to guard the landing? But what if the French caught them as the barges ran in? They would then have lost the only means of getting the infantry across. Perhaps if he risked just the one barge . . .

He jumped to the bank as they grounded among the reeds. He saw the jacketless men, and the service muskets – and he breathed a sigh of relief.

'Dawes, Third Foot, captain of the grenadier company,' said a man in his mid-twenties with cropped black hair.

Hervey took his hand, then put on his Tarleton and saluted. 'Cornet Hervey, sir, Sixth Light Dragoons.'

'We shall cross at once, if you please,' replied the captain, with resolution rather than certainty. 'You had better tell me what you can of the other side.'

'I cannot tell you much, sir, for I have only been at the water's edge. You will have to scramble about six feet up onto the quay itself: the river is low and the barges sit likewise, as you see. There's a steep ascent to a fair-size building, cobbled all the way – *very* steep in fact, but I would reckon the building a good place to occupy. I can't see how the French might take the quay, or even fire on it, without first clearing the place.'

'Very well, Mr Hervey, that will do. Now, do you suppose these barges will take a couple of dozen men each?'

'That is what the boatmen say. I will accompany you; I have a little Portuguese.'

The captain half smiled, as if pitying the youthful eagerness. 'No, Mr Hervey. That will not be necessary. You may leave this to the Third. I imagine you have other business.'

Could he argue? These were *his* boats, were they not?

'Sir, I think I ought to—'

'No, thank you, Mr Hervey. This is infantry business. Your horse will be waiting somewhere, no doubt!'

And the captain of grenadiers, with the weight of a hundred picked men behind him, brushed aside the cornet of light dragoons and jumped into the first barge.

CHAPTER NINE

FIELD PROMOTION

Two hours later

'Where in heaven's name have you been, Hervey?' Sir Edward Lankester sounded like a man irritated by a trifle, but to whom no trifle was unimportant. And he was tired, as they all were, but without Hervey's thrill of crossing and recrossing the Douro.

'We escorted Colonel Shaw to the river and—'

'Well, well, it has all taken a deal longer than I supposed, and now we are bidden to be two leagues east of here as many minutes ago.' Sir Edward detected muddle on someone's part, and he had a great disdain for disorder of any kind.

Hervey was a shade crestfallen. He had not expected words of praise (Sir Edward could not have known what they had been about at the river), but it felt doubly unfair that he should suffer his troop-leader's irritation on account of someone else's folly. But that was war, as Daniel Coates used to say. He wondered what would have happened if he had not found the troop at all as they made their way up the Douro valley: he didn't seem much missed – he could have stayed with the infantry. And there was heavy cannonading at the river, now. The *river* was the place to display, no doubt of it. Armstrong would have been in his element!

But Sir Edward evidently had other orders, and the battle moved on. He could still make his report, later, in writing. But what would he write? He could not speak of his own part in things. He could commend – he *must* commend – Corporals Armstrong and Collins, of course. For himself, if his service was in any way singular, he need not worry, for there would in due course be Colonel Shaw's despatch. But, looking back on things, with the infantry having to fight their way into Oporto, what was so special about rowing a skiff across the Douro?

'Hervey?'

He woke suddenly, having touched his helmet to Sir Edward and fallen back routinely to the cornet's place in troop column. 'What? Oh, I—'

Lieutenant Martyn, A Troop's second in command once more, now that the squadron was reunited, looked as fresh as a daisy, his uniform just as if it had come from a portmanteau, although he could not have had a great deal more sleep than the rest. 'I said that it sounded hot work in Oporto.'

'Ah,' said Hervey, supposing he had been nodding for several minutes. 'The infantry – they've found some boats and are crossing the river.'

'How do you know that?' asked Martyn, sounding almost accusing. 'No matter. That is what *we* are supposed to be about. Somewhere upstream, a ford or something. Do you not know of it?'

Hervey had to think; he was still not wide awake. 'No, I . . . that is, we didn't patrol east of the city. I don't recall why. I think the French were quite strong there yesterday.'

'The Sixteenth had a bruising, yes. We saw them on the way up. They say Stewart mishandled it.'

Hervey found himself unusually without appetite for Martyn's news. He wanted only to nod in the saddle. For some reason, Brigadier-General the Honourable Charles

Stewart was not popular with the regiment. Martyn had never ventured any opinion, only fact, but others had voiced theirs – that Stewart was a young man who owed his rank and place to the influence of his brother, Lord Castlereagh, the man who had secured command of the army for Sir Arthur Wellesley. To Hervey, General Stewart was not an especially young man – thirty-one, closer in age to Sir Arthur Wellesley than *he* was to Stewart; but others believed he had neither experience nor aptitude for generalship. That much was the common tattle of the mess, among the cornets at least, who after all only repeated what they heard.

'How so?' he answered, but with little enthusiasm.

Lieutenant Martyn shortened his reins as the troop broke into a trot. 'Don't know the particulars, but I had it from one of the Sixteenth yesterday that he ordered them to charge in the most unsuitable country. They were really quite badly cut up.'

Hervey wondered whether that meant as badly as the Buffs might be cut up, for the cannonade at the river was intensifying by the minute, and it could only spell the hottest fighting at the quay. The cavalry could have its tribulations, and bloody ones too, but they were not the normal currency of their trade. The Sixteenth were cut about, but it was by some mishap, a thing infrequent enough to provoke comment such as Martyn's now. The infantry, on the other hand, found heavy casualties an attendant misfortune. The cornets might disdain their legionary ways, thinking the cavalryman superior for his independence – or rather, for his worth other than mere volleying – but when Hervey saw a company going to it as he had the Third's grenadiers, he could not but admire them.

They rode east and a little north for a full five miles, in dead ground so as not to be observed from the far bank of the Douro, at the main in a trot, cantering occasionally where the going favoured it, and pulling up to a walk once or twice in broken country among the vineyards. It shook Hervey back to life, and while he had started the ride fretting for the action at the crossing, by the end he was seized again with the peculiar thrill that was the cavalryman's, riding not to the sound of the guns, but to some bold and distant deed that might make the work of the infantry easier – or even unnecessary.

They were not too late reaching Avintas, as Sir Edward had feared they might be, and as they slowed to descend to the Douro, they saw the little force which Sir Arthur Wellesley had hastened there, to the one crossing-point upstream of Oporto of which he had certain intelligence. A squadron of the 14th Light Dragoons stood in line in the shade of some cork oaks by the river, while two six-pounders from the horse artillery were unlimbering to the rear. Their purpose was not immediately apparent, however; at least to Hervey.

'What do you suppose is afoot, Martyn?'

'Deuced if I know,' replied the troop lieutenant, shielding his eyes from the bright, overhead sun. 'I can't make out any French at all.'

'I don't imagine they'll have given up a ford without a fight. Shall the Fourteenth dismount to flush them out?'

'What choice do they have? As far as I can see, it's a deal too trappy for saddlework.'

Hervey had thought the same.

'Ah, there's Stewart, by the look of things,' said Martyn suddenly.

Hervey saw a hussar officer cantering the length of the Fourteenth's line. From the animation which followed he concluded that the enemy was close. He wondered if General Stewart had seen their troop approaching. If he had, would he wait for them?

He saw him raise his sword arm and wave his sabre in the

direction of the village, and the Fourteenth take off into the trees. Perhaps there were but a few French, and the going not so trappy after all?

Musketry began at once. A Troop, with the advantage of high ground, saw it all: powder-smoke inside the grove – the French must have had sharpshooters not fifty yards from where the Fourteenth had stood! And the squadron's six-pounders could not support them; they had neither target nor clear line of fire.

'Christ!' snarled Martyn. 'Don't they see how *deep* is that wood? The deuced fools!'

Sir Edward Lankester saw. 'Into line! Draw carbines! Load!'

A hundred rammers clattered like a water frame.

'Advance! Right wheel!'

It was done adequately rather than neatly. The slope did not permit of the usual pivot, but with the aid of a deal of cursing by the NCOs, the troop managed to deploy in two ranks knee-to-knee. As junior cornet, Hervey took post on the right and rear of the second serjeant, in the second rank. He had no line of fire, but the job of the rear rank was to support the front, either with the sabre if the enemy closed, or by taking their place with loaded carbine if they were too hard pressed. He had no idea what they faced. Even to his subaltern eye the prospect of launching after the Fourteenth into such country was perilous to say the least.

In five minutes the first of the Fourteenth's men came staggering from the wood, unhorsed and bloody. In two more, half the squadron were out, badly bruised. The quartermaster spurred from the trees, bellowing at them to clear the front. Others followed, and loose horses – and then *voltigeurs*, emboldened by the effect of their musketry. At a hundred yards, Hervey knew, the advantage was all with the French. To close with them now would take the strongest nerve.

'Return carbines! Draw swords!' barked Sir Edward.

Nerve indeed, gasped Hervey! Out rasped a hundred sabres. His heart began pounding.

'At the trot, advance!'

The French opened fire immediately. The shooting was wild, but there was plenty of it. More than one ill-aimed ball struck. The horse next to Hervey's squealed as a bullet gouged through its mouth. A dragoon in front of him toppled forward stone dead. Others fell to his left – he couldn't make out who. It was like a parade in slow time. He wanted to dig-in his spurs and close with the *voltigeurs* – they all did – but Sir Edward Lankester knew what would follow if they galloped at the wood. He wanted his troop in hand. He had panicked the French into firing early, knowing he could close the distance at a fast trot before they could reload. He was gambling, but what choice did he have?

A ball ricocheted off Hervey's scabbard and hit the man next to him painfully but harmlessly in the thigh. Another struck the dragoon next to the right marker in the throat. He made a noise like a hissing kettle as he fell from the saddle, sword hanging from his wrist by the leather knot as his hand tried to close the wound. Hervey winced: Meadwell, a good man, smart and decent. Would someone help him?

Too late: the front rank was into the trees, sabres slashing. Hervey looked for a mark as they closed up behind them, but there was none. The *voltigeurs* wouldn't stand against steel. No one would if they could run instead.

'Halt! Halt! Halt!'

The rear rank pulled up just short of the trees. Hervey glanced left: it was a good, straight line, ready to support the front rank if they pressed into the wood or cover them if they withdrew.

'Front rank retire!'

Sir Edward burst from the trees, his expression keen, but for all the world as if he were drawing a fox covert. There was blood on his sabre, and on a dozen of the dragoons' that followed him out. Two or three had lost their Tarletons – not the best of caps for a fight in the woods – but they all looked in good order and high spirits. Hervey cursed his luck.

More dragoons began tumbling from the wood – the Fourteenth's. Many were bloodied, others bewildered-looking. It was plain to him: they had had a mauling. He was not surprised; none of the Sixth was. To plunge into a wood, mounted, was to give the advantage to the man on foot. Surely the Fourteenth had seen that, even without the benefit of high ground?

At last, General Stewart came galloping out, his two aides-de-camp hatless and blood-spattered. He looked like a man who knew things had gone ill. He sought to congratulate someone. 'Sir Edward! Splendid work! Capital! The French are driven back. We shall push them across the river just as soon as the infantry come up!'

Sir Edward Lankester returned his sword after dropping it to the salute. 'When the Fourteenth are all out of the wood, General, I propose we retire so that the guns have a clear line.'

'Just so, Sir Edward,' replied Stewart, looking over his shoulder at the Fourteenth's disordered squadron. 'And, I might say, one of your corporals deserves promotion as soon as may be!' He looked along the front rank. 'There, the right marker! He cut down a sharpshooter who'd have put a bullet in me for certain. Admirable address! Admirable!'

Sir Edward knew who was his right marker well enough, but he turned to see the object of the general's favour. With a nod, and in a voice just loud enough to carry to each flank, he announced, 'Corporal Armstrong, by desire of General Stewart, you are promoted local serjeant herewith!'

CHAPTER TEN
THE KING'S COMMISSION

Badajoz, late afternoon, Christmas Day, 1826

Hervey began peeling his last orange. They had been cork oaks at the affair of the Douro, good for *voltigeurs* to take cover behind, and low branches to entangle the unwary dragoon, Absalom-like. But when they had got to the other side – when the infantry had come up and swept through the wood – there had been orange trees; and what a feast they had had! Stewart had far exceeded his authority in promoting Armstrong, but that had been the least of his faults. The Fourteenth had lost half their men in that bungled affair. If the French had counter-attacked before the straggling squadron had cleared the gunners' line, there was no knowing how things would have gone. But they hadn't, and the infantry had come up, and the day had ended well. And not least for General Stewart, who had already botched things on the march north; another reverse might have proved fatal.

Hervey sighed. No, it would not have been fatal for Lord Castlereagh's kin, not for the brother of Sir Arthur Wellesley's supporter in London. There had been many, and greater, names in the pantheon of incompetence, secure in their positions in spite of any calamity because of some influence at the Horse Guards. In any case, Sir Arthur Wellesley had known how to deal with the problem of the

142

Honourable Charles Stewart: he had checked his impetuous confidence by hobbling him to the duties of the staff (and even there, Hervey learned years later, Stewart had been more hindrance than help). But checking Stewart had not been the end of it: there had been others who had sent brave men needlessly to their deaths. Slade, for one. What had Slade ever done but bungle things? And with a streak of malevolent cowardice that singled him out as being in a special category. Now he was lieutenant-general, with the rank to make war on his own, to dissemble and bungle on a campaign scale, to send men to their deaths in thousands.

Hervey angered, even as he sat confined. Would it be always thus? Would advancement in the army forever depend on this rotten system of purchase and patronage? Parliament couldn't care less: the nation won its wars, eventually; did it matter at what cost? Evidently not, for neither house showed any appetite for demanding generals' heads in return for soldiers' bodies – *legions* of bodies. Unless, of course, the general was known as a party man: there had been baying enough as the army stumbled back to Corunna, for Sir John Moore had been a Whig. The Tory Wellesley had heard party baying too, on occasion.

How different it had been at regimental duty in those early days in Portugal, with Armstrong promoted serjeant. There was scarce a man that had not lifted a glass to him – not because Armstrong had especially deserved it in the confusion of the cork grove (there was nothing singular in saving a comrade, except that Stewart was Stewart), but because of the aptitude he had shown on countless occasions since their first footing in the Peninsula.

Hervey smiled as he took the last of the peel from the orange. It had been a short-lived celebration, Armstrong's third stripe. Three days later, before the local rank could even be confirmed, he had been reduced to corporal again. A dispute in a Porto *tasca* over who was more use, infantry or cavalry, had come to blows, the sort of pointless debate in which no speaker could entirely believe his own proposition, yet each would submit to trial by combat to settle the question of honour. A serjeant of the 29th Foot (Worcestershire) had been chastened by a bloody nose, and the town commandant, charged by Sir Arthur Wellesley to maintain the strictest discipline, had insisted on condign punishment. Sir Edward Lankester had only been able to spare Armstrong from a regimental court martial by summarily removing the unsubstantiated chevron. Hervey smiled again, and wryly. *That*, he reminded himself, was regimental duty.

As to his own fortunes in the aftermath of the Buffs' brilliant and economic victory at Oporto, they had run no better than Armstrong's, for soon after entering the city, Colonel Shaw had been killed by the explosion of an ammunition tumbril. There had been no despatch commending him to Sir Arthur Wellesley, therefore. 'Here is your command. You will never have another like it!' – how the words had haunted him in the months that followed. The opportunity to display came rarely for the cavalry officer, just as Sir Edward Lankester had warned him. Poor Shaw: the commander-in-chief had lost a brave and resourceful observing officer; but he, Hervey, had lost the best opportunity he would have for the rest of the war!

He sighed a third time, cursed almost. He let events take him, that was his trouble. No, that was absurd: he had never waited for orders, and he had seized the moment to good purpose often enough. He frowned: that was why he was here now, was it not? Only in part. It was true that he would not be here if he had not opposed Colonel Norris's design, but, he told himself, no self-respecting officer of his arm could have done any other than press his case as he had. That was the purpose of the reconnaissance, was it not? Was he supposed to advance in rank by saying, instead, only what was welcome to the hearer? He knew some who believed it – until such time as they achieved a position of importance, they explained, whereupon they could exercise their independence of judgement to true advantage. But how did the independent mind not atrophy meanwhile? That was what he would know. And would the moment ever come when they judged the exercise of an independent mind more important than even *further* advancement, however remote it might seem? With such men, did not the sole purpose of advancement *become* advancement? Why did he not play their game, though? For nine times out of ten his judgement would be superior to any promoted in his place; and the *tenth* time – the tenth part – was a very small fraction of the whole business of command. Did he dissemble if he only did so one part in ten?

He shivered; the fire was getting low. It was Christmas Day and there was no chaplain, no company whatsoever. He had never spent Christmas Day alone; he found it remarkably discouraging. Were there any but felons confined as he was? None, he felt sure, who wore the King's uniform. And it was not entirely self-pity. He felt abhorrence at letting himself become a prisoner of the King's enemies (was 'enemy' not too strong a word for the men who kept him here?). He felt shame, indeed, and he dare not let his thoughts drift to home, to which in any case he had been stranger for so many Christmases.

How did Isabella Delgado spend this day? Warming by a great fire in Belem, in her father's easy and loyal company; mass at the Jerónimos; a walk in the royal gardens; a drive, perhaps, to Cintra; and dinner in agreeable company? He would have been glad to be with her at any of those diversions. Glad, to be sure, simply to be with her. He shivered again. Lady Katherine Greville – did *she* spend a good Christmas in Madeira? Would that he could picture it! Would that he were there, too! Did she curse him, now? He had treated her less than gentlemanly, he knew it. But alarm had suddenly seized him in Lisbon, when he feared himself drawn in excessively deep, and it had been all too easy to send her that dismissive letter – what was it, three weeks ago? Now, he half prayed she was thinking it . . . ambiguous. Had she ever intended going to Madeira in the first place, as she told everyone? Or had his coolness driven her there? He would never know, most likely. And he had such need of her capability now.

But what was the purpose of turning over the past, or the question of dissembling, when he would in all likelihood face the discipline of the Horse Guards? He doubted any amount of purchase or patronage could restore a career thereafter. Would it come to that, to court martial? What else could it come to unless he escaped soon? He could wish himself in Belem now, or Madeira, but above all he wished he were in Wiltshire. That was where his true duty lay, was it not? Home – a cold church but a warm hearth. How many times had he heard the Christmas bells in Horningsham? His stomach twisted: only once since joining the Sixth. Yet that season was imprinted on him as if he had never left – perhaps even stronger, for the changes which must have come, year by year, had never troubled him, so that his memory was the sixteen-year-old's, as perfect as may be. Except that there was now a dependent in that place, a daughter he was neglecting, even when he had his liberty. He could not say truly that he honoured his father and his mother, either, by his long absence. It was not so plain a commandment, perhaps, as the seventh, which he broke with astonishing ease; but break it he did. His condition, in all things, was not one in which he could take any pride.

He opened his Prayer Book with a heavy heart. It was at least something familiar; he would be transported for half an hour, perhaps even contentedly. He began with the day's lessons, then turned to the appointed psalm, 119 – *Beati immaculati*: *Teach me, O Lord, the way of thy statutes: and I shall keep it unto the end . . . O take not the word of thy truth utterly out of my mouth: for my hope is in thy judgements. So shall I always keep thy law: yea, for ever and ever. And I will walk at liberty . . .*

He smiled ironically. He could walk in liberty at this moment. It was only his parole that he would render up. But that would not be keeping the law as it fitted the soldier. He had pledged somewhere, if only in his own hearing, to keep it to the end.

He read on, until the closing verses: *It is good for me that I have been in trouble: that I may learn thy statutes. The law of thy mouth is dearer unto me: than thousands of gold and silver.* He shook his head. How *often* was the psalmist apt!

To Hervey's considerable surprise, and equal joy, the physician visited him a little before six o'clock. 'I could not bear to think of you dining alone this day, Major Hervey,' he had said, and with such warmth that Hervey was prompted to take his hand by return.

Indeed, after he had read the psalm, his cell had become a place of some cheer suddenly. His jailers had fetched more wood for the fire, and servants he had not seen before brought a bowl of candied fruit, and fine wine and cakes. And when the physician had said that he could not bear to think of Hervey dining alone, he had meant that he would dine with him. So Dr Sanchez and his 'charge' had feasted on roasted capon, beef and puddings, and Hervey had almost been able to forget his condition for an hour or two. They spoke freely, but of the past, which avoided cause for dispute or indiscretion, for Britain and Spain had been allies (in later years at least) in the long struggle against Bonaparte. The more they spoke, the more they found common ground.

'Oporto was a very fine affair,' said Hervey, taking a cigar. 'I did not realize it at the time, but it spoke everything of the Duke of Wellington. He had a reputation for caution, but that is to misunderstand. He was – *is*, I suppose – a safe general, and there is much difference between the two. A general may have his reverses, but a commander-in-chief must never be beaten.'

'To have the enthusiastic support of the people, in the way you had at Oporto, is greatly to be prized, Major Hervey. That was the undoing of the French in my country. You know, I hope, of the *guerrilleros*?'

Hervey blew the first of his cigar smoke towards the high ceiling. 'I do, but I confess I regard a great deal of what they did with utter revulsion. I saw unimaginable things on the way to Corunna, the most shameful things, but the butchery which followed after Oporto was an outrage. The duke begged the people not to molest the French wounded, but it had little effect. It was nothing to what we saw later in Spain, however.'

The physician nodded thoughtfully. 'But by Oporto, the Duke of Wellington had secured his reputation, it is true. A fine affair indeed, a brilliant affair, Marshal Soult ejected from Portugal to cower in Galicia a prey to the Spanish army. Such *audacity* on the duke's part!'

Hervey did not immediately respond. There was no doubting the duke's right to praise, yet Soult had *not* been destroyed; neither was he by the Spanish. True, he had had to abandon all his supply, just as Sir John Moore had, and many of his guns, but the fact was that Soult had escaped and would recover and be a thorn in the duke's flesh for four more years. Months after Oporto there were rumours the duke had thrown away his chance by disdaining the advice of a Portuguese officer who knew by what route the French would escape.

Escape – the word again. What might *his* route of escape

be? Was there some secret way, ancient but unmarked on any map, as Soult's had been, by which he might slip from these quarters and out of the castle, through the lines and across the border? Who might be his guide? He had high hopes of Sanchez, but there was a difference between hope and desperation.

He drew on his cigar. 'I did not speak of the horses and mules at Oporto, did I? The French abandoned them as they did everything else. As *we* had at Corunna – except that we destroyed all ours. Or, at least, we tried to. In truth we made a fearful thing of it. Poor creatures! But at Oporto they merely . . .' Hervey's French broke down.

Dr Sanchez inclined his head.

'I mean, they just cut through the . . . tendon at the back of the hock, just a sabre slice, leaving the animal to limp about. What is a man who contrives such a brute method, as if he were merely slashing a sheaf of corn?'

'Or who do murder and rape?'

Hervey shook his head. 'They had treated the people very ill, certainly.'

Sanchez frowned, but with a look of sadness rather than censure. 'I was thinking of my own city, Major Hervey.'

Hervey checked himself. Badajoz had changed hands several times in the course of five years of war, but he had no doubt what the physician meant. He lowered his eyes, and then looked back at him again. 'I think Badajoz the most shameful thing in the whole time we were in the country. I confess I recall it often enough still. I'd seen on that march to Corunna what our soldiers were capable of when there was a reverse, if the officers were not attentive, but I'd never imagined such scenes as I witnessed here that night. Shameful, unspeakable.'

Sanchez looked at him intently. 'So you were, indeed, here during the siege, Major Hervey?'

Hervey was puzzled by the manner of expression. What did he mean by 'indeed'? 'Yes, I was here.'

Sanchez said nothing for a moment. Then he brightened. 'I was at Talavera, you know.'

Hervey brightened too. 'Ah! *There* was a victory in the proper fashion! You were with General Cuesta?'

'I was surgeon in the Duke of Albuquerque's corps.'

'Then we stood not half a mile distant from each other! As I recall, I confess I found it infernally hot.'

'You recall it perfectly, Major Hervey,' said Sanchez, with a most companionable smile.

Hervey was now thoroughly warmed – the fire, the food, the wine, but above all the fellow feeling. Here with him was, if not a cavalryman, then a man who had served with cavalry. It was not necessary for him to explain everything, now: the physician would understand so much.

Talavera! Hervey smiled and shook his head. What a battle to have shared! There was nothing like it till Waterloo!

CHAPTER ELEVEN

CHARGE, AND
COUNTER-CHARGE

Talavera, 24 July 1809

The march to Talavera was not the happiest of times to recall, however. There had been celebrations enough after crossing the Douro – how the people of Porto had sung the praises of Sir Arthur Wellesley, and how the army had congratulated itself! But later had come reports, disappointing if not at first unsettling, that Soult's army had *not* been destroyed, that it had got away into Galicia, albeit badly mauled; and then the alarming news that the Spanish were in no position to finish Soult off, so that the marshal and his army were left in the Galician fastness to lick their wounds, which, once healed, would mean they could fight another day.

Why had the commander-in-chief let Soult escape, some asked openly. Were they going to be marching up and down Spain again at the beck and call of the French, as they had with Moore? But at least Soult was no immediate threat: Sir Arthur Wellesley was able to march south to deal with Victor's army, confident that Soult was unable to render his fellow marshal any assistance. It was, as Lieutenant Martyn pointed out, a taste of Bonaparte's own strategy: strike one army a blow so hard as to send it reeling, concentrate everything then on the destruction of the second, and when that was done, turn back to defeat the first in detail.

But the march from the Douro was hard – harder than anything Hervey could recall. The army was not yet forged; these were the second battalions, the army England had never intended to send on campaign. Three leagues in the day was as much as the infantry could manage. And on 'exterior lines', rations were in too short supply. They were hungry all the time. They had been hungry for a month. They were losing horses at a sorry rate, and mules even.

The Sixth, at least, had been tempered by the first campaign and the retreat to Corunna. The NCOs knew how to make a biscuit last and salt beef stretch, although the weather was very different now – burning sun, not driving snow. Most of the officers had learned the hard way what served in the drill book and what did not. They were 'roughed off' for the field, as Joseph Edmonds put it. As a consequence, the Sixth had not lost as many horses as the rest on the march to Talavera, and looked a deal better in the saddle.

Not all of them, however: Cornet Daly, for one. 'Damned screw of a horse!' he cursed, one scorching afternoon, jumping from the saddle and throwing the reins at his brown colt.

The subalterns had been riding together at the rear of the column. Lord George Irvine was in the habit of turning over the regiment to the serjeant-major and the quartermasters when no action threatened, and the officers had just halted for midday rest.

Beale-Browne, H Troop's lieutenant, at once angered. 'Mr Daly, you will not abuse your horse in that fashion!'

Cornet Daly threw up his hands in protest. 'The damned vet'nary won't do what's needed, and the horse's no damned good to me with a mouth like that!'

'Mr Daly! That is no way to speak of the veterinary surgeon,' snapped Beale-Browne, looking as pained as he was angry. 'I would that you moderated your language at once. It is most offensive.'

Laming looked at Hervey as they found shade under a jungled willow. 'I tell you, I never met such a blackguard. What does he complain of now?'

Hervey shook his head. 'His colt has lampas. John Knight told him it's because he's a youngster, and the teeth are growing. But to see Daly's hands I'd wager they're as much the trouble. He jabs and pulls at the bit as if the animal had no mouth at all.'

'And what is his complaint with John Knight?'

'He wants to fire the mouth but John Knight disapproves.'

Laming looked scornful. 'The insufferable conceit of the man! He gallops about the bogs of that country of his like some little Squire Western, and thinks himself superior to a man like John Knight. It is not to be borne!'

Hervey sighed. He kept Daly at arm's length anyway, although there were moments when an apparent interest in horses made for conversation, except that with Daly the interest invariably tended to the animal's celerity, to which he considered all else subordinate. Indeed, Daly was no one's boon companion. Quilley and he were thick, observed Hervey, but their association seemed more the necessity of the troop and the fact that they had joined together – and that, without each other's conversation, they would have been hard put to find any. They were, by common consent, an affront to the esteem of the regiment.

Daly snapped at his groom to bring his second charger.

Laming looked at Hervey again. 'No doubt he berates the tenants so. No dragoon will want to do duty for him long. Odious man! I wonder that Warde has not placed him in arrest a dozen times.'

'The colt's barely three,' said Hervey, shaking his head. 'It's too green an age to put a horse in hard work. The bones aren't strong enough. Jessye's four, and I wish she were two more.'

Laming clapped a hand on Hervey's back. 'You are an excellent fellow when it comes to horseflesh!'

Hervey frowned. 'I am sorry to disappoint you in other respects!'

Laming raised an eyebrow. 'It is not your fault, I suppose, that your Greek is elementary and your Latin very provincial.'

'Hah! I have not found it deficient for any purpose yet. How is your German?'

'The language of the Hun, Hervey, has no attraction for me.'

'I believe they taught your Romans a lesson or two when it came to fighting?'

'That is as may be. But I think it a very moderate achievement compared with the proper legacy of Rome.'

'You would be professor, then, when this fighting ends?'

'You would be parson?'

Hervey smiled. 'I take your point.'

Laming's second servant had brought a bottle of wine, the red of Estremadura, rough and warm but refreshing nonetheless, and infinitely to be preferred to the brackish water they had been forced to drink of late. The horses pulled at the parched couch grass as the two cornets sat with them, reins in hand. The sun was fierce, though not as bad as it sometimes was at this time of year, said their Spanish guides. The Sixth had lost twenty horses to the heat, and although the other regiments had lost many more, John Knight had been beside himself on a dozen occasions. The King's Germans weren't losing as many, he would thunder. Remounts were nigh impossible to come by. Why wouldn't the officers regulate things better?

'You know,' began Laming, intent yet on Cornet Daly, who had still not off-saddled his colt, 'I believe we cornets ought to speak as one to the senior subaltern.'

'And what might that do?'

'We should demand that we buy them out.'

Hervey was doubtful. He had heard of the practice, though never of any particular. He had no great objection: he probably stood to lose no money, if the regimental agents handled it well. 'Would that not take an inordinate amount of time?'

'I don't see why. These things can all be arranged among gentlemen.'

Hervey raised an eyebrow.

Laming sighed. 'I acknowledge the difficulty in that respect. But what say you?'

'If it could be brought off without rancour, then I say yes.'

Laming nodded. 'Very well, I shall speak to Martyn. He will have sound counsel. The sooner it's done the better, for the further we march from Lisbon the harder it will be to induce either of them to sell.'

That evening, the regiment encamped a league to the east of Talavera among olive groves, finding an old well which, after they had dug it out by pick and shovel, yielded enough water for both men and horses, though the relays had to work for four hours before watering was complete, and another three to fill the buckets ready for morning stables. 'Never did I know the back-breaking work that is a cavalry camp until this day' wrote Hervey in his journal:

> We halted at Three o'clock, the horses very tired and
> showing the want of meat and water. Our three days of
> marching rations are exhausted, and there was no corn
> to be had from the commissaries when they came at six.
> Neither have the men eaten today. They have taken
> every olive from the trees, which are abundant, but they

155

*are very sour. I myself have nothing at all, having eaten
the last of the pocket soup for breakfast. There is tea,
but no sugar, and little wine. We hope to stay here for a
day so that our supply may be restored, for it is as bad
with the rest of the army, they say, and worse. We hear
of a general action in the next few days, for the French
are in strength the other side of the Alberche, and, goes
camp tattle, 'King' Joseph Bonaparte himself is with the
army. How ironic it shall be when we fight a <u>Royal</u>
French army!*

'Sir! Will you come, please? Mr Daly's horse is down and
there's a hell of a to-do about it!' The orderly corporal
sounded angry rather than perturbed.

Hervey sprang up and buckled on his sword. He had hoped
for another half an hour with his journal before rounds as
picket-officer. 'Is the orderly quartermaster there?'

'Yes, sir. He sent me.'

Hervey stalked off for the horse lines, leaving Sykes to
the care of his journal.

'Where is Mr Daly?' he snapped.

'At the lines, sir.'

'Then why am I called?'

The orderly corporal hesitated. 'Orderly quar'm'er' told
me, sir.'

'*Yes*, Corporal, but why?'

'Mr Daly is right angry, sir.'

'With what reason?'

The orderly corporal hesitated again. 'He's taken against
the quar'm'er', sir.'

Hervey was becoming irritated by the evasion, but saw no
profit in fighting it. 'I wish they would save their anger for
the French,' he muttered.

It was getting dark, but the light of the campfires was
good. The olive trees may have yielded a poor supper but

they gave off a good blaze. Hervey could hear Daly cursing as he got near the end of H Troop's lines; he sounded drunk. Then he saw Daly's colt on the ground, like a mare foaling. The orderly quartermaster, B Troop's, stood erect and silent to one side, and beyond him half a dozen dragoons from the inlying picket, while Daly ranted, and swung his arms about.

Hervey could not begin to imagine what was the occurrence. 'Daly, what ever is up?'

Daly spun round, his eyes blazing. 'This man is insubordinate!' he raged. 'I've placed him in arrest.'

Hervey was not sure if a cornet could place the regimental orderly quartermaster in arrest. He was certain that it was ill advised. But why was the colt down? 'Serjeant Treve, what is the meaning of this?' And then, before the orderly quartermaster could reply, he rebuked himself for the distraction and turned back to Daly. 'What is the matter with your colt? Is the veterinary called?'

'Sir, he is, sir,' answered Treve, determinedly.

Daly cursed more. 'I'll call the vet'nary when I'm ready! This man must be confined, Hervey!'

Hervey bristled. Seniority among cornets might count for little, but he was damned if he was going to be spoken to like that by a newcome. *And* he was picket-officer! 'Hold your peace, Daly, if you will.' He turned back to the orderly quartermaster. 'Speak, Serjeant!'

Treve, B Troop's senior serjeant, a Dorset man, sixteen years in the regiment, remained at attention and spoke quietly. 'Sir, I was making my rounds and came on Mr Daly and his charger. The animal was down and in distress. Mr Daly was holding a cautery, sir. He said he'd fired out the lampas. I told the picket-commander to fetch Mr Knight at once, sir. Mr Daly protested that I was not to, but I said as it was my duty, sir. And then, sir, I regret to say, Mr Daly became abusive. Sir.'

157

'That's a damned lie!' screamed Daly, lunging towards Treve.

Hervey, boiling at the thought of the botched firing, stepped between them and held up his hand. Daly halted, swaying. Hervey wished there were another officer to take hold of him. 'Mr Daly, you will retire at once and report to the adjutant!' He knew it was a mistake as soon as he spoke, the proverbial red rag to a bull already enraged by the orderly quartermaster's correctness.

Daly lunged again – whether at Treve or Hervey, no one would ever be quite certain. The orderly quartermaster stood his ground. Hervey squared, and swung his left fist, striking Daly in the temple.

He fell – out, cold.

'Oh, God,' groaned Hervey. But better he than the orderly quartermaster. Could he have restrained Daly otherwise, though?

'What in heaven's name's going on?' came a voice behind them.

Hervey turned to see John Knight with a lantern.

'What's the infernal commotion? In the horse lines, of all places!'

Hervey began to explain.

John Knight was horrified. 'Stand easy, Sarn't Treve.' He handed the lantern to his assistant and knelt down by the motionless colt. 'Christ! What a fever,' he spat, running a hand along the sweating neck and shoulders. 'Light, Brayshaw!'

The assistant held the lantern close to the colt's head as the veterinary surgeon tried to prise the mouth open.

'Hervey, give a hand here.'

Hervey knelt, turning to the orderly corporal. 'Go and bring Mr Beale-Browne, please.'

'Ay, sir.'

'And tell him all you can!'

'Ay, sir.'

John Knight had managed to get the colt's mouth a little way open, but it took the two of them to prise it far enough for him to get a finger to the roof – risky business that that was. The colt struggled, legs lashing out. Hervey held the mouth wide for all he was worth.

'For heaven's sake, the palate's like . . .' John Knight took out his hand. 'Leave off, Hervey. God knows what I can do. Brayshaw, make me up a gargle for mouth canker: vinegar, two parts burned alum and salt, and one of bole armenic.'

'Sir.'

John Knight looked to where Daly lay sprawled. 'How does he?'

The orderly quartermaster answered. 'He'll be well enough, sir.'

John Knight huffed. 'Then more is the pity.'

All Hervey could do now was wait for H Troop's lieutenant. Daly had to be removed from the horse lines, and that was a job for his fellow troop-officers. He himself would have to make his report to the adjutant, and already he was wondering how it would be received.

He got up, spoke quietly to the orderly quartermaster, bade him dismiss the picket and continue his rounds, then turned back to John Knight.

'Christ!' spat the veterinarian again.

Hervey saw. The colt lay quite dead.

Next morning, Hervey made his report to the adjutant after stand-down. Lieutenant & Adjutant Ezra Barrow, 'the inelegant extract' as the blades had dubbed him, listened seemingly unperturbed. Extract he may be, but he was the commanding officer's extract, brought in by him from his old regiment, and therefore carrying authority without the need to display it. Barrow had seen much during his eighteen years in the ranks of the 1st Dragoons, but dispute between gentlemen-officers he was not well prepared for. To him, the officers' mess was still *terra incognita*. He had observed its native habits at a distance for many years, and they had seemed alien indeed; but now that he stood on the same ground as they, he sometimes felt he knew them not at all. He was adjutant, however, the lieutenant-colonel's executive officer, and he would attend to what was before him now as if it had been a mere case of indiscipline among dragoons.

Except that when he heard the words 'I was obliged to strike him', he realized that they were all treading in deep water. 'Striking' was a word with resonance, the mainstay of many a charge-sheet: 'striking a superior', 'striking a subordinate', 'striking an officer'. For a moment his head swam. Which of these charges was appropriate? A cornet had struck another cornet: he had no idea which of them was senior (it was a trivial thing among cornets anyway, was it not?). Might one officer be charged with 'striking an officer'? It was surely not the purpose of that particular formulation . . .

'A moment, Mr Hervey, if you please,' he replied, in the grating vowels of Brummagem. 'As I recall the serjeant-major informing me at stand-to, the orderly quartermaster informed him that you interposed yourself between Mr Daly and the same, and that Mr Daly then fell unconscious on account of his . . . hysteria.'

Hervey was surprised. Was that truly how it had appeared to Serjeant Treve, or was it the exercise of rough regimental justice? Either way, he could not let it stand, tempting though it undoubtedly was. 'No, sir, I did strike a blow, believing it necessary to prevent Mr Daly's hitting me or Serjeant Treve.'

Barrow sighed. 'You might have waited to make sure, Hervey. That way there'd be no doubt of what we're about now.'

Hervey was taken aback. 'I believe I might have weathered the blow without too much injury, sir, but Daly would now be facing a grave charge one way or the other.'

'Or not at all.'

'I have no doubt he was about to assault one or other of us. His whole demeanour spoke of it, then and before.'

'Your fellow cornets will not thank you, Mr Hervey,' said Barrow, shaking his head with a distinct look of disappointment.

Hervey was puzzled. 'What do you mean, sir?'

'I mean that one way or another Mr Daly would have been in such trouble as to lead to his employment elsewhere. That is what you have been plotting, is it not?'

'Sir, that is—'

'Have a care, Mr Hervey. I may not share your learning, but it is my business to know what goes on in this regiment, and I do not neglect it.'

'No, sir, of course.'

There was silence. A huge horsefly settled on Barrow's neck. Hervey strained to warn him, but stood at attention instead, waiting leave to speak. After what seemed an age, the horsefly left in search of other flesh. Hervey wondered why it had not stung – or how Barrow had not felt it if it had. For weeks they had been plagued by them. Was the adjutant's skin *literally* as thick as the cornets supposed?

Barrow sighed again. 'Mr Hervey, the veterinary surgeon has already been to see me. He wants Mr Daly to be charged for mistreating his horse. The serjeant-major believes he should be chastised for abusing Serjeant Treve in front of the picket, too. And no doubt *you* will expect charges regarding his menacing and assault.'

'No, sir. Daly was drunk.'

'I thought officers got intoxicated, Mr Hervey?'

Hervey considered himself in too precarious a position to

rise to the bait. 'No doubt Mr Laming would prefer the word, sir.'

'Ah yes, Mr Laming and his Greek. Very useful skill in an officer.'

'Except the word is Latin, sir.'

'Don't quibble, Mr Hervey.'

'I'm sorry, sir. I meant no disrespect.'

'I don't doubt it, otherwise I would have had your sword this instant.'

Hervey braced up again. He was not at all on firm ground, much less than he had imagined.

'Well now, for the time being there is no need to render this in writing, not until I have spoken to Mr Daly and then the lieutenant-colonel. You had better speak to Captain Lankester meanwhile. Is there anything else?'

'No, sir.'

'Very well, dismiss.'

Hervey replaced his forage cap, saluted, turned to his right and marched from under the shade of the olive tree, which was the adjutant's orderly room. He had had nothing but broth to eat in thirty-six hours, but that was not the reason he felt sick.

When he reported to Sir Edward Lankester, Hervey found that his troop-leader was already aware of the turn-out (indeed, the entire regiment appeared to be, according to Private Sykes).

Sir Edward looked pained. To the dismay of not being able to feed his troop – horses *or* men – was now added the distaste of one of his officers fighting with another. 'I know that it was not *brawling*, Hervey, but that is what the canteen will be saying. It does not do to have officers appearing at odds with each other. There are badmashes who would take advantage, if I may borrow a word from our Indian friends. It's not so very long ago that I recall speaking with you of advancement, and here we are now contemplating the very opposite!'

Hervey shook his head. He was a cornet of but a year – less; Sir Edward Lankester was a captain of much experience. But Corunna had steeled him in considerable measure. 'Truly I do not see what else might have been, Sir Edward, except to be knocked down by him. If I had merely stood in his way there would have been a struggle of some kind, just as repugnant, for he was much taken by drink. And I have at least spared him the charge of striking a subordinate, which I had every belief he might do.'

Sir Edward held up a hand. 'I don't doubt any of it. But are you able to say that your action was in no degree animated by the anger at seeing the horse?'

'No, I cannot, Sir Edward. But I do believe that it made not the slightest difference to the outcome. Daly was drunk and attempted an assault. I defended myself.'

'A little prematurely, some might say.'

'They would not if they had been there, Sir Edward.' He paused. 'And there were witnesses.'

Sir Edward nodded, thoughtfully. 'Ah yes, *witnesses*. The orderly quartermaster and the picket. How do you suppose that would serve – a serjeant and dragoons giving evidence against an officer?'

Hervey said nothing. It was a loathsome prospect. But he had imagined Daly would be facing two charges: causing unlawful injury – even death – to an animal in the King's service, and drunkenness (the latter offence obviating any graver charge of assault, threatened or otherwise). Why, therefore, was his troop-leader speaking of witnesses? 'Sir, I am revolted by the notion, but I believe I acted honourably as picket-officer. I trust that Mr Daly will do likewise now.'

Sir Edward sighed. 'There is the rub, Hervey. Warde has told me already that Daly intends bringing charges against you.'

Hervey felt sick again.

'But be assured, I don't doubt you for an instant. I shall go with Warde to the colonel to see if this may be resolved directly. For the meantime, I trust you will not speak of it. The very best thing will be to remain active: take a patrol north to see if there's anything to be bought by way of rations. Return by midday. Take Serjeant Strange with you.'

'Yes, Sir Edward.'

Hervey took his leave, feeling better for the expression of trust, except that by specifying Serjeant Strange, Sir Edward spoke of some doubt still. Strange was the steadiest NCO in the troop, probably in the regiment.

An hour later, in the shade of the same olive tree, the adjutant announced A and H Troop leaders to the commanding officer: 'Captain Lankester and Captain Warde, Colonel.'

Lord George Irvine looked up from his camp-chair. 'I can offer you no hospitality, gentlemen, but take your ease, if you will.' The first of the mules had come up with the regiment's baggage, so there were at least chairs for them to take, if nothing else. 'I compliment you both on your stables again. I thought the horses in extraordinarily good condition at muster, all things considered.' He smiled. 'Even John Knight says so.'

'Thank you, Colonel,' they replied.

Lord George shook his head, and looked grave again. 'Wellesley's going to have to fill some bellies, though, if he intends a general action. I'm assured there's bread and beef on its way to us, and, by God, not before time; but there's nothing of corn yet.'

'It could be worse, Colonel. There's plenty of couch grass, at least,' said Warde, holding up a cigar.

Lord George nodded, and again at the cigar.

Warde lit it – a quarter of a fine Havana, which was all

that remained of his supply after two months marching in what they had begun calling the Wilderness. 'I wonder if we might boil up these olives the Good Lord has provided. There are trees for miles, say the guides.'

Lord George looked encouraged. 'I think it a very serviceable suggestion.' He turned to the adjutant. 'Have someone ask John Knight if there be any objection to that.'

The adjutant went to find an orderly.

'Now, this wretched Daly affair,' continued Lord George, briskly. 'What's to do?'

Captain Warde spoke first. 'Well, Colonel, I questioned him after stand-down this morning. Beale-Browne had already alerted me to the business. Daly says that John Knight would not oblige him in the proper treatment of his charger – which he very imperiously, though correctly, asserts is his own property – so he was obliged to treat the animal himself. He apparently took a brand iron from the farrier, got his servants to assist him and performed the cauter with his own hand.'

Lord George nodded. 'John Knight has explained the procedure to me. Evidently the iron must have been red hot, and the horse, enfeebled by the work and short rations, succumbed to the great shock of it.'

Sir Edward Lankester's brow furrowed. 'Is John Knight approving the procedure in general? I have always considered it barbarous.'

'No, he's not. He very much *disapproves* of firing what he calls soft tissue, for the reason that it distresses the animal too greatly, and the cauter is prone to infection. But he conceded that his is not the universal view in this regard.'

Captain Warde looked troubled. 'Do we consider any of this relevant, Colonel? The charge is one of assault. I wonder, indeed, why Daly and Hervey don't just have it out with pistols.'

Lord George smiled benignly. 'I fear, my dear Edwin,

that such an eminently sensible course is closed to us. I'm certain Wellesley would have both of them court-martialled afterwards. No, the matter is relevant if there is to be any counter-charge of negligence, or misuse of an animal. In the case of assault, Daly has a right to bring such a charge, of course, and I am obliged to settle it by court martial. I should have no hesitation in bringing a charge of assault against *him*, since the picket-officer is my executive during silent hours. But it is all a pretty mess, and would be presided over by a judge advocate and officers from outside the regiment. *Will* be, indeed, for I don't see what discretion I may have on account of his scandalous conduct in front of dragoons.' He sighed, the intense distaste for such a thing perfectly evident. 'And all this with a general action promising!'

The adjutant had returned. 'Shall I summon Mr Daly to your orderly room then, Colonel?'

Lord George frowned. 'Yes. And soon, if we must. It were better that it were done quickly.'

'Very good, Colonel. And John Knight says that olives well boiled would be a capital thing, perhaps fed with chop.'

Lord George's spirits brightened a fraction. 'Well, gentlemen, that is something. Let us hope that ravens appear soon for our *own* stomachs' sake!'

In the afternoon, the adjutant summoned Hervey again. Hervey, finding his situation as 'hero' to the cornets a queer thing with the threat of court martial hanging over him, tried hard to appear neither anxious nor assured. Barrow's manner was unusually warm, but the unhappy explanation soon came: Cornet Daly was pressing the charge of assault, he said, and the lieutenant-colonel saw no alternative but to order a court martial, at which, Barrow hoped most fervently, the counter-charges of assault and mistreatment would be heard.

'In the meantime, Mr Hervey, the lieutenant-colonel wishes you to continue in your appointment, and to discharge your duty with the zeal he would expect of one of his officers.'

Hervey swallowed hard. 'The lieutenant-colonel may depend upon it, sir.'

'Very well, you may dismiss. Oh, and the major would speak with you. He's over yonder.' Barrow pointed to another olive tree twenty yards away, where the red pennant of the regimental major of the 6th Light Dragoons hung limp in the still air.

Hervey saluted and turned, then made for the major's tree. He did not see Barrow shaking his head slowly.

'Cornet Hervey, sir,' he announced, two dozen paces later.

Major Joseph Edmonds, sitting in a camp-chair cleaning his pistols, looked up. 'Well, *Cornet* Hervey, a pretty business, this. Sit you down.'

It was not what Hervey had expected to hear. He took the other camp-chair and removed his forage cap.

'I've been told everything. I've spoken to Treve and half the picket.'

Hervey supposed that only Edmonds could have had such disregard for the formalities as to speak direct with a serjeant and dragoons. He returned the steady gaze, now entirely confident.

'Treve said you were boiling.'

'That is true, sir. The horse was a sorry sight.'

'Treve said he was boiling more.'

Hervey almost smiled. 'I can easily imagine.'

Edmonds blew into the firing pan, then held the pistol up to the light to inspect the barrel. 'Daly is a thoroughly objectionable officer. He has every disagreeable feature of that class of man, and not one of the strengths, as far as I can see. I have no idea what are his means, but he signs credit notes as if they were nothing at all. I heartily mistrust his instincts, and I have told Warde this.'

Hervey was stunned by so decided a pronouncement from the regiment's second in command.

'But the trouble is, being Irish, when he's backed into a corner the only thing he knows to do is fight. And when he is bowed and bloodied, he'll get up and think nothing of it and expect to carry on as before. If the court martial goes against him – and I can't see how it can't – the sentence may yet be lenient, and we shall have him still.'

Hervey saw things perfectly well, but he could not see to what the major's words tended.

Edmonds laid down the pistol, and sighed. 'Funny things, courts martial, Hervey. Officers from other regiments don't always see things the same; which is, of course, why there *are* courts martial. But see – and this is the reason I sent for you – you are not to take alarm when the papers come. The colonel is perfectly convinced of the truth of the affair. He wholly agrees with me with regard to the character of Mr Daly. So you are to return to duties as if this were nothing, you understand?'

'Indeed, sir. That is what the adjutant instructed me, too.'

'Good. And not one word of this is to be repeated.'

'Of course, sir.'

Edmonds's brow furrowed. 'See, Hervey, we shall very probably face a general action in the next day or so, and I wouldn't lay odds on the Spaniards holding, in which case we'll be sorely pressed and may well find ourselves running for the sea again. Wellesley will have want of every high-stomached officer he has.'

Hervey glowed at the compliment. Edmonds had been his troop-leader for but a few months when he had first joined, and he knew his praise to be sparing. 'I understand, sir.'

'Well then, be about it!' He picked up his second pistol and began rubbing the barrel as if Hervey had already gone.

There had been a modest issue of rations for men and horses

late in the morning, and both had fed early in consequence. At six, relieved of further duty, and partially filled with bread and beef for the first time in days, Hervey sat propped against an olive tree and took up his journal.

25th July
nr Talavera de la Reina

Country very harsh and dry, and hills many, and with steep cliffs. There are olive groves, however, and vines, and these relieve barren appearance somewhat, but grass is poor and unlikely to sustain unless we graze by the Tagus. Intend visiting Talavera as soon as may be, to see its walls and towers, which are very ancient says Laming, also to buy silk from the royal factory there. We are told our eastward march towards Toledo is halted by the presence of a French army under command of Joseph Bonaparte himself, and that Genl. Cuesta is obliged to withdraw his advance divisions. Sir A.W. has sent fwd a division and Anson's brigade (23rd L.D. and 1st L.D. K.G.L.) to the R. Alberche to cover the retrograde movement of the Spanish, which vexes us all since the Sixth has not yet seen action except skirmish at Porto! We are brigaded with Genl. Fane's heavies (3rd D.G. and Royals), but are to join Genl. Cotton tomorrow (14th L.D. and 16th L.D.) to form line of observation between Talavera and the Alberche. They say Sir A.W. is well pleased at the prospect of a general action since the ground he has chosen on which to stand on the defensive is very favourable to the infantry and also to the guns. I do not recall the place, though we first passed this way with Sir John Moore last November, and there is so great a difference between that season and now that I do not believe I should recognize any but a town of some substance.

All the rivers are v. low, and some altogether dry.

J and L are new-shod today and both sound, also my
mule Pedro. Sykes has a fever but is not too ill and will
not report himself sick for fear of being left behind. Sir
E.L. sent me on forage patrol in morning. Found
nothing but olives. Commissaries brought in some corn
and grey bread and beef, but no wine. Water is sweet,
however, and we do not have to boil it with tea.
Commissary officers are in high dudgeon for apparently
Sir A.W. berates them for lack of address, the Spaniards
all being well victualled.

In spite of vexations too shaming to record, I am
tolerably well, and look forward keenly to the morrow.

All next day, the Sixth stood to the east of Talavera without
a sign of the enemy, although they heard skirmishing
beyond the Alberche, and occasional cannonading, off and
on until the evening. They had shade, at least, and some
water, for as well as the olive groves there were big oaks,
and the Portiña, which ran from north to south behind them,
although for the most part it was a dry ravine, did have
pools adequate for watering. Where there were no trees
there was stubble, the corn cut a month before by
the Spanish, anxious lest what was left of it fall to the
French, for Marshal Victor's men had already made a fine
harvest for themselves. They had even made shelters from
the stooks, such was the harvest's abundance, so that as far
as the Alberche and beyond, the plain was filled with what
looked like yellow bell-tents.

Early in the afternoon, Major-General Sir Stapleton
Cotton had ordered his regiments to off-saddle by half
squadrons, but the whole brigade saddled up again for
stand-to at last light, and remained saddled until midnight.
No other order had come to the Sixth in the entire day, and
little news. Cotton himself had stood throughout with

Colonel George Anson on the far side of the Alberche, but he had been unable to send back any intelligence of the battle to the east other than from observation, and *that* very little. General Cuesta's troops were retiring, seemingly in good order, and neither Anson's cavalry brigade nor the infantry divisions of Generals Mackenzie and Sherbrooke forward of the Alberche received any change in orders from Sir Arthur Wellesley, so there was no occasion for alarm. At dusk, therefore, Cotton had ridden back to his brigade, ordered the Sixteenth to post videttes along the dry bed of a stream which ran parallel to the Alberche half a mile to its west, and told the Sixth and the Fourteenth to sleep.

Hervey slept until the welcome order to off-saddle came at midnight, and then he had slept without interruption until five o'clock, when Private Sykes roused him with a canteen of hot goat's milk, with the compliments, he said, of one of the King's Germans. Hervey, to whom the sound of the trumpet's reveille this morning was not so sweet as usual (he had been in a very deep sleep following two nights with next to none), knew he ought to ask how his groom had come by the milk – and, indeed, for how much – but could not summon the strength for the inevitable, lengthy explanation. Sykes was an able servant, but a pedantic one. Instead he leaned half up on an elbow and sipped the pleasing cup. Barely more than a year ago he would have woken to the sound of the chapel bell and the imperative voice of a schoolmaster. He had not disliked Shrewsbury, neither had he actually liked it; he had endured it, usually cheerfully. As well dislike the rain on Salisbury Plain! But now he knew what he truly liked, because when the trumpet roused him it thrilled him also. It did not matter that he was hungry, or cold, or wet, or tired: the prospect of the day, booted and in the saddle, with dragoons who looked to him, a man set in authority (all be that of limited degree – at present), was unfailingly reviving.

A sip or two of the goat's milk, the brain come fully awake, and he was thinking of the day ahead. A general action, he hoped; bigger, perhaps, even than Corunna. Not for a moment did he doubt the outcome, in spite of the major's warning. Nor did he doubt himself, even though he faced court martial when it was over: 'sufficient unto the day is the evil thereof!' It was in large measure his watch-phrase – and that of the other cornets too. That was the benefit of youth. That was why infantry regiments gave their colours into the hands of sixteen-year-old ensigns, and their companies to youthful captains – ensigns and captains of good family, with the means to purchase a commission and the ardour to do their duty to the bitter end. That was how he understood it, at any rate – the *bright* side of the purchase coin! What were his complaints at the lack of means to advance by purchase, or his opportunity to display for merit promotion, when the army was facing a general action this day? The commander-in-chief must rely on every man with the King's commission. Purchase was, at least, a stout bond of surety!

Every man? Yes, sighed Hervey – as near as made no odds. Even Daly and Quilley. But why repine over those two? What did they matter on a day like this, when the entire army would be drawn up against the French? And, in truth, Daly and Quilley would face shot and shell exactly as he would, and the sabre's edge, too, if the Sixth were blessed with a charge. And then Daly and Quilley might buy a lieu-tenancy over his head, the one by extortion of his miserable tenants, the other by some gambling debt in White's Club! Well, damn their eyes, Hervey cursed! Was he himself worthy of promotion if he could not win it in action?

These were the cornet's waking thoughts on the day of the general action at Talavera de la Reina.

CHAPTER TWELVE

THE SMOKE AND THE FIRE

Talavera, later

All morning the Spanish had filed past Cotton's brigade on the road from Cazalegas three leagues beyond the Alberche, making for Talavera, which the Sixth had now learned was to be the right of Sir Arthur Wellesley's line of battle. Indeed, for most of the morning the Sixth had been speaking of nothing but the admirable defensive position the commander-in-chief had chosen. He had selected, so to speak, a bottleneck, where the Tagus, flowing west from Toledo to Talavera, and thence to Alcántara and the Portuguese border, meandered north a little, nearing the steep escarpment of the Sierra de Seguilla, and then parallel to it for about seventy miles. By choosing to stand on the defensive at the top of the bottleneck rather than further down – further west – Sir Arthur Wellesley not only held the city of Talavera de la Reina, he gave himself room to withdraw, if that became necessary, with his flanks secure on the one side by the wide, deep Tagus, and on the other by the rugged sierra. That, at any rate, was the opinion of Joseph Edmonds. Prudent a choice it was, he told the subaltern officers, whom he had assembled by way of field tutelage. 'A commander ought never to fight a general action unless he believe there to be a good chance of victory,' Edmonds said. 'But neither should he do so without the certainty of being able to retreat in reasonable order should victory be denied him.' Nor did the commander have only the enemy to take into consideration; there were his allies too. With the Spaniards, Edmonds added, nothing could be certain. Some days they would fight like tigers; other days they had the stomach of a fat kitchen cat.

Hervey studied the trudging ranks – dirty white uniforms as far as the eye could see. Two centuries ago, the Spanish infantry could count itself the finest in the world; now they looked no better than a peasant levy. No army in retreat ever looked its best. Hervey knew it from Corunna; and there they had been retreating with scarce a shot from the enemy. What sort of a mauling these men had had he could only suppose. There had been no forerunners, bandaged and bloody, to speak of any action. The rumour was there were so many French that withdrawal to better ground – ground suited to the defence – was the only course. But *that* was the rumour before which they had retreated to Corunna, was it not? So the Moore-baiters had it yet. And this Spanish general, Cuesta – he was too old and obese, the word was. But he must know his business? In any case, with Sir Arthur Wellesley the two armies would be a worthy match for 'King' Joseph and Marshal Victor, would they not? The position on which they would give battle here spoke volumes in their favour. Hervey was sure there could be no occasion for dismay.

He had only to consider the ground. As the major said, it was admirably chosen – a battle line three miles long, its right, the walled city of Talavera de la Reina, resting on the Tagus, its left on a steep escarpment, and the entire front protected by the dry bed of the Portiña river. With so much cover of vineyards, olive groves and corks, as well as the natural entrenchment of the Portiña, it was a position *made* for the infantry. It wanted only for a better orientation, for the armies would be facing due east, into the sun. But then, what did that matter to the men in red coats, who wanted only for an opportunity to get to close quarters with the French? They had all seen the position when they came up the day before, and were relishing putting it to the test. However, the true genius of the place, as Edmonds pointed out, lay in the centre of the line, where a ridge ran east–west parallel to the Tagus on the right and to the escarpment, the Sierra de Seguilla, on the left. The ridge was cut in half by the Portiña, running north–south, and the western half, the Cerro de Medellin, was higher than the eastern, the Cerro de Cascajal. On the north side of the ridge was a narrow plain of heath, pasture and arable, and a few dry streambeds. Edmonds had asked the cornets what they concluded by this, to which Laming had at once correctly answered that the British guns on the Cerro de Medellin commanded the narrow plain to the north, the Cerro de Cascajal on the far side of the Portiña, and the greater part of the distance to Talavera, whose own guns would easily overlap.

'Capital, Mr Laming!' Edmonds had replied, slapping his thigh with uncharacteristic exuberance. Then he had narrowed his eyes. 'And what else?'

Laming had had no answer. Neither had two further nominations. Bruce and Wyllie made attempts, but unsuccessful.

'Mr Hervey?'

Hervey searched hard for what else there might be, other than the restatement of Laming's conclusion in different form. He looked uncertain as he spoke. 'If the French were to take the Cerro de Medellin, it would no longer be possible for us to hold the position?'

Edmonds smiled wryly. 'Ah, yes, indeed, Mr Hervey. *That* is the material point. Mark, gentlemen, that the Cerro de Medellin is the very hinge on which this position turns.

175

Once lost, the position will fall, exactly as the heaviest door will fall for want of a serviceable hinge.'

A smile came to the lips of Conway, the senior subaltern. 'Then the commander-in-chief had better post the Fourteenth on the hill to fill it with screws!'

The laughter was loud as the lieutenant-colonel rode over.

'I love a good joke, gentlemen. I would have the whole regiment share it on the morning of a general action. But I think there is little opportunity now, for if you look yonder . . .'

Hervey and the others seized their telescopes and turned towards the Alberche. He saw smoke spread for a mile and more across the front, half a league away, the very smoke of Ai: *And when the men of Ai looked behind them, they saw, and, behold, the smoke of the city ascended up to heaven, and they had no power to flee this way or that way; and the people that fled to the wilderness turned back upon the pursuers.* Were there Joshua-men out there, even now, he wondered. How were they to know what the enemy did beyond the smoke unless there were spies there – or cavalry? *And when Joshua and all Israel saw that the ambush had taken the city, and that the smoke of the city ascended, then they turned again, and slew the men of Ai.* But what burned? There was no city. Hervey peered through his telescope, but he could make out nothing at all.

'The corn stooks, gentlemen – the shelters: *that* is what burns,' said Lord George. 'The question is, do *we* fire them to cover our withdrawal, or do the French to cover their advance? Either way, gentlemen, it is the time for cavalry. To your troops, please!'

A quarter of an hour later, the Sixth were ranked in two lines by squadrons. 'Mark, Hervey, Lord George's promptness in this,' said Lieutenant Martyn. 'For no orders have come from Cotton.'

Hervey did mark it. And he relished what it might bring.

Martyn continued to search with his telescope. 'Our advance division is withdrawing, evidently. See!'

Hervey saw redcoats a mile away, marching towards them in good order, and unhurried. The columns of Spanish would be well past, now; just a few stragglers limping by. One of Cotton's gallopers had said the main body of them were marching by the southern road, which meant that Talavera must be teeming with troops; and no doubt they were already hard at work fortifying the city. What was it that Sir Arthur Wellesley would ask of his cavalry, therefore? If the brigades to their front were not being pressed hard, as evidently they were not, there would be no need of cavalry to cover the withdrawal. Was it the intention, then, to wait for night, and for the brigades to come into the main position under cover of darkness? In which case, too, there would be no need for cavalry. Hervey sighed: that would be disappointing in the extreme, for not only would they be deprived of an action, they would have the indignity of being mere spectators to the infantry's battle (and of bearing the taunts thereafter).

Just as Hervey was about to ask Martyn's opinion, Lord George came up. The commanding officer's charger, a liver-chestnut a full hand higher than Jessye, moved with an extension that spoke of both the animal's quality and his rider's purpose.

'Sir Edward, send someone to see what goes there,' said Lord George, giving the merest nod in the direction of the infantry. 'It would be well to know if we have given up the Alberche once and for all.'

'Very good, Colonel.'

Sir Edward felt no need of elaboration, couched though his orders were in the most gentlemanly and imprecise terms. Lord George's *intention* was clear, and he could trust to his captain's discretion how it was to be accomplished.

The infantry may have the most of the fighting, Hervey reflected, but they did it with enough words of command to fill a book. The cavalry had their own manual, with evolutions as complex, but there remained the imperative for prompt and independent action, requiring discrimination and celerity – the cavalry *coup d'oeil*. He sat a little taller in the saddle, and surveyed the field.

'Mr Laming, Mr Hervey,' said Sir Edward, without turning his head. 'Take a serjeant's detachment apiece and make contact with the infantry to discover what the enemy does and what the divisional commander's intention is there. Mr Laming, take as your left boundary the road to our front, and, Mr Hervey, it is to be your right boundary, both to use it as you will. But the Alberche is to be the limit of any reconnaissance. I would have a first report within the hour, if you please.' Sir Edward's tone and manner reflected that of the lieutenant-colonel, but a degree sharper.

Lieutenant Martyn, though no order had been addressed to him directly, stood in the stirrups and turned his head. 'Serjeant Crook, Serjeant Strange!'

In less than a minute, the two patrols – nine men each plus serjeant – were raising dust on the road down which the Spanish had marched all morning.

After half a mile Hervey swung north across the heath, which a few days before had supported so many sheep that it reminded him of Salisbury Plain. Now they were gone. Where, he had no notion. Not into the Sixth's stomachs, that was certain. The smoke was getting thicker; he could see nothing at all beyond the Alberche. He could not even make out where exactly was the line of the river. If the French were crossing, they did so much further to the south, where it joined the Tagus, and where a bridge would save them wet feet. From his map he knew the Alberche ran south-west before bending more to the south for a mile until its confluence with the Tagus, and the road he had first ridden down, his boundary with Laming, swung due north at the bend, so if he crossed the road he knew he must turn half-right in order to come up to the river. Otherwise he would err north and find no one. He had never seen smoke so thick, not even in Wiltshire when the farmers burned the stubble. It had drifted so far that he could no longer see Laming's patrol. He was becoming anxious about keeping direction.

Crack!

A dragoon clutched at his shoulder, with a look more astonished than pained.

Before Hervey knew what had happened there was a volley. Then bluecoats swarmed from the smoke, and his gut twisted so much that he near clutched it. 'Draw swords!'

He heard them rasp from the scabbards behind him, then thought better of it.

'Threes about!'

He turned, to see the movement already done, save for Serjeant Strange, who reined round calmly, keeping his sword vertical as if on parade.

'Away!'

They spurred into an untidy gallop, Private Porter still clutching at his shoulder with his sword hand.

There was no time to worry for him. Hervey's one thought was to put a safe distance between them and the *voltigeurs*. Musketry followed their every stride. A ball whistled through the crest of his Tarleton.

After two furlongs they pulled up, but it took Serjeant Strange's bark to get them to front, sharp.

Hervey returned his sword and took out his telescope. The smoke was drifting again but he could just make out the French infantry turning south towards the road. Had Laming seen them, or heard?

'We had better see what the others do, Serjeant Strange.

179

We'll make for that ruin yonder.' He nodded to what looked to be a substantial farmhouse a hundred yards to their right. He could see redcoats to the rear of it, some of them lying down. 'Can you ride back to the troop unaided, Porter?'

Private Porter could not speak.

'Go with him, Corporal Welsh,' said Hervey, shaking open his map. 'Make your report to Captain Edmonds. Tell him that I intend standing at the . . . Casa de Salinas.'

Corporal Welsh closed with Porter to support him, and then turned back for the troop. Hervey and the rest struck off at a canter in the opposite direction. He felt the deficiency of the report all too well, but what more could he do than send word of first contact and what he intended? He could hardly speculate as to how they had collided with the *voltigeurs*: the French might have crossed the Alberche under cover of the smoke, or the '*voltigeurs*' might even be cavalry come down the north bank from Escalona, dismounting to advance through the smoke. It seemed unlikely, but it was possible. Would wet feet not have run into Anson's brigade, however? They were in close watch of the river for just such a crossing.

He soon had his answer. As they closed with the brigade resting behind the Casa de Salinas a heavy musketry opened from the trees a hundred yards beyond. Scores of redcoats fell to the first volley. Many who jumped to their feet were instantly struck down. The fire continued – increased – as more French poured from the woods, blazing away as they found their line. Order among the redcoats dissolved.

Hervey galloped for the ruins, head low on Jessye's neck. He pulled up in cover, saw they made it without loss, dismounted and scrambled atop a broken-down wall to see what assailed them. Only then did he wonder if he exceeded his orders.

Serjeant Strange clambered up beside him. 'Irish, sir, Connaughts,' he said in the measured voice of Suffolk. 'They're good men packed tight in ranks with a serjeant's spontoon to prod them, but the devil's own without it.'

Hervey looked back. They were running now, as if the hounds of hell were after them.

'They'll not re-form until they gets behind a standing line, sir. Mightn't *we* go and form?'

Hervey inclined his head. 'I reckon we're more useful to them here, Serjeant Strange.' He did not add 'if we ourselves aren't cut off '.

As suddenly as the French had appeared there were green jackets on the far side of the road.

Serjeant Strange saw them first. 'Sixtieth, sir, yonder! A welcome sight, they.'

Strange's capacity for understatement was ever arresting: Hervey sighed with relief as he saw the other battalion of General Donkin's brigade – Rifles, not so regulated as musket-infantry, and, resting in the cover of trees, evidently not thrown into confusion by surprise.

The Sixtieth opened a counter-fire. It soon told. The French checked and began falling back.

Here was their chance of escape, Hervey realized. If they galloped now, they would be clear away before the French could come on again. For all he knew, too, *voltigeurs* might already have worked themselves further round to the south. But where was Laming?

'Look, sir!' Serjeant Strange pointed up the road.

Laming and his men were galloping flat out for the ruin. Hervey saw what must happen, but hadn't the slightest means of averting it. In seconds they were galloping across the Sixtieth's front. Three horses went down, their dragoons hit in leg or side.

Hervey's men began waving and cheering. 'Here! Over here!'

Laming's patrol pulled up hard in the cover of the ruin. Hervey jumped down from the wall and ran to his fellow cornet.

'The French are *pouring* across the river,' gasped Laming, for once not troubling to maintain a pose. 'There's no sign of Anson's brigade. They must've crossed well to the north.'

'That were *our* men firing, sir,' said Serjeant Crook, jumping from the saddle, his horse in a worse lather than any. 'Bell and Owens is down.' He glanced at the others. 'And Horncastle.'

'Good God,' said Laming, horrified by what he had just led them into. 'We'd better go back.'

'You and me, sir, and Corporal Hart,' insisted Crook. 'The others should stay here.'

'Yes, very well.' Laming was glad of the advice, his thoughts still on what had happened. 'Shall you wait here, Hervey?'

'I shall.' He did not add 'unless we are driven out'.

The Sixtieth's fire was slackening. Hervey watched as Laming, Crook and Corporal Hart galloped back to where the dragoons had fallen. He did not see the little group of staff officers galloping up from Talavera until they had dismounted and begun scrambling up the wall next to him. The profile of the foremost was unmistakable, however – hawklike.

Shots rang out from the right, almost behind them. Hervey turned to see French sharpshooters swarming through the scrub, out of sight to the Sixtieth. Sir Arthur Wellesley at once jumped down from the wall and turned and looked at him, though without a word. Serjeant Strange had fired his carbine by the time the commander-in-chief's foot was in the stirrup, and he had reloaded and fired a second time before Hervey realized they could have no support from the Sixtieth.

'Mount!'

Serjeant Strange fired both his pistols, deliberately and in turn, while the others eagerly complied with Hervey's order.

As they edged round the rear of the farmhouse, Hervey saw Laming coming back down the road – and none too hurriedly – two of the dragoons lying lifeless across the saddle. He glanced back at the sharpshooters. The ruin stood in their line of sight: they could afford to take it at a trot and give Laming some support – but not for long.

'Thank you, gentlemen,' said Lord George Irvine, gravely but surely. 'Admirably clear reports. I compliment you on choosing the position of observation, Mr Hervey. I am saddened by the loss of two men, and to our own fire, but I fear it is ever thus in our business. You acted very properly, Mr Laming. I commend your address in recovering them.'

The two cornets saluted, reined about and rode back to the right of the line, with Sir Edward Lankester leading. When they were halted again, Hervey turned to his troop-leader and spoke in a lowered voice. 'Serjeant Strange acted throughout with very marked coolness, Sir Edward. He stood firing his carbine as we remounted at the ruin, totally unbidden.'

Sir Edward did not reply at once, looking straight ahead as if thinking matters over. 'It should, of course, be un-remarkable, but I fear it is not. Strange is a singular NCO; he shows address and judgement in high measure, as well as loyalty.' He did not add 'and courage', for that was meant to be the common currency of the rank. 'I never had dealings with him much, but Edmonds speaks well of him always. He's a Methodist, of course, but he's not preachy. I've a notion his quality is from the impulse of his religion.' And then he smiled, in a resigned sort of way. 'Not like Armstrong. Not at all like Armstrong.' He shook his head. 'And yet each in their way is the finest of the rank. Except, of course, Armstrong does not *have* the rank!' He sighed. 'When we will have occasion to restore it, I would not like to say. Strange will be serjeant-major, I've no doubt, but

Armstrong will be fortunate to be promoted quartermaster.'

Hervey said nothing. Despite the intimacy before Oporto, when Sir Edward had seemed to share more with him than mere duty required, Hervey still had an impression of a taciturn disposition, and remained uncertain as to what his troop-leader's confidences tended.

Half an hour later, at two o'clock, with the French momentarily checked by Major-General John Mackenzie's brigade, behind which the Irish had rallied, the Sixth received orders to withdraw to the line of defence. General Cotton's voice, composed but stentorian, carried to right marker and left flanker alike: 'Lord George, the Sixth to do rearguard, if you will. Allow me to retire one half of one mile with the Fourteenth. The Sixteenth I have already sent back. Anson's will be covering the infantry.'

Lord George Irvine touched the peak of his Tarleton to the brigadier. 'Very well, Sir Stapleton.' Then he turned to his regiment. 'Number One and Number Two Squadrons, skirmishers out!'

Sir Edward Lankester and Captain Thomas Lennox, C Troop leader, repeated the order to their squadrons.

Out from the ranks trotted a dozen corporals and dragoons, drill-book fashion – *The Regiment in the Withdrawal*.

'Flankers!'

Two dragoons from right and left squadrons trotted out a hundred yards to either flank, ready to do the skirmishers' job there if the enemy worked round unseen.

In ten more minutes, Hervey saw Colonel Anson's brigade – the 23rd Light Dragoons and the 1st Hussars of the King's German Legion – coming up from Talavera at a fast trot. Now General Mackenzie's division (he had command of a second brigade as well as his own) could begin to withdraw.

Ten minutes later, with Anson's cavalry in a tight masking formation two hundred yards to their front, Mackenzie's men were marching back towards Talavera. Hervey turned in the saddle to see how far General Cotton and the Fourteenth had got: a quarter of a mile, and retiring very deliberately at the walk. He could not understand why the French made no move, having been so bold in crossing the river in the first place and surprising Donkin's men.

Not a minute later he understood all too well, as horse artillery began firing from the olive groves where the Sixtieth had stood not an hour before. The shot fell short of Anson's brigade, half a mile to the right of where the Sixth stood, but not by much.

'Tricky of them, that,' said Sir Edward, in a bemused sort of way, and taking out his telescope. 'They gave no notice with cavalry.' He searched the entire front. At a range of a thousand yards the damage would not be too great: Anson's men would be able to see the shot approaching, and evade. It was well, however, that the French had no 'Monsieur Shrapnel' to provide them with exploding shot. He frowned. 'I wonder if we shall see them dare to follow in the open.'

The 6th Light Dragoons now became spectators at a field day, except that it was conducted with shotted guns, and carbines with ball-cartridge. Every officer had out his telescope, and every dragoon strained his eyes to see the evolutions. French skirmishers – *chasseurs à cheval* – came out of the olive groves and began exchanging fire with Anson's. At three hundred yards they troubled each other even less than the guns troubled the main body. After a quarter of an hour of ineffective cannonading and musketry, the artillery limbered up and trotted out from cover protected by two strong squadrons of *chasseurs*.

'A fine sight indeed,' declared Sir Edward, ruefully. 'And very artfully concealed they were.'

Hervey saw; they *all* saw. This would have been the

moment for the British gunners, but every troop had been sent back behind the Portiña.

'Anson has no alternative but to charge or retire,' said Sir Edward, searching the olive groves intently. 'And I'll warrant there'll be another four squadrons in yonder trees waiting for him.'

Hervey had not thought of that. He cursed himself, for as soon as Sir Edward spoke it appeared obvious. The cavalryman's art lay as much in determining what you could *not* see from what you could.

'I hope he'll not be tempted,' added Sir Edward, in a tone that said he might.

But Anson was evidently not to be lured. He turned his brigade about and began following General Mackenzie's infantry.

'I think we had better conform,' said Lord George, lowering his telescope. 'Fours about!'

The commanding officer's trumpeter relayed the order: falling crotchets, G, E, C, G, dotted quavers and semis on C then E, and a long C for the executive. The Sixth about-faced, four men wheeling as one the length of the line, with the officers riding round the squadron flankers to take up position again. It was a deal more involved than each man simply turning about, but it kept the proper order of things.

'Walk-march!'

The trumpeter repeated the command: just six Cs and an E, an easy call.

Once the ranks had dressed after striking off (it always took longer when they had been standing for any time), Lord George made to keep up with Anson's brigade, for he was otherwise being left too far forward on an open flank.

'Trot!'

Repeating quavers doubled the Sixth's speed. Bits jingled, scabbards clanked, NCOs barked. To Hervey, it was the best of music.

The French began firing again. Hervey glanced left and rear, expecting to see more cavalry coming from the olive groves, but there were none. He saw Anson's brigade halt and front. Would this unnerve the French, keep them at their distance? Or would Anson's men have to charge? There were no supports showing themselves yet, but they could remain concealed and still have time to close with the *chasseurs* if Anson did charge. It was a fine judgement, Hervey saw. The trouble was that General Mackenzie's infantry had half a league and more to march before the Portiña, and they would not be under cover of Sir Arthur Wellesley's guns for another mile.

'Walk!'

The order took him by surprise. He flexed the reins late. Jessye obliged but stumbled slightly, putting them two lengths ahead of the quartermaster, bumping Serjeant Strange's mare. He felt himself colour.

'Halt!'

He reined rear until he was in line.

The quartermaster scowled. 'Welcome back, Mr Hervey, sir.'

He deserved the rebuke, he knew. If *he* didn't keep his attention how could the other ranks be expected to? He saw the nearest dragoons smiling. They enjoyed seeing a cornet checked by the quartermaster. It didn't matter how aptly an officer did his duty on patrol if he couldn't keep his place in close order.

'What do *you* find so amusing, Harris?' growled A Troop's quartermaster.

Private Harris wondered how the quartermaster had been able to see from his position in rear. But, then, that was why he was a quartermaster, was it not? 'Nothing, sir.' It sounded feeble.

'Nothing, is it? Well, just think on this, Harris my lad: there'll be a regiment and more of sabres in those trees yonder, and any minute now they'll be coming out with the sole intention of sticking one in you. That is if *I* don't stick mine in your arse beforehand!'

'Sir!' Harris sounded chastened.

Hervey reflected on the propriety of humour in the regiment. A quartermaster might make a remark at a cornet's expense, and for others to hear, but the quartermaster's humour was the final word; it needed no acclamation from the ranks. In a matter of moments the cornet might in turn have to give the quartermaster an order, perhaps unpalatable, and would have it obeyed without demur; but a cornet would stand rebuked for carelessness for something a trained man would not be permitted without equal rebuke. It did not bear scrutiny, but it worked. He had *seen* it work, and in the most exacting conditions; what was there left to know in the management of men after Corunna?

But why had they halted?

'Regiment, fours about-face!' There was an edge to Lord George's voice now.

The Sixth went through the same evolution as before, but reversed, so that in a minute they were standing exactly as they had prior to the retirement. Hervey quickened: would they charge?

Major Edmonds rode from centre-rear, round the right marker, to where the lieutenant-colonel stood coolly observing the French.

'I think Anson's going to have a deuced awkward time of it, Edmonds,' said Lord George, pointing. 'Look yonder: there's another troop of guns coming up on his flank.'

Edmonds saw. 'Anson's right to be wary of charging. There's bound to be twice as many in the woods.'

'My opinion exactly, Edmonds. I think we had better give him support. Mackenzie's men are evidently tired, too. Cotton will be home safe shortly.'

'Indeed,' said Edmonds, shading his eyes against the sun.

'Curious there's no appetite to follow us up. Haven't they seen we've no guns, d'ye think?'

Lord George nodded. 'I had thought of that. Perhaps they imagine we're masking them, which is why I think we may be of assistance simply by remaining in line with Anson.'

'What do you intend if the French break cover?'

Lord George shrugged ever so slightly. 'We must see, but if there's opportunity to charge, then I shall take it!'

Anson's brigade stood their ground in open order for a full ten minutes. One ball alone did damage, striking the head clean off a man's shoulders as he tried desperately to rein round. But the second gun troop, a thousand yards to the brigade's right, had now begun unlimbering, so that fire would converge and be the harder to evade. General Mackenzie's infantry, meanwhile, had managed another half-mile, giving Anson the opportunity at last to withdraw far enough to tempt the French gunners out of range of any supports in the olive groves.

The Sixth watched with the keen interest of spectators at a field day as Anson's brigade turned about. The King's Germans were unquestionably handier would have been the majority opinion; the Twenty-third had fresher horses, it seemed, for there was a good deal of napping and barging. But the brigade turned tight nevertheless, and sharp though unhurried.

'Very coolly done, I must say,' declared Lieutenant Martyn. 'The brigadier judges it very fine.'

Lord George waited until the nearer gun troop ceased firing and the horse teams came up, then resumed the Sixth's own progress rear. 'Regiment will retire. Fours about!'

Round they went again, and tighter this time for the practice.

'Walk-march!'

And then, after fifty yards, 'Trot!'

Anson's brigade had retired a full half-mile in the meantime, before stopping once more to cover the infantry's last mile to the Portiña. Both troops of French guns followed up quickly and came into action as soon as the brigade formed front again.

'Halt!' called Lord George.

The Sixth pulled up from the trot, untidy but fast.

Lord George intended losing no time. 'Front!'

The squadrons turned like a weathervane when the wind veers suddenly. It was an urgent manoeuvre, and every man knew there must be cause.

They saw the cause as they came full round: the nearest gun troop stood half a mile off, a squadron of *chasseurs* to each flank, and an empty mile and more between them and the olive groves.

'Singular,' declared Sir Edward Lankester. 'They are deuced confident of themselves!'

He spoke the thoughts of his squadron, for every man could see as he did: before, the French had been bold; now they had been rash.

'Forward!'

The command thrilled through the ranks – so much more welcome to the dragoon's ear than 'retire'. And Lord George's trumpeter sounded the call with relish.

'Trot!'

The bumping and barging began again, horses extending unevenly to keep with the fast pace Lord George was setting.

In four hundred yards they halted, having wheeled a quarter right without any command but from the sword. Without the pivot it was uneven, but much the faster.

'Draw swords!'

Five hundred sabres flashed from polished scabbards. The movement was meant to unnerve the enemy, a calculated display, its timing of the essence. These French had dared so much in coming forward with so few supports; Hervey wondered how they would take to this notice of the charge.

'Forward!'

Lord George would press them for an answer.

'Trot!'

It was knee-to-knee proper now, stirrups clinking with the next man's, scabbards bouncing about and clanking without the weight of the sword, shouts of 'Pull back there!', 'Get up on the left!' It was a sight that awed more at a distance.

The next order would all but commit them to the charge. The guns were a quarter of a mile away, trained off the Sixth's line of advance at Anson's brigade. The French had seconds only to decide their course, or it would be decided for them. Hervey could barely contain himself as he saw the *chasseurs* incline to face them.

Lord George did not hesitate. 'Gallop!'

At last it was come, his first true regimental charge! Four squadrons – eight troops at a good strength, in first and support lines, with the lieutenant-colonel at the fore and every officer in his place. The strangest thoughts came to him: two thousand iron shoes pounded the hard earth, each one but a nail from failing – how the regiment's farriers held the fortune of them all in their rough and ready hands! He had to check himself: it was not *yet* the charge. It was possible, even now, for Lord George to hold up, the gallop still in-hand, sabres still sloped.

The French did not advance to meet them. Would they turn and run? Hervey felt his gut tighten with every stride. There were two hundred yards to close with the *chasseurs*. When would Lord George give the word?

'Steady, damn your eyes! Stop your racing! Hold hard there!' Officers and NCOs alike cursed to keep the lines straight. Hervey saw a horse from C Troop bolt, its rider heaving on the reins for all he was worth. One in front of him stumbled then somersaulted headlong, tumbling the horse next to it and the one right behind. Hervey swore with relief at the near-miss. This was *so* much harder than Sahagun! The ranks were so close – too close? And the approach was so long! Would the French turn?

Now they had the limbers forward, hitching up the guns. Seconds more and they could gallop them safely rear.

One hundred and fifty yards: the *chasseurs* drew their sabres. Hervey swallowed hard. They *would* stand their ground!

Up went Lord George's sabre. 'Charge!'

His trumpeter blew the rising triplets as best he could.

Up went five hundred sabres, just as the drill book said, lofted high to meet cavalry with a powerful cut (the point was kept for infantry, to spear like tent pegs).

The Sixth ran *ventre à terre*, the fastest Hervey had known. The collision would be terrible, the destruction appalling. He prayed Jessye would not stumble or collide head-on when they closed. He could only do so much to direct her.

Less than half a furlong: he could see it all. They would overlap both flanks of the *chasseurs* by a dozen yards, just as the drill book prescribed. Jessye was pulling, but nothing to what every other trooper was.

Fifty yards: they broke! The *chasseurs* broke! They turned, they ran – back, left, right, any way there was space to run. The guns were pulling away, but exposed now to five hundred sabres.

Every man pressed his horse for the last turn of speed. The lines bowed and buckled, the cursing and swearing inaudible now – only the wild shouting.

The front rank veered left a fraction, exposing the second by a dozen men. Hervey found himself with a clear front and chasing the *chasseurs*' left-flankers. But he shot so fast between two of them he almost missed his strike: Cut One – right, diagonal-down left – a clumsy slice to the nearside, slashing the man's sword-arm from behind. He reined hard left to the support of the front rank, where he was meant to be. It was all confusion.

But the leading squadrons were already galloping on after the guns, despite the disordering of the second line. Some of the *chasseurs* had pulled up or turned, letting the squadrons charge past. Many were clutching at wounds, and many more were pretending to.

Hervey was almost knocked from the saddle by the rear two squadrons as they raced through like the wind, eager for blood and seeing it fast disappearing. They thrust and cut as they passed, making more for the surgeons' list, but those French who had not run for it suddenly saw their chance: they would fight their way through what was left of the leading squadrons' second line. In an instant, Hervey and his fellow supports were thrown onto the defence.

A man rode at him with his sabre at Guard, eyes burning. Hervey met him with Cut Three – right, diagonal-up left, driving the horizontal guard high and exposing the man's rein-arm to the covering corporal. But the coverman wasn't there. Hervey felt the cut at his shoulder blade as the *chasseur* followed through like lightning. There was no pain, just the sensation of blood, and then another *chasseur* was hacking left and right towards him. Hervey jerked his wrist up, sabre to Bridle Arm Protect. Just in time – the French blade arched down and drove-in his sabre hard, slicing deep into Jessye's left ear. It would have cut through the headstall had the leather not been doubled with chain; then the bit would have fallen from her mouth and he would have been helpless. He gasped. Another *chasseur* lunged at him with the point, but Hervey's coverman swooped from the nearside and dashed the sword from his hand.

And then the French were gone. A dozen dragoons were

suddenly by themselves, the flotsam of the clash, the rest of the Sixth three furlongs away dealing terrible destruction to *chasseurs* and gunners alike, or lying on the ground as lifeless as the scores of Frenchmen and horses. Two of the dragoons nearest him were so blood-soaked he could not name them; another was bent double in the saddle. What did he do now?

'Mr Hervey, sir!'

His covering corporal had circled and come up behind him again.

'Are you all right, sir?' Well might he be anxious, for his officer's bloody back rebuked him for not being in position.

'I'll be well, Corporal Toyne.' Hervey was more determined than certain, for he felt his left arm weakening. But he must appear unperturbed, just as would Sir Edward Lankester.

'I'm sorry, sir: she ran out as we bent left.'

In truth, Hervey had no sense of dereliction in his coverman. The charge had become a barging race, and he himself had lost the front rank, which *he* was meant to be supporting. 'You were there to parry that point, Corporal Toyne. I'm deuced grateful for that.'

He closed to the doubled-up dragoon. 'What's wrong, Bunting?'

Private Bunting tried to lift his head.

Hervey saw the blood oozing between the dragoon's fingers as he clutched his stomach – and the grey matter among the red, a hideous disembowelling. 'Take him rear, Abbott,' he said to the man next to him, trying not to betray any hopelessness. Then he turned away while he still had control of his gorge.

'Hadn't I better bind up your shoulder, sir?' asked Corporal Toyne.

Hervey was tempted, but he couldn't give in, not now. There was fighting still, and no bugle had sounded 'recall'.

'We'd better catch up the troop. Form line, Corporal!'

By the time they closed on the rest of the regiment, the fight was over, and Lord George's trumpeter was blowing the octave leaps for 'rally'. Hervey found himself strangely composed by the return to order, for it was just as the manual prescribed: *When the shock of the squadron has broken the order of the opposite enemy, part may be ordered to pursue and keep up the advantage; but its great object is instantly to rally and renew its efforts in a body.* Yet he was abashed that he rallied from the rear rather than from the front.

However, no one seemed to have missed him. But then, how *could* anyone know where men were in an affair such as that?

'Very well, Mr Hervey,' said Sir Edward, seeing him touch his sword to his lips. His voice was barely raised. 'Right-mark for the second rank, if you please. Just there will do capitally.' He nodded to where, then turned his head again. 'Your jacket, sir, requires attention. See to it as soon as may be!'

Hervey's mouth fell open. The remark would have stung when first he joined the Sixth, but now, after his Corunna steeling, he recognized his troop-leader's manner for what it was. An officer might be carried from the field, but otherwise he was to bear his wounds unremarked and preferably unnoticed. Indeed, an officer was never *wounded*: an officer was *hit* – like a gamebird. That, at least, was the code of the 6th Light Dragoons (Princess Caroline's Own). He smiled, helplessly.

When they had retired west of the Portiña, dressed wounds of men and horses alike, mended tackling, refastened shoes, and attended to all the other requirements of a regiment of cavalry that had clashed with a couple of hundred *chasseurs* and brought in or spiked six guns (and were required to be ready at once to do the same again if needs be), Hervey sat under an olive tree, put his sabretache on his knees and wrote to Wiltshire.

Talavera de la Reina
27th July

My dear Dan,

I enclose herewith a separate account of our progress to this place, which is the furthest we have advanced eastwards this time. But today we had an affair or two of cavalry, in which the regiment as a whole utterly routed two strong squadrons of Chasseurs à Cheval, and took six guns. Earlier this day I was so close to the Commander-in-Chief that he looked directly at me. He is smaller than I had imagined, compared with Sir John Moore I mean, but very active. He was almost captured, had he not been able to spring so fleet into the saddle! After our affair of the guns, which was by way of covering the retirement of a division of infantry most sorely tried in advance of the city, we crossed the Portina river, a dry stream about a mile to the north of the city, which the Spanish have garrisoned. It is not a little steep sided, about four feet deep, and more in places. One of the dragoons had a fall, his horse broke a leg and he himself has broke his skull, which was very ill luck since he had gone through the skirmish with the chasseurs with not a scratch. We are dismounted now and stood-easy (it is Six, and the sun is still high directly to our rear) amid olive groves, very extensive, so that one might ride to Talavera without showing one-self to the front. They extend half way up the Cerro de Medellin, which is a promontory, affording the same cover therefore. In front of us are the Guards and Col.

Kemmis's brigade, in which are the 40th, where John
Ayling is ensign, for whom I was doul at Shrewsbury,
and an excellent fellow. He hailed me as we rode in and
I shall mess with them later if duties allow. We stand-to
at Nine.

I did not say that a Frenchman cut Jessye's ear badly,
so that I feared she must lose a part of it, but our
veterinary surgeon, John Knight, is so skilled with
needle and thread that he has sewed her up
admirably . . .

He wrote nothing of his own predicament. The wound he would not have dreamed of mentioning, and certainly not the prospect of a general court martial. The one would have caused anxiety to the old man, the other dismay, and Hervey could not be sure that he would not speak of it with his people at Horningsham. And in any case, the wound was nothing that the surgeon's needle – as John Knight's with Jessye's ear – had not been able to repair. His tunic was another matter, but Private Sykes had found the baggage animals and brought his second coat forward. Hervey had wanted to keep it for the court martial, but Sir Edward Lankester's strictures would not now permit him.

It was a strange thing, he mused as he began readying himself for stand-to: he hoped fervently that the regiment would be in the thick of things tomorrow, yet he hoped as much that his uniform would not be spoiled. What queer things indeed an officer must be sensible of! But at least he would be well turned out to mess with the Fortieth. And after today, with the affair of the patrol and the charge at the guns, he would not trouble himself with thoughts of court martial. What could he do but smile at the peculiar fortunes of war?

CHAPTER THIRTEEN
TIMES PAST

Belem, the Feast of Stephen, 1826

Brevet-Colonel Charles Laming settled into the rear-facing seat of the Delgado travelling carriage, on the right-offside, as a gentleman ought, so that he faced Isabella diagonally, allowing her the forward prospect and the shaded side during the journey eastwards to Elvas. He had lost no time in securing leave of Sir William Clinton in order to go to the assistance of his old friend. The general, indeed, had been wholly supportive, declaring that if Hervey were not released very promptly then he would take it upon himself to effect his release by whatever means he thought fit. Sir William, as a lieutenant-general, had wide discretion (even if he could not be entirely certain what his orders from London amounted to), and he did not intend that any of this ill news should reach the Horse Guards until it was resolved satisfactorily, and to Hervey's advantage, since the dispositions he was now making for the army of intervention were based in large part on Hervey's own assessment of the situation.

In ordinary circumstances Sir William would not have been so sanguine about losing his deputy quartermaster-general. Laming had been promoted to the staff on account of his uncommon facility to render into few words, and with absolute clarity, the thoughts and intentions of politicos and senior officers. Throughout the years of unrest in England, which had continued in one form or another since the end of the war with Bonaparte, he had penned instructions to the army acting in support of the civil power, and his precision and foresight had saved many an ugly situation from turning into disaster. It was said that if it had been Laming who had drafted the orders for the Northern District that day in 1819, when the crowds had gathered to hear 'Orator' Hunt, there would have been no occasion for the coining 'Peterloo'. These talents had kept him from regimental duty, and then had come the opportunity for advancement, on the list of another regiment, and eventually a substantive lieutenant-colonelcy on the quartermaster-general's permanent establishment. Laming had seen a good deal of action as a subaltern, but none since Waterloo.

The years of his cornetcy came easily to mind, however, as he continued his reacquaintance with Isabella. Her English was fluent, with nothing of the accent of someone who spoke it only occasionally. She was, after all, 'Mrs Broke', as well as 'Dona Isabella Delgado'.

'Colonel Laming, this is very good of you – to accompany me to Elvas, I mean,' began Isabella, as the travelling carriage picked up speed. 'And to have Major Hervey's corporal, too. We have lost a little time by this delay, but my father says we may journey through the night. He would not hear of it before, when I had no escort.'

From what Corporal Wainwright had told him of the first affair in Elvas, when Hervey and Isabella had confronted the Miguelites in the middle of the night, Laming scarcely imagined she had need of an escort. 'I am glad you waited, ma'am. This is a more agreeable way to go than posting astride.'

She smiled. 'I was speaking with my father last night, Colonel, and he seemed to recall that you once shot one of his footmen?'

Laming turned bright red. The mess had never let him forget it. 'Ma'am,' he spluttered, 'I—'

She smiled the more. 'Do not trouble, Colonel. I merely wanted to know if it *were* you. I recall that you were very kind to the man.'

'*Kind*, ma'am? I had filled his back with shot!'

'Oh, come, Colonel. It was a very little shot and he made a rapid recovery. I meant that you sent him comforts, and visited him.'

Laming was now more composed. 'I did what any man should, ma'am. And I must protest, as everyone at the time was quick to point out to me: the footman had strayed far from his line.'

'Yes, Colonel; my father reminded me of that, too.'

Laming settled back into the plush of his corner again. 'We were all most grateful for your father's hospitality. Some of the best sport I ever recall, partridges faster than Congreve's rockets!'

Isabella nodded, approving. 'And, now, I recall it was you whose sister came to Belem?'

Laming was at last able to smile. 'Indeed, ma'am. She spent a very happy winter here.'

'I believe I recall, too, that your sister . . .' She inclined her head.

'Frances.'

'Yes. That Major Hervey was much taken with Frances.'

It was true. And Laming had been hopeful that the affection might become something more, for although his fellow cornet had not had a penny to his name, he was a man he would have been pleased to call brother-in-law. 'Yes, there was a strong affection. But we were very young!'

'Indeed we were, Colonel!'

Laming was discomfited again. 'Ma'am, I did not mean that—'

'Colonel, do not trouble yourself. We are none of us in our *première jeunesse*!'

Isabella's smile was so warm, Laming could not quite catch his breath. So used was he these past few years to fashionably tight lips that her want of inhibition caught him off-guard. He had never married, and such intimacies had been largely denied him. His pleasure now was more than he had imagined.

'Major Hervey's wife, Colonel – can you tell me anything of her?'

Laming regained his composure. 'I can indeed, ma'am. She was a most excellent woman. If I tell you she chose to accompany the regiment to Canada in the depths of winter, while she was with child, that will speak of her quality. It was, of course, that which occasioned her death.'

'I know a little of it, Colonel. Would you tell me more?'

Laming unfastened the front of his pelisse coat. The carriage-warmer had taken the chill off the air, and he found himself able to relax more. 'I will tell you what Hervey himself would approve, ma'am, but there are some things which go profoundly hard with him, even after the passage of ten years.'

'Of course.'

He took off his gloves, looking pensive, then tapped his knee with them, as if signalling for the off. 'At that time, the regiment was commanded by the most disreputable man I have had misfortune to meet – a coward, jealous of Hervey's reputation and ability. They were soon at odds. He sent him across the border into America, to co-operate with their army against the native Indians. Henrietta joined him at a later date, leaving behind the child with a nurse, but the commanding officer took objection and sent her away from the fort back to Canada. She was not long gone when her party was ambushed by Indians.'

Isabella's face betrayed her horror. 'I did not know the

end was so . . .' She looked out of the window for a long moment. 'And I imagine that Major Hervey blames himself in some part?'

'You have it perfectly, ma'am. He cannot quite get it from his mind that had he been either more obliging to the lieutenant-colonel, or else had exposed him for the villain he was, then Henrietta would be alive today.'

Isabella nodded. 'I can see that it would go very hard with a man like Major Hervey.'

She took off her gloves, revealing elegant hands. Laming found it difficult to picture them holding a foil, as Wainwright had spoken of. He saw the rings that showed she had once been married – perhaps married yet, in her own mind.

'And what of the child, Colonel?'

'What? Oh, the child . . . yes – a daughter. I confess I don't recall her name. Hervey's sister is guardian.'

'She lives with Major Hervey?'

Laming raised an eyebrow. 'There again, ma'am, you touch on a nerve – although you must understand that he and I have not been close these past years. Our duties have taken us different ways, he to India, principally. But those who know him better say that their separation causes him much unrest.'

'Of course, of course. I imagine Major Hervey is the sort of man who is torn by . . . *conflicts*, do you say?'

Laming nodded; it was the most apt word.

'By conflicts of his duty almost every day!'

Laming smiled, ruefully. 'You are most perceptive, ma'am. I am of the opinion – as are many – that if Hervey were able to find it in himself to be a little more accommodating to those superiors he finds himself in disagreement with, he would by now be brigadier-general.'

Isabella returned the smile. 'I can suppose it. But then, my own country would now be sorry for it, since Colonel

Norris, evidently, was incapable or unwilling to do more than rebuild a few old forts!'

'No doubt, ma'am. It seems a pity, though, that it should come to this: you and I having to travel to Elvas.'

Isabella frowned. 'It is no hardship for me, Colonel, I assure you.'

Laming let the remark go. It was no hardship for him either. Indeed, rather the opposite. His worry was that, from all he had heard in London and Hounslow, his old friend's restlessness was manifest in the situation before them now at Elvas; or, more to the point, at Badajoz. He had seen others the same; not men with Hervey's capability, that was for sure, but others who had let some deep disquiet in their lives run them hard against everything that ought to have been their support. Ultimately, they had fallen apart, like a horse that would not take the bit. He smiled to himself, for the remedy was plain – even to him, a bachelor.

He looked out of the window at the once-familiar road. It was *far* from hardship to take it again to Elvas. They had marched this way with Sir John Moore (and in this season), and he had thrilled to the sight of the mountains, the rivers, the forests, and to the call of the eagle – everything that had been so different from the green face of England, which to that date had been his sole experience. Elvas, he fancied, he could remember well: they had rested there a good deal. Badajoz less so. Badajoz had given them comfort after Talavera; that much he could recall perfectly. But Badajoz had also been the place of sheer, bloody murder, and he could scarce bare to think of it.

His eyes began closing – the little stove, the gentle rocking of the carriage. Forget Badajoz the night of the storming; obliterate the memory. Think on Badajoz as it had welcomed them after Talavera. Think on *Talavera*! What a battle to have shared with his old friend: nothing its like until Waterloo!

CHAPTER FOURTEEN

THE NIGHT HORSE

Talavera, late evening, 27 July 1809

'Stand down one in three, off-saddle and feed by half-sections.'

Sir Edward Lankester, pleased with what he saw at evening stand-to-arms after their fighting withdrawal, and that Lord George Irvine had seen likewise, patted his handsome sorrel on the neck as the squadron officers closed to him. Drawn up to the west of the dry riverbed of the Portiña, beyond a screening line of olive trees, willow and cork oak, they might be in a different world from the infantry's. Here they could rest, unobserved by the enemy, his guns unsighted. The other side of the trees, the domain of the redcoat, there could be no such ease; not, at least, until darkness, and even then the regiments would have to picket strongly, for the French might think the day had been theirs, and victory only a night attack away.

'A memorable day, I think, gentlemen. But it will be the more so tomorrow, I'll warrant. For tonight, we shall stand down the remainder after dark, and I would that the men get a good sleep. The regiment is to send additional gallopers to each of the divisions, our squadron one each to Hill's and Campbell's. Hervey to the former, if you please.' He paused, looking at him, as if to ask if he felt up to the exertion.

Hervey nodded.

'Bruce to the latter. Are there any questions?'

There were none.

'Very well, gentlemen, to your duties.'

Hervey was disappointed. Had he been assigned to Campbell's division he might have seen Ayling – and perhaps a little action, since the division stood beyond the Portiña still, in the centre of the allied position. They would be Wellesley's ears for the night, Sir Edward explained. But Hervey had no idea where was 'Daddy' Hill's division – only, as Sir Edward said, 'up there', on the Cerro de Medellín, the ridge that ran east–west in the middle of the position: just about the quietest place to be in the entire allied line, he reckoned.

'Loyalist, please, Sykes,' he told his groom. Loyalist may not pass the riding master's inspection as a charger 'fully trained', but Jessye had earned her night's rest after the day's exertions.

A cannonade like thunder startled the Second Division's staff, not least the general himself. 'Great heavens, gentlemen! What can be their purpose at this time of day? I'm surprised they see anything; there'll be no light at all in another hour.'

Hervey, just come, looked at his watch. By his reckoning there were another *two* hours of daylight yet, but he hardly thought it the thing to correct the divisional commander; at least, not in front of his staff. He had only just shaken hands with him.

The general's hand was a surprise. But, then, as Hervey knew, the commander of the Second Division was no ordinary man. Major-General Rowland Hill was not yet forty, but he had the appearance and manner of one considerably older. Hervey could see why he was called 'Daddy', even without his reputation for the care of his men. His face was ruddy, not in the least stern – indeed, to

Hervey's mind rather cherubic – his voice was soft, and his eyes kind. It would have been easy to imagine that here was a country squire in the uniform of the local militia.

It had not been Hervey's first encounter with this redoubtable infantryman. On the second occasion, when he had galloped for Colonel Long at Corunna, Hill and his brigade had stood like a stone wall astride the road to the harbour, so that Sir John Moore had taken one look at them and then turned to gallop back to the centre, confident he need have no fear for his left flank.

'I know you, sir. We have met in more agreeable surroundings,' said Hill, closing his telescope and turning back to face the temporary addition to his staff. 'Mr Hervey and I, gentlemen, share the inestimable advantage of an education in that finest of counties, Salop.'

The staff smiled politely at the diversion, while Hervey puzzled as to how on earth the general could recall his meeting a schoolboy two years ago. It was not even as if he had received a prize when Salop's most distinguished soldier had visited his school. He bowed, acknowledging, and stood in respectful silence.

The general turned back towards the guns. 'Well, gentle-men—' he began.

The guns thundered again. All the staff now turned, telescopes raised.

'A mile, d'ye suppose? A couple of batteries?'

'But not heavy, General,' said one of his aides-de-camp. 'It's scarcely throwing up earth yonder.'

Even with two hours to go before sunset, the shadows were beginning to lengthen appreciably. Hervey imagined that every man's thoughts would be turning to the night. The 'gentlemen in red', the junior ranks at least, would be thinking of sleep: it was all scrub and couch grass, not bad bedding for the night, if they were permitted to lie down; but the officers would be thinking there was not a deal of cover either; whether day *or* night, that was not the best of arrangements. General Hill's division formed the second line of Sir Arthur Wellesley's defensive position, although the brigades of the first line were still taking ground – which was as well, Hervey observed, for the French shot was arching across the Portiña from the Cerro de Cascajal and plunging onto the crest at the eastern end of the ridge, where the French gunners must suppose the outposts of the first line to be. It fell too far east to be any real threat to the division, but Hervey knew that General Hill would be occupied by what the fire portended. He looked at his watch – a quarter to seven.

'It is not at all auspicious,' said the general, scanning the ridge. 'I can still see no one. There ought by now to be pickets up there, at least. I would that Wellesley were here.' He snapped closed the telescope. 'I'd better go to find him.'

The aide-de-camp beckoned for their horses.

Hervey reckoned they had perhaps an hour and a half to find the commander-in-chief before the light failed; the moon would not be up for four hours and more. He shortened stirrups before mounting: he had stumbled about enough on Salisbury Plain in the dark to know what they might be in for.

As soon as they descended to the pasture south of the *cerro*, a terrific musketry opened from the direction of Talavera. The sun was low to their right, but the powder flashes were still vivid. The little party pulled up sharp.

'I think that is our answer, gentlemen,' said General Hill, calmly. 'The French are trying to persuade us they will attack tonight on the left, while the real attack is against the Spanish.'

'Will they hold, sir?' asked Hill's aide-de-camp.

'Talavera's a strong enough place, Harry,' replied the general (audible, just, to Hervey standing four lengths rear).

207

'But there's a mile of open line to the junction with Campbell's brigade, and Cuesta's men are unpredictable, frankly. Cuesta himself is unpredictable!'

Without warning, he dug his spurs into his charger's flanks; the ADC and escorts had to kick into a fast canter to catch him up. Loyalist began napping as Hervey pressed him hard to follow.

The shadows were long when they found the commander-in-chief. He was exactly where General Hill had supposed he would be, with the right-flank brigade, Campbell's, watching calmly as Spanish soldiers poured rear from the line between the redoubt and the city. Hervey saw them, and with some dismay after what General Hill had said. He looked about for Cornet Bruce, but there was no sign of him.

'Ah, Hill, what is the pounding on your flank?' asked Sir Arthur Wellesley, nodding to the salutation.

General Hill replaced his bicorn, fore and aft. 'I cannot rightly make out, Sir Arthur. The batteries on the Cerro de Cascajal are pounding empty ground on the east of the ridge. I came to ask what are your dispositions for the first line, for I can discern nobody yet, not even a picket.'

The commander-in-chief kept his eyes on the rearward stream of Spanish. 'Have no fear, General: the Germans will soon be there, and there'll be a brigade of cavalry in the valley beyond you.'

'In that case I will ride up the line to find them, Sir Arthur – the Germans, I mean.' He paused, staring now at the Spanish, who continued to pour from the line, although a good many of their comrades stood their ground yet, keeping up a brisk, if ragged, fire. 'This is a pretty business!'

'It is the most curious affair,' replied Wellesley, very composed. 'A great host of French dragoons came up to the trees not a quarter-hour ago and discharged their pistols – to have the Spaniards show themselves, I suppose. And they obliged them handsomely: the whole line blazed away! Well, it is no matter: if they will but fire as well tomorrow, the day is our own!' He shook his head just perceptibly. 'But as there seems to be nobody to fire back at just now, I do wish they would stop it.'

'You have sent someone, Sir Arthur?' asked General Hill.

'No, they are Whittingham's men. He'll see them right, I have no doubt. Only look at the ugly hole those fellows have left in my line!'

It was as plain to them as may be, long shadows or not: there was a gap in the allied line a furlong and more. Hervey reckoned the French must have the sun in their eyes not to see it.

Brigadier-General Alexander Campbell, in the Government sett of his old regiment, the 74th Highlanders, and sitting astride a tit of a mare that even the commissary would not have looked twice at, could bear it no longer. 'General, I think I had better take the Seventh there. If those fellows keep running they'll take the rest with them.'

'No,' said Wellesley, shaking his head. 'I shall want the Seventh here soon enough. But I wish you would go to their second line and try to get them to fill it up.'

Campbell raised his hat and turned his charger. 'Hill, I'd be glad of another galloper, if you would. I've had to send mine with word to the next division.'

General Hill nodded to Hervey. 'By all means, Campbell. I shall return to mine. I perceive you will have the fight of it here tomorrow, if not tonight. I wish you well.'

Hervey was disappointed. He had hoped to learn more of affairs here; it was not every day a cornet might listen on the conversation of the commander-in-chief. He saluted and took off after the brigadier and his major obediently.

'Great heavens!' cursed Campbell, his nostrils flaring, his

eyes wide. In five minutes he had discovered what Sir Arthur Wellesley could not observe. 'A whole brigade's worth of them running! The supports have gone as well!'

Hervey was equally astonished. The scrub, to the rear of the olive groves which marked the front line, was alive with men making west at the double. Many of them had thrown off their hats and downed their muskets. They looked like stags running before hounds.

Brigadier-General Alexander Campbell was having none of it, despite Wellesley's caution. He drew his sword and took off at once into the middle of the rout, laying about any man within reach with the flat of it. Hervey and the brigade-major, likewise swords drawn, stuck as close as they could, fearing at any moment a Spaniard would turn on his abuser and shoot him from the saddle.

The brigade-major all but grabbed at Campbell's reins. 'General, it's no good! We must get help!'

'Damn it, Gorrie, I'll flay 'em back to their posts! I'll damn well shoot them to their duty!' Campbell let his sword drop by its sling and drew his pistols instead.

Hervey and the brigade-major dutifully drew theirs, Hervey certain it would be his last. There were a thousand Spaniards in musket range, and not all of them had thrown down their arms.

Campbell fired into the air. A few men checked; others further away, seeing a madman not an adversary, changed direction. He drew a bead on the closest Spaniard still running, and fired. The man fell stone dead.

There was a split second only to marvel at the marksmanship before a ball whistled past Hervey's head, then several more. It was pointless trying to find the culprits – there were dozens of muskets levelled at them.

'General, we must run for it!' the brigade-major insisted.

There was a sudden and decided fusillade behind them.

Hervey turned to see a long line of cavalry approaching, enveloped in smoke.

'Thank God!' sighed the brigade-major. 'See, General, the Spaniards have brought up their cavalry.'

Brigadier-General Campbell, feverishly reloading his pistols, seemed not to have heard.

'General!'

At last he turned, his face as red as his coat. 'And not before time,' he rasped. 'I'd hang every other man if he were mine!'

Hervey shifted uneasily in the saddle. While he could admire the general's courage and determination, the sanguinary rage was more than a little alarming.

Campbell slapped his mare hard with the flat of his sword – if not quite as hard as the unfortunate Spaniards – and took off as suddenly, almost leaving Hervey with his thoughts. 'Thank you, Cornet! You may go back to Hill now,' he called over his shoulder, as if he were dismissing a pilot at the end of a day's hunting.

Hervey touched the peak of his Tarleton punctiliously, glanced about gingerly, then inclined left so as to make straight and fast for the Cerro de Medellin.

By the time he found General Hill's headquarters – a two-mile ride – it was dark but for the campfires.

'Stand easy, Mr Hervey,' said the assistant quartermaster-general. 'The French guns blaze away every so often, but things are quiet. Keep your horse saddled, though.'

'Yes, sir. General Hill might wish to hear that the Spanish are getting back into their place on the right flank.'

'Very well, I shall inform him.'

Hervey turned and went to look for Private Sykes. In a division of infantry he knew it ought not to be too difficult to find a man with a horse, but the night was now so black that it was difficult to make out anything more than half a dozen paces away.

'Sir?'

'Is that you, Sykes?'

'Yes, sir. I heard Loyalist blowing. There's coffee over here, sir. Picket's got a brew on all night.'

'That would be welcome indeed, Sykes.' He glanced over his shoulder to fix exactly the general's campfire in case he were summoned.

'I wondered where you was, sir, when the gen'ral came back.'

Hervey smiled, ruefully. 'I think in the despatches it might say "liaison with our allies".'

'Sir?'

As Sykes took Loyalist, there was a sudden musketry due east – three hundred yards, perhaps four. Hervey grabbed the reins again and began running back to General Hill's headquarters.

The general was already giving orders to Colonel Stewart, his second brigadier. 'Yours to the support of Low's brigade, then—'

The firing ceased as abruptly as it had started. General Hill waited for several minutes before changing his mind.

'Very well, Stewart: as you were. A false alarm. These Germans fire too readily. You may go back to your brigade, but keep a sharp watch.'

The brigadier took his leave.

'Mr Hervey?' said the general, peering at him in the light of a good blaze.

'Sir!'

'Thank you for your report. Have you taken coffee since coming back?'

'No, sir, I was—'

The firing began again, but from atop the crest this time, the flashes quite clear.

General Hill growled. 'The old Buffs, as usual making

some blunder! I do wish these fellows would contain themselves better. Fetch my horse, please.'

An orderly brought him his black gelding and helped him into the saddle.

'I'd better go and put them right. They'll have lost all direction, I fancy.'

Hervey clambered astride Loyalist while General Hill and one of the brigade-majors took off as if it were daylight. He had the devil of a job keeping with them, Loyalist napping again, wanting his head in the pitch blackness.

Four hundred yards at a fast go, and uphill, and the general shouting, 'Cease firing there, you men! You face the wrong way! Cease firing!' Hervey could only wonder at the impulsiveness of infantry generals: they made the cavalry's work that day seem timid by comparison.

The firing suddenly faltered. Loyalist started as black shapes loomed.

One grabbed the general's reins. '*Se rend, monsieur!*'

Hervey drew his sword, spurred at him and cut hard on the offside. There was a cry and the black shape fell.

'Away!' yelled Hill, hauling on the reins.

They dug in their spurs for dear life. Shots followed left and right. Hervey lay low across Loyalist's neck and prayed they wouldn't stumble. He didn't see the brigade-major fall, nor the musket ball strike the general's horse.

Down the slope they hurtled – four hundred yards, rats running in his stomach as fast.

'Stand to!' bellowed Hill as they galloped in. 'Stewart, your brigade at once, please! Open column of companies! I've no notion where the Germans or Low's men are, but the French have the crest!'

Colonel Stewart began barking orders as General Hill dismounted. Hervey made to follow, but the general had other intentions. 'Find Wellesley and tell him what's up, Hervey!'

* * *

It was a simple enough order, but devilish difficult. Where *was* Wellesley? Would he still be with Campbell's brigade on the far flank? Surely not, if the situation had quietened there? Yet Campbell would know where he had gone next – that was something. Would he even be able to *find* the flank brigade, though? It was pitch dark, and there were two hours to moonrise. And he had not yet been about a battlefield at night, with nervous sentries firing before a challenge. This was not like Corunna. He must think very carefully.

He decided to descend the ridge riding due south – at least the sky was clear and he could see his stars – and then strike due east until he found the second line. Someone there must know where was the commander-in-chief.

They scrambled down the ridge, Loyalist choosing his footing carefully. They made the bottom without too much trouble, striking left and east at the olive groves and following the tree-line for a furlong and more until the groves began climbing the side of the *cerro*, so that Hervey knew he was near the line. Then he took a fix on a good star due east, and pushed on into the trees. He heard firing on the heights above him, and prayed it was 'Daddy' Hill's men worsting the French. Could it be otherwise?

After five long minutes he found the rear of what he reckoned must be the Third Division. 'Galloper!' he called. 'Second Division galloper!'

'Here, sir!' answered a picket-serjeant, lofting a torch. 'Second Twenty-fourth.'

Hervey jumped down thankfully: here was an NCO who knew his business. 'General Mackenzie's division, are you?'

'His brigade, sir. The general's been here this very minute.'

The Twenty-fourth's picket-officer came up. 'What is the firing, do you know?'

'The French are on the ridge,' replied Hervey, nodding left. 'Do you know where General Mackenzie is?'

'With the lieutenant-colonel, I think. I'll take you.' He held out a hand. 'Davies.'

'Hervey, Sixth Light Dragoons, galloping for General Hill.'

'A horse-holder if you please, Serjeant Allott,' said Ensign Davies.

Hervey handed Loyalist's reins to one of the picket, though not without hesitation. It was the maxim of the prudent soldier never to be parted from his kit, and the horse was the cavalryman's kit, *sine quo non*. But he could hardly trail through a battalion of infantry at night leading a charger.

Ensign Davies was sure-footed about the olive groves. It was not long before they found the Twenty-fourth's lieutenant-colonel, General Mackenzie with him. Davies stood to attention, and saluted. 'Picket-officer, sir. A galloper from the Second Division.'

General Mackenzie turned. 'What is the alarm up there?'

Hervey saluted. 'The French have the summit of the ridge, sir. General Hill is driving them off. He has sent me to find the commander-in-chief, sir.'

'He went there the minute the firing began.'

Hervey checked himself, somehow disbelieving that Sir Arthur Wellesley had been ascending the *cerro* as he himself had been descending. He almost asked, 'Are you sure?' Instead he saluted again. 'With your leave, sir.'

The general nodded. 'My compliments to General Hill. He shall have my best support on his flank.'

'Sir.'

Hervey picked his way back with Ensign Davies, easier now that his mission was accomplished – or, rather, obviated. 'You had hot work of it this afternoon,' he tried.

215

'We did, by God! You saw?' replied Davies, sounding as if he would go again this instant.

'We were on your left flank.'

'I did not see it. I did not see anything but smoke and shot. You fellows have the better view of things astride.'

Hervey hoped he did not mean they merely looked on, especially since things would have gone so much the harder with the Twenty-fourth had the Sixth not charged. But it was scarcely the time to put him to rights about that. 'The work of cavalry is for the most part unobserved,' he consoled himself.

Loyalist was waiting quietly as they got back to the picket's fire. Hervey took the reins and thanked the holder, a private man who looked surprised to be addressed directly. Then he turned to Ensign Davies again. It was a strange feeling, for he knew there was every chance he would not see him again: an ensign in the centre of the line during a general action would face a great deal of metal. 'I hope you have a quiet night. And good fortune for the morrow.' He held out a hand.

Davies took it. If he feared for the morrow he did not – would not – show it. 'As long as we have powder enough it will be well. Come and dine with us afterwards.'

Hervey smiled. 'Thank you. I shall.' He climbed into the saddle (Loyalist preferred him not to vault, as Jessye allowed), touched his peak, and turned back the way he had come.

The moon was an hour and more away yet, but the sky was lightening. When Hervey found the same trec-line he had taken east, he squeezed Loyalist to a trot – quick, but in-hand. The horse started napping again, and Hervey began wishing he had taken Jessye instead. Loyalist had done him well in the gallop on the *cerro*, but there was no surety in a

216

charger half trained, and picking about the army in the middle of the night was not a thing to be doing with a nappy gelding. The musketry atop the *cerro* was increasing. There would be nothing he could do, but his every instinct was to gallop there. Loyalist sensed it and broke into a canter. Hervey would not allow it, though, checking with rein and leg until the horse was back in-hand again. Half trained Loyalist may be, but there was no excuse for bad manners. But he lengthened the stride a fraction: General Hill might have more duties for him – he ought not to delay beyond a safe moment.

In a few minutes more he saw the open pasture. Then he heard the crack as Loyalist squealed and faltered. He pulled up at once and sprang from the saddle. Loyalist stood calmly as Hervey felt around the impaling: twelve inches of olive branch the diameter of a musket ball stuck-out from just beneath the sternum like a bolt from a crossbow. How deep it had gone he could not know, but blood was already oozing from the wound. He realized there must be force to it, for the entry was clean, no tearing.

What could he do? Could he find John Knight? Where *was* the regiment? If he left the shaft in, would it help staunch the flow? But what damage did it do inside? If only John Knight were here . . .

He must pull out the shaft. The surgeon always removed a missile. That was the way, was it not? Thank God Loyalist stood calm! Perhaps, then, the damage was not so great? But then, when he got the shaft out – and he must have it *all* out, and cleanly – he must staunch the bleeding somehow. How could he do it without someone to hold Loyalist still? And he had nothing but his blanket to staunch with. Perhaps if he cut it up . . .

Loyalist was grunting now, but he stood motionless. Hervey slashed the blanket into handy rags with his sabre. When he was done he felt the wound again. The blood was copious. He was sure the shaft had gone deep. And now it was wet and he would not have the purchase on it . . .

Should he pull fast or slow? If he pulled fast it might break; if slow, Loyalist might shift with the pain and break it anyway. He dried his palms as best he could, looped the reins round his right arm and grasped the shaft with both hands. 'Good boy,' he whispered, then drew firmly and evenly, praying it would come out in one.

Loyalist grunted but stood stock-still. Hervey felt the point of the shaft anxiously: it was sharp – it hadn't broken inside. 'Thank God,' he muttered. But a good six inches had penetrated. If four inches would kill a man, it did not take a horse anatomist to understand the damage.

Blood was running freely now. Hervey pressed the rags into the wound as best he could, but at once they were soaked through, so that in a few minutes he had used every piece of his blanket. The horse was becoming unsteady on his feet; Hervey had to lean hard against him. In a few minutes more, Loyalist dropped to his knees; the hocks followed soon after, and then he rolled to his left side, breathing shallow.

Nothing Hervey could do would staunch the blood. Could John Knight have done anything? Knight could clamp a vein or an artery – he had seen him do it – but how could *he* here? He couldn't *see* anything, even if he had had clamps – or even a knife to make an incision. All he could do was kneel by Loyalist's head as his lifeblood emptied into the earth. There was musketry all about the *cerro*, men dying alone in the dark; he did not think about them, only that a noble animal like Loyalist should not die ignobly or alone. He thought to finish things with a pistol, but there had been enough of that at Corunna (and the shot would likely raise alarm with General Mackenzie's brigade). No, there would be no ball in the brains, for Loyalist was not in pain; that was evident. He must stay by his side, reassuring, until the time.

In half an hour Loyalist was quite still; there was no more breathing. Hervey struggled with the lump in his throat, and cursed. There was nothing he could do now but salvage what furniture he may and make his way back to the *cerro*. There he would take Sykes's trooper and send his groom back to the Sixth for Jessye. The moon would be up soon: Sykes ought not to have too hard a time of it. He envied him, indeed, for what was there for a cornet to do in the thick of night among infantry? There hadn't even been need of him to fetch the commander-in-chief. He swore. Galloper duty, the cornet's thrill, had been a pointless affair. But that, he knew (because first Daniel Coates, and then Joseph Edmonds, had told him), was one half of the true nature of war – a terrible, pointless wasting. He cursed again, and stopped struggling with the lump in his throat.

And he had thought himself steeled by Corunna!

CHAPTER FIFTEEN
THE WORK OF CAVALRY

Next morning, 28 July 1809

A hand shook his shoulder, roughly. 'Reveille!'

Hervey had sweated through the day before, and through the night, but now he shivered, his instinct to pull the cloak about his shoulders again. He sat up. The moon had set, but the sky was lightening in the east: it would be full dawn inside half an hour. He had slept for three hours, perhaps, and he ached for more. His shoulder throbbed. The wound had been nothing, but the stitching had been rough. He was hungry, too. He had with him some liquorice sticks and a flask of brandy, nothing else. The supply animals had not come up by the time he had left for the Second Division, and General Hill's infantrymen had no rations to spare. But the night's alarms had thrown everything into confusion; it looked as if no one on the Cerro de Medellín would fight his battle today on a full stomach – or even half of one.

He got up, folded his cloak and started to saddle the little trooper Sykes had handed over to him. Trixie, his groom had called her, after his sister. Poor Sykes: he had drawn the mare only the day before, John Knight having cast his post-Corunna remount on account of bog spavin. Loyalist had been almost a hand higher, but Trixie was sturdy enough, and steady, reckoned Hervey. She stood loosely tethered where he had slept, calmly cropping the rough grass. *Her* belly at least would be filled, even if with poorish fodder. He was relieved that Loyalist's saddle fitted well, and he managed to get the girth and surcingle tight without the biting that some of the older troopers were prone to. She even lifted her head for the bit. A very tractable mare, she was. It pleased him, drawing the sting of the night somewhat. He hoped she was as handy.

He buckled on his sword, tidied himself – ablutions waited until stand-down – checked the girth again and climbed into the saddle. She stood still for him, a good sign; he flexed the bit, she dropped her head nicely, and he squeezed his legs just a fraction. She answered well. Hervey had no idea of her provenance – even if she were country-bred – but he was relieved at her quality: he did not fancy seeing out his duty with the Second Division astride a screw. He was only surprised she had passed into the riding-master's hands and then out again.

He saluted the AQMG and nodded his 'good morning' to an aide-de-camp he had not seen before. General Hill was just mounting, so he halted at a respectful distance with his dawn thoughts. The sky was no longer black but grey, the urgent time when the minutes seemed to race. When daylight came, the country would be exactly as yesterday, the lie of the land unaltered in a single detail. But the enemy had not been inactive during the night: what would be the scene before them? How many French would be drawn up ready to attack? How many guns would there be on the Cerro de Cascajal? More, for sure, than the British disposed here.

Half a dozen other mounted figures now rode up. Hervey strained to see who. He braced as he recognized the profile of the commander-in-chief, cloaked and wearing a bicorn. What had kept him here the night? Had the Cerro de Medellin been in such peril that the commander-in-chief had kept vigil while he himself slept? He felt a sudden guilt; but, then, no one had told him to do other than sleep. No one, indeed, had told him anything at all. Or had Sir Arthur Wellesley come up to the *cerro* for the dawn stand-to? In which case it could only mean that it was here he expected the French to show themselves first. Hervey felt the thrill of a man discovering he was unexpectedly in the place of decision.

It was so obvious, now that he thought about it: *here* was the place to see the battlefield, not down among the olive groves. Here, the commander-in-chief could direct his battle, seeing the moves the French made, judging which were real and which were feints, speeding gallopers this way and that with his orders. But Hervey supposed he would see none of it, for his own orders were to return to the Sixth as soon as daylight was come. Could he do so without General Hill's leave? But could he remain here longer without incurring his troop-leader's wrath? There would be nothing for the cavalry to do until the infantry had clashed. In any case, had not the order gone out for the cavalry brigades to forage after dawn? He would hardly be missed in foraging . . .

He could not yet make out the hands of his watch face; by the look of the sky, he reckoned it must be half-past the hour, perhaps even a quarter-to, for first light was at five. And at first light a white horse was grey, not black: the staff dragoon's with Sir Arthur Wellesley, now, was black (if, of course, it was the same animal he had seen yesterday). First light was the time when the routine of the night – pickets, sentries, sleep – changed to that of the day, when regiments mustered and stood-to their arms, when the pickets and sentries came in, when general actions began. He calculated that it would be two hours and more before the first dragoon drew his sabre to cut anything but grass. He hoped fervently that General Hill would not dismiss him now, therefore.

Sir Arthur Wellesley and General Hill moved off with their staff towards the eastern crest of the *cerro*. Hervey followed hesitantly, expecting at any moment to be told to rejoin his regiment.

One of the aides-de-camp, a lieutenant from General Hill's own regiment, rode up alongside him. 'Was it you with the general last night?'

Hervey was cautious, uncertain of the ADC's purpose. 'If you mean when the French first attacked, yes.'

'Then I am especially pleased to make your acquaintance. Gartside, Ninetieth,' said the ADC, holding out a hand.

Hervey took it. 'Hervey, Sixth Light Dragoons.'

'The general owes his liberty to you, I understand, if not his life.'

In truth, he had not given it much thought, such was his dismay at losing Loyalist. 'It was a close shave, I own. I am sorry for your major, though. He must have been hit by a ball as we galloped home.'

'He was dead when we found him. I'm only sorry I was not with you: the general had sent me to Tilson's brigade for their evening state, which we'd not had.'

Hervey nodded in commiseration. 'What I don't understand is why we were surprised. How had the French passed through the first line? And with scarcely a shot?'

'There wasn't a first line, not to speak of. The brigades had been posted very ill.'

'I imagine they're better posted now?'

'Indeed. Wellesley and the general were abroad for two hours after we pushed the French off the ridge. Both our brigades are now forward. Tilson's is right, on the crest, and Stewart's left so the French can't envelop the wing. There's supposed to be a brigade of cavalry in the valley over yonder to support him, but I don't know who.'

Neither did Hervey. Cotton's, with which the Sixth were

brigaded, were covering the junction with the Spanish on the right, and Fane's heavies would surely be needed in the centre? 'Anson's, perhaps.'

'Well, when they show, no doubt one of us will be sent to them. But I should say, the general spoke very favourably of you, you know – after the skirmish last night, I mean. There'll be a promotion in it.'

Hervey was flattered, if doubtful. 'Really, Gartside, it was nothing out of the ordinary. We must have made two dozen cuts apiece in the Sixth yesterday afternoon!'

Lieutenant Gartside put a hand to Hervey's shoulder. 'My dear sir, we all of us know the work of cavalry goes unobserved. When it comes to promotion, one cut in the right place is worth a hundred out of sight. Be pleased you have made both sorts!'

Hervey was still doubtful, but he would hope. If it did not bring promotion, it might at least serve his reputation when it came to the court martial and Daly.

Ten minutes later, with the sun flushed up, Lieutenant Gartside pronounced his final words on the matter. 'See, Hervey: those are the fellows who will give us our opportunity!'

The sun was full in their eyes, but Hervey could make out the French well enough. Opposite the Second Division, on the Cerro de Cascajal, were more guns than he had ever seen. He took out his telescope to observe. The gunners were standing to attention by their pieces, as if all was ready and waiting for the command 'fire'. He scanned right, to the low ground the other side of the Portiña. Regiments of blue-coated infantry stood facing the British line as far as the redoubt at the junction with the Spanish, all ranked in column of battalions for the attack, guns to the fore. Behind them were cavalry in numbers he could not begin to calculate. Corunna looked but a skirmish compared with this! The rats in his stomach began running again.

Lieutenant Gartside beckoned him further forward until they drew close to one of Sir Arthur Wellesley's ADCs. 'Gordon, my dear fellow!'

A captain, four or five years Hervey's senior, no more, wearing the uniform of the Third Guards, turned in the saddle. 'Gartside – good morning.'

To Hervey, he sounded as cool as the commander-in-chief looked.

'I heard you were come out,' said Lieutenant Gartside, with an easy smile. And then he looked at him more intently. 'My dear Gordon, are you quite well?'

'The devil, I am, Gartside. I've not been well since leaving Lisbon. Something has taken hold of me, and I wish it would leave go!'

'I am sorry for it. It's deuced noble that you should turn out, feeling so out of sorts. May I present Cornet Hervey, of the Sixth.'

The ADC turned further in the saddle, and nodded. 'How d'ye do, sir.'

Hervey touched his peak.

'Gordon was with Sir David Baird at Corunna,' explained Gartside.

Hervey at once knew all. Baird had been Moore's deputy at Corunna. This was the Gordon who had taken the victory despatch to London, and got a brevet for it. It ought to have been another's honour, they had all said, since Baird himself had been carried from the field early in the day, and General Hope had seen the battle to its end. But Baird had insisted that his nephew take the despatch – and, no doubt, had arranged this appointment to Sir Arthur Wellesley, too. But Hervey was not disposed to dislike a man merely for his good fortune. After all, Captain the Honourable Alexander Gordon had paraded this morning, in the most evident discomfort, and that said something of his quality, did it not?

Gartside was not deterred by either Gordon's reserve or Hervey's. He knew the one well enough, and was already coming to like the other. 'Gordon, are you able to tell us what are the army's dispositions? We came up here last evening and saw nothing.'

Captain Gordon, while keeping a sharp eye on the commander-in-chief, was happy to oblige his old-school-fellow. It was simply explained, he said. From their vantage point, here on the Cerro de Medellín, they could see the mile of British line along the Portiña clearly enough – and with a good telescope they could see the Spanish, too, three-quarters the distance again to the walls of Talavera. The junction was guarded by the bastion of Pajar de Vergara and its batteries (Hervey had seen it the evening before) and the divisions were formed, conveniently alphabetical, right to left from the bastion to the *cerro*: Campbell's on the right, then Mackenzie's, then Sherbrooke's; and then Hill's on the left flank. Two brigades of cavalry – Fane's and Cotton's – would stand in the centre of the second line between Mackenzie's division and Hill's, while Anson's was ordered to the north valley.

'I am very much obliged, Gordon,' said Gartside, turning to Hervey.

Hervey imagined himself as well served now as any galloper in the army. He nodded. 'Thank you, Captain Gordon.'

The ADC turned and looked at him. 'Was it you who cut out Hill last night?'

Hervey was surprised the news had travelled. 'It was.'

The ADC nodded, and with just a suggestion of a smile. 'Then you did the army a service, if I'm not very much mistaken.'

A thunder-blast of cannon seemed to rock the entire *cerro*. Then came the whistling-buzzing shot, tearing the air about them, pounding the forward slope and throwing up fountains of earth, showering the commander-in-chief's party with sods and stones – and worse. A bloody arm fell in front of Hervey, its fingers stretched out like a fan. Instinctively, for it was the way Joseph Edmonds had trained them (and to take his eyes from the disembodied limb), he took out his watch: it was twenty minutes past five o'clock.

The redcoated battalions of the forward brigade swayed visibly under the bombardment – thirty guns were firing, by the ADCs' common reckoning. But the batteries were now joined by others further down the slopes of the Cerro de Cascajal, so that soon there was a continuous fire, and all concentrated on the eastern end of the long ridge of the Cerro de Medellin.

Sir Arthur Wellesley turned to General Hill. 'Very well, have them withdraw behind the crest and lie down. But have the light companies hold their ground: I must have skirmishers to break up the columns when they advance.'

General Hill had taken the precaution of having the brigade-majors join him for stand-to. He nodded to them, no words necessary, then he touched his hat as the commander-in-chief spurred off to inspect his other divisions.

Smoke drifted across the valley of the Portiña, obscuring their view of the batteries, but likewise spoiling the gunners' aim. General Hill sat coolly astride his black gelding on the reverse slope, far enough behind the crest for protection, but, standing in his stirrups, able to observe the movement of the French – and his light companies. After twenty minutes without flinching in the storm of shot, he snapped shut his telescope suddenly, and scowled. 'The French have excess of fortune this morning. So many guns firing blind and still telling! And every shot thickening the smoke. I can no longer see the light companies!'

'Recall them, General?' asked his AQMG.

'Ay, George; let us have them in. And quick about it.'

The AQMG reined about and repeated the order to the brigade-majors.

In less than a minute the regimental buglers were sounding 'retire'. As a rule, General Hill did not permit field orders to be passed by bugle. The drill book was emphatic on the matter: *Signals are improper in exercise, because dangerous and apt to be mistaken in service.* Except that in his experience signals were rarely mistaken by the enemy! But what alternative did he have this morning, with so much smoke? This morning he did not mind by *what* means his skirmishers were recalled. If the French heard the urgent, repeated Gs, so be it! The light companies would be sure to.

Ten minutes later, Hervey saw the first men filing home through the blackening smoke, arms sloped, regular as if on parade.

General Hill exploded. 'Damn their filing! Let them come in anyhow!'

Lieutenant Gartside blinked. 'I do believe that is the first time I have heard the general swear.'

With so severe a cannonade, Hervey could not but imagine the general had cause.

Then, in a few minutes more, the fire abruptly ceased. The only sound was of the wounded, and these remarkably composed. After such thunder, the silence was eerie. Hervey felt his stomach tighten.

'There can only be one reason,' said Hill, standing tall in the stirrups, and shielding his eyes from the already strong sun as he peered into the smoke. 'The gunners'll not be able to see their own men. Their infantry must be half-way to the top.'

'Bring forward the brigades, sir?' suggested the AQMG.

'No, George, not yet. I want to see the colour of their facings before I stand ours up. The smoke's to our advantage now.'

Anything that hampered the gunners' aim was to their advantage, thought Hervey. He wondered again if he ought not to be seeking his leave: the Sixth would surely not be foraging long, now that action was joined?

The guns did not remain silent for long, however. They commanded more than just the forward slope of the Cerro de Medellin: they could as easily enfilade the Portiña. But they were not yet ready to switch from the Second Division entirely. The right flank of Colonel Stewart's brigade, extending partway down the southern slope of the *cerro*, stood exposed, the only troops of the division not concealed on the reverse slope or masked by smoke. Two guns on the left of the French battery had direct line of sight, and these now opened an unnervingly accurate fire on the first battalion of the 48th (Northamptonshire) Regiment, followed by others firing blind – and lucky.

'They shall have to bear it,' said Hill resolutely, but sadly. 'Either that or lie down. The French will be upon them soon.'

Hervey watched, appalled, as shot tore into the Forty-eighth's ranks, the men dragging their fallen comrades rear and then closing the gaps, so that with each minute the line moved a little further to the left. 'Why do they close up? Why do they not lie down, or stand open so the shot has less effect?'

'Because they might not stand at all unless in close order,' replied Lieutenant Gartside, grimly.

Hervey could scarce believe the steadiness. These men would rather stand shoulder-to-shoulder and suffer the consequences than disperse and suffer less! He began praying the cannonade would cease; the Forty-eighth had already borne more than a regiment ought to endure.

General Hill judged it the moment. 'Now, George!'

Hervey saw the French helmets cresting the ridge as Major-General Tilson's brigade rose to its feet, followed by

Stewart's and Donkin's. The French had suffered not at all as they ascended the slope; *now* the ranks of redcoats would exact their revenge.

Hervey heard the first command – 'Fire!' – and then all hell itself seemed let loose.

Five minutes, ten, fifteen . . . he had no idea how long it was. The French tried to answer, but in close column of divisions they could not bring enough muskets to bear against battalions in line only two ranks deep. And even as the columns tried to deploy, riflemen of the German Legion came doubling up the south slope to pour well-aimed fire into their flank – General Mackenzie and his promised 'best support'.

'*Bayonets!*' shouted Hill.

In an instant, four thousand muskets were turned into pikes. The lines of red surged forward, the columns of blue wavered, the British charged – and the French broke. They ran back down the slope to the Portiña, but not fast enough. Hundreds of them fell to the points of steel which pursued, half crazed.

General Hill and his staff followed as far as the crest of the *cerro*. Smoke hung about, if patchy, but Hervey could see redcoats at the Portiña, and some even across it, hunting their quarry right back to the reserve line. He had seen nothing its like before, but his instinct told him what must happen next: the whole of the British line would advance, and the whole of the French line would break.

He was wrong. As suddenly as the French had broken at the crest, the reserve line sprang to life, and the fleeing blue-coats turned on the hunting bayonets, as a wildcat turns on its pursuer.

General Hill saw but the one outcome. 'Curse their ardour, George! What *do* the officers do there? Sound "recall"!'

* * *

230

In the relative peace of the olive groves, Hervey, now returned to duty with the Sixth, sought to recount what had happened. 'They were horribly pounded by the artillery as they made their way back up the hill, Colonel.'

'And there was no opening for cavalry?' Lord George Irvine wanted to know every detail.

Hervey shook his head. 'I do not think two horses could have crossed the Portiña together at that point, Colonel. Where they *might* have served, perhaps, is in the valley north of the ridge. There was a whole regiment of *chasseurs* there, and able to withdraw in perfect order.'

Lord George frowned. 'Anson's supposed to be there. He's still foraging, I suppose. There's nothing for us here the while. I believe I shall go to Cotton and propose taking the regiment instead. Has Hill applied to Wellesley, do you know?'

'I do not know, Colonel. The general was obliged by a wound in the head to leave the field. That is when his colonel ordered me to return here. General Tilson has taken the command.'

Lord George nodded. 'Very well, Hervey: you may rejoin your troop. Doubtless you were of use to Hill, but I can ill afford any more detachments.'

Hervey took his leave a shade disconsolately. Lord George seemed peeved that he had been absent on duty – why else complain of detachments? – and appeared to imagine he had been but an observer. With General Hill *hors de combat*, perhaps invalided home even, what chance was there of any recognition now?

Half an hour later, with no move by the enemy except the continued pounding of the Cerro de Medellín, Lord George Irvine received the nod from Major-General Stapleton Cotton. He summoned his troop-leaders and gave his orders in the space of but a minute. The squadrons were well drilled, and the skirmishing of the day before had put a confident address into them, too.

'To the left, *form*, in column of threes!'

Hervey thought it a pity there was no one to observe how regular the line turned to the north. These things spoke of capability, especially when so much of what they otherwise did went unremarked.

'Walk-march!'

The bugles sounded as if on parade.

'Trot!'

The jingling-jangling began – the music of a regiment of light cavalry on the move. It could lift the dullest spirits. Hervey was happy to be back, even where there was not 'the opportunity to display'.

Lord George Irvine led his regiment along a track which ascended the Cerro de Medellin about a mile west of the Portiña, close enough to see the Second Division's brigades on the reverse slope – riding through their baggage-lines indeed. At a distance, the battalions looked regular enough, but the dressing-stations nearer to were prodigiously busy. Hervey had recoiled the first time he heard the phrase 'the butcher's bill'; seeing the surgeons at work, now, the words seemed cruelly apt.

The Sixth broached the ridge and began descending the northern slope, and still there was no sign of Anson's brigade. Hervey, at least, was glad: they would have a good gallop here – he was sure of it.

In five more minutes, as the track levelled, they began forming right into line, four squadrons abreast, the left with its flank resting on a muddy stream. The valley bottom was perhaps half a mile wide, but the stream divided it neatly in two, and it was plain to all that north of it the French could have little opportunity to manoeuvre, even cavalry, since the ground was broken by ditches and dry watercourses, and the pasture was very rough. South of the stream was more promising: the going looked better for two furlongs and more, but beyond it was impossible to make out because of the scattered trees.

'Sit easy!'

The officers reached for their telescopes.

Hervey searched right to left: fore-ground, middle-, and distant-, as Daniel Coates had taught him on Salisbury Plain. But this morning there was moisture in his telescope, the lens part-misted, so that he took longer than the others with his surveillance. He could see nothing except where the ground began to rise at the head of the valley a mile and a half away – what he took to be the French flank-guard squadron. 'Do you see ought other than the cavalry yonder, Laming?'

'Not a thing,' drawled his fellow cornet, telescope still raised. 'You would have thought the place would be alive with *voltigeurs*.'

'The *cerro*'s deceptive,' said Hervey, trying to find where the moisture had got into his spyglass. 'We're too much under it, here. Atop they command the valley. If the French try to envelop the flank, all the Second Division has to do is incline its left brigade to meet them. But it *is* strange that the French do not probe. Do you suppose they don't have so many men after all?'

Lord George Irvine rode up to the troop, arresting speculation. 'Sir Edward, we'll watch for another quarter of an hour, and then I would have you send patrols to discover the lie of the land.' He nodded front, giving Number One Squadron leader his freedom of manoeuvre.

'Very good, Colonel,' replied Sir Edward, touching the peak of his Tarleton again. 'Do you happen to know where is the closest of our artillery?'

'I do not, but I intend discovering.'

'It would be a decidedly fine thing if the Chestnuts would accompany.'

233

'A *very* fine thing. I expect they'll show. Meanwhile I imagine we'll have to content ourselves with what the Second Division is able to dispose. But it ain't easy firing down into a valley like this.'

The Second Division's gunners would have no occasion to test their skill in support of First Squadron, however, for as soon as Lord George had finished speaking, a cloud of dust a mile west down the valley signalled that the Sixth's prospects had changed. 'I think Colonel Anson's brigade approaches, Colonel,' said the adjutant, standing in the stirrups to observe.

All heads turned rear.

Hervey cursed to himself. Now they would not get their gallop.

'I trust they have breakfasted well,' said Lord George, dryly. 'Well, Sir Edward, I think we may resume our former station.'

It made little difference to Sir Edward Lankester where the regiment took post, as long as they were not supports. He disliked contemplating the hindquarters of another regiment: much better a clear view of what to be about – and if they stayed here, Anson was sure to post them behind his own. 'You do not want me to take a look at the ground, then, Colonel?'

Lord George shook his head. 'No; our duty's to get back to Cotton. I shall tell Anson he must see the ground for himself.'

'Dismount!'

Troop-leaders repeated the order left and right, the length of the Sixth's double rank, and five hundred horses, as one, felt their backs ease.

General Cotton, standing close by with his staff, raised his hat by way of 'welcome back'.

Hervey looked at his watch. He wanted to be able to make

a very exact entry in his journal this day. It was approaching eleven o'clock, and still, by the sound of it (he could not actually *see*, for the olive groves), the French had made no move against the centre of the allied line. The gunners on the Cerro de Cascajal continued to pound away at the Second Division, although the regiments had long withdrawn behind the crest of the ridge again, save for the outposts. Why did Marshal Victor not attack?

'Deuced odd,' said Cornet Laming, while discovering that his brandy flask was empty. 'If Joseph Bonaparte really *is* in the field, you'd think Victor would want to put on a show after being thrown off yon ridge.'

Lieutenant Martyn thought otherwise. 'I don't believe the French are in earnest,' he said, the little knot of First Squadron subalterns all eager for his superior opinion. 'I had it from one of Wellesley's ADCs last night: Bonaparte *frère* will stand on the defensive and wait for Soult to come up in rear of us. So Wellesley will have to attack, which he's scarce strong enough to do, even if the Dons could be relied on. That, or else he'll have to withdraw. And it would be a deuced difficult business since there's only one bridge across the Tagus.'

'How many French are there, do you suppose?' asked Laming.

'Wellesley believes in excess of fifty thousand.'

'Whereas we have twenty!'

'Just so.'

'And the Dons thirty.'

Rather fewer now, reckoned Hervey, thinking of last night's dismal affair.

'Then why *do* the French attack 'gainst such odds?' asked Laming, even more incredulous.

Martyn looked at him as if the answer were obvious. 'Because they can fright the Dons into staying behind their walls in Talavera, and throw their whole weight against *us*.

But numbers alone won't carry the day. They have to do it with determination.'

Hervey thought he had seen plenty of that at first light. He wondered what were the implications of his lieutenant's appreciation. 'Does that mean the cavalry will reinforce the flank, Martyn? Or shall we stay here?'

The speculation occupied them for a good ten minutes, but what Lieutenant Martyn could not know, because Wellesley himself did not, was that Joseph Bonaparte was not without his own concerns for his lines of communication – for his own capital, indeed. Much as the Sixth might scoff at their allies, and old General Cuesta in particular, there was one Spanish general at least who showed an appetite for the offensive: intelligence had reached Joseph Bonaparte that very morning that General Francisco Venegas and the army of La Mancha was before Toledo, and would not be long in marching on Madrid. 'King' Joseph had but a day or so before he must send fifty thousand men to defend his royal seat. And true though Martyn's intelligence from Wellesley's staff had been, it was already out of date, for soon after sunrise, the commander-in-chief had received word from his observing officers that Soult was still a week's march away, perhaps more.

Forward of the olive groves, in the centre of the British line, Sir Arthur Wellesley was even now pondering the consequences of this most welcome intelligence. At length he turned to his quartermaster-general. 'Murray, have someone go to Tilson and tell him to keep a sharp watch for *voltigeurs*. I am certain Victor must try to turn our flank. He has no other way. All else here in the centre will be humbug!'

CHAPTER SIXTEEN
A BATTLE FOR A PEERAGE

Later

At the turn of a creaking wheel, the 6th Light Dragoons were transformed into the most contented regiment at Talavera. A bullock-cart had come up, and with it a smiling Serjeant Bentley. That he had not been there after muster at first light, the hour at which breakfast would have been most welcome, did not now matter. If Bentley was smiling it meant that his 'progging' had been successful, for they all knew there were no commissary rations to be had until the evening (the Spanish had only just agreed to let Wellesley have what he had asked for a week ago). The Sixth, as other regiments, had been reconciled to making do with what they carried at 'first line' – which was no more than biscuit. But Lord George Irvine had judged it the moment to use his gold, and Serjeant Bentley had been despatched to the rear with more coin than he would see in three years of being paid regularly. Now he was returning with nothing left of it – but with bread, red wine and brandied peaches; enough for the entire regiment.

Lord George did not need to buy the admiration or affection of his men. Their discipline was well regulated, they were keen for the fight, and, given what had happened so far, they could trust their officers. But they were sore

237

hungry, and in any case, it did no harm for a man to think himself in a regiment well provided for. If Hervey felt any guilt at eating peaches and drinking passable wine, when the poor, wretched infantry on the Cerro de Medellin had only stirabout made with maggoty biscuit and brackish water, the pleasure of his exceptional feast overcame it. Besides, the infantry were always the first to get at the spoils after a battle, were they not?

'By, sir, but I feel the better for that!' declared Corporal Armstrong, stowing a piece of bread the size of his fist into a mess tin – 'for a rainy day, sir'.

'So do I, Corporal; so do I,' said Hervey, reaching for his own mess tin to stow the little of his that remained, grateful for the example of prudence. He looked round to see how many others were reserving any portion of the issue. He saw few. He fancied it was telling – the difference between the private-man, whose actions were regulated by orders, and the canny NCO, expected to think for himself. Canny NCOs were not found everywhere, he knew: Joseph Edmonds had said there were a couple of dozen 'wise virgins' in the regiment, as he called the seasoned campaigners, and the rest would never have their lamps filled.

Not only was it a feast, it was a breakfast of real repose. The guns had been silent for a quarter of an hour, the odd report in the direction of the Cerro de Medellin sounding like nothing but the random shots of a shooting party. The entire field, indeed, was quiet – peaceful, even, like the middle of the night. Lord George Irvine, having fed his regiment, could now give them the order to rest.

Hervey lay down, altogether mindless of the ache in his shoulder now that that in his stomach was gone, and at once fell asleep.

A marrow-chilling roar of cannon woke them, horses and men alike. Shot tore through the olive groves, flat and low.

Hervey sat bolt upright, though barely awake. A man from B Troop had his head taken clean off not twenty yards away; what remained of him seemed to stand an age before toppling backwards. Two dragoons next to him threw up noisily. A ball hit a trooper square in the chest: the mare back-somersaulted twice before coming to rest stone dead with her legs rigid in the air. Another struck a gelding withers-high, carrying off the saddle but leaving the horse with its mane standing on end but otherwise unharmed. One ball touched the outstretched arm of Cornet Burt in D Troop, neatly amputating the lower part at the elbow. The French might not be able to see them, but raking the cover this way was sure to wreak havoc.

'Down! Get down!' shouted Sir Edward Lankester.

Hervey sprang up, seized Jessye's left-fore and began pulling on her neck. He had done it once before, but no horse liked lying down except on its own terms. He had to start pulling at the off-fore as well. Somehow he managed. Others would not shift, rooted, terrified, or else oblivious. Two more tumbled like skittles in the time it took to get Jessye's shoulder to the ground.

For a full twenty minutes the Sixth bore the fire. Shot fizzed, whistled and buzzed over them, or tore through flesh as if it were paper. Dragoons took shelter behind their grounded troopers. Hervey did likewise. He felt ashamed, but then a mare was disembowelled not twenty yards from him, her dragoon sheltering unscathed, and he stopped feeling and began praying.

The silence came as suddenly as had the cannonade. Dragoons jumped to their feet without an order, getting horses up, throwing on saddles. Then came the rattle of musketry.

'Mount!'

It was more an understanding than a command. No corporal shouted, no serjeant barked; the lines seemed to form and dress of their own accord. The lieutenant-colonel had but one decision to make: carbines or sabres.

To a man, the Sixth were itching to draw swords. Through the olive groves were the enemy – and, beyond, the guns which had just felled their comrades. Going at them with cut and thrust was what they wanted, the way they liked, at a good lick, knee-to-knee, spurs dug in.

But Lord George Irvine was no mere *sabreur*. If the French broke through the Guards the other side of the olive groves, then it would be volley-fire that would check them, not slashing and hacking among the trees.

'Carbines!'

Dragoons began priming firelocks, and the officers withdrew to the flanks. Hervey wished he had one: a pistol served well at three lengths, but no further. He went through the motions with his service pair, however; he might as well add to the volley, and, anyway, the drill quietened the mind. Hearing a battle rather than seeing it was a strange thing. A tutored ear ought to be able to read its course: what could he make of it? The musketry was ragged, and all along the line in both directions. He imagined *voltigeurs* were skirmishing the length of the Portiña, with counter-fire from the light companies, and single, aimed shots from the Sixtieth's riflemen and the German Legion. Then came a terrific volleying – by battalion, it sounded like: double rank, five hundred muskets discharged as one, and then the rear rank advancing and giving another volley while the first calmly reloaded, ready to begin again. He had seen them, at practice and in earnest. They drilled like a machine, deafened the more and smoke-grimed with each discharge, lips blackened and mouths parched with every bite of a cartridge, but working on mechanically, ramrods clattering like flying shuttles in a power-mill, as if the noise and the smoke actually helped them forget themselves. And then the French volleys in reply: weaker, for they advanced in column and could not deploy so many muskets, but plenty of them still.

He could not, *would* not, picture the effect of those volleys, French or British; his sole thought now was whether the Guards would throw back the columns. Was it possible the French could break through those lines of red? He had seen the infantry volleying at Corunna: unless the artillery had knocked them down, he could not see how *anything* could breach those red walls. But that was the question: how well had the Guards weathered the storm of shot?

Out from the olive groves trotted Major Joseph Edmonds on his barb, calm yet determined-looking. Lord George Irvine had posted him with the divisional commander to read the battle on his behalf. The eyes of every man in the Sixth were on him: was it success the other side of the trees, or was it destruction?

'Well, Edmonds?' asked Lord George, calmly.

'The Guards have thrown them back. Sherbrooke's going to order the advance. I believe we ought to be moving forward. Cotton's man is telling him the same.'

General Cotton was fifty yards away, conferring with his staff. He turned, lofted his sword and signalled the advance.

'You don't think it over already, Edmonds?'

'I think not, Colonel. There are plenty of reserves the other side of the Portiña, and a great host of *chasseurs* uncommitted still. Sherbrooke'll have to judge his advance carefully.'

Hervey and the rest of them were straining to hear the exchange, but the orders came soon enough.

'Regiment will advance!'

They surged forward into the olive groves as the cannonading began again. This time the shot went another way. Hervey wondered why.

Out of the trees, the other side, a view of the field at last, smoke everywhere. He gasped at what he saw. Before them were two lines of red – *bloodied* red – men lying where they had fallen. Not shoulder-to-shoulder, thank God, but in lines quite distinct, as if they had fallen at attention. Beyond, between the lines and the Portiña, it looked like a patchwork of earth-brown and blue – *bloodied* blue (and bloodied earth, too). It was not possible to advance in a straight line without trampling a dead or dying Frenchman.

Batteries thundered left and right, French and British – it made no difference: the noise was stupefying. It actually seemed to penetrate, like a bullet: he could *feel* it. Jessye felt it too. She stood stock-still, mane on end, ears back. This was battle fiercer by far than Corunna. He began shivering. It was infernal, ghastly, like a representation of hell. If only could they draw their swords and charge into the mêlée – *anything* but just sitting here!

Hervey struggled to make sense of things, for every gun, French and British, seemed to be turned on the same place. Those on the Cerro de Cascajal fired in enfilade at the British as they plunged in pursuit into the bed of the Portiña, while those in the bastion of Pajar de Vergara were enfilading from the other direction as the French clambered out.

What he did *not* see, next, for the thickening smoke and fountains of earth, was the sudden reverse. The lines of red, disordered by the scramble across the Portiña, and by the artillery, and by the headlong chase beyond, stopped dead in their tracks, as if they had run up against a giant wall.

The batteries ceased firing abruptly as the gunners tried to realign their pieces. The smoke cleared just enough for Hervey to see red coats – and then many more blue, swarming like wasps on fallen plums, so that he was certain every red coat would disappear.

Then through the smoke he saw General Mackenzie's brigade rising from the Portiña, advancing in support of the Guards. Seeing the tide turning in front of them, they halted and ported arms, knowing perfectly what must come.

Lord George Irvine perceived that the battle was changing too. 'Return carbines! Draw swords!'

Now there were redcoats running back, Guards and Line alike, and the French pursuing. General Mackenzie's brigade let their reeling comrades through, then presented muskets when the line of fire was clear. They volleyed. It was like a whipcrack among errant hounds. The French wavered then halted. Behind the brigade, the Guards were re-forming, and the Line regiments too. Hervey could scarce believe it: they had looked so broken. Soon there were rolling volleys tearing into the mass of bluecoats. One whole division began giving way – slowly at first, retiring steadily, but then at the double. They fell back so quickly that they exposed the right flank of the division next to them.

General Cotton saw his chance. 'Brigade will advance!'

Lord George Irvine raised his sword and pointed it towards the French, turning his head to look for the acknowledgement of his squadron leaders. Every man cheered.

The brigade billowed forward in line, a picture of eagerness. They crossed the Portiña at the trot; and then there was no holding the pace. They took off at the charge, three regiments in line, directly into the open flank of the leftmost division.

It was Hervey's first time against infantry. He pointed rather than lofted his sabre, as the manual prescribed, and dug in his spurs – if only to encourage himself against the bayonets. The steel could yet impale every last one of them. *Could* impale them – *if* the French formed square, or even threw out a flank.

But they didn't. Instead, the dragoons fell on a cowering column, the muskets shielding faces rather than thrusting.

The slaughter was easy at first, the points of five hundred

sabres finding their mark, if not all fatally. Hervey took a man in the shoulder, and then made a powerful cut against another who was crouching with his musket on-guard, catching the side of his head and slicing off the ear before cutting through the stock and into the neck. Soon there were too many men on the ground, horses unable or unwilling to press on. Everywhere, the French were throwing down their arms and shouting for quarter, while others at the rear of the column were taking cover among the scattered olive trees. Some were trying to re-form, bravely, volleying as best they could before retiring. Dragoons lunged at them all the harder, as if their pride were affronted.

'Rally! Rally! Rally!'

It was all Hervey could hear. He began shouting himself: 'Rally! Rally! Rally!'

He saw a man fall dead from the saddle close by, and realized there was musketry yet, though it was impossible to hear.

'Rally! Rally! Rally!'

He saw the troop quartermaster using the flat of his sword against his dragoons with as much vigour as he had used the edge against the French, and cursing them worse, until somehow the squadrons began to re-form at last. There was cheering from the infantry behind them, certain the day was now theirs.

Back from the smoky mêlée, in full view of all, appeared Corporal Armstrong, leaning from the saddle, fist clenched firmly on the epaulette of a *général de division*. General Cotton cantered over, saluted the Frenchman with his sword, then turned to Lord George Irvine. 'Lord George,' he called, boisterously, and for a good part of the Sixth to hear. 'Have the general escorted to the rear by two cornets.' Then he scowled and pointed at Armstrong. 'And make that man serjeant!'

* * *

The brigade retired in good order, leaving the Portiña to the infantry. Hervey tried to fathom the French attack. If it had been but a demonstration, to tie down men in the centre while Joseph Bonaparte moved against the flank, it had been a bloody and determined one. Hadn't Martyn said that the French would press the Spanish instead? But what did he, Hervey, know of a general action? Corunna had been nothing to what he had just seen. And although they had checked the assault – thrown it back, indeed – the day was not over, and it certainly was not yet theirs. The fight continued on the right, evidently, with the redoubt at Pajar de Vergara thundering away again. Was it now the turn of General Campbell's flank brigade, and the Spanish? Hervey wondered how soon it would be before the Sixth were called to support them. He looked at his watch (he was *determined* to give the most accurate account in his journal). It was four o'clock. Where could the day have gone?

A galloper sped along the front of the brigade, throwing up dust knee-high as he reined hard to a halt in front of General Cotton and handed him a written order.

'Norbury – one of Payne's men,' said Cornet Laming knowingly. 'I wonder what our division commander wants.'

'I expect we're to go once more,' said Hervey.

The squadron leaders were already closing on Lord George Irvine as General Cotton rode up again.

'Lord George, General Payne desires me to send a regiment to the left to reinforce Anson in the north valley. That, apparently, is where Wellesley believes the principal attack will come. The Spaniards are sending a division, and Albuquerque's cavalry too. Fane's heavies will go as well, as soon as may be able. How many did you lose just now?'

Lord George tilted his head, as if to say he was uncertain. 'Forty-odd, but I think we'll have the most of them back before evening.'

'Very well. You know where is Anson, and the ground there. I should be obliged if you went at once.'

Lord George touched the peak of his Tarleton. 'Of course, General.' Then he gave the briefest of orders to the squadron leaders.

Sir Edward Lankester returned to his squadron and repeated the brigadier's instructions word for word. Hervey could scarcely believe their luck in being singled out. This was indeed a general action on the grand scale, and *he*, Cornet Matthew Hervey, only lately an ink-fingered boy at Shrewsbury School, was to be in the middle of it! With what *pride* might he write home that evening!

'To the left, form, in column of threes!'

The Sixth began the manoeuvre by which they would leave General Cotton's command to come under Colonel Anson's. Hervey felt his stomach churning. He could hardly contain his delight.

'Walk-march!'

The bugle repeated the commands. Every trooper was on its toes, sensing they would have another good go soon.

'Trot!'

Jessye, and four hundred and something others, could hardly wait for the leg when the bugle repeated the Cs, and the regiment began forging back the way it had come only that morning. Except that it might have been an age ago.

They were riding *away* from the sound of the guns rather than towards. It felt strange. But it was not long before Hervey realized he could hear the guns on the Cerro de Cascajal again – not just the muzzle-roar but the shot too, and louder by the minute, so that in twenty, as they broached the Cerro de Medellin in the same place as they had in the morning, it sounded as if every gun east of the Portiña was firing onto that flank. He wondered if the French expected to pound the Second Division from the ridge. Would the battle continue into the night, therefore? What would happen then? Before, he had supposed that a contest was decided – finished – by last light. But so regular was the French artillery, and so numerous their infantry, he could easily imagine the 'machine' continuing through the night, just as did the 'factories' – the power-looms and the steam-hammers. During the retreat to Corunna they had scarcely had a night's sleep for alarms and excursions, but those had been small affairs, fifty sabres or so. Here, tens of thousands were moving about the field with the facility of hundreds. The British infantry fired like a machine; was it too fanciful to describe the manoeuvring of the French thus?

Over the Cerro de Medellin, descending now its north slope, the Sixth saw what was the reason for their new orders. When they had left the valley in the morning, it was empty. Now there were so many French – two divisions, by Lieutenant Martyn's rapid reckoning – that it seemed another army had been hiding and awaiting its moment.

But a closer look would tell them different. As they halted behind Colonel Anson's brigade, the officers took out their telescopes. Two divisions there might be, but they did not come on with the *élan* of those which had just attacked in the centre. There were Spanish troops on the north side of the valley, on the steep slopes of the Sierra de Seguilla, threatening their open right flank, and a British battery on the north-east shoulder of the Cerro de Medellin, able to enfilade them for much of their advance. And a mile to their front, *tempting* them, it seemed, to advance, were the Duke of Albuquerque's cavalry. Little wonder the French came on gingerly, thought Hervey. Had they yet *seen* Anson's brigade?

He had not closed his telescope when a galloper sped down the slope from behind them, making straight for the brigadier. Hervey recognized him as one of Sir Arthur

Wellesley's – the same he had met in the grey dawn of that morning.

'You're very welcome, Gordon,' said Colonel Anson, returning the salute. 'What are we expected to make of those French yonder?'

'The commander-in-chief desires that you attack them directly, Colonel.'

'*Does* he, by Jove!'

'He is of the opinion that they will not stand. One of the divisions is Ruffin's, and they have been worsted twice already.'

Colonel Elley, the cavalry division's adjutant-general, was standing next to the brigadier. 'If you can force them into squares, Anson, they'll be cut up something savage by the Second Division's guns.'

Colonel Anson was not entirely convinced, though he was willing enough for a fight. If Fane's heavies had arrived, as he had been told they would, there could be little doubting the outcome. But one brigade of cavalry against two divisions of infantry . . .

'Very well, though I'm not certain of the ground. We shall advance with caution.'

'I'll spy out the ground for you,' said Colonel Elley.

Anson nodded gratefully, then called the commanding officers.

His orders were simple enough, the object and the route apparent to every man, so that barely a minute later the brigade was trotting onto the plain and wheeling to the right in two lines.

Hervey (and, he imagined, the other cornets) thrilled to the prospect of a second brigade action in a single day. And this time it would be a model, since the approach was a good three-quarters of a mile: they would do it as a field day, not like the scramble at the Portiña – all properly regulated and as the manual prescribed. Directing regiment was the 23rd Light Dragoons, looking exactly as his except for their yellow facings. Left were the 1st Hussars of the King's German Legion, sitting tall with their 'muff-caps', as the dragoons called them; and the Sixth formed the support line. Hervey fancied there could be few finer sights than fifteen hundred sabres on the move.

Ahead, he could see Colonel Elley already selecting the line of advance. It was unusual, he knew – not at all as the manuals prescribed. If any were to be in advance of a brigade it should be skirmishers, not a field officer. But the ground was open, there could be no *voltigeurs* concealed, and there were no *chasseur* skirmishers to harry him. And in any case, what did *he* know of the true practice of the brigade in the advance?

'I wonder that Anson doesn't select his own line of advance,' said Lieutenant Martyn, as they settled to the trot.

Hervey was pleased to have this affirmation of his own opinion.

'Could it be the brigade's *not* scouted forward? Surely not!' Lieutenant Martyn could hardly contemplate so elementary a failure. His own troop had been about to ride the ground when the Sixth had been ordered back to the centre.

In five minutes, picking their way purposefully along Colonel Elley's cleared line, they had covered half of one mile. The batteries on the Cerro de Cascajal now decided they were in range.

The brigade saw the puffs of smoke long before they heard the reports, and the shot before the reports. The Twenty-third, seeing the line of fire, began veering left and increasing pace. The shot bounced harmlessly. The hussars of the German Legion, conforming to the directing regiment's movement, likewise bore left, but after a minute or so came under a galling fire, if from extreme range, from *tirailleurs* at the foot of the Sierra de Seguilla, and they too quickened their pace. Colonel Anson found himself conforming rather than leading, so that, half a mile from their objective still, the whole brigade broke into a premature canter. Up on the Cerro de Medellin, the Second Division began cheering them – lines of redcoats with muskets and shakos held high. It seemed to urge on the Twenty-third to an even faster pace. Soon they were close to a gallop.

Lord George Irvine struggled to maintain proper supporting distance, while keeping the regiment in check so that he alone would judge the moment to release them for the charge. Hervey, finding Jessye easy in-hand as usual, stood in the stirrups for a better view. The long grass minded him of Salisbury Plain, and he reckoned the ground might yet be as broken and treacherous. But as long as the Twenty-third and the Germans were driving across it, what had he to worry about but the odd rabbit hole? Jessye was sure-footed enough on that account. But there were darker patches in the heath, and that meant water. And where there was water there would be ditches. For all the exhilaration of it, he began wondering if the pace were not too hazardous.

Colonel Elley stumbled on it first. Cantering fast but just in-hand, he managed to check. Then, with a great effort, he cleared the gully, landing well and swinging round to signal frantically.

Too late. The Twenty-third were running fast, *too* fast. The Germans were no better. They blundered onto it – a wide, dry watercourse the length of the brigade's front. Some managed to clear it – a twelve-foot leap; some managed to circle; others tumbled one way or another down the side – eight feet at its deepest. Many were unable to scramble out again. Their second line, warned, tried to rein up, but most of them surged into the struggling remains of the first.

The French gunners were onto them in an instant, and the leading infantry of the left-hand column opened a biting musketry.

The Twenty-third's colonel would not wait and rally, however. He pressed on with any who had leapt clear or managed to scramble out. They were not more than a hundred, and strung out behind him for a furlong and more.

Lord George Irvine still had the Sixth in-hand, and despite the mêlée the troop-leaders were able to choose their lines. Those troopers that could, jumped; those that couldn't slid down into the gully and scrambled up the other side without too much trouble.

Jessye cleared it by a foot and more. 'Good girl!' shouted Hervey, as if he were galloping with Daniel Coates on the Plain.

There were few fallers, and none who looked back. Lord George pulled up, re-formed the lines at the trot, and then pressed on.

But the thin and ragged ranks of the 23rd Light Dragoons were half a mile ahead, and the Germans too. Half the Twenty-third now tore in at the hastily formed square of the *27ᵉ Léger*. They fell in dozens, men and horses. The rest, in a swarm rather than a formation, chased behind Colonel Elley, who had swung left between the *27ᵉ*'s square and the *24ᵉ* of the Line's, which the Germans now threw themselves against. For Elley had seen what no one else had – the French cavalry coming to the belated support of the infantry.

Lord George had no choice but to follow him, unless he wished to impale the Sixth on the infantry's bayonets.

Elley and the remnants of the Twenty-third hurtled into the leading brigade of *chasseurs* with such momentum that the French line parted rather than meet them. But as the dragoons ran on to the second line, the first closed round them, pincers-like.

Lord George did not hesitate. With a furlong to run, he lofted his sabre and shouted, 'Charge!'

The collision was appalling – exactly as Lord George meant it to be. Horses fell; riders disappeared beneath kicking hooves and dead flesh. Hervey all but closed his eyes as they ran in. He couldn't use his sword for want of a man to strike at: all was confusion. But the French were thrown over by the shock of it; that was certain. He could hear the bugle – 'rally'. Every sense told him to disengage.

He looked for his coverman, reining round to leave the hacking mass. Then he saw Laming, and three *chasseurs* at him.

He dug in his spurs harder than ever before. Jessye almost leapt the distance. His sabre struck powerfully – Cut Two – and the nearest *chasseur* lost his rein-arm at the shoulder.

His coverman swooped past and sliced at another, severing the sword-wrist.

Laming, with but one *chasseur* to deal, could now drop his guard. He brought up the blade like lightning – Cut Three – cleaving the man's jaw from below.

Hervey circled, tight. 'Are you well, Laming?'

Laming nodded. 'Thank you. I really am most greatly obliged – to you both.'

Three men lay irrecoverably wounded at their feet, with nothing to staunch the copious flow of blood. Hundreds of others lay dead or mutilated not yards away. Yet Cornet Laming insisted on the proper courtesies. Hervey smiled by return.

They had surely confounded Joseph Bonaparte now? If only the commander-in-chief had been there! He would heap laurels on the Sixth, for sure! After all, the word had been that this was the battle in which he would raise himself to the peerage. And his cavalry had served him well – if, as ever, unobserved.

CHAPTER SEVENTEEN
A BACKWARDS STEP

Badajoz, 3 September 1809

A month and more had passed – a month in the saddle, a march *away* from the French rather than towards Joseph Bonaparte's capital. And this after decisive victory in the field! It had not been as the army hoped. But unlike the retreat to Corunna, the regiments' self-esteem, and therefore their discipline, had not diminished. The army had not run before the French, as they had believed they were doing eight months before: Talavera was a famous victory; every man felt it. They had the measure of the French now. The infantry knew they could stand and volley, and throw back the columns which had marched all over Europe. The cavalry knew they were more than a match for twice their number – if chastened rather by the disarray of Anson's brigade and Sir Arthur Wellesley's rebuke in consequence (but what was wrong with high spirits, they asked?). The French artillery was the problem. Sir Arthur Wellesley had not the weight or the number of guns to pitch against them, and little prospect of acquiring more. And their Spanish allies were . . . at best unpredictable.

But Hervey and the other officers of the 6th Light Dragoons knew there were the makings of a successful strategy to evict the French from the Peninsula. Major

Joseph Edmonds had *told* them. 'Think of it,' he had said one evening at mess. 'They cannot merely *sit* on all those bayonets of theirs; this ain't the sort of country. Bonaparte – major or minor – has got to defeat Wellesley, not just parry him. As long as the Spaniards can tie down French troops at Madrid and places, Wellesley can draw the rest on to ground of his own choosing. And I can't see, from what I observed at Talavera, that they could overthrow him thence.'

'And he will have the Portuguese, Edmonds; let us not forget that,' Lord George had added.

They had all agreed: the Portuguese would be worthier allies. To all intents and purposes they were British troops – British-armed, British-dressed, British-drilled, British-led. They could fight. They seemed to *want* to fight. The mess had even raised their glasses to them: 'A toast – His Majesty's Lusitanians!'

And so, in spite of a retrograde march as long as Sir John Moore's to Corunna, Sir Arthur Wellesley's army was unbowed. They were not running for the sea; they were seeking favourable ground, and there they would bloody the French, just as they had done at Talavera.

Hervey had rediscovered the invigorating sense of being clean. Not clean-shaven (for that he was most days), nor clean-bodied (once a week there had been, as a rule, opportunity to strip-bathe in a bucket), nor even clean-vested (for he had managed that several times in the last month). It was, however, the three in combination that had eluded them ever since leaving Lisbon. At Badajoz, the day before, the cavalry had gone into billets – and not bad billets, although it was ever the regimental maxim that a modest billet was better than a good bivouac. With that respite from the march came the opportunity for thorough ablutions, and for 'interior economy', as the business of putting the regiment's administration in order was known. The walls of Badajoz were washed on the northern side by the Guadiana, and bathing in that wide, gentle river, with soap, and clean linen to change into (and the prospect of regular bread and meat), made every dragoon think himself a new man – a new man capable again of the greatest exertion, whereas but a day ago he had thought himself capable only of sleep.

Not that any dragoon expected great exertion. No walls they had seen since first coming to the Peninsula compared with Badajoz's – not even at Elvas. The ditches, moats, ramparts and bastions, the river on the north side, the Rivellas stream on the east, were a picture of impregnability. The French would not attack here. No one ought to.

Hervey, like the rest, was enjoying this new sense of liberty, and, the officers' duties being done for the day until evening stables, he felt able at last to address himself to a deficiency which had troubled him for the month past. In his billet, a comfortable house near the walls, he picked up his pen, hesitated for a moment while trying to decide whose letter should be first, and then began to write.

My dear Dan,

I cannot know if this letter will arrive before my last (on 27th July) wherein I told you of the day's skirmishing with the French before the city of Talavera de la Reina. Hereafter I shall number these so that you may tell at once when there is an interruption in my reports. Since that letter, as well you may have read in the newspapers, we have fought a general action, which is to be called __Talavera__, and they say that more men fought here than at Blenheim! Think of that, Dan, for your own cadet has seen a battle as great as that. They say that Sir Arthur Wellesley will be made an Earl! I send you herewith a fair copy of my journal for the day, which I was able to set down within forty-eight hours of the end of the action, for the army was greatly knocked up on account of the fighting, and there was some rest. General Craufurd came up from Portugal with the Lt Brigade which they say made a most prodigious march as fast almost as cavalry, and they were received with great cheering all across the field, the like of which I never heard. And it was as well that they did for the Army has lost five and a half thousand. It was the most dreadful business, and the collecting of the wounded and burying the dead fair wore us out. The ground was so hard we could not dig, and so many dead we had to place in dried beds of winter torrents and cover as best we could, while many more and the horses were gathered in heaps and burned, a dreadful thing to do, but there was no other course for the sun was very hot. I confess the smell was intolerable. And many of the wounded, British and French, for both were treated the same, perished while lying in the blazing sun, in want of water, dressing, and shelter.

The excitement of battle over, we all felt severe stomach cramps. But for some bread and peaches we had nothing for most two days. We cursed the commissaries greatly, but it was not all their fault, for bread had been baked for the Army before the battle, but the Spaniards had broken into the stores and made off with it, and many of these left the field altogether. Early next morning about 25 of the Spanish deserters, all dressed in white and accompanied by priests, were marched up in front of the Army and shot. One was a young lad, and he dropped before the party fired, but it was no use, for after a volley at 10 paces distant had been given by about 50 men, the whole party ran forward, and firing through heads, necks, breasts,

&c, completed their grisly work.

Since then we have been much about the country between Talavera and the Portuguese border, for Marshal Soult has marched from the north of the country where he had been reinforced since the battle at Oporto, and has collected an army of fifty thousand, which greatly threatens our lines of communication with Portugal since General Joseph Bonaparte has not been besieged in Madrid as it had been thought after the battle, and is able to fasten the Spanish of General Cuesta at Talavera, so that in dividing our forces we should be very materially at risk, and especially so now that it is certain that Soult has <u>fifty</u> thousand not twenty as was first supposed. We have marched up and down but now we are where Sir Arthur Wellesley intends staying. It is said that we should have marched on to Elvas, which is not many miles westwards of here, but that abandoning altogether Spanish soil was too hard a thing for the commander in chief after such a victory as Talavera . . .

Hervey wrote three pages of news, attached four more (the fair copy of his journal account of the battle), and then composed a second letter, to Horningsham. This was an altogether less dramatic account of the past month, with little narrative of the action to and fro, and even less of the battle itself, merely a line that 'I was much about the field with my regiment but never in any danger'. One event he felt compelled to write of, however, even though his people knew nothing of the man, for he had never before mentioned him.

Late in the day of the battle we were obliged to advance across country which had not previously been spied out, and which proved to have several hidden watercourses, some quite deep, and the brigade ran faster than was

> *prudent, so that one regiment (the 23rd Lt Drgns) lost*
> *so many men fallen as to be severely disordered, and*
> *ours coming up in the support line lost some as well, on*
> *the left flank, and one cornet, Quilley, I am afraid broke*
> *his neck . . .*

He wrote by way of expiation. Such had been the contempt for Quilley by the time of Talavera that there had been a general sneering at the news of the fall, ascribing it to a 'what can be expected?' lack of horsemanship. But when it became known that Quilley was dead, a certain sense of guilt – or perhaps it was merely distaste – had silenced all comment.

Hervey, indeed, had felt a good deal of shame at his first thoughts (that he wished it had been Cornet Daly instead). That was a part of his news that he could not impart to Wiltshire, either to his family or to Daniel Coates. For Talavera, for all that the steeples might be rocking in England now, had not been the occasion for amnesty: the court martial merely awaited opportunity. Hervey's pleasure in going into quarters at Badajoz was therefore greatly tempered by the knowledge that at last there *was* the opportunity.

CHAPTER EIGHTEEN
AN OFFICER'S WORD

Badajoz, evening, Innocents' Day, 1826

Hervey looked at the letter from Elvas again. It had been in his hand not a quarter of an hour, but it was intriguing him the more with each minute. The veiled speech and the knowledge that it was not the writer's mother tongue – although as fine as ever he would expect to read from someone whose first language was not English – was increasing his doubts.

Elvas
28th December

My Dear Friend,

It pains me greatly that ten whole days have passed since your noble act, and yet you are still confined. I assure you, as I have each time, that I do not spare myself in seeking your return to Elvas in accordance with what I trust are your wishes. I am comforted to know that you are well treated, as I would expect of our great neighbour, Spain. These are confounding times, and I pray that proper relations shall be restored before long between two countries which are of one Catholic heart.

Hervey shook his head again as he re-read the sentiment. He recognized both the sincerity and the need to assure the censor – to engage his sympathy, even – but the words, truly, were too finely crafted, even for Dom Mateo, though he had no reason to suppose the letter was not his. In any case, the news it brought, heartening as it was, could scarcely have been from another, even if the singular puzzle over the identity of the 'fellow of long acquaintance' would now vex him. At least the identity of the other arrival at Elvas could be in no doubt:

> *I am overjoyed to tell you that unofficial and friendly*
> *emissaries from Lisbon have arrived here this very*
> *hour. The one who has connections here, and in whose*
> *company we first made our acquaintance, shall be of*
> *exceptional assistance on account of family. The other*
> *is a fellow of long acquaintance to you, in a position of*
> *some authority and influence now. But more I cannot*
> *say until the greater comings are made generally*
> *known, for to do so might tempt hasty action, or*
> *diminish the consequence at the highest level.*

So, Isabella Delgado was in Elvas! Hervey felt more re-assured than he had in days. Why, he would have been hard put to say; except that there was about Isabella a great air of capability and judgement, as well as connections with the bishop's palace in Elvas, which in turn meant connections in Badajoz – perhaps even in Madrid. However, such an oblique reference to the identity of the second arrival could suggest no name to him more likely than any other, except the mention of authority and influence. 'Authority' ruled out Kat. *Thank God*, for Kat's charms and talents did not seem to him well matched to the frontier. There were any number of officers who might answer to the description, especially since he had no idea of the magnitude of the authority and influence Dom Mateo had in mind. There were *generals*, indeed, who might feel some slight obligation to him. But could a general be an 'unofficial' emissary? He thought not.

'The greater comings' was maddeningly ambiguous. Hervey saw perfectly well that the words could refer to the visit of senior officials (and with that, public humiliation and the Horse Guards' discipline). But might they refer to comings to Portugal, rather than to Elvas? And might 'greater' mean greater in number rather than rank? In other words, had a British army landed in Lisbon?

Dr Sanchez came about six. Hervey did not know if he had seen the letter (Sanchez had brought all the others, but this one had come by an orderly – which had first put Hervey on his guard somewhat). He thought to judge his moment before revealing its receipt or contents.

They sat down to wine, the physician in distinctly good spirits.

'You know, Major Hervey, I have been thinking about Talavera since you recounted it to me. I believe I must have seen your regiment that day. The Duke of Albuquerque's corps stood in the valley north of the ridge you spoke of. I confess I recall it very well, in fact, since I was astonished – and I was not alone in that sentiment – that our corps made no move.' Sanchez shook his head, not pained, but evidently embarrassed. 'But what did *I* know, a mere regimental surgeon? And it was a long time ago.'

To Hervey, it was *not* a long time. A year ago he might have thought so, perhaps, but not now, not cloistered, in-carcerated – whatever might be the word – in Badajoz. He was troubled by the good doctor's perspective. If he were to enlist his help, he had to persuade him that the alliance of their two countries was of recent mind – *continuing*, indeed. In fact, he had to convince him that the two of them were men of one body.

He believed he could, for the sense of obligation to one who had shared the dangers of that day at Talavera would be profound in a man of Sanchez's manifest sensibility. Sanchez, the regimental surgeon, may have carried a scalpel rather than a sabre, but he was of the 'Yellow Circle' still.

His very next words appeared to prove it. 'You did not say what of your wound. I imagine it was but superficial?'

Hervey smiled. 'The shoulder blade prevented the sword from cutting too deep. Our surgeon said I was lucky, although I did not feel it, for it hurt like hell, and I could hardly flex my rein-arm for days after.'

'I imagine there to be no ill effects now?'

'No, none at all. Indeed, it was all quite better before we reached Badajoz.' As he said it, he felt the smile turn hapless.

Sanchez nodded. 'Until you reached here. Just so. But not for the last time, of course.' He looked saddened.

Hervey imagined he knew the cause. His own remembrance of Badajoz, in spite of the pleasant days they had had on first reaching the city, was hardly agreeable. Some of the later memories haunted him yet. Sanchez's own memories, even if hearsay, would be infinitely worse: four sieges (the first French, the others British), and the terrible final storming. It was not to be recalled. But – and here was the gamble – Hervey judged that it might serve his purpose to do so, for the very horror of the final storming of Badajoz might touch something deep in a medical man. It would be risky reminding a proud Spaniard of his ally's depredations. But, as Sanchez himself had said, it was a long time ago. He might not recall too well the details; he might not even have been there.

'Would you take more wine with me, doctor?'

Sanchez nodded. 'I would.'

He had appeared to hesitate, as if overcoming a prohibition. Hervey sensed his purpose working out.

'Major Hervey, there is something I should speak of.'

'Yes, doctor?' Was this the moment Sanchez would pledge himself?

Sanchez sighed, sounding heavy-hearted. 'I am distressed to tell you this . . . I had hoped it not necessary . . . I . . .'

Hervey was now uneasy. 'Speak, doctor; let us have the worst!'

'Major Hervey, the authorities here are talking of bringing you before a military tribunal.'

Hervey's jaw dropped. 'On what charge?'

Sanchez shook his head again. 'I do not know. I heard mention of . . . espionage.'

Hervey did not reply. The outcome of such a trial, if unfavourable, was known to them both well enough. He felt his spirits plummeting like a stone into a deep, dark well. A military tribunal at Badajoz: the wheel had come full circle. Nothing could be more painful to a soldier's pride than to be arraigned before a military court. He had never spoken of the first time, with anyone – not with Daniel Coates, nor even with Henrietta. In a pocket of his writing case there was, still, a sheet of paper, a convening order for a court martial seventeen years old – his age, almost, at the time of its signing. He did not rightly know why he kept it. His penance, perhaps. But had he not redeemed himself a hundred times since then? A military tribunal – a court martial: the wheel had, indeed, come full circle, and he dreaded being broken on it.

COURT MARTIAL

A General Court Martial shall convene at Badajoz on the 10th day of September, 1809, in pursuance of a warrant from Lieut.-General Sir A. Wellesley, commanding his Majesty's Forces in Spain, to hear charges against Cornets M. P. Hervey and F. K. Daly, both of his Majesty's 6th Light Dragoons (Princess Caroline's Own).

PRESIDENT,

Colonel Sir JOHN PATTINSON, Bart.

MEMBERS,

Lieut.-Col. J. A. CHATTERTON, C.B. 3rd Drag.
   Guards.
Brevet-Major C. TOWER, R. Artillery.
Major P. MITCHELL, 4th Reg.
Capt. A. J. APLIN, 88th Reg.
Capt. F. HAWKINS, 88th Reg.
Capt. WARBURTON GREY, R. Engineers.
Capt. J. S. SECCOMBE, R. Artillery.
Capt. the Honbl. F. PURDON, 7th Reg.
Lieut. R. J. INCE, 60th (Royal Americans).
Lieut. W. PODMORE, R. Artillery.
Lieut. C. ZWICKY, 97th Reg.
Lieut. A. J. NEWTON, 48th Reg.

JUDGE MARTIAL

DAVID JENKYNS, Esq.
Deputy Judge Advocate General.

As the regulations required, Hervey and Daly had been placed in close arrest the evening before the court assembled, though each separately. They were not incarcerated, rather were they confined to quarters in agreeable houses near the Las Palmas gate, close to the convent that would serve as the court. But it did not go well with either man to have his liberty suspended: Hervey felt the deepest humiliation at having Cornet Laming sit the evening with him as escort, while Daly fulminated against 'the ungentlemanlike refusal to accept his parole'.

264

In the morning they dressed in best regimentals, but without sword, belt or headdress, which were carried instead by the escorts. At the convent, Hervey met his defending officer, Lieutenant Martyn, and walked with him to an ante-chamber to wait for the court to assemble. Cornet Daly was already there. He made no sign of greeting, looking straight ahead, so that when they were asked to form up ready to march into court, Hervey found himself taking position in front of him, as his marginal seniority demanded, with added discomfort.

One pace behind Hervey was Laming, however, a re-assuring thought if not an altogether happy one. 'Prisoner, attenshun.'

Laming said it so softly that Hervey barely heard. 'Be a good fellow and speak up,' he said, turning his head to the side.

In doing so he saw Serjeant Treve, who had been orderly quartermaster the night of the incident, waiting to be called in evidence. John Knight was standing nearby, too, and Private Brayshaw, his assistant, and the orderly corporal of that night, and the inlying picket-commander, and several dragoons who had been on guard – all waiting to give evidence. Inside the court, he knew, there would be spectators, from the regiment and from the army. He felt sick with shame.

'Prisoner, quick-march.'

Hervey, *prisoner*: it was scarcely to be borne. He had done his duty, and it was come to this. When would they hear of it in Wiltshire, or at his school? The ignominy stretched before him like the open sea.

'Halt.'

Again, Laming could hardly bring himself to breathe the word of command. Hervey halted by some instinct rather than obedience.

Behind them, Cornet Wyllie from C Troop, Daly's

escort, gave the commands very decidedly.

Hervey looked directly at the president. He did not know Colonel Pattinson, as was only right, but he had heard of him. He had been with Sir John Moore at Shorncliffe and had a reputation for discipline, if not quite of the ferocity of General Craufurd. He wore his bicorn low on his brow, betokening, thought Hervey, an angry disposition towards the proceedings. He could have no objection to the colonel's being president, however, though that was his right, as it was Daly's too.

He looked at the other officers in turn, twelve of them, making thirteen in all, the minimum required for a general court martial. The junior member was Newton, lieutenant of the 48th (Northamptonshire), the regiment that had done more than any to save the day at Talavera. What would he make of a quarrel between cornets of light dragoons – an affair of peacocks? Next was Zwicky, from the 97th (Queen's Germans); what might his notions of high honour make of the conduct of two British officers? The other two lieutenants, Podmore in the blue of the Royal Artillery, and Ince in the green of the Sixtieth's rifle battalion, he imagined would think much the same. The captains, three in red, two in blue, looked as if they would share the opinion, but more vehemently. Hawkins, second of the two Connaught captains, had a raw powder-burn across his nose and left cheek, vivid evidence of a fighting disposition. What would he care for a brawl in the horse lines, safe behind the infantry's pickets? Would he know that the Sixth had had their share of fighting too, had gone hard at the French time and again, first with Moore and now with Wellesley? It was the old trouble – the work of cavalry, light cavalry especially, went unseen for the most part. It was too easy to think of them trotting here and there looking as if they were off to escort the Prince of Wales at Brighton. No one had seen them on the march to Corunna, though they had held the French cavalry at bay and bought the infantry precious time. But they had not been there when Sir John Moore had finally given battle, for he had sent his cavalry rear. There was nothing to earn the contempt of a soldier more than to be absent from a battle.

Captain the Honourable F. Purdon, 7th Foot, the Royal Fuzileers, a peer's son from (it was said) Sir Arthur Wellesley's favourite regiment: what would *he* make of a drunken squireen and a parson's son who resorted to his fists? The Sixth's reputation would be tarnished, whatever the outcome. And the tarnishing would be under the gaze of their new commanding officer: Lord George Irvine was taking his seat behind the prosecuting officer's table.

Hervey now glanced at the two majors. They looked every bit as severe as Joseph Edmonds. Finally, he turned his eyes to the lieutenant-colonel, the only cavalryman, from the quartermaster-general's department of Sir Arthur Wellesley's staff. He presumed the exclusion of any other was deliberate, perhaps because it was difficult to find anyone who did not know something of the affair; perhaps because another officer of light dragoons might be prejudiced in his opinion.

The president broke the silence. He read out the warrants for the convening of the court martial, then turned his gaze directly on the accused. 'Do either of the prisoners have objection to me or to any other member of the officers here assembled for the purpose of trying the cases before the court?' He addressed the question directly to the two defending officers.

Lieutenant Martyn, standing to Hervey's right, turned to him for an answer.

Hervey shook his head.

'Mr Hervey has no objection, sir.'

Lieutenant Beale-Browne asked the same of Cornet Daly. There was an exchange, *sotto voce*, but evident enough.

'Mr Daly objects to Captain Aplin on the grounds that his family and Mr Daly's are in dispute over certain matters.'

The president looked at Aplin.

'I am not aware of these matters, sir,' replied the Connaught captain. 'Neither that my family has any business with Mr Daly's. I myself do not know him, but I am ready to stand down, of course, if Mr Daly believes I might be prejudiced.'

The accent was not dissimilar to Daly's own, thought Hervey, but neither was it exactly the same.

The president turned back to Lieutenant Beale-Browne. 'I myself would not consider there to be sufficient evidence of the likelihood of prejudice on the part of Captain Aplin, but the prerogative is the prisoner's.'

There was another whispered consultation. Hervey thought Beale-Browne sounded agitated.

'Mr Daly is still of the opinion that Captain Aplin be not a member, sir.'

The president stifled a sigh. 'Very well. Captain Aplin, you are released. Court orderly, be so good as to summon the waiting member.'

Hervey imagined that Daly had not served himself well by insisting on Aplin's replacement, and could not help being pleased by it; except that officers sitting in judgement were sometimes contrary and might take it as evidence that Daly was of a very 'independent' mind – which to any thinking officer could be no bad thing.

The waiting member was a lieutenant of the 29th (Worcestershire). He entered by a side door, stood at attention and saluted.

'State your name, if you please, sir,' said the president.

'Hyacinth Hames, sir.'

Cornet Daly smirked noisily.

The president rounded on him. 'Mr Daly! This is a court of law and you are in contempt of it.'

Hervey started. Character appeared to be outing: he almost felt sorry for Daly.

'Well, sir? Have you nothing to say?'

'I meant no offence to the court, sir,' replied Daly boldly.

The president looked even blacker. 'Do you have objection to this officer?'

'No, sir.'

The president looked at Hervey.

'None, sir.'

'Very well then. Court orderly, be so good as to inform the judge martial that the court is assembled.'

'Sir!'

The court orderly, a lantern-jawed serjeant of the 1st Guards, spun round and marched out. The members placed their swords on the long table before them, removed their hats and took their seats. The president nodded to the escorts, who in turn propelled their charges to chairs, one in front of the other, facing forward on the right-hand side of the court.

'His honour, the judge martial!' barked the court orderly.

The court rose as the bewigged representative of the judiciary entered. He and the president exchanged bows, and then both sat down, the judge martial to the president's right.

Then the judge martial rose again, followed by all the members except the president. He bowed once more, and looked at each member in turn. 'You shall well and truly try and determine according to your evidence in the matter now before you, between our Sovereign Lord the King's Majesty, and the prisoner to be tried. So help you, God.' He next gave a bible to the president, together with an ivory board the size of a cartridge case, on which was printed the oath. 'I require, on His Majesty's behalf, that each now swear upon the holy evangelists to this effect.'

The president, Granby-bald, and in consequence looking

twice as severe as before, rose and growled his way through the solemn declaration: 'I, Sir John Pattinson, do swear that I will duly administer justice, according to the Rules and Articles for the better Government of His Majesty's Forces, and according to an Act of Parliament now in force for the punishment of Mutiny and Desertion, and other Crimes therein mentioned, without Partiality, Favour, or Affection; and if any doubt shall arise, which is not explained by the said Articles or Act of Parliament, according to my Conscience, the best of my Understanding, and the Custom of War in the like Cases. And I further swear, that I will not divulge the Sentence of the Court until it shall be approved by His Majesty, the General, or Commander-in-Chief; neither will I, upon any Account, at any time whatsoever, disclose or discover the Vote or Opinion of any particular Member of the Court martial, unless required to give Evidence thereof, as a Witness, by a Court of Justice in due course of Law. So help me, God.'

The president sat down, and the judge martial proceeded to swear the remainder. To Hervey it was interminable. He tried to assess, from the tone and stance of each member, what might be his attitude to the proceedings, but evidently the gravity of the law was amply conveyed by the process, for every officer spoke as if he were facing the Awful Day of Judgement. That was reassuring in one respect, but he found it disconcerting nevertheless.

At the conclusion, the president rose again and likewise swore the judge martial.

'I, David Jenkyns, do swear that I will not, upon any Account, at any time whatsoever, disclose or discover the Vote or Opinion of any particular Member of the Court martial, unless required to give Evidence thereof, as a Witness, by a Court of Justice in due course of Law. So help me, God.'

They both sat, and the president turned at last to the prosecuting officer, nodding his assent to proceed.

Lieutenant & Adjutant Ezra Barrow rose to his feet solemnly. He was something of a veteran of courts martial, but this was his first time in a position of authority. 'Mr President and gentlemen, there are before the court three charges. First, for that he, Cornet Frederick Keevil Daly, of His Majesty's Sixth Light Dragoons, Princess Caroline's Own, on the 24th July, 1809, in the field at Talavera de la Reina, did occasion injury by wilful neglect or commission resulting in death to a horse in His Majesty's service. Second, that he did abuse a subordinate, namely Serjeant Treve, regimental orderly quartermaster that day, and attempt an assault upon him.' The adjutant laid down the sheet and took up a second. 'The third charge relates to the other prisoner: for conduct unbecoming the character of an officer and a gentleman in that he, Cornet Matthew Paulinus Hervey, also of the Sixth Light Dragoons, on the same day and in the same place did strike without cause Cornet Frederick Keevil Daly.' The adjutant laid the second sheet on the table before him, bowed, and sat down.

The president turned to the table opposite the adjutant's. 'How do the prisoners plead in respect of each of these charges?'

The two defending officers rose. Lieutenant Beale-Browne spoke first. 'In respect of Cornet Daly, sir, on both charges, not guilty.'

The president waited for the judge martial to make the formal entry in his ledger, then looked at Lieutenant Martyn.

'In respect of Cornet Hervey, sir, not guilty.'

'Very well, be seated, gentlemen. Mr Barrow, continue, if you please.'

The adjutant rose and took up a third sheet, this time of manuscript. 'Mr President and gentlemen, it is with feelings of deep regret that I am compelled to appear before you this day as the prosecutor of two officers under the orders of the

271

lieutenant-colonel commanding His Majesty's Sixth Light Dragoons. But however unwilling he be, under all the circumstances of the case about to be submitted to your investigation, the lieutenant-colonel considers that he would not be conscientiously discharging the duties of command entrusted to him, or furthering the good of the service, were he, from considerations of protecting the good reputation of the regiment, to hesitate in coming forward and laying the whole of the conduct of two of his officers before you. And he trusts that calm and dispassionate consideration, which it is sure to meet with before a court composed of officers, will conclude in a right judgment in this extraordinary matter.'

Barrow paused, as his manuscript indicated he should, and looked at the president and members – as did every man in the room.

It did the trick: they each nodded gravely, publicly, at least, disowning any thoughts of frivolous prosecution or – as some of the tattle in the army had it – a trivial affair of dandies over a horse. Without doubt, however, Barrow's Birmingham vowels had already persuaded some members that not *everything* was elegance about Princess Caroline's Own. For his part, Hervey was a little surprised by the adjutant's evident command of legal formularies, though dismayed, too, by their length.

'Mr President and gentlemen, the charges relate to an incident almost immediately before the general action at Talavera de la Reina, following from a continuous period of many weeks' marching, of which the members of the court will be only too perfectly aware. Although the horses of the regiment were in pretty good condition, as its veterinary surgeon would testify, Cornet Daly's second charger, a brown colt, was suffering from lampas. As a result—'

The judge martial looked up from his ledger and turned to the president.

The president had anticipated the enquiry, however. 'Mr Barrow, would you explain, for the benefit of the court, what precisely is lampas.'

The adjutant lowered his page of manuscript. 'Mr Knight, the veterinary surgeon, will be able to give a complete description, sir, but in essence the lampas is an excrescence on the first bar in the roof of the horse's mouth, not common but prevalent in younger animals from irritation occasioned by the growth of or changes in the teeth. It may also occur in horses at work from inflammation set up by injuries from the bit. I trespass further on the veterinary surgeon's ground when I say that in the past the treatment was frequently the burning out of the excrescence, but that recent practice has tended away from this, and to treat instead by frequent washing of the mouth with an acerb mixture.' He waited for acknowledgement that his explanation would suffice.

The president looked at the judge martial, who nodded. 'Very well, Mr Barrow. Would you say that the nature and treatment of this condition is of essential substance in this trial?'

The adjutant smiled slightly. 'Sir, my own knowledge of both is not greatly more than that which I have just rendered to you, and I have not found it difficult to reach a conclusion.'

The president, while not reflecting the smile, evidently found the reassurance welcome. 'Very well, but I may require the veterinary surgeon to give his professional opinion in the matter separately to any other evidence, and if necessary at an early stage should it become apparent that the court has need of it.'

The adjutant looked not the slightest perturbed at the prospect of departure from his carefully prepared script. 'Of course, sir. If I may continue now?'

The president nodded.

'Mr President and gentlemen, as I was saying, Cornet

273

Daly's colt was suffering from lampas, to an extent that made it unfit for service. The veterinary surgeon prescribed the washing treatment I referred to, refusing Mr Daly's request for firing. Later that evening, Mr Daly took it upon himself to burn out the lampas. The veterinary surgeon will testify that in his opinion the procedure was done ineptly, and that in consequence the animal died from a condition which he will refer to as "the shock".'

'One moment, please,' said the judge martial, turning to the president for his approval, and then back to Barrow. 'You say, Mr Barrow, that the veterinary surgeon is of the opinion that the procedure was done ineptly. Is there any suggestion that it was unauthorized? An improper procedure?'

Again, Barrow did not flinch. 'The horses of the regiment, be they owned by government or not, are deemed to be in the King's service, and the veterinary surgeon is responsible to the lieutenant-colonel for the treatment of all sick animals. To that extent, Your Honour, if a treatment is not authorized by the veterinary surgeon, it is an unauthorized procedure – an improper procedure, yes. And in the case of Mr Daly's colt, the veterinary surgeon will testify that he specifically forbad the firing.'

The judge martial wrote in his ledger very deliberately. His knowledge of the military was limited, and it was his first trial in the field. It was, indeed, the first trial in the Peninsula at which a judge martial had been present, and the first in which the new rules of procedure – *controversial* rules of procedure, lately enacted by parliament – were to apply. Sir Arthur Wellesley himself had asked for a judicial presence, so that courts martial could conduct their business expeditiously rather than having to send the proceedings to England for review. Judge Advocate Jenkyns was not about to invite the wrath of the commander-in-chief on account of any mistrial over a point of law. At length he stopped writing. 'Thank you, Mr Barrow,' he said, in a noncommittal tone, then turned and nodded to the president.

'Very well, Mr Barrow,' said the president, sounding perfectly certain.

'Sir. After Mr Daly had burned out – had *attempted* to burn out – the lampas, the regimental—'

The judge martial stopped writing again. 'Which is it to be, Mr Barrow? I should like to be certain. Did he burn out the excrescence or no?'

Barrow hesitated. 'It is my understanding, Your Honour, that Mr Daly failed to burn it out. But to what extent he failed I must refer to the veterinary surgeon.'

Hervey, sitting bolt upright still, felt an anxious twinge at the way the questioning appeared to be going. Did the judge martial believe that Daly had a right to attempt the procedure? It would be but a short step thereafter to consider the colt's death to be the unavoidable consequence, the occasional price, of a practice accepted by some parts at least of the veterinary profession. It boded ill.

'It's not true!'

Daly's protest stunned the court.

'I burned it out good and proper!'

Daly's escort clapped a hand to his shoulder, and Lieutenant Beale-Browne tried to stay the protest by seizing his arm.

'That so-called—'

The president growled. 'Mr Daly! Compose yourself, sir! You will conduct yourself as if on parade. You will have ample opportunity to state your case.' He turned again to the adjutant. 'Continue.'

Whatever doubts he entertained still about the wisdom of accepting a commission, Lieutenant & Adjutant Ezra Barrow, sometime serjeant-major of the 1st Dragoons, perfectly concealed it. And if Lord George Irvine, who had brought him in from the Royals, had ever entertained a moment's doubt as to his man's capability in the arcane proceedings of courts martial, he could now rest, for Barrow stood erect throughout the interventions and the altercation with not a flicker of distaste or dismay. 'Mr President and gentlemen, the prosecution will call as witness Serjeant Treve, who was regimental orderly quartermaster that evening, and who will testify that on doing his rounds of the horse lines he came across Cornet Daly and the colt, which was lying distressed, and that he instructed H Troop's duty dragoon to summon the veterinary surgeon. At this Cornet Daly protested, very strongly; indeed, intemperately.'

'That's not true! Treve was—'

The president exploded. 'Mr Daly! I have warned you once already, and I would have thought that sufficient for any man! If there is another outburst I shall convict you summarily of insubordination. Do I make myself clear, sir?'

'Yes, sir.'

'Mr Barrow, if this is indicative of the state of discipline in the Sixth Light Dragoons then I am very much of the opinion that we shall not arrive at any satisfactory judgement in the matter before us.'

The adjutant bridled at the imputation, as did the Sixth's assembled officers, Lord George Irvine not least. Restraint prevailed, however, helped to no small extent by the judge martial, who leaned over and whispered in the president's ear.

When Colonel Pattinson resumed, he sounded, if not exactly chastened, more circumspect. 'Mr ... Beale-Browne, be so good, sir, as to instruct Cornet Daly to direct any remarks to the court through you, his defending officer.'

Lieutenant Beale-Browne, already on his feet, bowed. 'Very good, sir.' He had thought for an instant to beg the defence of Irish temperament, but then thought better of it.

The president turned back to Ezra Barrow, with a distinctly dyspeptic look. 'Proceed, Mr Barrow; and as succinctly as may be.'

The adjutant had no intention of proceeding otherwise. He had spent the previous day, and had been up half the night, preparing his summary of evidence. His milieu was the stable, the parade, the field day and the orderly room, *not* the 'literary' world of officers and lawyers; and he was damned if he, ranker lieutenant or not, was going to be found wanting. He may not have had an education, but the Methodists had taught him to read and write, and if he could speak it, he could write it; and if he could write it, he could now read it.

'Mr President and gentlemen, as I was saying, Cornet Daly protested strongly to Serjeant Treve that he was *not* to summon the veterinary surgeon, and when Serjeant Treve repeated the order to the duty dragoon, Cornet Daly ordered Serjeant Treve to place himself in arrest. At this point, Serjeant Treve instructed the orderly corporal to inform the picket-officer, who was Cornet Hervey.'

The president and the judge martial, and all the other members of the court, looked directly at Hervey – or so it felt to him. Daly's interventions, Hervey reckoned, could only serve to demonstrate a disposition to excitement, to pugnacity even, although it seemed to him that the judge martial at least was minded that a botched firing was a matter of judgement rather than of discipline. The adjutant's choice of words to describe what had happened next would therefore be crucial. Hervey could only trust in the assurances of support which Edmonds and Lankester had given, albeit some time ago now. Barrow was prosecuting officer, after all: he could hardly stay his hand.

Be what may, the eyes of the court were now turned to him. He did not calculate that to sit at attention would be to demonstrate a proper, regulated, officerlike demeanour, for that was his instinct; but he knew it to be the right one *particularly* at this time, and the more so in contrast with Daly's. He had not one scrap of sympathy for him now.

The adjutant continued. 'Cornet Hervey, on arriving at the horse lines, perceived the colt to be lying on the ground, and asked what had happened, and if the veterinary surgeon had been called. To which Cornet Daly made violent objection, and insisted once more that the orderly quartermaster be placed in arrest. In the exchanges which followed, Cornet Daly made a threatening gesture towards Serjeant Treve and was struck a blow by Cornet Hervey.'

Hervey winced, but hoped not visibly. The account was correct, but so succinct as to suggest he struck without cause. He looked the president in the eye, however.

'That, Mr President and gentlemen, concludes the summary of evidence. The prosecution intends calling four witnesses, first Serjeant Treve, then Veterinary Surgeon Knight, then Corporal Rawlings, the regimental orderly corporal that day, and finally Corporal Mains, the picket-corporal. The prosecution may, however, have recourse to calling an additional four non-commissioned officers or dragoons.'

The president looked at the judge martial, who nodded, then back at the adjutant. 'Very well, Mr Barrow, distasteful as that may be.'

Distasteful – NCOs and men testifying against an officer: that would be the feeling of every officer in the court. Hervey groaned inwardly. But he had seen the look on Treve's face as he waited to be called. Treve was as upright as they came – sixteen long years of service and good conduct; everyone spoke of him as being of the best. And now he was to be subjected to examination by the adjutant, and in front of his commanding officer and a whole court of outsiders. Would it have come to this if he, *Cornet* Hervey, with but one year only in the King's uniform, had better regulated his actions that evening? Might he have done so? Had it been at all possible? So far he had not doubted it, but the process of court martial could gnaw at a man's certainty.

Serjeant Treve, in full dress, spurs ringing loud on the flagstone floor as he marched, halted before the members' table, and saluted.

'Remove headdress,' barked the court orderly, startling the judge martial.

Serjeant Treve removed his Tarleton helmet and placed it under his left arm. The court orderly handed him a bible, and held a board up to him, on which the oath was written.

'I swear, upon the holy Evangelists, that the evidence which I shall give shall be the truth, the whole truth and nothing but the truth; so help me, God.'

'Be seated, Serjeant,' said the adjutant.

The court orderly placed a chair before the members' table.

'State your name, rank and appointment, Serjeant.'

'Walter Treve, serjeant, quartermaster B Troop, Sixth Light Dragoons, Princess Caroline's Own, sir.'

'Were you, on the twenty-fourth day of July this year, regimental orderly quartermaster?'

'Sir.'

The judge martial looked up. 'Is that a "yes" or a "no", Mr Barrow?'

'It is a "yes", Your Honour. In the Sixth Light Dragoons the custom is that the affirmative is so-stated.'

'And the negative?'

'The same, Your Honour.'

The judge advocate sighed as he smiled. 'Mr Barrow, you will appreciate, I am sure, the difficulty which may arise in a court of law were such a procedure to be followed. How is the difference discerned?'

'Everything is conveyed in the tone of the response, Your Honour.'

'Well, Mr Barrow, for the benefit of those of us un-practised in the no-doubt admirable custom of the Sixth Light Dragoons, perhaps we may adhere to the common form of affirmative and negative – a simple "yes" or "no"?'

'Sir.'

The president stifled a smile.

'Serjeant Treve, were you that evening orderly quartermaster?'

'Sir, yes, sir.'

'Thank you.'

'I am obliged, Mr Barrow,' said the judge martial, taking up his pen once more.

Barrow made a small bow, then resumed. 'Tell the court what you found on visiting H Troop's horse lines.'

'Sir. I found the brown colt belonging to Mr Daly lying with its head on the ground, shivering, and Mr Daly standing by holding a cautery, sir.'

'And what did you say?'

'I asked Mr Daly what had happened, sir. He replied that he had removed a lampas from the horse's mouth.'

'What then did you say?'

'I said that the horse looked in distress, sir. I asked if the veterinary were called.'

'And Cornet Daly replied?'

'Mr Daly said it weren't necessary, sir.'

'Did you press Cornet Daly upon this point?'

'Sir, I did, sir.'

'And what was Mr Daly's reply?'

Serjeant Treve hesitated. 'He said as how he didn't need me to tell him what was wanted for a horse of his.'

'Were those Mr Daly's exact words?'

Treve hesitated again. 'Not exactly, sir. Mr Daly put it more blunt.'

The judge martial looked up. 'I think we had better have them out, Mr Barrow.'

Barrow frowned, though he had known it must come. 'Serjeant Treve, tell the court exactly what Cornet Daly said.'

Treve looked directly at the president. 'Mr Daly said, "I

don't need a fucking little serjeant to tell me how to cope with a horse." '

The president raised his eyebrows.

'What was your reply?' asked the adjutant.

'I said, sir, as there was no cause to speak to me like that, that I was orderly quartermaster and it was my duty to report any sick or injured horse at once to the veterinary surgeon. Sir.'

'And how did Cornet Daly reply to this?'

'Mr Daly said as how the animal wasn't sick or injured, and that it was *his* charger and *his* business, sir.'

'He used those exact words?'

'Again, sir, Mr Daly swore. I believe he used the same word three or perhaps four times, sir.'

'Was this in front of witnesses?'

'Sir, the orderly corporal and the duty dragoon. Some of the picket came by, but that was later, sir.'

'What did you then do?'

'I instructed H Troop's duty dragoon to inform the troop farrier and the veterinary surgeon that there was a horse down and in distress, sir.'

'Did Cornet Daly say anything further?'

'Mr Daly told me to place myself in arrest, sir.'

'And what did you do?'

'I instructed the orderly corporal to bring the picket-officer, sir.'

'So you were then alone with Cornet Daly?'

'Sir, yes, sir.'

The adjutant turned to the members. 'Mr President and gentlemen, the prosecution does not intend questioning Serjeant Treve on the period in which there were no witnesses present.'

The president nodded, but the judge martial looked doubtful. 'For what cause, Mr Barrow? Each of the parties gives evidence under oath.'

Hervey became aware of whispering behind him, Cornet Daly to Lieutenant Beale-Browne.

Barrow resumed. 'Your Honour, it is the prosecution's opinion that no good shall come of it.'

'No good? Mr Barrow, the court is concerned not with "good" but with the law.'

Hervey hoped it would be concerned rather more with justice. And he hoped the judge martial would press to hear the evidence, for he had heard that Daly had become entirely obnoxious during the time before the picket arrived.

'Nevertheless, Your Honour, the charge against Cornet Daly is substantially proved by the officer's conduct before witnesses, and with Your Honour's permission, I will not – at this point at least – examine the witness as to the private exchanges.'

'Mr Barrow, let me remind you that it is the court which will decide whether or not the charge be proved. Nevertheless, if it is the wish of the prosecution then so be it. Proceed.'

Hervey sighed, but inaudibly. It seemed to him that Barrow was letting off Daly lightly. Why should Treve's word, on oath, be doubted? He would be as guilty of perjury as Daly.

'Thank you, Your Honour. Serjeant Treve, tell the court what happened when the picket-officer came.'

'Sir. Mr Hervey was picket-officer, sir. He came after about ten minutes, not more. He asked what had happened to the colt, and if the veterinary had been called. Sir.'

'Go on.'

'Mr Daly said as how it was *his* business and he wanted Mr Hervey to place me in arrest, sir.'

'Go on, Serjeant!'

'Sir, Mr Hervey asked me what I had said to Mr Daly, and I told him what I told you earlier, sir, and said that Mr Daly had been abusive. At that point, sir, Mr Daly said it was a lie and stepped towards me and—'

'*Stepped* towards you, Serjeant?' The judge martial, who alone of those sitting at the members' table had seen the written witness statements, sounded incredulous.

Hervey was glad of his diligence.

'Sort of . . . lunged towards me, sir, as if with a sword, though I could see he hadn't one, sir.'

'Did you believe it to be in a menacing fashion?'

'Sir, yes, sir.'

'You thought Cornet Daly was about to strike you?'

Hervey almost breathed his relief.

But Treve hesitated. 'To be honest, sir, I cannot recall if I believed Mr Daly was intent to strike me, sir. But he was very angry.'

Hervey groaned.

'Mr Daly had taken much drink, sir.'

'*Oh*, indeed?' The judge martial looked at Barrow. 'There is no mention of that elsewhere.' He turned back to Treve. 'Did you see Mr Daly consume this drink?'

Barrow's eyebrows were now rising. He and the lieutenant-colonel had hoped to keep this out of the proceedings.

'Sir, I did not, sir.'

The judge martial turned to Barrow again. 'Unless the prosecution intends calling witnesses to testify in very particular terms as to this assertion, I rule that the remark be struck from the record, and that the members of the court take no notice of the assertion. Mr Barrow?'

Barrow shook his head. 'There is no intention to call witnesses, Your Honour.'

The judge martial now turned to the defending officer. 'Mr . . . Beale-Browne, may I take it that Cornet Daly will not be entering any plea in mitigation to this effect?'

Lieutenant Beale-Browne's first instinct was to check the

certainty of this with Cornet Daly, but he recognized the difficulties of doing so in front of the court. 'No, Your Honour.'

'Very well, then. The remarks will go unrecorded and are to be entirely disregarded by the members of the court. Proceed please, Mr Barrow.'

Lieutenant Barrow found the page in his notes. 'Serjeant Treve, what happened when Cornet Daly ... *lunged* towards you?'

'Mr Hervey stepped in front of Mr Daly, sir.'

'And?'

'I didn't actually see that well, sir, it being dark, but Mr Daly seemed to be very angry and lunged again, and then I saw him fall to the ground. At that stage, sir, the veterinary came.'

It was the truth, Hervey knew, and if it was not the whole truth then that must be because Treve genuinely could not have seen. The court must conclude that his own blow was gratuitous.

The adjutant turned to the president. 'I have finished with this witness, sir.'

'Very well, Mr Barrow. Mr Beale-Browne, do you have any questions of the witness?'

Hervey was conscious of renewed, and urgent, whispering behind him, and wondered what might be Daly's objection to a most impartial account. How he wished the adjutant had questioned Treve about Daly's condition that night: it could only have helped his case. Except, of course, that to do so would have risked suggesting the regiment's discipline was defective, as the president had already intimated, and that would go hard with mess and canteen alike.

Lieutenant Beale-Browne stood up. 'Only one, sir. Serjeant Treve, the language in which Mr Daly addressed you: though it sounds indelicate, no doubt, in a court

284

such as this here, now, was it unusual for the horse lines?'

'Sir, with respect, it is most unusual to hear an officer speak in that way.'

There was a degree of throat-clearing in various quarters. Beale-Browne, having done Daly's bidding in asking the question, might now have withdrawn decently, saving himself – and others – the risk of ridicule. But strong though his own distaste for Daly was, Lieutenant Beale-Browne perceived he had a duty to perform, and when this business was over, from which he knew that none could emerge with much honour, he was damned if he was going to give anyone the opportunity to find him wanting. 'Serjeant Treve, have you ever before heard Mr Daly speaking in the language, let us say, of the horse lines?'

Treve hesitated. 'Sir, if I might put it this way, Mr Daly, sir, is known for his colourful language.'

There was more throat-clearing. Hervey groaned inwardly again. Daly would now appear to the court as the quintessential Irish squireen, fond of the bottle, as all his fellow countrymen – 'splendid fighting men, if unruly' – his language strong, but affectionately so. Hervey felt the court turning against him even before he had had the opportunity to speak.

'I have no more questions, sir.'

The president looked at Lieutenant Martyn, who rose quickly.

'I have no questions, sir.'

The president turned to the judge martial, who shook his head, and then to the members of the court. None had any question.

'Thank you, Serjeant; dismiss.'

Serjeant Treve sprang up, replaced his Tarleton, turned to his right and saluted, then left the room at a brisk march.

The adjutant got to his feet again. 'Mr President and

gentlemen, I wish to call as witness Veterinary Surgeon Knight.'

The president nodded, and the court orderly went out to summon him.

A full minute passed. Hervey was aware of half a dozen whispered asides and exchanges, but he said nothing, looking straight ahead throughout, conscious that the members before him must now think the regiment to be little more than a collection of—

The heavy oak doors opened and John Knight entered. He had the gait of a man used to marching in his own company, his right arm describing curious and erratic patterns as he swung it, his left elbow sticking out as if to barge someone out of the way, and the hand grasping a borrowed sword scabbard without its slings. His right spur was adjusted too high and the roundel was jammed, so that only the left spur rang as he marched, which made for added curiosity among the members of the court. He came to a halt, more or less precisely, and saluted by placing several fingers to the point of his bicorn.

'Remove headdress, sir,' said the court orderly, voice lowered.

Knight took off his hat and handed it to the serjeant, who, surprised, found himself trying to hold it while handing him the bible. It was managed, but not as a serjeant of Foot Guards would have preferred, and to the amusement of the junior members.

The court orderly cleared his throat pointedly, composing himself and the court for the due gravity of the swearing-in.

'I swear, upon the holy Evangelists, that the evidence which I shall give shall be the truth, the whole truth and nothing but the truth; so help me, God.'

Hervey heard Daly whispering to Beale-Browne again, and insistently. He could not imagine to what he might already be objecting.

'Be seated, Mr Knight,' said the adjutant, respectfully.

The court orderly brought a chair. Knight sat down, letting his sword clatter to the floor, and crossed his legs.

'Please state your name, appointment and qualifications.'

'John Knight, veterinary surgeon, Sixth Light Dragoons, licentiate of the London Veterinary College.'

'Would you tell the court what happened on the evening of the twenty-fourth of July in respect of a colt belonging to Cornet Daly.'

'At about nine o'clock I received an urgent summons to attend at H Troop's horse lines. On arrival there I saw Daly's colt lying on the ground – as well as Daly himself, I might add. I attended at once to the colt, but the animal had died.'

'Did—'

The defending officer rose, hesitantly.

The president glowered at him. 'Yes, Mr Beale-Browne?'

'Sir, I . . . I beg you would forgive the interruption, but . . . Mr Daly would know why it is that the veterinary officer was sworn, since he is an officer.'

The president was taken aback. He turned to the judge martial.

'Really, Mr Beale-Browne,' began the judge martial, laying down his pen and taking off his spectacles. 'Such enquiries are not appropriate at this time.'

Beale-Browne cleared his throat apologetically. 'I am sorry, Your Honour, but Mr Daly is very desirous to know why it is that an officer is sworn to tell the truth, which is not the usual practice, his word being always taken for the truth.'

'Mr Beale-Browne,' replied the judge martial, sounding more than a shade irritated, 'it has not been the practice for an officer to take an oath in a regimental court martial, but it has ever been the practice in a general court martial. And, I might add, parliament has very recently passed an act requiring the same of regimental courts martial. So, I hope that is an end to it.'

Beale-Browne looked deeply embarrassed. 'Thank you, Your Honour.'

The president sighed, audibly. 'Proceed, Mr Barrow.'

Barrow bowed. 'Mr Knight, did you ascertain the cause of death?'

'Yes. It was from the shock, occasioned, in my opinion, by the introduction of a red-hot cautery into the animal's mouth.'

'By whose hand?'

'Daly's; the cautery was still in his hand, and he later admitted he had used it.'

'Had you earlier spoken with Cornet Daly on the subject?'

'I had, earlier in the day. The colt was suffering from lampas. Daly wanted me to burn it out. I refused. I disapprove of the practice.'

'If you *had* approved, would you have instructed a farrier or would you yourself have done it?'

'I most certainly would not have instructed a farrier. The procedure would require a very particular skill.'

'Thank you, Mr Knight. I have no further questions.'

The adjutant turned again to the president, and bowed.

'Mr Beale-Browne, do you have any questions of this witness?' asked the president doubtfully.

Beale-Browne was still in an agitated, whispering exchange with Daly.

'*Well*, sir?'

'I beg your pardon, sir. I have but one question. Mr Knight, is the universal opinion of your profession against firing of lampas?'

'By no means.'

Beale-Browne cleared his throat apologetically again. 'Might I press you to more?'

'It was in my time a procedure taught at the London Veterinary College, but progressive opinion is against it.'

'Then you would not dismiss Mr Daly's opinion as being without foundation?'

'No, but I would dismiss his skill as a veterinary practitioner as without foundation, and that is the material point.'

Beale-Browne had seen it coming. He had seen it coming before he rose, but Daly had insisted. He wondered, now, how to make a retreat without looking too bruised. It did not help that he was uncertain of the law, but he had one more line of enquiry. 'Mr Knight, there is nothing in law, so far as I am aware, that prevents a farrier from attempting such a procedure. He regularly attends to the horse's teeth, for instance?'

'That is my understanding.'

Beale-Browne cleared his throat again. 'Mr Knight, besides the many learnèd books by veterinary surgeons, you will know the work of Mr Francis Clater, in particular *Everyman his own Farrier*?'

'Of course. In the main an admirable book.'

'And in that book, in the part addressing the lampas, it says that the cure is generally performed by burning it out with a hot iron.'

'Indeed it does. But it goes on to say that it requires care and a man of judgement to perform operations of that kind, and that in general farriers are too apt to take more out than is necessary.'

There was a murmur of appreciation in the 'public seats' for the evident depth of John Knight's professional opinion.

'But the law nevertheless does not prevent it?'

'As I have said, Mr Beale-Browne, it is my understanding that the law does not, but that is not an end to it: by regimental standing order, no farrier is allowed to make any surgical intervention without the express approval of the veterinary officer.'

Beale-Browne was crestfallen, and becoming desperate. He fired one last round, even *sounding* hopeless. 'And burning out the lampas is a surgical intervention?'

John Knight huffed. 'If it ain't medical then it's surgical, and I'm damned if I can see how anyone could administer medicine with a cautery!'

The president cleared his throat very pointedly. Knight had overstepped the mark, but with provocation. 'I think we have reached the end of this line of questioning, Mr Beale-Browne?'

Beale-Browne made a determined effort to hide his mortification. 'Yes, sir.'

But he conceded too soon. The judge martial had a question. 'Would that standing order be known to every officer?'

John Knight half shrugged his shoulders. 'I cannot say. My business is the horses and the farriers.'

The judge martial turned to the man most likely to be able to answer.

'No, Your Honour,' said the adjutant. 'There are general standing orders, which every officer and non-commissioned officer is required to be conversant with, and standing orders particular to certain duties or appointments. The order which the veterinary surgeon refers to would be a particular.'

'Thank you, Mr Barrow,' said the judge martial, in a manner suggesting that he ought not to have been the one to ask the question. He glanced at the president, and then back to Barrow again. 'If Mr Beale-Browne has now finished, you may proceed.'

Barrow bowed. 'Thank you, Mr Knight. Be pleased to dismiss.'

The court orderly brought the veterinary surgeon's bicorn. Knight gathered up his sword, noisily, bowed rather than replacing the hat and saluting, and then left the court with the same single spur ringing with every other step.

The president raised his eyebrows in mild amusement. 'And now, Mr Barrow?'

'Mr President, at this time I would call Cornet Daly to give evidence.'

Hervey heard the urgent conferring again, but it went on longer, and sounded even more insistent.

'Mr Beale-Browne!' snapped the president.

Beale-Browne rose, hesitantly. 'Mr President, sir, I . . . Mr Daly requests that he not be sworn.'

'*What?*' The president's brow was deeply furrowed.

The judge martial looked up from his ledger. 'Mr Beale-Browne, I have already explained: it has ever been the practice for evidence to be given upon oath in general courts martial.'

'Yes, Your Honour, but Mr Daly maintains that it is unbecoming for an officer's word to be doubted.'

The judge martial sighed, but with apparent sympathy. 'Mr Beale-Browne, there are many who share that opinion, but the law is what it is, and it is that an officer give evidence upon oath.'

Beale-Browne leaned across the table to confer once more with Daly. Hervey was the only man in the court unable to see Daly's head shaking furiously.

The president thumped the table with his fist. But it was Barrow who spoke. 'Mr President, the prosecution is content not to call Cornet Daly, if the defending officer is of like mind.'

Lieutenant Beale-Browne looked like a drowning man who had been thrown a lifeline. 'I should be content, sir.'

Barrow almost smiled. 'Very well. Mr President and gentlemen, the prosecution's case is concluded.'

The president looked bemused. 'No further witnesses, Mr Barrow? No closing address?'

'No, sir.'

'Very well. Mr Beale-Browne, you are free to conclude.'

Beale-Browne rose again, wearily. 'Mr President and gentlemen, er . . . Cornet Daly would wish to state that he believed he had every right and skill to attempt the burning out of the lampas, and that the death of his charger was the unfortunate but not uncommon outcome of any surgical intervention. He would state that he did not abuse Serjeant Treve, rather did he speak generally in the direct language of the horse lines, and that he had no intention of assaulting the serjeant at the time that he was struck by Cornet Hervey.'

The silence that followed was so pronounced that the judge martial looked up, curious, and then at the president. 'Is that it, Mr Beale-Browne?'

'I do believe it is, Your Honour.'

The judge martial laid down his pen. 'Well, upon my word, I never came across anything so contrary. Mr President, I beg an adjournment in order to consult with myself on the matter before us.'

The president looked relieved. 'Very well. The court stands adjourned. All shall remain within the environs.'

CHAPTER NINETEEN
LONG SHADOWS

Badajoz, 29 December 1826

It was so cold that a hoar-frost whitened the hangings of Hervey's bedchamber. He lay still, listening for a sound that might tell him someone was come with news, welcome or otherwise. Since wine with Dr Sanchez the day before, hourly he had expected him to return with either a letter from Elvas telling him that his release was arranged, or else a summons to attend the tribunal. He had slept little, partly on account of the cold, but in larger part because his mind had wandered, back and forward, over a decade and more, from one misjudgement to another, every excess and indiscretion. They oppressed him, and yet none of them, in his imagining, compared with what was to come. How could it be that he had not learned his lesson until now, and that it should come to so low a point? He had learned the easy things well enough – the business of his profession, the drills and such like – but all else, when he contemplated it from the perspective of his present condition, appeared as nothing so much as failure.

He had lost a wife. It was ten years ago, but her memory – and the cause of her death – was ever with him, if routinely shut out. It had been his fault that Henrietta had died. Others might be blamed, but it had been his actions that had brought it about. He could not escape the fact (and he had never tried). He had a daughter, for whom he barely made provision beyond the material. How might he ever be father-hero to her when he did not see her from one year to the next? He slept with another man's wife – or rather, he *had* slept (and how much did he wish she were by his side now?). When the tribunal here had finished with him, and the court martial in Whitehall, he might yet be named in the high court by a cuckolded husband. He would never be able to show his face to his family again. How could he even decently face the day?

He had been apprehensive that first time, the court martial at Badajoz, but not truly fearful, as now. It was not that his memory failed him (he was certain), rather that to be arraigned as a cornet was one thing, and quite another to be tried as brevet-major, Companion of the Most Honourable Military Order of the Bath. The irony in how things had turned out could not escape him. No doubt the one-time Cornet Daly would this day be hunting freely from his rackety estate in Galway, a careless, bibulous local hero, who regaled his fellow squireens with stories of slaying the French. Doubtless, too, he wrecked a good horse every season, and thought nothing of it beyond the cost of replacement. For what was an animal's distress compared with his pleasure?

Why was it that some men had no sense of shame, no *true* sense, while others could be eternally burdened by it? Daly's face when the court martial had pronounced without withdrawing – how could it not have registered abject shame? Hervey could see it still, the brazen scorn at the judge martial's plain words: 'A man of violent temper wielding a cautery is no little threat. I direct that the case against Cornet Hervey be dismissed.' Then, when the court reassembled half an hour after withdrawing to consider its verdict on the remaining charges, Daly had marched in for all the world as if he were come to buy a horse at Tattersalls.

And when the president read the words, 'To Charge One, Guilty! To Charge Two, Guilty!', there remained about him a defiant air, as if the proceedings, the regiment, the entire army, did not ultimately matter, for he, Frederick Keevil Daly of Kilconnell, would jaunt on. Even when the president announced punishment, 'that he be dismissed the service', his only thought – his question to the court, indeed – had been whether he might recover the value of his commission.

Now, at such a distance, and for an indulgent moment, Hervey might admire the man, for where had his own unbending principles landed him? But in truth he was resolved that if he escaped his present predicament, and if he escaped a court martial, and the attention of Sir Peregrine Greville, he would amend his ways. He would amend his ways so thoroughly, so root and branch, that there could be no possibility of finding himself in a contingency such as this again. Nor, indeed, would there be any neglect of the Commandments or the proper regulation of family.

It was a very remote prospect, however, his 'deliverance'. That, he acknowledged. But the very thought of amendment lifted his spirits, as if, indeed, he were at some meeting of Methodists. He smiled, and thought of his sister. And then he chided himself again: had Elizabeth ever been wrong in her estimation of things? Had she ever had other than a right judgement? He had laughed at her for her evangelical principles, but they had never let her into deep water. Elizabeth would show him the way; he could trust in that.

He picked up his Prayer Book and opened it again at the collect for the previous day, for it had anticipated his new-found resolve: *Mortify and kill all vices in us, and so strengthen us by thy grace, that by the innocency of our lives, and constancy of our faith, even unto death, we may glorify thy holy Name.*

If only Joshua could be so apt! In these last, empty days,

he had read Joshua closer than ever, almost as if the book might reveal his means of escape. A great soldier was Joshua, a cunning soldier, a soldier who overcame as much on his own side as on that of the enemy. But he knew no Rahab in Badajoz to let him down from the walls, no spies to find such a person within the city.

Dr Sanchez came at noon. He did so full of apology for his absence, for his failure to keep his promise of an early return. 'It has been a difficult time, Major Hervey, difficult for me to explain. I beg you would forgive me and trust that it was not through choice that I did not come earlier.'

It did not matter to Hervey what had prevented the physician's visiting, for whatever he had imagined were the possibilities in their recent intimacy, he had begun to conclude that Sanchez was not a man for turning: no honourable man could hazard his family by such a thing, and the physician was nothing if not an honourable man. 'It has been an idle time, I confess, sir.'

Sanchez glanced at the open bible on the table. His face softened as he drew up a chair and sat down. 'Joshua, Major Hervey?'

'Joshua, yes. A great soldier.'

Sanchez unbuttoned his coat, despite the chill which the new-laid fire had not been able to dispel. 'Do you believe, Major Hervey, that Joshua's trumpets alone brought down the walls of Jericho?'

Hervey was intrigued. He thought to answer obliquely. 'With God, all things are possible?'

'Fie! Major Hervey! I had thought your study of Scripture would yield some more profound insight.'

Hervey smiled again. Was Sanchez merely making conversation? It was a curious attempt at diversion. 'If you wish, señor, I will tell you what I understand may have happened at Jericho.'

296

'Indeed I would hear it. It seems apt, here in Badajoz, don't you think?'

Hervey was even more intrigued. Did Sanchez mean the aptness was historical or of the moment? 'Apt? Possibly. Unlike the French, however – or, I imagine, your countrymen now – the Canaanites were terrified at the prospect of meeting the Israelites. They were resigned to their fate even. Does not Rahab the harlot say, "Our hearts did melt, neither did there remain any more courage in any man"?'

'Go on, Major Hervey.'

Hervey hesitated. The subject was closing to home. 'The first object in laying a siege is to persuade the besieged that resistance is futile. The walls of Jericho would have meant little if the defenders had not had the courage to fight.'

Sanchez nodded, but with the appearance of sadness. 'Would that the hearts of the defenders of Badajoz had melted!'

Hervey presumed he meant the night they had stormed the city. But he supposed it just possible that Sanchez referred in a roundabout way to the Miguelites. He would lead a little more. 'Yes, would that they had. But Jericho was sacked, as you recall, and all but Rahab's family put to the sword. It was an offering to God, was it not – a first fruit of the conquest of Canaan?'

'Badajoz was an offering too – an offering to the basest instincts of war. Was not Badajoz the first fruit of the conquest of Spain?'

Hervey's brow furrowed. 'Hardly *conquest*, doctor!'

'Forgive me. The campaign that rid Spain of Bonaparte – *both* of them – and for which my country is ever grateful for the assistance of yours, I assure you. But Badajoz paid the same price as Jericho.'

Hervey shook his head. 'I recoil at the image of Jericho put to the sword, doctor, as I do at that of Badajoz. And yet the slaughter of the innocent here that night is somehow all of a piece with the slaughter in the breaches. You can have no idea how hard our men had to fight to overcome the walls. They did not tumble down, as at Jericho.'

Sanchez nodded again, gravely. 'I know, perhaps, better than you imagine, my friend.'

Hervey stayed silent; he saw no cause for pressing him.

And then the physician brightened. 'But you, I think – I *know* – did not use the edge of the sword against the people of Badajoz.'

'Certainly not.'

'Quite the contrary, indeed.'

Hervey looked at him intently.

'See, my friend: I did not visit this morning, but it was not from neglect. I have the means of your escape. It will be quite easy, but we shall need help from Elvas.'

Hervey fought against his exhilaration. He needed to know how Sanchez had the means, and why. The declaration was so much more surprising for his having concluded that the physician was not his man. 'Why do you do this?'

Sanchez held up a hand. 'There may be opportunity to explain later. For the moment I would beg you to trust me, and attend carefully to what I say.'

Hervey inclined his head; what was there to lose?

'Very well. Now understand this,' began Sanchez, unusually imperative. 'The castle is impregnable – in the minds, at least, of the authorities. The guards are few and confident of surety. Men may come and go quite freely as long as they have the password, which changes but weekly. The next change will be in two days' time, when I shall learn of it. But, of course, I may not simply walk out of the castle with you. In any case, how then might you get to Elvas?'

Hervey was certain he would have no trouble getting to Elvas. 'A third party must enter and overcome the guards on the way out?'

'That is a possibility, although not without its difficulties. I had in mind your taking my place and leaving with a visiting party.'

Hervey looked doubtful. 'I rather think it the stuff of books.'

Sanchez shook his head. 'I see no reason why it should not obtain here, Major Hervey. I have observed the guards. They are, as I say, confident – *complacent* – in their surety. There is, after all, no threat to the fortress, and the officers do not intrude upon their duties greatly. No, I have seen the guards at work: they are content to count the numbers entering and leaving the citadel. Sometimes they do not even count.'

'Forgive me, doctor. I did not wish to sound unthankful. As long as we have the means to fight our way past the guards if things go wrong . . . But how may we leave you here? Your fate would be an unhappy one!'

Sanchez held up his hands. 'That is a detail of which we may speak in due course. The first thing we must do is communicate the password to Elvas. I am unable to do so, for reasons you may suppose. But you have free communications by letter, as we see. You have, I presume, a code?'

Hervey shook his head. 'Matters did not progress to that.'

Sanchez looked disappointed. 'Ah, I had imagined—'

'Except . . .' began Hervey, thoughtful. 'There *is* a code . . . but I don't have it. But if I ask Elvas to send me the code-book of the Corpo Telegráfico . . . do you imagine the authorities will let it pass?'

'Ask for *many* books. That way there stands a chance it might not be noticed.'

Hervey took up a pen. There was paper still on the table from his half-hearted attempts to maintain his journal. He began writing, quickly, an everyday account of his time these past few days, nothing to raise a suspicion. Then he inserted the request for the code-book, trusting that the veiling did not obscure his meaning, other than to the censor:

But time weighs heavily upon me. Send me books to read,
as many as you may spare, for I am without any
diversion. Send, if you can, Folque's book, that I may
learn more of the language while I am confined. And we
may speak to each other of his ideas.

Hervey read him the letter, in French.

'Admirable, admirable. It will arouse no suspicion whatsoever. And your general will understand?'

'He will understand, I trust. We spoke of Folque enough.'

'Who is he?'

'A general of engineers. He planned the army's signalling system, and its code. Wellington used it throughout the Peninsula.'

'Very well. I will take your letter to the lieutenant-governor at once. If he has not heard of Folque either, Elvas should have it by the morning.' Sanchez rose.

Hervey fixed him with a scrutinizing look, though far from hostile. 'Why do you do this?'

The physician replaced his battered old tricorn, and put a hand to Hervey's shoulder. 'Badajoz, my friend. Because of Badajoz!'

It was no explanation at all: Hervey was uncomprehending still. Why would this man do this, risk his own life, indeed, when a British army had behaved so infamously in his own city? He shook his head.

'That night, the night of the storming here: the shadows are yet long.'

'But—'

'Another day, Hervey; another day, perhaps.' Then he lifted up the letter, waving it and smiling, hopefully.

CHAPTER TWENTY
FIRST FRUITS

Badajoz, midnight, 6 April 1812

Five years, Sir Edward Lankester had said it would take to eject the French from Spain. 'The long point', he had called it – 'no bolting Reynard and running him fast to the kill'. Three of those years had passed, and here they were at Badajoz, barely a league beyond the border with Portugal, exactly where they had been three summers ago. 'Believe me, Hervey, these French marshals will show us more foxery than you'd see in a dozen seasons in Leicestershire.' On such a night as this, Sir Edward's words seemed extraordinarily prophetic.

No, they were not *exactly* where they had been three summers ago. This time they were *before* the walls rather than within. Hervey could not help but smile at the realization, chilling though it was. In truth, however, it was not quite as it seemed, and he knew it – they all knew it. Sir Arthur Wellesley was a hunting man; he was now thoroughly acquainted with his hounds and his huntsmen, and he had the measure of his quarry at last. After Talavera, elevated in the opinion of his army (and by the King to Viscount Wellington), he had secretly constructed the lines of Torres Vedras in case he would have to defend Lisbon. Then for twelve months he had dashed about La Mancha as

301

the Spanish junta collapsed, so that the following October, when he perceived he could rely on Spanish support no longer, he withdrew to the lines, breaking his pursuer, Marshal Masséna, by scorching the earth for fifty miles so that for a whole month Masséna's men sickened and starved within sight of the lines before turning-tail back for Spain.

And so the third year, 1811, had begun with high hopes. They had soon been dashed as the French captured Badajoz and the other border fortresses, closing the door into Spain again. Wellington had lost no time, however, investing Badajoz within two months. But the siege had failed, and a second a month later. Winter quarters, still at the border, still no nearer Joseph Bonaparte's capital, had been cold and bitter indeed. Wellington knew he could not stay long. And so at the beginning of January 1812, although the ground was hard as iron, and sleeting snow did his army more ill than could the French, he had opened the siege of Ciudad Rodrigo. The fortress fell to a fierce assault ten days later, and Wellington – the whole army – had then turned with confident but brutal determination to the *third* siege of Badajoz.

'Who the *devil* are you, sir?' barked a voice from the smoky blackness. 'Get out of my way!'

Sir Edward Lankester had had enough. General Cotton had ordered his squadron forward, dismounted, to the support of the Third Division, but they had stumbled about for an hour in the pitch dark, the guide useless. The walls of Badajoz looked but a stone's throw away, and the noise was infernal – the sudden shots, the numbing explosions, the terrified screams of the wounded, the terrifying screams of the assault troops, the jeering-cheering of the French who threw them back. And yet the detachment of dragoons could find no part in it because they could not find the provost marshal's men. 'Do *not* address me in that way, sir! I have not been informed that it is a ticket affair!'

'Damn your eyes, sir! I am General Picton!'

Sir Edward was not in the slightest discomposed. 'Then I am very glad of it, General, for we are damnably lost and have no idea of our purpose. Perhaps you will permit us to join you?'

'Is that *you*, Sir Edward?'

'It is, General.'

'Where are your horses?'

'The other side of the river. Do you have need of them?'

'Don't be a damned fool! What are you doing here?'

'We are wanted by the provost marshal, it seems.'

'Well, God alone knows where he is. Or cares. These walls are the death of us. Colville's division and the Light can make no headway in the breaches. And God knows how Leith's fares on the other side. You can come with me. I need officers to take charge. How many have you?'

'Three.' He would not ask 'to take charge of what?'

'Well, keep your dragoons where they are and keep as close to me as you're able.'

That soon proved harder than it sounded. General Picton wore a black coat and a forage cap, and there were more men crowded into the ditch at the foot of the castle walls than Hervey would have imagined possible. A powder keg fell on a man a dozen yards away, killing him instantly. His comrades stamped at the burning fuse like frantic Spanish dancers. A grenade exploded beyond, and there were another ten men screaming.

This was not Hervey's idea of fighting; it was nobody's idea of fighting. What was it about Badajoz? Three sieges in twelve months, days of battering away at the walls, and still not a man through its breaches! And here were the Third Division now trying to scale the walls, for the breaches were mined, barred with *chevaux de frise*, and swept by cannon – swept all the easier for not having to fire through embrasures. It was madness, yet still they were trying. The ladders did not even reach the top of the walls! Hervey saw a man climbing onto the shoulders of another, and then another onto his, as if his life depended on it. What could propel a man so, only to be met with a musket-butt in the face and a thirty-foot plunge onto the bayonets of his comrades below?

But life did not depend on it. On the contrary – the piles of dead below the walls showed that. Hervey knew that something else drove them forward. Threats? Perhaps. Pride? Possibly. Promise of reward? Maybe. A dreadful blood-lust, concocted of revenge and filthy living in the trenches? Undoubtedly. It was a volatile mixture, one that could be boiled up only occasionally and under the severest regulation. Hervey's blood did not yet boil, neither did pride nor promise of reward overwhelm him yet. No one threatened him, for sure. What in the name of God was he going to do here?

'Where is General Picton?' came a voice from behind, and with it a hand grasping hold of his cross-belt, a welcome point of recognition in an otherwise black and hellish stew of uniforms.

Hervey got to his feet again. 'He's here about somewhere,' he replied, trying to make out where his troop-leader had gone. He saw no occasion for asking who the enquirer was: if an officer wanted the divisional commander then he must have reason. 'Keep touch; I'll try to find him.'

He began edging forward, stepping over a man lying face down, and onto another lying face up, who let out a cry so agonized that Hervey jumped back before striding over him.

'Sir Edward!' he called, but muted.

What was the good of calling for one man in all this? But what alternative did he have? It was confusion as he had never seen it.

'Sir Edward!'

'Here!'

304

Hervey fell as he turned towards the voice, jarring his knee so hard as to make his head swim.

'What the devil are you doing?'

Hervey, clutching his knee, struggled to catch his breath. 'An officer, Sir Edward, for the general.'

'From Lord Wellington,' added the voice.

'I've no idea where he is. Neither has his colonel. He told me to wait here. What is it?'

The officer was perfectly composed, if alarmed nevertheless by the chaos into which he had quite literally stumbled. 'Lord Wellington wishes the Third Division to make a further attempt at an escalade. The Fourth and Light Divisions can't pass the breaches.'

Sir Edward pushed back the peak of his Tarleton. 'Hamilton, is that you?'

'It is. Sir Edward Lankester?'

'What is *happening*?'

'I don't rightly know, but I never saw Wellington look so ill. Nothing but reports of failure for two hours!'

'How does he expect Picton to get into this place *over* the wall if two divisions can't force the breaches?'

'I don't know *how* he expects it, but there's nothing else to hope for.'

'Good God! Brave men's breasts! It's not enough, Hamilton; it's not decent.'

'I know, Sir Edward, and doubtless does Wellington. But, I tell you, there's nothing else but to withdraw.'

A voice barked from the ink darkness: 'Who goes there?'

'General?'

Picton had come barging through the crouching mass of infantry, cursing left and right, threatening with his sword, frustrated as no other that he could not thrust it into a Frenchman atop the walls.

An ADC's lantern threw just enough light for a measure of recognition.

'General, Captain Hamilton is come from Lord Wellington,' said Sir Edward, almost as if making an introduction in Hyde Park.

'Well,' growled Picton, 'what has the commander-in-chief to say? Astonish me!'

'The Fourth and Light Divisions are utterly stalled, sir. He does not believe they will be able to make their way through until daylight. And General Leith's division has made no progress on the far side, either. He wishes you to press a further assault, for he believes that were the castle to be taken now the whole fortress would be ours.'

Picton heard him in silence – or rather, he said nothing, for the bedlam continued. At length he spoke, and softer than any had heard him in a month. 'Very well.' He turned to his ADCs. 'Go fetch the brigadiers.'

Picton lapsed into silence again when they had gone.

For the first time, Sir Edward saw the dressing on his shoulder. Picton clutched at it and swayed.

'General?'

He seemed reluctant to part with his thoughts.

'General, are you well?'

Picton snapped-to. 'Nothing, Sir Edward. It is nothing at all!'

'What would you have me do? Should we not seek a little cover – what's left of the palisade there?'

'No. If once we retire a yard we'll never recover it. Now hear: this will be a desperate business, but I shall forfeit my life if we don't carry it, and the brigadiers the same. Once we gain the castle the sole object shall be to assault the breaches from the rear. By then we'll have lost a good many, the officers especially. You will therefore act as my staff, you and your officers – and *drive* them to the breaches. I want no heroics from you until then. That is the most imperative order.'

'I understand, General.'

'Well then, let us see what Kempt and Campbell can do with their brigades, damn them!'

It was nigh impossible to see anything in the Stygian ditch. Hervey stumbled and cursed as they edged their way back to make room for the 5th (Northumberland) bringing up more ladders. Every powder flash blinded him for a minute and more, and even with night eyes it was too dark to see the top of the walls. How could these men scale them, not knowing what was up there?

'Hold hard,' said Sir Edward suddenly. 'I won't push past any more of them. It's bad enough wearing blue in a place like this.'

Hervey was surprised, for besides not being able to make out one colour from another on a night like this, Sir Edward as a rule displayed supreme indifference to such things. But then, this was Badajoz. Two assaults had failed already; if they failed again, the army would stop believing in itself. There could be no failure this time, whatever it took. That was what Picton had meant. It no longer mattered how many men died scaling these walls. If the bodies piled up in a mound, then their comrades could climb on them to reach the top – a ramp of redcoats, doing more in death than they had managed to do alive. And if that was to be, then it were better to go at it quickly, to take one's death early, with the blood coursing, rather than waiting till it ran cold – easier by far to storm the walls with a hundred men following than to *follow* and see the bodies of the fallen. Hervey smiled grimly: there was always the chance of being first in Badajoz. Someone must earn that accolade!

'Sir Edward, I wish to go with the Fifth.'

'Hervey, we have work to do,' replied his troop-leader, a shade impatient. 'And besides, they would never let you.'

'Surely, sir, they—'

'Hervey, listen with close attention to what I say. Those

brave fellows in red are legion. If the Fifth don't scale the walls, the Seventy-seventh will, and if not them then the Eighty-third behind them, or the Ninety-fourth behind *them*. That is the purpose of the infantry of the line, and there will be many a fine officer dying to remind them of it. *Our* purpose is precise and limited. We will face our turn for oblivion when the walls are stormed.'

Hervey was abashed. 'Sir.'

'Very well,' said Sir Edward, but more encouragingly. 'Now, where are the covermen?'

Eight officers and NCOs of the 6th Light Dragoons crouched in the bottom of the ditch as cheering redcoats sprang forward. Ladders slammed against the walls; men even began climbing the stonework with their bare hands, getting nowhere but keeping up the momentum of the surge of red. In the torchlight, Hervey saw the Fifth's commanding officer climbing the nearest ladder, his men close behind shielding his head with bayonets. Soon there were so many redcoats clinging to the ladder that even if the French had been able to get a hand to the top rung they would not have been able to tip it back. Did the ladder even *reach* the top? Hervey could not tell. But there was no check in the movement upwards, and for a moment he thought the French must have abandoned the walls. Then came a very deliberate fusillade. Men at the bottom fell clutching wounds, but none from the ladders. The Fifth's light company answered, the musket flashes atop the walls showing them where to aim. Hervey realized the light company's marksmen had been waiting for this: now they could sweep the walls and keep the defenders back while the grenadiers climbed.

'Clever Fifth!' he heard himself say. (*And he dreamed, and behold a ladder set up on the earth, and the top of it reached to heaven!*) 'Clever, brave Fifth!'

But these were no angels ascending. Neither did they *descend*: there was no check in the ascent of the lieutenant-colonel's ladder.

Suddenly there was shouting from the top: 'Old Ridge's in! He's *in*!'

Grenadiers were all but running up the ladder now.

Hervey was as humbled as he was thrilled: the first man into Badajoz was not a thrusting ensign or a raging corporal, but the Fifth's own commanding officer, Lieutenant-Colonel Henry Ridge, leading his regiment sword-drawn as if on parade. And he, Cornet Matthew Hervey, crouched in the ditch below!

The light company stopped firing, and there were no shots from the top. Had the French left the ramparts? When would it be their turn?

'Leu-in, leu-in the Fifth!' shouted the brigadier, waving his sword and grasping the rung of a ladder. 'Follow-up, Seventy-seventh!'

Hervey rose on one knee: a *brigadier* in – now was the time, surely?

'Hold hard,' said Sir Edward, calmly. 'Let the Fifth fight the French out of the castle. We go after the Seventy-seventh.'

Hervey chafed as hundreds more redcoats surged to the walls. He was certain it would be over by the time their turn came, for Picton had said the French could not hold once the castle had fallen. He could hear firing again: the last desperate attempt to throw back the Fifth? What a thing it was to be waiting so close!

General Picton came, pushing, shoving, cursing worse than before. Everywhere there were torches, no need of the dark now that the walls were his. Yet he was a man angry with everything and everybody.

'Get in there, Campbell!' he barked at his brigadier. 'Get every man you have in there!'

He pulled a grenadier from the bottom of a ladder and lashed at another two with the flat of his sword. 'Laggards, laggards! Make way there!'

He cursed every rung to the top. He was still cursing as he jumped over the parapet and ran along the walls to the castle, checking only when he came upon Colonel Ridge lying dead at the gates.

General Phillipon was a defeated man. He had calculated (and disposed his troops accordingly) that even if the fortress walls were overcome he could still hold the castle until Marshal Soult came to his relief. But he knew that if the castle fell, the rest of the fortress would. Kempt's brigade as well as Campbell's had scaled the walls and fought the defenders out of this last redoubt with bloody loss, and they had held it against ferocious counter-attacks. The bugles that had been blowing since the first drummer gained the ramparts were now being answered by Leith's on the other side of the city, and they told Phillipon that the game was up. An hour after midnight, unseen, he gathered about him his staff and escort, rode north from the centre of the city through Las Palmas gate, and crossed the old Roman bridge over the Guadiana to take refuge in Fort San Cristobal, which guarded the right bank.

Sir Edward Lankester and his party had followed close after General Picton, waiting occasion for their services, but hoping it would not come. Hervey thought the general was tiring, for he did not curse and swear as before, neither did he drive the brigades to the breaches. The escalade had been exhausting and the butcher's bill large. Once his men had forced the castle gates, the French had fled or laid down their arms, and those at the breaches would know to do likewise soon. The impulsion of the assault was gone, the bullet spent. He, General Thomas Picton, fifty-four years old, his wound now telling, had done everything Wellington had asked of him, and more than could have been expected. That he was still alive was a surprise to him, as it was to others. His staff wanted him to rest: it was now up to the regimental officers to rally their companies, round up the prisoners, deal with the wounded, collect the dead. What else was there for a divisional commander to do but rest?

But his division, which he had in large measure *driven* over the walls by the sheer strength of his will, now had a prodigious thirst. Men who had laboured in the trenches for weeks, wet through, perishing cold, their comrades blown apart by howitzer shells even as they worked; men who this night had waded knee-deep in the dark across the mill dam, whose comrades had fallen into the swollen Rivellas stream and drowned, or had jumped into ditches thought dry, only to discover their error too late; men who had been shot at from two sides at once as they filed between bastions, who had been spattered with the ordure of comrades as bombs were tossed among them, who had been stoned or speared from the ramparts like beasts in a primitive hunt, whose messing-mates had fallen from ladders thirty feet onto bayonets, or been butted and stabbed in the face as they gained the top – and all of them fearing oblivion at any moment by the touch of a quickmatch to a mine: men whose impulsion was not diminished but turned in another direction. And not against the French. For all that the defenders had made them pay well over the odds for every yard of the assault, the men in red coats did not exact any special revenge. What they wanted – and what many were determined to have – was reward, not revenge. There was money in Badajoz – French and Spanish. They had not been paid in months; why should they not take their arrears now? There would be drink, too. They had had nought for weeks but a warming measure of rum each morning, and fighting was a thirsty affair. There would be *plenty* of drink in

Badajoz, and whether it was French or Spanish, they would have it. There were women, too.

It began within minutes of taking the castle. Those still under discipline made for the rear of the breaches with their officers, as Picton had ordered; many more ran straight into the deserted streets. It was three o'clock when Sir Edward Lankester realized what was happening: there was shooting throughout the city, long after the last Frenchman would have surrendered. Although Picton had diverted him to the assault, it was the provost marshal who had summoned him forward, and he could not exempt himself now from the original orders. But where *was* the provost marshal?

What, anyway, could a troop do, asked Lieutenant Martyn, if the better part of four divisions was dissolving in disorder?

Sir Edward appeared to grit his teeth. 'There are women and children and old men in this city, and they're Spanish too – our allies. We can *do* what we can do.' He turned to his senior NCO. 'Serjeant Hawkins, go bring up the troop. Muster in the castle yard.'

Hervey was relieved they would be doing something, at least. After Corunna, he knew full well what the worst might be. Should they even wait until the troop came up? The regimental officers would be having a hard time of it in the streets: could they not try to help them?

'Hervey, go and see if a picket has been placed at the castle gate,' said Sir Edward, sounding weary.

'Sir.'

'And no further, mind.'

'No.'

'Sir, the captain said no further!' Corporal Bancroft, covering, was not so much fearful for his own safety but for his reputation.

'You saw that place, Corporal.'

'Ay, sir, but what'd we 'ave been able to do?'

The nuns had been unfortunate in the extreme. Their convent was at the very exit from the castle. But the location had also been a blessing, since their defilement had not been prolonged: Kempt's reserve battalion had come out and put an end to the riot.

'I don't know,' replied Hervey, sharply. 'We can do what we can!' He pressed on, sword drawn.

Hatless men in tattered red coats, filthy, bloody, lurched out of the shadows or from doorways, clutching bottles and other plunder, inviting Hervey and Bancroft to join them, pointing to where there was more.

Bancroft grabbed his arm as Hervey lunged at them with the flat of his sabre. 'No, sir! Steady on!'

A scream made both men turn on their heel.

'What in *God's* name . . .' gasped Hervey.

They sprinted for the house. Its door, like the others in the street, lay battered down. Hervey leapt it, while Bancroft took post to cover his back.

Oil lamps and candles lit the brutish scene: two Connaught privates, and a mother and three daughters – Hervey wondered they hadn't screamed more. The bigger man lunged at him with a bayonet. There was no room to fence. Hervey dropped his sword, drew his pistol and fired in a split second. The man fell back across the girl's body, blood bubbling from the hole in his chest, legs and arms twitching like a dancing puppet. The second rushed at him. Hervey swung his pistol-butt at the man's head, but a mutton fist felled him. Corporal Bancroft pointed with his sabre as the man tried to leave, but the same fist grasped it and wrenched it aside. Bancroft drew his pistol. Then he dropped his aim – save it for a man trying to come *in*.

The women (in truth, the daughters looked but in their teens) were now hysterical. Hervey held up his hands to calm them, assuring them he had not just killed the man to take possession of them himself. He pulled the lifeless Connaught to the floor, freeing the third daughter. But her throat was cut, and her nightdress slit top to bottom. There was nothing he could do but restore her modesty. He pulled down a curtain and laid it over her, and then in the most broken of Spanish he told them to put on their cloaks and come with him. The mother at once began protesting – *imploring*. Then he understood.

It was madness to try bringing the murdered sister as well, but he saw the woman would not leave her. And so he shouldered the bestial evidence of the Eighty-eighth's riot, and prayed they would have it easy for the hundred yards to the castle.

CHAPTER TWENTY-ONE

RESOLUTION

Badajoz, 31 December 1826

'When did you know it was I? How?'

The physician smiled a little, as much as to say that Hervey ought not to be surprised that such a thing could be known. 'Soon after I looked inside your Prayer Book, when the guards took it, I thought it probable. It seemed unlikely that there would be any other by your name in the British cavalry. And then, as we began to speak about the past, I became more certain. But only listening to you now could I be assured.'

'I am much moved, señor.'

'A daughter murdered, Major Hervey: one does not forget the details, I am sorry to say.'

Hervey, pained, looked down. 'No, of course.'

Dr Sanchez poured himself another glass of wine. 'But let us talk no more of it, my friend.' He lowered his voice. 'There is interesting news from Lisbon – or rather, *of* Lisbon. From Madrid.'

'Oh?'

Sanchez lowered his voice still further. 'Several brigades of English troops are landed.'

Hervey brightened. 'Indeed!'

'I rather think this may hasten your release, parole or no.'

Hervey frowned. 'I would far prefer escape by the method we have set in-hand. If I am released it will mean ceremony, and . . .' He paused. 'Do you have any more of the tribunal?'

Sanchez shook his head. 'I have heard not a word. But then, Major Hervey, truly I am not privy to these things. I do know, however, that the governor of this place is called away – perhaps to Madrid, I am not told – and nothing would be likely before his return. We have several days in that regard, I believe.'

'But not a day to lose.'

'No, there is never a day to lose, Major Hervey,' said Sanchez, quietly but emphatically. 'Well, it is but a day's wait now for the new password. Your scheme of codes has worked admirably well.'

It had. Brigadier-General Dom Mateo de Braganza had seen at once what was Hervey's design, and had sent two portmanteaux of books, including General Folque's manual of semaphore codes, together with a trial message. Hervey had replied in a long letter of thanks, with numerals from the code-book carefully interspersed, and had received a reply by return which told him of the plan to steal him away, and the identity of his 'fellow of long acquaintance'. Tomorrow, when Sanchez learned the new password, Hervey would send it in a letter asking for some dictionary or other, and then the escape would follow before dawn two days following.

'Was there any intelligence of where these brigades would go?' he asked, unable even now to distance himself from the matter of strategy that had propelled him here in the first place.

'If there was, it was not given to me,' replied Sanchez, shaking his head. 'I imagine one must come to Elvas? It is the logical place.'

Hervey groaned. 'It is a long story.'

'How so?'

He had no wish to appear evasive: here was a man risking his neck, after all. But the precise extent of the physician's loyalty he could not gamble on. 'I found myself in dispute with others over where the troops should go.'

But Sanchez had no interest in the details. 'Well, we must pray they will have no recourse to arms. It would be a dreadful thing indeed for an old ally.'

Hervey presumed Sanchez referred to the Portuguese, although he might easily have in mind his own countrymen: the alliance with Spain against Bonaparte had come late, and had always been uncomfortable, but they had indeed been allies.

In truth, Sanchez was obliged by a debt he felt personally to Hervey, not to the British. That there would have been no debt had it not been for the infamous conduct of a part of the army at Badajoz, he was not inclined to dwell on. He bore no grudges. Like many of his countrymen, he professed to liking Englishmen while disliking the English.

Hervey approved his wish for peace, however: let them pray, indeed, that there would be no recourse to arms. '*Oremus.*'

The physician smiled. 'Ah, Major Hervey, would that your Latin came from your Prayer Book!'

Hervey returned the smile. 'It does, but a very little. I rather fancy we were taught the nobler texts. I recall quite a trade in epigrams when I was a cornet. But I am very unpractised now.'

'And your Greek? I am afraid there was scant choice if not in Spanish in the little library here.'

'My Greek is very ill. I confess I struggled a good deal with the New Testament you so thoughtfully provided.'

'Not, perhaps, so great a failing in a soldier?'

Hervey smiled again. 'No, I don't suppose it is. If there is war in Greece then I might be able to forage in pentameters;

317

otherwise I imagine it to be little loss. Doctor, I was grateful merely for the sentiment; and as I said, it occupied my mind – *considerably*!'

Sanchez held up his hands, conceding the point. 'But now, to return to your friends in Elvas, is it not very gratifying to learn that such a man as Colonel Laming, and a lady of rank, have hastened to your aid?'

Hervey took another large measure of wine. It warmed him, the taste of the familiar from hearth or mess. 'I hardly know what to think. *Laming*, I am not perhaps so surprised by. We served together for some years, but he went elsewhere when the regiment was in India. Dona Isabella is "at home" in Elvas; her uncle is bishop. I imagine she accompanied Laming as interpretress. But, yes, it is quite a turn-up.'

Sanchez finished his wine, and made ready to leave. 'Well, you shall see both, and soon. I will leave you to your books, now, Major Hervey. I have calls to make.'

'Of course, doctor.'

Sanchez rose, looking thoughtful again. 'Do not trouble yourself with unhappy memories of this place, Major Hervey. We Spanish understand what is the nature of war. You know well enough what our *guerrilleros* had to do. And after Badajoz, we did not once retrace our footsteps, did we? Were you at Salamanca?'

Hervey smiled. 'I was at Salamanca. *And* I saw Madrid the following month.'

'Exactly! And thence to the Pyrenees . . .'

Hervey shook his head. 'You forget: we could not take Burgos. We had to withdraw again to the border.'

Sanchez raised his hands and his eyebrows: he had forgotten. 'But *Badajoz* never changed hands again!'

'No, and we ran the French hard and fast the following year. I made my first footing in France in October.'

'Five years!' said Sanchez, shaking his head. 'A long time in the life of a young man.'

Hervey shrugged his shoulders. 'It would be crueller now for me, I assure you!'

Sanchez grasped Hervey's shoulder. 'Major Hervey, my *dear* friend, forgive me! I understand perfectly: every day for you here must seem like a hundred. I am certain your release shall be soon!' He gathered up his coat and hat. 'I beg you would excuse me now. I leave you to your thoughts of tomorrow. Be ready with that book of codes when I return!'

Later, when all was silent in the repose of the afternoon, Hervey took up a pen and began a letter home – or rather, to the place where his sister held the guardianship of his daughter, and increasingly the care of their ageing parents.

As from Lisbon

31st December 1826

My dear Elizabeth,

I much regret the long delay in writing to you and to answering yours of— the letter is not to hand, forgive me. Your salutations, as those of our entire family, in respect of the King's honouring me with his order of the Bath are most gratefully received, I assure you, and required an earlier expression of gratitude from me than here. However, the past weeks have been a very great trial, I fear to tell you, though I would beg at once that you do not worry, for all is now well. I have, perforce, been unable to write to you – I will not trouble you with the causes now, for they are tedious and better explained à tête. But I have had opportunity and occasion for serious reflection and consideration of my situation, especially as it touches on you and

Georgiana, and I am resolved on return to England at once to put all arrangements onto a sound and proper footing, and so to arrange my military duties as to have a proper regard for the need of a daughter for her father, and, I might say, of a sister for her brother, and for the parents of a son who has too long been absent from them. I do not yet know how this is to be accomplished, for there are certain questions which the Horse Guards shall require answer of me when I return, neither do I make any particular proposals in respect of Georgiana . . .

He made no particular proposals, but he knew what was the right course. A governess, which in part Elizabeth was, would without doubt satisfy the requirements of a daughter who, by maternal right at least, would at some time enter good society – indeed, very high society. But a governess (even *he* was aware) did not satisfy the natural needs of a child. In truth, he knew that none could but the actual mother. However, a new wife, if she were good and loving (and why should a man choose otherwise to be his wife?), would better serve Georgiana than any hired woman might. His course, therefore, was very clear. How he would set it was another matter.

He wrote on, several pages of inconsequential 'sketching', letting his sister down lightly after the portentous beginning – a record of Nature, of architecture, of the manner of the people, anything which might convincingly fill a letter to someone he must own to using very ill indeed. For if he might contemplate marriage, and with considerable expectations, he knew that his sister's prospects were meagre – a meagreness largely of his making. At length he reached a point at which he considered he might decently finish, and signed his name in the most affectionate manner he was capable of.

Then he sealed the letter, addressed it, and poured more wine. He was not diverted by any book, even Folque's, for without the password to encode it was the dullest volume in the world. Instead he drew close to the fire, wrapping his cloak about his shoulders and giving his wine-warmed thoughts over to the course he would set – the course for Georgiana.

CHAPTER TWENTY-TWO
VEILED SPEECH

Next day

'But how, Major Hervey? Why?' Dr Sanchez was despairing: he had been given the new password and had come at once.

Hervey shook his head, trying not to betray the despair to which *he* was tending. 'I don't know. They came this morning, shortly after breakfast. They've never searched before. They took every book – sparing my Prayer Book, that is. They had that long enough before.'

'I will go at once to speak with the captain.'

Hervey sat down. His boots wanted polish, the silver and brass about his tunic was dull, and his shirt was no longer white. These things he had attended to as best he could, but he was daily more conscious of the decline. That the means of his deliverance should be plucked from him now, so close to his triumph, was a cruel blow: the sea of despair was once more stretching before him – perhaps even wider than before.

But he would fight it. So close . . . there must be a way! 'I've been trying to imagine what they might make of Folque's signal-book – if they've found it. Would it be apparent what I was about? I think not.'

'It might raise a suspicion, not least because it's

part-written in English. But see, when I go to the captain, if the books are simply collected, without examination, I can secrete your book and return with it.'

Hervey was fighting despair, but he kept his reason: if the authorities had grounds to remove his books, they would be suspicious of any 'friend' of his. And if they discovered him with the book, the game would be truly up. 'Easier said than done, I think, doctor. But what agitates me as much is the thought they might stop the correspondence with Elvas.'

'Exactly so. I will go at once.'

Hervey held his cloak for him. 'What *is* the parole?'

Sanchez glanced at the door. 'Napoleon,' he whispered.

Hervey sighed. 'It is all the more dismaying for its being so simple. I suspect it might even be in Folque's vocabulary – no need to spell it out at all. Concealment would have been easy.'

'Vexing in the extreme.' Sanchez put on his hat and turned to go, but then he changed his mind. 'See, Major Hervey, might you not be able to convey the word in another way? So singular a name is surely susceptible to allusion?'

The same thought had just occurred to Hervey; also the peril. 'I could veil my words, yes; but the consequences of conveying the wrong meaning would be disastrous.'

Sanchez looked disappointed. 'I see the danger perfectly; I had not thought—'

'*No*, wait!' said Hervey, his face now animated, and happily. '*Laming* – I do believe that self-regarding scholar may be our deliverance! Doctor, you recall I spoke of cornets trading epigrams?'

'I do.'

'Well, one of those – and deuced clever – conveys exactly the parole, no doubting it! Laming will not have forgotten, for it was his own.' He sat down and snatched up a pen. 'Doctor, go to the authorities, if you will, and ask if they will take a letter on the usual terms. Do not trouble them for the return of any book: it could only rouse suspicion, and we have no need of Folque now.'

Sanchez needed no urging. He clapped a hand on Hervey's shoulder, as much to reinforce his own resolve as his friend's. 'Very well! We *shall* succeed!'

When Sanchez had gone, Hervey began to write. He had said it, and he was as sure of it as may be: Laming, even after so long a time, would not have forgotten such an intriguing acrostic. It remained only to insert the obviously contrived phrase.

He did not have to ponder long: Joshua would serve him. He smiled at the thought of the great spy-master continuing his work here. Joshua would not bring down the walls of a fortress, but he might yet 'let him down by a rope'!

My dear Laming,

How very good it was to learn that you are here, to pursue some classical purpose – study of the Roman bridge at Elvas, perhaps? Or is it something of greater antiquity in the bishop's library? I myself had not the time when of late in the palace, but then my Greek, as you may imagine, is now very poor. Do you recall our efforts when we were younger? I try, however.

I am very well treated here and await my release agreeably, although I am not able to read and write as I should wish. Nevertheless, I content myself with the recollection of our former studies, and believe I may give you my word *in this. I have been reading so much of the Book of Joshua, whom you will know to be a childhood hero of mine, perhaps as much to me as to the people of Israel. Indeed, to those who know, the* word is thus: *with but one remove, Joshua, the destroyer of whole cities, was the lion of his people . . .*

He filled two pages with thoughts on Joshua, with emphatic underlinings in insignificant places, so that the pertinent phrase did not stand out by its curious sense. He was especially careful not to refer to Jericho, or indeed to any other city which a sharp-eyed censor might connect with Badajoz. It would be a cruel irony, he mused, to have the letter withheld for an unintended parallel.

When it was finished, he asked the guard for the letter to be conveyed to the castle authorities, as usual. The guard took it without hesitation, as he had the others; and Hervey breathed a silent sigh of relief.

It was much troubling Dom Mateo that the Spanish were being so punctilious in maintaining the posts and couriers. Colonel Laming was less inclined to puzzle over it since the French border had remained open in the days before Waterloo, and the mails had moved freely between Paris and Brussels. Closing a border was no small thing, he declared. As often as not it was prelude to a formal declaration of war. Were Spain to do so, it could only be regarded by Lisbon – and now London – as a hostile act.

'I pray you are right,' said Dom Mateo. 'I fear, though, that the present arrangements greatly favour the Miguelistas.'

'They favour us too, General; at least in respect of Major Hervey.'

Dom Mateo nodded. 'Indeed, they do, Colonel. But, I hope, for not very much longer: not half of one hour more, I think.' The semaphore had already signalled the crossing of the Badajoz courier.

Dom Mateo picked up his copy of the code-book and turned its pages. He looked pleased with himself, at last. They had been dark days since the taking-prisoner of Hervey. He had seen off the Miguelistas' half-hearted attempt to overawe the garrison at Elvas. It had been extraordinarily easy, indeed: no more than a display of the gunpowder at his disposal – proving the guns in the bastions, and *feux de joie* from the walls by the *pé do castelo*. The Miguelistas and their Spanish friends had not stayed long after that. They had had no siege train: had they truly believed the garrison would desert to them as soon as they showed themselves? Dom Mateo's chief of staff believed it to have been only a reconnaissance in force, but Dom Mateo himself was more sanguine: he was sure their *ruse de guerre*, although it had been exposed as one (and Hervey was paying the price), had fatally unnerved the invader. And now that British troops were actually making their way here, he was certain there could be no usurpation from within Elvas or from without. He would have Hervey back in the fortress by the time they arrived, and there would be no diplomatic embarrassment, for the Spaniards could hardly protest against the rescue of a British officer taken on Portuguese soil. Not that he cared one jot about ruffling the feathers of diplomatists; but he did care for the reputation of his friend.

Dom Mateo felt content as he turned the pages of General Folque's manual. It had been great good fortune indeed that he and Hervey had spent the morning together, a month past, with the Corpo Telegráfico. But then, he had always been of a mind that good soldiers made their own fortune.

When he read the courier's despatch, half an hour later, Dom Mateo was at once bewildered. Indeed, he was quite dismayed, throwing his arms about in extravagant gestures. 'There is *nothing* – nothing but a page observing the habits of the birds in the garden at Badajoz! Is Hervey suffering some derangement, you suppose? Where is the parole? He says nothing at all!'

Laming was engrossed in his own letter.

'What say you, Colonel?'

'I . . . I beg your pardon, General: I did not hear.'

'I said, why is there no parole? No code, nothing!'

Laming smiled wryly. 'Then his letter to me is all the clearer. Hear, General: he writes, "I am very well treated here and await my release agreeably, although I am not able to read and write as I should wish." Evidently the code-book has been taken from him.'

'Then how are we to learn the parole?'

'Hervey tells me, General. And unless the censor in Badajoz has both a perfect grasp of English *and* Greek, then he tells me in a code every bit as clever as Folque's. The password is Napoleon.'

'Here, let me see.' Dom Mateo almost seized the letter. He read, his brow furrowing deeper with every line. 'Where? Where is this code?'

'There, General,' replied Laming, pointing to the sentence, and smiling still.

' "The word is thus: with but one remove, Joshua, the destroyer of whole cities, was the lion of his people". What is Joshua to do with it?'

Laming shook his head. 'Joshua is merely the . . . decoy. You understand "decoy", General?'

'Yes, yes, I understand the word right enough. But how is it decoy here?'

'General, remember that Hervey had to write in such a way as not to arouse suspicion. Talking of Joshua is commonplace enough, I surmise. The code is an acrostic – the term, I imagine, is the same in Portuguese? When we were cornets, we played these games. The true phrase is "*Napoleon*, the destroyer of whole cities, was the lion of his people". When Hervey writes "with but one remove, Joshua" he means me to substitute Napoleon for Joshua!'

'You are certain of this?'

'I am, General.'

'But how do you know it is Napoleon who replaces Joshua? I have never read of it! Whose is the saying?'

'General, I beg your pardon. I did not say: it is a clever play on Greek words.' He picked up a pen and wrote carefully. 'Here, sir. You see, by writing "Napoleon", and then removing the initial letter for each successive word, the sentence is made: Napoleon, the destroyer of whole cities, was the lion of his people.'

ΝΑΠΟΛΕΩΝ ΑΠΟΛΕΩΝ ΠΟΛΕΩΝ ΟΛΕΩΝ ΛΕΩΝ
ΕΩΝ ΩΝ

Dom Mateo shook his head, quite diverted by the acrostic's simplicity. A man did not have to be a Greek scholar to appreciate it. 'Ingenious, Colonel Laming; quite ingenious. My compliments to you, and of course to Major Hervey.'

'It is schoolboy conceit, General; but then, we were very lately out of school.' Laming paused, and then pressed home. 'It is settled, then? Two of your men, Dona Isabella, the corporal and me.'

Dom Mateo looked more resigned than content. 'It goes hard with me, Colonel Laming, but I must concede you are right. It would indeed be an embarrassment for your government as well as mine if I were discovered in Spain. You will have one of my couriers, and a captain of my own regiment – he was with the Corps of Guides, a proud, excellent fellow.'

Laming was relieved. In truth, the embarrassment might be the greater if he himself were to be discovered, but although he would own that he knew the country not one tenth as well as did Dom Mateo, he still fancied he knew better how to spirit his old friend from the castle at Badajoz. That had been the way of things in the Sixth. 'Very well, General. And you will give me a man who knows the unguarded crossing?'

'You may depend on it, Colonel. It is little more than a mule track. We use it frequently. The Spanish cannot watch every mile of the border, even if they have a mind to. The road has never been used by them.'

'And the courier's papers are all that will be needed to pass within the town?'

'I am assured of it. And Dona Isabella has Spanish enough to deal with any official. You will be especially careful of her safety?'

'I shall have the very highest regard for her safety, General. I should not for one moment contemplate her accompanying us if I believed we might do this without her.'

'I understand perfectly, Colonel. The Spaniards will be disarmed by her sex, for all that their experience ought to put them on their guard instead.'

'*Deo volente.*'

Dom Mateo nodded, and made the sign of the Cross. '*Deo volente.*'

They assembled at two o'clock. Laming was by no means certain that the plan could work *with* Isabella, let alone without her. There were just too many points at which they could be challenged, and at any one, despite official papers and Isabella's Spanish, there would be no escape following discovery – not without a deal of bloodshed at least. And if they had to negotiate all these points of challenge on the way to Hervey's quarters, they would have to do so by return – *and* with a fugitive. They had their diplomatic papers, and they travelled in plain clothes (borrowed, and strange-looking as these were), but at root it was a plan reliant as much on Spanish ineptness as clever Greek wordplay; Laming had seen enough in the Peninsula to know that ineptness was not a quality which could be relied on. But he perforce wore the mask of command, and he now smiled and waved confidently as they rode out of the headquarters.

They walked for a quarter of an hour, breaking into a trot once they were out of the east gate of the fortress. Dom Mateo's captain led, then came Laming with Isabella at his side, then the courier – who did not know of the plan, but who would be recognized by the Spanish authorities and therefore assist their progress – and at the rear Corporal Wainwright led a packhorse, its burden less than it appeared, for the animal was the means by which Hervey was to escape. Laming worried that a suspicious sentry might think it too fine an animal to be bearing a load instead of a rider, and might remove the baggage and see a riding- rather than a pack-saddle. But he worried too much, he told himself: why *should* a sentry be suspicious, for a party of travellers must be accompanied by some baggage, and if they could afford to engage a decent packhorse then why should they not? Indeed, he would tell them that it was a spare riding-horse! These were little things, he knew, but they were of the essence: they properly occupied the mind of a man charged with such an adventure – especially when it had been so many years since he had taken to the field.

But no one spoke. The captain of Dom Mateo's own regiment had some French but little English, in spite of his proud lineage with the Corps of Guides. The courier had nothing but Portuguese and a little Spanish, and Wainwright waited only to be given an order. Isabella seemed wholly absorbed in thoughts of her own. Laming's thoughts, left to themselves therefore, were becoming increasingly ill com- posed. What was troubling him now was moral not physical, and that he always found much the harder. He had con- sidered the question before they set out, but now, alone on the road, the challenge of what had before been merely theoretical was all too concrete. What should be his priority if it came to a fight? Or rather, *who* should be his priority? The cold fact was that he himself, if he were to fall on the Spanish side, would be the cause of the greatest embarrassment to His Britannic Majesty's government. But, now committed, he would put himself beyond that calculation: he could not spare himself for the loss of his old friend, and certainly not for the loss of Isabella Delgado. As for the others, the captain was important only until they had succeeded in crossing the border (he was certain he could find his own way back); the courier was of no importance once they had gained entrance to the castle; and Corporal Wainwright . . . a coverman was required not infrequently to cover with his life. Laming balked, however: it had all been so much easier on the battlefield. But, it was better that he had it out now than have to come to a judgement while wielding a sabre. He turned and looked at Isabella. Truly, she was a very handsome woman; and with pluck to admire as much, if not more. She was indispensable, at least until Hervey was sprung; but it was inconceivable that she could be left behind.

So, in their silence, they left the kingdom of Portugal and entered that of Spain. It was easy, save for a little stumbling in single file through a secret, wooded valley, and by four o'clock they had the walls of Badajoz in sight.

Laming was at once filled with dread. It had been nigh fifteen years, but still the walls spoke of death – and failure. Twenty feet high at least, thirty for much of the curtain, and even more in places, they had twice defeated Wellington's men, and only by unleashing the very hounds of hell had the duke been able to overcome them the third time. He grimaced at the memory. He had played no great part, but he had been witness to it. And to what had followed.

He braced himself. 'I recall it best from the other direction, Dona Isabella,' he said, sounding, he hoped, matter-of-fact.

'When it was in Spanish hands therefore?' she replied, urging her horse up alongside his.

Laming was gratified by her attention at last. 'Indeed.

The next occasion was bestial. But I would not dwell on it.'

Isabella smiled. 'Oh, I imagine I know more than you suppose, Colonel Laming.'

He supposed she did. 'Hervey had to shoot a man, you know. One of our own men, I mean.'

Isabella looked pained. 'I did not know that. What a terrible thing to have to do.'

Laming nodded, and he took note of her resolve. Isabella had not recoiled at the revelation: she had presumed it to be necessity – cruel necessity. Truly, she was a woman of uncommon mettle, a silver lining in the great black cloud that was this audacious adventure.

The air was cold and clear, and the prospect of the city now distinct. He recognized the tower of the cathedral, and the Tête du Pont, the fort guarding the bridge across the Guadiana; he could even see the gate at the other end, Las Palmas. He wanted to halt and take out his telescope, as he would have done in 1812, but he was not here as a soldier; he was a diplomatic traveller, said his papers – there was no cause for surveillance. It was perhaps as well, for as they joined the post road which connected Elvas and Badajoz, he saw the *alcázabar* quite plainly, the castle where Hervey was confined, and looking every bit as formidable as that night of the assault. It chilled him to the marrow, the sight as well as the recollection.

In half an hour more they were close enough to the bridge to make out its traffic. Laming saw that it flowed mainly towards the Las Palmas gate, as he had hoped, since the day was drawing to its close. That worked to their advantage, as he had calculated, but he hoped it would ease by the time they needed to recross. How he wished the approaches were not by bridge at all, or at least not by just the one: when it came to the escape it was this or nothing, for the Guadiana stood between them and Portugal for more miles south than they could ride. Fording it was impossible at this time of year, if at any, and swimming – three hundred yards at the very least – perilous beyond question. Perhaps without Isabella Delgado ... *No*, he would not allow himself to think like that. When the time came, no matter if the alarm had been raised, one way or another they must get across that bridge.

CHAPTER TWENTY-THREE
BRAVE HORATIUS

Later

The sun was beginning its evening descent behind them as the little party approached the Tête du Pont. General Phillipon had taken brief refuge nearby when Badajoz had fallen – the Sixth had been close when he surrendered his sword the next day – but Laming could give it barely a passing thought. They were approaching the first of the half-dozen certain occasions for challenge, and therefore exposure. For himself he felt no fear; for his 'command', and the enterprise, he was almost contorted by it.

But the guards at the bridge merely returned the courier's wave as the party clattered onto the cobbled ramp. They recognized him well enough (his passage was as good as daily). Laming had brought him forward for just this purpose – to reassure if Dom Mateo's man at point somehow aroused suspicion – but the ease of passing, with no check whatever, surprised him yet. It augured well for their recrossing.

At the other side, at the gate of Las Palmas, it was the same: a wave, no undue interest in any of them, even Isabella (there were several Spanish girls on foot happily distracting the soldiery). And then they were inside the fortress-city itself. No one would challenge them now unless they drew attention to themselves. All they had to do was make their way to the *alcázabar*, and once inside its walls they would follow the courier, and then Isabella would lead the way to Hervey's quarters, dealing with the challenges which were sure to come. The courier had told them precisely where he was confined (the Spanish had made no secret of it); it would not be difficult – the third, top, floor of the building overlooking the garden. Laming wondered again if they might not have taken the courier into their confidence; but Dom Mateo had been insistent – he would trust no one but his own, and the man was not even a soldier.

In twenty minutes they were at the gates of the *alcázabar*. It might have been less, but there were a great many people in the streets. Laming was already worrying about making their way back: if the alarm was raised, there would be a signal, so that the bridges over the Guadiana and the Rivellas would be closed. With a press of people in the streets it could take a half-hour and more. But then, if it took them only *five* minutes, and the alarm was sounded, they would be just as hoist . . .

The sentry did not recognize the courier. He took his papers and studied them carefully. Then he called for his corporal.

Laming's heart pounded.

Isabella threw back her hood and rode forward as the corporal came out of the guardhouse.

'Tio Pepe!' called the corporal, seeing the courier and slapping the sentry playfully on the back, assuring him that it was only old 'Tio Pepe' from Elvas.

Laming held in his sigh of relief as the corporal beckoned the party through. There were nods, smiles, waves: he was too relieved to despise the laxity which would have brought a swift court martial to any of the Sixth's NCOs.

* * *

They dismounted in the middle of the great courtyard. A groom came to take the courier's horse, as usual, but Isabella politely declined his offer to bring more holders. They would not stay long, she explained.

As the courier took the despatch bags to the post office, Laming, Isabella and Corporal Wainwright made for Hervey's quarters, leaving Dom Mateo's captain to guard the horses – and their retreat.

To Laming's surprise and equal relief there was no sentry at the entrance to the building. It would be an even greater blessing on the way out, he reckoned, for if there was any mishap, a sentry at the entrance would be able to rouse the whole courtyard in an instant.

They climbed the spiral stone staircase quickly but quietly (better to give no warning of their approach, with or without the password). On the first floor there were three guards, all seated. They stood as Isabella appeared, but did not challenge.

Laming was too relieved to be suspicious.

As they reached the second floor, a door opened and an officer appeared in what looked like levee dress. He glanced at them, at Isabella principally, looked as if he would question them, and then instead bowed and said simply 'Señora, señores' before making his way past them and down the stairs. Laming wondered if his face betrayed anything of his thoughts: he had been certain the game was up. He looked at Isabella. She appeared as cool as if she had title to the place. He nodded, and they began the final flight of stairs.

The light on the upper floor was poorer, no window but a high lancet, and few candles, but Laming saw at once the pistols on the table next to the two guards, and the sword-bayonets in the cross-belts hanging over the backs of their chairs. The men, though clearly startled, made no attempt to recover them, relieved, perhaps, that it had not been their serjeant.

Isabella spoke. 'I am come to question Major Hervey.'

The guards looked at each other.

'It is authorized,' said Isabella curtly. '*Napoleon*.'

They looked at each other again. Why should a woman come to question the prisoner? Why had they not been told before?

Laming saw he had but seconds only. His hand began moving to his pocket.

Then one of the guards, grumbling loudly, reached for the key which hung by a nail on the wall above the table. The other looked uncertain still, but the first guard put the key in the lock, hesitated a moment, then turned it and pulled open the door.

'Wait here, please, señores,' said Isabella.

If the guards had had a mind to search the party, Isabella confounded them utterly. She was not carrying anything, and they could hardly search her person. And the two men, of whom they might be rightly more suspicious, were not in any case going to enter the prisoner's quarters. There was nothing they could do but trust they were doing right; here, very evidently, was a lady of rank. Who were they, mere private-men, to question her?

Isabella advanced. The guard held the door open, then closed it after her.

Laming and Wainwright each whipped out a brace of pistols. Wainwright's were pressed to the turnkey's neck before the door was locked. The second guard looked so frightened that Laming only had to gesture to get him on his knees.

Hervey flung the door open. It had been many years: unlike Corporal Wainwright, he had not seen Laming at Hounslow, and never had he imagined that circumstances such as these would reunite them. Laming's eyes were wild, and his jaw set firm – as at Talavera when they had had to hack him out of the fight with the *chasseurs*. For his part,

337

Laming saw only the uniform of the Sixth, and at that moment wished with all his heart that he wore it still.

There was no time for elaborate greeting: there were two guards to deal with. Hervey held out his hand, Laming indicated that both his were full, and the ice was broken with grim smiles.

Wainwright had brought lint and silk cord. The intention was not to do harm, simply to disable and confine. That way, Laming had calculated, the Spanish were least likely to make diplomatic complaint.

'I'm glad to see you, Corporal Wainwright,' said Hervey, nodding in return to the salute. Then, covered by Laming's pistols, they began stuffing the lint into the guards' mouths, binding it with cord, tying their hands behind their backs and pushing them into Hervey's erstwhile cell.

Laming braced as he saw the unexpected figure in the middle of the room.

Isabella shook her head, as if to say there was no cause for concern.

'Laming, this is Dr Sanchez, without whom you would not be here.'

But Sanchez himself looked anxious – indeed, very anxious.

Hervey sought to reassure him. 'I had no idea it would be so soon. Shall we bind you, as the guards?'

It was a calculation requiring more time than they had. But Sanchez feared staying more than fleeing. 'I will come with you.'

Laming shook his head. 'We do not have a horse.'

Sanchez understood. 'I have a horse. But it will take me time to fetch and saddle it.'

Laming nodded. 'It is better that he goes now. The guards will know him. It should be easy.'

Hervey gripped Sanchez's arm reassuringly. 'Go, my

friend. We will wait here five minutes, and then we must all leave.'

Laming watched him go, and uneasily. This was something he had not foreseen. Would he have let him go if he had been able to consider it thoroughly? But what could he do, for Hervey would not have him bound against his will?

The minutes crept by. At least the guards made no sound. But Laming grew more uneasy. It had ever been the cavalry rule that no gain repaid delay. He had lived by the precept long enough, and Hervey even more. He would not have believed that any cornet – let alone a colonel and a major – would have settled for such a thing. Why, indeed, did he defer to Hervey now? 'We *must* go. The guard commander might come at any moment. It's fatal to delay further.'

'I said we would wait five minutes, Laming. There are two more. In truth he needs fifteen.'

'Then let us at least descend the stairs. Better to wait at the door. There was no sentry.'

Hervey frowned, and began putting on the coat which Wainwright had brought. 'Very well. But let me lead.'

'*I* shall lead, Major Hervey,' said Isabella emphatically.

Laming cursed silently; was this his 'command' or not? But Isabella spoke sense: the password and imperious Spanish were needed, not brawn and pistols. 'Dona Isabella shall lead. I shall follow, then you, Hervey, and Corporal Wainwright.'

Wainwright locked the door behind them as Hervey picked up two pistols from the table, checked they were primed, and seized one of the swordbelts.

Laming shook his head. 'It is too conspicuous.'

Isabella took it from him, slung it over her shoulder and pulled her cloak about her to conceal it. 'Come,' she said.

Laming stifled his protest. 'Very well.'

They began their exit as quietly as they had come.

Laming now realized that the staircase, although square rather than circular, descended (unusually) clockwise, giving the advantage to the man below, pistol or sword in-hand, rather than to the one above. He wished he had gone first.

But then, Isabella knew she would have the advantage of surprise, for who would imagine a woman to have any fighting intent?

The floor below was empty, as before, and they passed quickly along it to the other end.

They descended to the first floor, where the guards had let them pass without challenge on the way up. Laming saw they were not the same. But that was good: they would not count an extra man, if they counted at all.

The guards rose, as the others had, and looked at Isabella, curious.

'Thank you, we are leaving now,' she said, assuredly.

The older of the two guards touched his peak. '*Sí, señora. Contraseña*?'

'Napoleon!'

The man touched his peak again and stepped aside. Laming, Hervey and Wainwright each looked him in the eye as they passed, and nodded.

Laming was still anxious. They must have taken ten minutes already to come this far, he reckoned: he wanted to quicken the pace.

Isabella would not be hurried, however. She took each step as if she were descending to a carriage in front of her household.

As they turned the final corner, the door into the court-yard now but a couple of dozen strides away, Laming saw the same officer in his levee dress as on the way in. He reached for his pocket, certain they would be discovered.

Isabella, too, hesitated a moment, then thought better of it, curtsied, lowered then raised her eyes to what she prayed was her best advantage, and continued walking.

The officer, hatless (a bicorn under his left arm), halted and made a low bow. '*Señora!*'

As he rose, she tried fixing him with her eyes as the others passed. But gallant – and manly – though the officer was, he was too well bred to ignore other gentlemen for the sparkle of fine eyes. He bowed again – '*Señores!*' – and looked at each in turn.

They too bowed.

He looked again at Hervey, and his forehead creased into the inevitable question.

'The English officer is taking his recreation with us, señor,' tried Isabella.

Laming was astounded by her composure: she was so convincing!

But not entirely. The Spanish officer continued to look puzzled. '*Señora*, forgive me, but I know nothing of such an arrangement, and I am captain of the guard.'

'It is by arrangement with the general,' replied Isabella.

Laming was even more astounded: Isabella thought as nimbly on her feet as he had heard she could dance with a foil in her hand!

The officer smiled awkwardly. 'Of course, señora, forgive me. But you will understand: it is my duty to see all these things are arranged perfectly. May I ask you to wait here for just a little time while I acquaint myself with these new orders. Please, be seated.' He indicated the chairs by the wall.

Neither Laming nor Hervey could follow the exchange precisely, but the import was clear. Both began moving hands to their pistols.

But Isabella decided things. Her sword was out of its scabbard in an instant, the point at the officer's neck. It made the merest crease in the flesh under his chin, but enough to convince him of her skill. Three pistols now pointed at him, too, so that he must know that death would come at once if he made the slightest sound.

And yet, if one pistol were to fire, the castle guard would be upon them before they could cross the courtyard. He may have been duped by fine eyes, but the captain of the guard was no coward – and he would *not* be disarmed by a woman! He jerked his head back and grabbed for the sword.

Isabella's reflex was quicker. She lunged. Before he could let out a sound the point burst through his windpipe.

Laming sprang with his pistol, felling him with a single blow, the barrel drawing blood while the first drops ran yet an inch down Isabella's blade.

She recovered her sword calmly, though when Hervey saw her face he knew what it had done. Her eyes were distant, her olive skin pale as ivory. He wanted to support her.

'Get his body behind those chairs, Corporal!' snapped Laming, his own hand shaking, though no one saw. 'Hervey, what's happening outside?'

Hervey, jolted, made for the open door. He saw Dom Mateo's captain of dragoons and the four horses. 'Your man's there with the horses, but there's no sign of Sanchez.'

'Well, it's too late now,' rasped Laming. There was no profit, either, in wondering what would have happened if they had waited another two minutes above stairs. For all they knew, the Spanish officer might have been making his rounds.

Hervey did not demur. He looked anxiously at Isabella, but she was unfastening the swordbelt. He handed her a pistol, without speaking.

They walked out into the courtyard with no apparent haste, and the captain of dragoons nodded to say that all was well. Corporal Wainwright pulled a knife from his pocket and cut the faux-baggage free from the 'packhorse'. The courier came out of the despatch office, in ignorance still of his companions' design, or even of the purpose, handed a piece of silver to the groom holding his horse, and mounted in anticipation of a leisured ride back to Elvas.

Laming helped Isabella into the saddle. She rode astride, as many a continental woman; he reckoned it might give her the advantage if she had to aim her pistol on the off-side. The thought amazed him.

He mounted, and beckoned urgently to the others to do the same. Corporal Wainwright, ever correct, waited by his horse as Hervey looked about for the man who had been accomplice to his escape.

He looked in vain. Laming, agitated in high degree now, beckoned furiously.

Hervey at last sprang into the saddle. Though despairing of leaving his friend, he felt keenly the sudden sense of liberation, the contact with leather again like a friendly voice welcoming him home.

Then, *relief* – the noise of iron on cobbles, and the sight of Sanchez and his cob . . .

'*Deo Gratias*,' muttered Laming, as he nodded to the courier to lead on.

Laming looked at his watch as they approached the Las Palmas gate again. It had taken less than half an hour from the time they had entered the *alcázabar*, yet it felt five times as long. They were making too slow a progress. The press of people was even greater than before, a sort of early-evening promenade before the light failed and the chill of the night air took hold.

There was another half an hour to dusk, perhaps three-quarters, but no more. And then it would be dark quickly, and they would have to ride the road a good way before the moon came up. Was that cause for worry? The courier knew the way, and the captain of dragoons knew the secret crossing. Laming would choose which when the time came. But for now, every step was the greatest trial, for at any moment the alarm might sound. How long could it be before two guards were discovered absent from their post, or an officer dead and only very partially concealed? If only he dared speak, dared share his thoughts; but to risk a word of English, even in this crowding babble, would be folly. No, they must ride for the bridge confident in their own daring, confident that the authorities could not expect there to be Englishmen in possession of both the parole and the means of passing themselves off as Spanish.

He trembled at the very audacity of it. Indeed, *now*, the plan looked not so much audacious as reckless – so many things to go wrong, so few alternatives but to press on. Perhaps, though, that was the very reason for their success so far – no opportunity for diversion, only the need for utter resolve. *That*, and Isabella Delgado! He could scarcely believe how much they owed to her. Without her, even if they had been able to overpower the guards, the cat would have been out of the bag by now, and a hue and cry that would have blocked every street in the city.

A bullock-cart full of wine butts creaked agonizingly slowly through the Las Palmas gate, blocking all traffic onto the bridge. Laming saw it was clear beyond, however: they could take it at the trot, make up a little time, without drawing undue attention to themselves. If only the alarm did not sound. If only . . .

One of the bullocks, lame, began bellowing in protest at its load, or at the goading of its driver and the sentries. In the confines of the gate-arch the noise was so bad that Laming's horse – and then the others – became nervous, stamping and snorting, trampling several people in the press. The dragoon captain's began rearing. He sat it well, though, calmly, letting his hands and weight forward rather than fighting her. But one of the bullocks strained so hard at the yoke that the one behind fell to its knees, terrifying the mare so much that she threw herself back wildly, hooves flying from under her on the smooth cobbles. The captain fell clear as his mare toppled onto her back, but his head hit the cobbles hard.

The sentries rushed to him, pulling him clear of the mare as she struggled to get to her feet. They opened his cloak and collar to give him air. Then one of them stood up, as if he had seen a ghost.

Laming saw it too. Not a ghost, but a red coat, the prideful dolman of the Corps of Guides. He cursed him for a fool beneath his breath.

In the instant the guards saw red, Laming saw his fence change from hurdle to palisade.

The guards drew back: who wore red but the British? And why did they wear it concealed? They raised their muskets, gesturing at the riders.

Isabella, brave as the lioness, saw where her duty lay. She urged her mare forward. 'This man is a spy,' she declared boldly, but keeping her voice low. 'He is our most *important* spy and we must get him to Elvas as soon as may be!'

Neither Laming nor Hervey understood, though they knew the word 'spy' well enough, but the expressions on the faces of the guards told them that all was not yet lost.

'*Spy*, señora?'

'Yes! Spy! Look, he comes-to. Help him back into the saddle!'

Hervey held his breath. Why did they not challenge?

'Señora, I must call the serjeant. We have no orders.'

Laming began moving his hand slowly to his pistol, Hervey likewise: the guards evidently accepted Isabella as a woman of rank, but were wary still. Could they know of 'the English prisoner', that there might be an attempt to rescue him? It was possible: there was but the one bridge over the Guadiana, and only the one way onto it. This would be the way the prisoner would bolt if he was able to break out of the *alcázabar*.

345

A crack like thunder braced the guards, as if bellowed at by their corporal.

Laming's heart fell: the signal gun! He gripped his pistol, but he stayed his hand yet. What would the gun compel the guards to do?

A second gun fired from the walls of the *alcázabar*. The guards rushed to close the gates, heaving on them as if their lives depended on it. Men came tumbling from the guard-house across the square.

Hervey leapt from the saddle, reins in-hand, Wainwright following. 'Go!' he shouted at Isabella. 'Go, doctor!'

They dragged the half-conscious captain through the arch despite the protests of the guards backing away, wary of the unsettled horses. Laming grabbed the fractious mare's reins and pulled her after them, barging aside one of the guards just in time to slip through as the gates slammed shut.

They were safe for the moment, long enough at least to get the captain back into the saddle. He had come-to: he was well, he protested; it was nothing, they need have no fear, they should make at once for the other side.

Hervey and Wainwright heaved him astride his mare. She settled at last as he gathered the reins, though a stirrup evaded him. He looked dazed still as the rest of them remounted and kicked for the other side.

This was the way General Phillipon had galloped to free-dom the day after Badajoz, and it had been a short liberty, gone to ground in Fort San Cristobal until Wellington's men found him the following morning. Could they now get as far as the fort, even? Hervey, too, was beginning to doubt it. At the other end of the bridge was the Tête du Pont – not a gate, but a strongpoint nevertheless. It straddled their line of escape; except that its purpose was to guard the bridge from assault, not command what passed on it. But there would be soldiers there. How many, he couldn't know: perhaps they only garrisoned the place at times of danger? But if it *were* garrisoned, the signal gun must have told them to do something. He dearly hoped it would be to take post facing the approaches rather than the bridge itself.

'Kick on!' snapped Laming. 'We take the bridge at the trot, and at the other end we wheel sharp left for the road to Elvas. No looking back!'

Hervey marked his old friend's determination. If any fell there would be no going back for them.

'Major Hervey, sir: look!'

Hervey turned to see the gatehouse walls alive with men. He was thankful that Wainwright, at least, took more notice of his duty than Laming's commands.

They had not gone fifty yards before a volley sent musket balls whistling about their ears. Laming at once pressed to a faster trot, though the cobbles were treacherous. Hervey looked back again and saw the gates opening. He expected cavalry to burst out after them like hounds in full cry.

There was cavalry, all right, but they seemed loathe to follow.

Hervey saw why. At the far side the guards were mustering, not with cavalry but a cannon. Would they sweep the bridge with grape when they knew there was a woman with them – and an English officer? He could scarce believe it. But how would they know who they fired at? The signal gun told them there were fugitives, and evidently the drill was to rake the bridge.

Laming would not surrender, however. 'We must ride them down before they're ready!' he shouted, pistol aloft and spurring into a canter.

Hervey kicked hard after him. If only they had sabres: the mere promise of steel could make a guncrew panic!

There was another volley from the Las Palmas gate. Hervey looked round to make sure Wainwright and the captain were with him still.

They weren't. The captain's mare lay sprawled on the

cobbles, her quarters crimson, her rider under her. Hervey cursed and reined hard round.

'No, sir! Go on, I can do it,' shouted Wainwright.

But Hervey had left a man behind a dozen years ago, at Waterloo. He would not do it again.

'Go on, sir!' insisted Wainwright. 'There's Mrs Delgado!'

What was he thinking? It was Isabella they must get away. The rest, himself included, must take their chance. He turned the gelding even sharper and kicked hard for the far end.

In seconds it was a desperate, close-quarter business. The gunners cowered, but a line of bayonets was doubling from the Tête du Pont. Laming, reins looped and both pistols cocked, rode straight at the gun. 'Go on!' he shouted to the others. 'See her safe!'

Isabella, Sanchez and the bewildered courier raced past him, but Hervey pulled up and thrust his pistol at one of the gunners. '*Espada! Espada! Presto!*'

The terrified gunner gave it him, expecting a ball in the chest at any moment.

'*Espada!*' demanded Hervey again, and another of them gave up his sword, to Laming.

Now they felt as if they could fight rather than just fire and run. But two dozen bayonets were no odds to sport with.

'Come on, Hervey, we've got to get her away!'

Hervey looked back across the bridge: Wainwright had the captain astride his own mare. He was determined. 'We've got to hold those bayonets off the bridge, Laming! Leave these: let's front *them*!'

Laming didn't hesitate. They rode straight at the line, breaking it in two places, then turning and charging back to break it in another two. That was what dismayed infantry – spoiling 'the touch of cloth'! Another go and Hervey was certain they would scatter them.

He looked back at the bridge. The gunners hadn't given

up. They were already ramming. The gun would soon be loaded-primed. He saw Wainwright struggling to lead his mare, saw the puffs of smoke from the ragged musketry at the far end of the bridge, and then the captain bowled from the saddle like a running hare to buckshot. At two hundred yards it could only have been luck, but a ball in the back at that range was the end. He saw Wainwright crouching by him – it seemed an age – until he was certain of what Hervey could only suppose. Then Wainwright sprang back into the saddle and spurred for the Tête du Pont.

But the way was barred. The gunners were determined. The bridge-end bristled with handspikes, spontoons, muskets, and half a dozen of the bayonets with the nerve to run that far. The ventsman was putting in the primer-quill; in seconds more it would be 'Stand clear!' And then a hundred one-ounce iron balls would mangle every bit of flesh on the bridge.

'No!' bellowed Laming. 'No, Hervey!'

Hervey jerked the bit, and the gelding pulled up. It was futile.

Wainwright, too, saw there was no way forward or back.

Hervey reeled as a man lunged at him from the cover of the brush, the bayonet tearing through his cloak and into the saddle. He plunged the straight, thin blade of the artilleryman's sword between collarbone and neck. As the man fell lifeless, Hervey looked back in dread for his covering corporal.

His jaw fell open. Wainwright, with not even a sabre as goad, was urging his little Lusitano onto the parapet. Then, Horatius-like, he leapt, astride her still, into the deep, dark Guadiana.

CHAPTER TWENTY-FOUR
BATTLE HONOURS

Badajoz, late afternoon, 7 April 1812

'Sixth Light Dragoons, draw swords!' Lieutenant-Colonel Lord George Irvine, turned-out as immaculately as if on Horse Guards, gave the words of command with the confidence and pride of one who did so under the gaze of both his own and the defeated commanders-in-chief.

Five hundred sabres were drawn from their scabbards with a flourish, to rest, vertical, awaiting the next order.

'Sixth Light Dragoons, *salute*!'

The private-men remained braced, as the officers brought their swords first to the 'kiss' and then down and outwards, flat-side offered, to their chargers' right flank.

There was no band, no double lines of infantrymen at the 'present'. The Earl of Wellington (as lately he had been created) showed courtesy to General Phillipon; he did not render him military honours. Had the French surrendered *before* the assault on the fortress, they would have been able to march to their captivity bearing arms and colours. Since they had forced the issue – *and* after a practicable breach had been made – they were lucky to be spared their lives.

Not that there wasn't a deal of respect – grudging respect – for the tenacity with which they had defended the place:

the army had turned its anger on the Spanish in the city rather than on the beaten French.

Out of the San Cristobal fort, to which he had galloped over the Guadiana bridge in the early hours, when Wellington's redcoats had finally taken the *alcázabar*, General Phillipon and his staff rode at a parade-walk. At fifty yards, the distance Hervey now stood from him, he looked every inch one of Bonaparte's generals – the braid, the sashes, the plumes, the ribbons, all resplendent in the late-afternoon sun. A little closer and Hervey would have seen the tired truth, as did Lord Wellington now as he received the general's sword. Defeat went hard with such a man.

When the Sixth were stood down half an hour later, Sir Edward Lankester sought Hervey out. 'The provost marshal's men will want a deposition from you regarding the Spanish girl. Larpent intends putting up the gallows.'

Hervey nodded. Wellington's judge-advocate-general was a punctilious man; he would suppose there were accomplices to the murder. 'Of course, Sir Edward, but in truth I saw only the one man – and he can say nothing.'

Sir Edward smiled, but grimly. 'The deposition is for your own benefit, Hervey. You can't go about shooting His Majesty's soldiers without remark!'

'No, of course not, Sir Edward! I meant that—'

'I know what you meant. Had I the means last night I'd have had a dozen of them shot down. It was infamous.'

'Just so, sir.'

Sir Edward fingered the loose bevel on Jessye's throat plume. 'This needs the armourer's hammer.'

'Sir.'

'After they've seen to the sabres. God, what a sight they were!'

Hervey raised an eyebrow. The fifty yards between

351

Wellington and the regiment had worked not solely to Phillipon's advantage.

'Lord George wants to see you.'

'See me, Sir Edward?'

'Yes, *see* you! Do not have me repeat myself.'

Hervey blinked. It was easy to forget that Sir Edward Lankester could be as tired as any of them. He saluted, handed his reins to his groom, and went to find his commanding officer. He did not see Sir Edward smiling wryly.

'Mr Barrow?'

The adjutant spun round, still holding his charger's near-fore. 'What is it, Hervey? I'm deuced busy!'

'Sir Edward said the colonel wished to see me.'

Barrow gestured to his groom to take the horse's foot. 'Dry it and lime-bag it,' he said wearily, then turned back to Hervey. 'Come with me.'

They set off for the regiment's headquarters.

'What does the colonel want to see me for?'

'I'll leave that to him,' said the adjutant, firmly.

Hervey knew he was guilty of no offence – in any case, the adjutant would have been first to notify him of it – but he was becoming anxious nevertheless. He had never spoken directly to the commanding officer before, other than the usual civilities in the mess.

'Mr Hervey, Colonel,' Barrow announced, at the door of the white-walled hut which served as regimental headquarters.

Lord George looked up from his writing table. 'Come in, Hervey. Thank you, Barrow.'

The adjutant left them, which Hervey knew to be irregular, but Lord George, though tired, did not look like a man about to deliver a reprimand.

He saluted. 'Good afternoon, Colonel.'

'Good afternoon, Hervey. Stand easy, take off your hat.'

Hervey did so gratefully.

'Now, last night: you were witness to murder. The Eighty-eighth's colonel has asked to speak with you on it. I have agreed, and the provost marshal has no objection.'

'Very good, Colonel.'

'A dreadful affair, but it was an act of courage on your part that prevented further outrage.'

Hervey said nothing. He knew that the mother and her two daughters had been interviewed already by at least three doctors, a chaplain and one of Judge-Advocate-General Larpent's men.

'You shall have a promotion.'

Hervey's spirits leapt. And then they sank again as he realized it would be promotion for shooting a man in red rather than the enemy – a cruel irony after three years' fighting. 'Sir, I had not expected—'

'No doubt, no doubt,' said Lord George, leaning well back in an old leather chair. 'The promotion is not in the Sixth, I regret to say.'

The words were like a cold douche. Hervey's stomach tightened.

'There just isn't the vacancy. It would be in the Royals.'

A promotion in Lord George's old regiment (and evidently, therefore, of his arranging) – Hervey knew he was rewarded *and* honoured. 'I thank you, Colonel. It would be a great privilege.'

Lord George nodded.

'But I could not accept.'

'*What?*'

Hervey was surprised his commanding officer appeared not to understand. 'Colonel, these past three years I have come to know a good many men in the Sixth, and to trust them – and they me, I believe – and I would see the war to its end in their company. With respect, Colonel.'

Lord George leaned forward again, and sighed. 'Sit down, Hervey.'

Hervey pulled a wooden stool towards the writing table.

'I greatly admire your sentiment, but there can be no promotion in the Sixth for a year at least. I don't say the war will be ended by then, but it can't run much longer in Spain now that Badajoz is ours.'

Hervey shifted awkwardly. 'I understand, Colonel.'

'Do you? This lieutenant's vacancy is solely on account of circumstances in the Royals. Their colonel has asked me if I have a nomination. That is unlikely ever to occur again.'

Hervey felt his certainty only increasing. 'Colonel, with the very greatest of respect, I request to remain in the regiment.'

Lord George shook his head, but he smiled just perceptibly, too. 'Hervey, I shan't call you a damned fool, though others might. You may, of course, remain cornet in the regiment. And, I might add, I myself shall be pleased of it. You have scarce put a foot wrong since we came to the Peninsula.'

'Thank you, Colonel.'

'Very well, you may go. And you may tell Sir Edward that he may collect his champagne when next we are in proper quarters!'

Hervey returned the smile as he replaced his Tarleton, and saluted.

As he walked back to A Troop's lines, the sun now low in the sky behind him, he gazed east. The men with bayonets had broken open the door to Spain (Lord George had said it). Now it would be a run to the French border. They might get a footing in France itself before the allies in the east could get across the Rhine. Might they even ride to Paris? He could not say how many miles that would be, but already they must have marched a thousand – *more* – since first they had come to the Peninsula with Sir John Moore. He knew full well, as Lord George had said, that some would call him a damned fool to turn down promotion – and in a regiment like the Royals. But how could he leave men with whom he had shared so much? Perhaps there would not be so much fighting with the bayonet now? But in that case there would be more work for the cavalry to do . . .

Hervey wondered what his troop-leader would say – Sir Edward and his 'long point'. Perhaps, indeed, the point had not yet begun: perhaps they were only now going to bolt their fox, from his earth in Badajoz. Monsieur Reynard would then be running over country he knew well, and they would be hunting him with followers strung out all the way from Lisbon.

No matter which way he looked at it, Hervey was sure he had made the right decision. Three sieges it had cost the army to take this place, and now he could turn his back on it for ever and fix his gaze, albeit by his map still, on the Pyrenees.

CHAPTER TWENTY-FIVE
UNHAPPY RETURNS

Reeves's Hotel, Rua do Prior, Lisbon, 8 January 1827

Private Johnson put more wood on the fire, and shook his head. 'I bet it won't be any colder there, that's all I can say.'

Hervey took less consolation in this dubious proposition than his groom might suppose. 'Thank you, Johnson. I think, however, the prospect of England is not a warming one.'

'Well I'm fed up wi' this place. Tha d'n't know 'ho to trust.'

'I beg your pardon, Johnson, but one knows very well whom to trust.'

Johnson frowned. 'Tha knows what I mean, sir.'

Hervey sighed. 'Yes, I know what you mean.'

'Will tha be gooin' to see Mrs Delgado again?'

'Yes,' Hervey replied, warily. 'But not for a day or so, I would imagine.'

'I like Mrs Delgado.'

'Yes, Johnson, so you have never failed to inform me.'

He had not minced words with his groom for years. Indeed, Johnson was less a soldier-servant, more *family*, of sorts. Hervey knew well enough what were Johnson's thoughts: they were simple, probably too simple. But what *was* there to stop him riding to Belem and asking for

Isabella's hand? It was what he desired, was it not? There would be vexations, on account of Isabella's religion no doubt, but they could be overcome. There was no woman he admired more – save his sister. And Isabella excited in him as much passion as any he had felt in . . . well, it was better that he make no comparison in that regard. Did he *love* her? He believed he did. Why was he not certain? Because a part of him – the part that loved in the way he had once known – had died in the snowy wastes of America along with Henrietta.

But what of Isabella herself? What could be her feelings for him? They had not spoken on any terms of intimacy; she had given no sign. He was long past any diffidence that would inhibit a proposal on these grounds, but how might he love a woman – take a woman as his wife – who did not at heart share his regard or passion?

Or was that the adolescent's, the romantic's, notion – the very thing he had resolved to be done with? If there had been one profit in his caging in Badajoz it was (he flattered himself) an understanding of his condition. That, and a resolution to put unsatisfactory matters to rights. He had hoped to be spared any public discipline, yet he knew in truth that atonement without penance was not possible. Especially was this true where Colonel Norris was concerned. Perhaps he ought not to be too dismissive of Norris's tiresome caution. Men had died, after all, in the course of his own designing.

'An' I don't see why there should be all this trouble either.' Johnson sounded quite decided.

'There was only ever a possibility of avoiding trouble, as you call it, if things remained in Lisbon. I was lost as soon as the Horse Guards learned of it, let alone the War Office.'

'Will Corporal Wainwright get in trouble?'

Hervey shook his head at the thought of his covering corporal on the bridge: the courage was one thing, the presence of mind quite another. 'I cannot think even Colonel Norris could see anything but honour in what Wainwright did. I'm determined he shall have some reward.'

'Ah wish ah'd seen it. Why didn't 'e just jump wi'out 'is 'orse, though?'

Hervey shook his head again. 'He said he thought he would be a burden without her!'

Johnson nodded, perfectly understanding. 'An' 'e's still only a young'n!'

'Indeed, Johnson.' He started searching again among the paraphernalia of uniform piled ready for packing. 'Where is my button-stick?'

'But that doctor were brave an' all.'

Hervey looked up. 'You know, Johnson, it was fifteen years ago, the business at Badajoz. I could never have imagined what long shadows it cast. I didn't tell you the other two daughters died of fever before the war was ended, and that his wife took her own life not long after. He might have been a broken man – or, at least, a very bitter one. Yet I never met a *kinder* man.'

'Will 'e be in trouble, d'ye think, sir?'

Hervey shrugged. 'He cannot very well return to Spain, at least for a while. Mr Forbes at the legation is taking good care of him. They spoke of some employment in the Americas. I shall see him again before we leave, I hope.' He threw up his hands in frustration. 'Where *is* that button-stick?'

Johnson laid down the bellows. 'Why don't tha let me do that, sir. Sit down and 'ave thi coffee while it's 'ot.'

Hervey sighed. He had no need of the button-stick anyway, except to occupy his mind. He sat in the armchair by the smoking fire and poured out some of the thick black brew which Johnson had perfected over many years of improvisation with the most unpromising of raw materials, and then picked up the letter again. 'I must tell you frankly, Johnson: the Duke of York is greatly angered. Lord John Howard tells me all in this, here.'

Johnson took up the poker again, and scowled. 'Ay. But t'Duke'd never 'ave known if Colonel Norris 'adn't told 'im.'

'Except that the Spanish ambassador has probably also protested.'

Johnson stopped poking the fire, and turned with a look of uncharacteristic anxiety. 'Sir, tha doesn't think tha'll be—'

'What?'

'Well, I don't know rightly – whatever it is as 'appens to an officer.'

'Cashiered?'

'Ay, sir.'

'Quite possibly. I imagine the Horse Guards would not go to the trouble of ordering a general court martial otherwise.'

'An' tha's not worried?'

Hervey half laughed. 'Johnson, in truth I'm so dismayed by how we seem to arrange things in the army that I hardly care *what* happens. I believe I may say that I would not do the same again, for I see all too clearly how things have become, but in all honesty I cannot regret what I did, for it was all I had learned in these eighteen years a soldier.'

'Ay, well said, Major 'Ervey. An' Gen'ral Clinton says 'e'll speak for thee, doesn't 'e?'

'Oh yes, have no fear, Johnson. There'll be testimonials enough. But if the Duke of York is as angered as Lord John says he is, it will be to no avail. He's an old man, and a sick one too. His opinions are more decided by the day, and they are not favourable to junior officers who take things upon themselves, especially in the face of their seniors.'

'All this is because of Colonel Norris.'

'All this is because of *me*, Johnson. I cannot escape the responsibility.'

Johnson stood up and looked at the fire despairingly: no wood he could find in this place gave off any heat. 'Very Christian that is, Major 'Ervey. Some consolation to thee, I suppose.'

Hervey scowled back.

'An' why 'asn't tha been to see Mrs Delgado an' 'er father?'

'What has that to do with it? I told you anyway: I have been, and shall go again as soon as I am able. You forget, perhaps, I am in open arrest.'

'Colonel Laming's been to see 'er.'

'I am glad to hear it. But I cannot call on her and her father before Colonel Norris gives me leave.'

'Tha knows they might go to England? On account o' t'trouble 'ere.'

Hervey looked surprised. 'No, I did not. How did you come by this?'

'Colonel Laming's man.'

Hervey's eyes widened. 'I compliment you on your sources, I'm sure!'

'Ay, 'e 'eard they'd be gooin' by t'end o't'month.'

'Well, I have not seen Colonel Laming these last few days, I regret to say.' Hervey sounded especially thoughtful. 'He has important duties with General Clinton. He says he will come by tonight, all being well.'

But what came instead that night was a letter:

Head Quarters,
Valle de Pereira Barracks
8th January 1827

My dear Hervey,

I am prevented by only the most urgent duty from calling on you this evening, for there are matters with

which I would acquaint you in person, and so I am
obliged to depose these matters here instead, and would
beg your indulgence, confident that you of all men will
know the urgent delicacy of what we are about. You will
be pleased to learn, for every good reason, that Sir
William Clinton is inclined to base his dispositions in the
very largest measure upon your design, for he has
learned from M. Saldanha the Minister of War that the
Miguelites will next renew their offensive in Minho and
Tras os Montes, but that M. Saldanha is confident of
the Portuguese army so long as there are English troops
not too distant who would thereby demonstrate to the
Miguelites that whatever success they might enjoy in the
provinces it would never take them to Lisbon. Half our
army is therefore to march forthwith to the Mondego,
and shall have its Head Quarters at Coimbra. The
remainder shall occupy the Tagus forts with a view to
securing the peace of the capital and to be in a position
to reinforce the garrison at Elvas if that front should
become active. The Spanish announce that they are to
form an army of observation of fifteen thousand men in
Estremadura, this to guard against advance from
Portugal, which notion is of course entirely without
justification, and it is the opinion of M. Saldanha that
the true purpose is to check the Miguelites, which they
protest they are now certain to do. In any case, there is
to be no occupying the lines of Torres Vedras, save for a
very few forts. Instead if the division on the Mondego is
obliged to withdraw, or withdraws to shorten its lines of
communication in the event of the Regent's forces
driving the Miguelites from Minho and Tras os Montes,
it will occupy a line from Leiria to Santarem, much as
you proposed, with an advance guard at Thomar. In
almost every detail, therefore, Sir William has adopted
your design, and he asks me to assure you that he is

*most conscious of it. I do believe this will mean an end
to your animadversion, for he is sure to write in these
terms to the Horse Guards.*

 *The second matter on which I write is one of some
delicacy too, although a different kind. I have resolved
to end my state of bachelorhood, and if Isabella
Delgado returns a favourable reply to my offer of
marriage then it will be ended sooner instead of later. I
confess to you – and here, perhaps, I am able to confess
more than I might were we to speak together – I confess
that I have formed a most ardent affection for her. She
is, without doubt, the most admirable woman of my
entire acquaintance, and I pray that she will judge my
circumstances to be to her favour. I go tomorrow to
Belem, and you will wish me every good wish, for you, I
know, hold her in the highest regard also. My one regret
is that I did not press my suit all those years ago when
first we made the acquaintance of the baron, but then
circumstances were hardly to my favour, whereas now a
colonel instead of a cornet asks his daughter's hand . . .*

Hervey laid down the letter, his hand trembling.
Favourable circumstances indeed! Lieutenant-colonel, with
a colonel's brevet – and more promotion to come, no doubt.
What would Isabella's reply be? What *should* it be, for her
daughter had no father, and she no husband?

He sat down heavily in an armchair. What did *he* offer?
Captain, a major's brevet, and the prospect of a court martial
that might end in cashiering. He did not even have the *right*
to propose, let alone contest so favourable an offer as
Laming's – his friend of nigh on twenty years, the man who
had risked everything to rescue him from Badajoz, and who
even now was working for his deliverance from an injustice.
It would be the basest thing, would it not?

Despite Johnson's coaxing, Hervey lapsed into a long silence. In his resolution to put his affairs in order, and to 'lead a new life', he had allowed himself to imagine that Isabella Delgado might somehow play a part in it. Indeed, in the hours before his release he had begun to imagine her playing a very decided part. She would be mother to his daughter (she was loving and well practised in motherhood already); she would be an agreeable companion in every way (and, he imagined, a zealous lover); and she would be his strength through the public degradation that would follow from the Horse Guards' discipline.

She would be none of these, now, and he could see no prospect of any other who would take her place.

CHAPTER TWENTY-SIX
A GRAND OLD DUKE

Gravesend, 13 January 1827

Hervey came down the gangway of the steam packet into the bustle of the Peninsula quay and began making his way through the crowd of hawkers and porters to the Duke of York Inn, where he intended buying a ticket on the first mail to London. As he rounded the corner into the high street, he stopped sharp in his tracks. The inn sign was draped in black.

'The Duke of York, is he dead?' he asked one of the ostlers in the forecourt.

'Ay, sir. A week ago and more. Dead, but not yet buried!' The man might have been surprised by the enquiry had not Hervey been so evidently new-arrived in the country.

'Not yet buried?'

The man smiled dryly. 'They says as they can't bury 'im since they can't find enough sodjers!'

Not enough soldiers! Hervey shook his head in despair. But then, was hardly surprised when the country had had to send a battalion of Guards to Lisbon, and call on the garrison at Gibraltar too. England was at peace, but she hadn't enough soldiers to send to Portugal *and* to bury a field marshal! But what should he care? Was the commander-in-chief's demise not a merciful release for them all? He may have been 'the soldier's friend', but the army was not prospering. And it might mean – *might* – that the convening order for his court martial would be rescinded. An ignoble thought, he chided himself: a field marshal was a field marshal.

But what, in truth, *did* he care now? He cared, certainly, about being cashiered! He would be defiant if it did come to defending his actions, but a court martial would find against him if that was what the convening officer wanted. It was the way. He could not count on a last-minute surrender to conscience and honour, as had happened at Badajoz (if that had indeed been the impulse for Cornet Daly's action). At best he might hope for a commission elsewhere – black infantry in the tropics, perhaps, the white man's grave. He could not afford to go on half pay; that was certain. Would that be the court's offer – the fever colonies or the Inactive List? He shuddered at the thought. And would Isabella Delgado have come with him, if she had accepted his offer of marriage? Would her father, the baron, have permitted it? No father ought to! How could he have even contemplated asking her, or taking Georgiana?

He shuddered again. He shuddered at the disarray which was his life, things more disordered than ever – and only a fortnight ago he had been full of resolution to put all to right! A black-draped name was a powerful *memento mori*: he did not have for ever to master his life. *Memento vivere* had been Cornet Laming's dictum all those years ago, and *Colonel* Laming was certainly grasping life to advantage now! Hervey knew his duty (or thought he knew) – to family and to those he counted his friends (which in a sense included every man of the regiment). And to himself, too: duty was not a matter of mere abasement. That, however, was the order of his priorities now, and he must keep it thus until he could truly declare his affairs in order.

Nothing was possible, however, unless the charges

against him failed. *That* was his immediate objective; the rest might then just follow.

He managed to get an outside seat on the three o'clock up-mail, and settled as best he could for the four-hour journey to the General Post Office in Lombard Street, his thoughts on nothing but the tactics of his grand, improving design. When he arrived, and had himself and his travelling baggage transferred to the United Service Club in Charles Street, he wrote at once to Lord John Howard and sent the letter by messenger to White's Club. By return he received a reply saying that Howard was dining with Lord Palmerston and would be pleased if he would come at nine.

Hervey bathed and put on undress, leaving the United Service on foot at ten minutes to nine, and reaching St James's Street as the watchmen were calling the hour. Inside, he was shown to a small ante-room, where, ten minutes later, Lord John Howard and his party came, all wearing mourning bands, including Lord Palmerston.

Palmerston, though seven years his senior and Secretary at War for almost twenty, had to Hervey all the appearance of a blade, of a man not yet tired of the diversions of mess, dance or field. He was tall and uncommonly handsome, even by the standards of the army's fashionables, and there was something about his eyes that spoke of a certain way-wardness, as well as of high intellect. Hervey could not help but warm to him at once. He knew right enough of the quarrels and petty jealousies that had subsisted between the Horse Guards and the War Office, but he imagined that the fault lay at least half-way with the Duke of York, for it could not have been easy for the old field marshal to defer to an independent-minded and brilliant young politician – all be he a Tory one.

Palmerston nodded upon Lord John Howard's introduction, and with an easy expression. 'You are well, I trust, in spite of your ordeal?'

Hervey knew he should not have been surprised by the Secretary at War's knowledge of his 'ordeal', yet he had not actually imagined his name spoken of in Whitehall, certainly not outside the Horse Guards.

'Perfectly well, sir.'

Palmerston saw his confusion, and enjoyed the tease. 'I have been very well informed of events. You have most zealous friends at court.'

Hervey glanced at Lord John Howard, who shook his head, denying the honours.

'Lady Katherine Greville has been a most assiduous agent, Major Hervey. I believe I may have learned as much from her as from any official source.'

Hervey coloured slightly. Lord John Howard smiled.

'Do sit down,' said Palmerston, as he perched on the arm of a chair.

Hervey was, indeed, wholly taken aback by the revelation of Kat's unimagined intervention. Did he owe, therefore, these benevolent circumstances to her? He could only wonder at the change in them. On the Gravesend coach he could imagine only a frosty interview with the adjutant-general at the Horse Guards.

'Tell me first' – Hervey's ears pricked at 'first', the promise there would be more – 'how were the troops received at Lisbon?'

'I did not see them arrive, Lord Palmerston, for I was at the frontier as they did so, but what little I was able to observe on return was perhaps disappointing. There was something of a sullenness, I should say, though that may well have been as much a reflection of the unhappy situation in Portugal as of anything else.'

'But no flags were put out for us, so to speak?'

'I would say not.'

Palmerston nodded thoughtfully. 'Mm. But few of us expected any different. These things are never quite as ambassadors' eloquent entreaties have it. Well, Major Hervey, I am sorry not to be able to examine you more on the expedition, but the House sits late this evening and I am required there directly. However, I would know one thing. In your happy escape, was any countryman of ours left for dead?'

'No.'

Lord Palmerston inclined his head. 'You are certain of it?'

'Yes. A Portuguese officer was killed, no other.'

Lord Palmerston turned to Lord John Howard.

'Colonel Norris's despatch spoke of a corporal, Hervey,' said his friend.

Hervey was at once angered. 'My covering corporal was lost for a day after he made his escape jumping into a river, but he is perfectly well, and on his way to Hounslow barracks as we speak.'

Lord Palmerston looked at him intently. 'I am relieved to hear it. It would not serve to have a soldier killed by the Spaniards. It would give rise to a very proper indignation.' He rose.

The rest of the party followed, Hervey wondering where might be this indignation (the death of a soldier was not usually cause for much notice).

'On the basis of what you have informed me, Major Hervey, I shall issue instructions to rescind the convening order for general court martial.'

Hervey bowed. 'I am very much obliged, Lord Palmerston.'

'Very well, I hope there may be opportunity to speak further with you on the situation in Portugal, but for the present I bid you good evening.'

Hervey bowed again. 'Goodnight, Lord Palmerston.'

Lord John Howard motioned him to wait as he accompanied the Secretary at War to his carriage.

When he returned it was with a distinctly breezy air. 'Hervey, it is uncommonly good to see you! What an affair it has all been; I was very glad to have your account of it. Norris has been writing in vitriol. But he's a fool. He doesn't understand there could be communication other than official.'

'But he was the Duke of Wellington's man,' replied Hervey, eyebrows raised. 'It is very strange.'

'I cannot explain it, but so is Sir William Clinton the duke's man. And his despatches have not been favourable in regard to Norris's mission, I assure you.'

Hervey accepted a second glass of champagne, though his stomach was very empty.

'In truth, the Duke of York was vexed by the whole enterprise. He was set against sending troops in the first instance, as at heart was the Duke of Wellington.'

'The duke *will* be commander-in-chief?'

Howard raised his hands. 'There are all sorts of rumours. The King is supposed to be of a mind that he himself should be, or failing that the Duke of Cambridge.'

Hervey's jaw dropped.

'I know, the notion is absurd. They are rumours, that is all. Nothing is decided.'

'But how, then, may Palmerston give instructions to the Horse Guards in respect of me?'

Howard sat back. 'Ah, perhaps I should have explained. Until the King appoints a new commander-in-chief, the Secretary at War assumes the position.'

'That is very singular.'

'Yes. I think no one was more surprised to discover it than Palmerston himself.' He smiled. 'But he is greatly diverted by it.'

'*I* am only surprised he should be acquainted with so

trivial a thing as a major's court martial, let alone that he should presume to act so decidedly in the matter.'

'Oh, I would not say it was trivial, not in the circumstances – sending troops to Lisbon, I mean. Palmerston works prodigiously hard, too, for all his casual air. And *The Times* has it, of course. Portugal is of great moment, indeed.' He smiled again. 'Nor would I underestimate the influence of Lady Katherine Greville.'

Hervey shifted uncomfortably. 'Just so.' He wondered who else Kat had written to. These things could not always work to his advantage.

'And I think, in a month or so, when we are coming out of mourning, I shall ask you to dine here with Palmerston. He may have no prospects in government, but I would not say he will be without influence.'

Hervey nodded politely. He would not be too fastidious if it were to bring him a little favour. 'If Palmerston *does* rescind the convening order, shall that decision be final do you think?'

Lord John Howard pondered the question. 'The warrant bore the late Duke's signature: he insisted on signing everything to the last, as if to show he retained his faculties. The adjutant-general had already ordered the warrant be held in abeyance until the new commander-in-chief took office. If it is Wellington, I think you may be assured you will have heard the last of it. If it is Cambridge, then I believe the warrant might go forward, for he would not likely contradict his late brother. There again, if Palmerston dismisses the charges quickly, then I do not see by what instrument they *could* come before the Duke.' He sat forward again, as if to reassure. 'But it would be by no means certain that a prosecution would succeed. Not from the papers which I have seen.'

'The humiliation would be the same!'

'Oh, come, Hervey! Half the country, at least, would consider you hero! *Does*, I should say.'

Hervey started. 'What do you mean?'

Howard saw that he had presumed too much. 'Then you have not seen *The Times*?'

'No!'

'Two days ago.'

'Did it say I was made prisoner?'

'Yes.'

Hervey sprang up. 'I must send an express. May I do so from here?'

'Of course. To where?'

'To Wiltshire, naturally!'

At breakfast the following morning, Hervey received a message from Lieutenant-General Lord George Irvine, colonel of the 6th Light Dragoons, wishing him to call at once at Berkeley Square. He therefore adjourned his scrutiny of the morning newspapers to the United Service's hairdresser, and an hour later, at ten-thirty, presented himself at Lord George's London house, expecting censure and worse, and an invitation to contemplate service in another corps. In his choppy progress to Gravesend, and his cold but more agreeable one to London, he had not thought of this possibility, that his own colonel would request his resignation. He should have, and as he walked to Berkeley Square he could not imagine why he had not, for although the most public humiliation would come from the Horse Guards, even official absolution from that quarter might not be enough as far as regimental propriety was concerned. He had not imagined that Lord George Irvine would know of matters at this time, but he ought to have, for as soon as a convening order for a court martial was signed the business would have been as good as gazetted. He believed that Lord George held him in high regard: Spain and Portugal, and then Waterloo, were trials not shared by many. But the colonel of a regiment could afford no excess of sentiment, and only a very little favouritism.

Hervey pulled at the bell, resolutely. He was grateful that he did not have to knock, for it would have sounded all too much like the fateful summons.

He had to wait several minutes, which he did with perfect patience, if not ease, before a footman opened the door (it was morning, after all, when footmen had other duties but to wait to receive visitors). But the delay proved a happy one, for when he was at last admitted, Lord George Irvine was standing at the door of his library, and the warm delight in his expression told him at once that whatever might be required of him it would be with the greatest civility.

'My dear Hervey! How very good it is to see you!' he called, advancing with his hand held out.

Hervey bowed as he took it. 'Good morning, Colonel.'

A footman removed his surcoat, and Lord George ushered him into his library. 'It's deuced cold, Hervey; as bad as anything I recall in Spain. Sit ye down by that fire. We shall have coffee directly.'

The bookshelves were extensive, there were portraits of Lord George's long ancestry on the fashionably striped walls, and the furniture was both practical and elegant. Here, Hervey saw, was the library of a man of affairs and of society, a senior lieutenant-general, and a member of parliament. Above all, however, Lord George was pater-familias of the 6th Light Dragoons, and he still looked the active cavalryman – lean, vigorous, strong. Hervey was warmed as much by his hale manner as by the fire beneath the graceful carrera chimneypiece – as if he were at home in Wiltshire. It had been quite five times colder in Spain on more occasions than he cared to remember, but Lord George's cheery dismissal of the memory of those days seemed to speak volumes for his disposition towards him now. Nevertheless, he took his seat near the flames with some apprehension, as well as gratitude: it was still deuced cold out (exactly as he had told Johnson that it would be).

'Now, I am glad you are come so soon. I know you arrived only yesterday, so there is no need of explanation. I expected to receive your card today, but I wanted to see you at the first opportunity. I've to leave for the north in a day or so.'

The footman brought coffee.

Lord George did not wait for him to retire. 'Now, I have it all, I believe, from that admirable John Howard, and I have had occasion to visit with Bathurst, who is always a staunch ally in such matters, and he has shown me what the ambassador in Lisbon has written. And, of course, we have *The Times* to give us a faithful and full account.' He smiled. 'It appears to me that you did everything I would have expected of an officer, especially one who finds himself under an ass of a staff colonel.'

Hervey breathed a deep sigh of relief, as much surprised as gratified by the candour. Lord George had relinquished executive command of the regiment soon after Waterloo, and had only lately assumed the colonelcy; their dealings hitherto had been those of commanding officer and cornet. 'Thank you, Colonel. I learned but last night that there was a notice of my detention at Badajoz in *The Times*.'

Lord George huffed. 'A notice of little consequence! It was without the usual rhetoric. But I *am* assured that no ill came to any man?'

Hervey steeled himself to the explanation. 'John Howard would, I'm sure, have spoken from the deposition I made in Lisbon. A Spanish officer was killed during the escape, and a loyal Portuguese officer. I believe it was reported – and by the Spanish authorities too – that one other of our number was killed, by which I presume was meant my covering corporal.'

Lord George's ears pricked.

'He leapt his horse from the bridge across the Guadiana. We managed to cut our way through the Spaniards – they were not the best of men – but it was soon dark and we were unable to find him. The Spaniards turned out the garrison to search up and down the bank, and the Miguelites as well. We had the devil of a job evading them. But he was unhurt, and the horse too, and they made their way back to Elvas the day following. He's the most excellent fellow – as fine, I think, as was Serjeant Strange.' He presumed Lord George would need no reminding.

'Hareph Strange? Excellent man indeed.' Lord George needed no reminding. Nor that the death of Hervey's covering corporal would have mirrored the circumstances of Serjeant Strange's. 'What happened to his widow? Something of a gentlewoman, was she not? You made arrangements in that regard, as I recollect.'

'She is mistress of my father's school in Wiltshire, Colonel.'

'Ah yes, admirable.' He lapsed into thought again. '*Hareph*: queer name. I don't believe I ever heard its like. Abraham's tribe, I suppose? Strange was a preacher, was he not?'

'The descendants of Judah, Colonel,' replied Hervey, only grateful that the long hours in his father's pews could have such practical benefit. 'Strange's people were Baptists. It was Mrs Strange's father who was the minister.'

'I compliment you on your recall.' Lord George looked into his coffee cup, which was empty. 'But we digress. I hear you met Palmerston last night.'

'I did, Colonel. He told me he would rescind the court martial order.'

'Capital! Capital indeed! It had been my intention to call on Wellington today.' The footman returned and began refilling their cups. Lord George took another sip, and then

374

placed his down very decidedly. 'Hervey, I may say that I would be obliged if you rejoined the regiment at Hounslow as soon as may be. There's no lieutenant-colonel appointed yet, as doubtless you know. Neither do I see any prospect this side of three months, for even if Wellington is in the Horse Guards the day after the funeral, he won't have opportunity to approve the command lists for weeks. Strickland holds the reins meanwhile, and damned fine he holds them too.'

It was of the greatest moment to Hervey who would be the next lieutenant-colonel, yet warm though the interview was, he did not think it apt to press Lord George to an opinion. 'I shall go there this day, Colonel.'

Lord George shook his head. 'No, no, there is no cause for that. I should want you to take your ease in London for the week. Give the regiment time to learn that all is well.'

Hervey saw how the business must have preoccupied him, despite his air of unconcern. 'Very good, Colonel.'

Lord George brightened. 'And I would have you join us this evening at dinner if you are not engaged.'

'I am not engaged, Colonel.'

'Capital!' he replied, rising. 'Strickland will be dining, too. It will be an admirable opportunity for the two of you.'

Hervey was entirely diverted by the prospect. 'Indeed, Colonel.'

'Then I shall take my leave, since Mr Canning addresses the House at midday, and I would hear him.'

Hervey prayed that Lord George would hear nothing that might incline him to a change of mind. He could scarcely credit the rapid improvement in his fortunes, and it was all down to the influence of men of rank and position. True, they would not have been inclined to angle in his favour had they no regard for him – his stock had stood high in the regiment for a long time – but it served to remind how precarious was the matter of advancement when there was no enemy to decide these things.

As he left Berkeley Square, he felt the clouds of the past month rolling back. Now he would be able to turn his attention to the promises and resolutions he had made in Badajoz.

CHAPTER TWENTY-SEVEN
A FAMILY REGIMENT

That evening

Dinner was at eight, on account of the late sitting of parliament. Hervey arrived promptly at seven forty-five, the first of the Irvines' guests. Lady George greeted him as cordially as had her husband that morning, as an old friend, without the circumspection imposed by rank, and very slightly maternal. She had not seen him in half a dozen years – or was it more, she asked – but in the regiment these things did not matter: the years fell away, allowing the fellowship to be renewed immediately, as if there had been no interruption. Hervey felt the comfortable sense of permanence, a distinct homecoming. There was champagne, well chilled despite the bitter cold outside, and a hot punch. He was at once in exceptional spirits.

'So tell me, Major Hervey, how is your daughter?'

Cheery though the enquiry was, Hervey felt awkward addressing it. 'I confess I have not seen her in some months, Lady George, though I know her to be generally in good health. My sister has charge of her. I don't think you ever met.'

'No, I don't believe we did. How old is your daughter now – what is her name?'

'Georgiana, ma'am. She is . . . she will be nine years in but a few weeks.'

'She is very fortunate, then, in having an aunt as governess.'

'I think so too, ma'am.' But he was less certain that his sister might be counted fortunate, though doubtless to someone of Lady George's age and circle Elizabeth was as perfectly engaged as may be in the event of not having secured a husband.

His hostess's eye was caught by the arrival of the second guest. 'Ah, Lady Lankester it must be!'

Hervey turned. It was almost a year exactly since he had last seen her. Then she had been in mourning weeds, the newly married, newly widowed wife of Lieutenant-Colonel Sir Ivo Lankester, lately commanding officer of the 6th Light Dragoons, killed in the assault on the fortress of Bhurtpore. It had been a painful meeting, Eustace Joynson, acting in command, and the squadron leaders calling at the Governor-General's residence in Calcutta, where Lady Lankester lodged, to pay their respects. *More* than to pay respects, indeed: it had been to make her acquaintance, for Sir Ivo had returned with his bride after the regiment had marched for Bhurtpore. *Salve et salvete*: could anything be more cruel? And Lady Lankester had been with child, Sir Ivo's heir. Or was the child female? He ought perhaps to have known. He was not sure, even, if an unborn male *was* the heir. To whom did the baronetcy descend? He chided himself. What did these things matter? What mattered was the health of mother and child. The thought was suddenly painful, but then he braced himself for the formalities, allowing his mouth to describe a smile.

'Lady Lankester, do you know Major Hervey?'

Lady Lankester did not so much smile as maintain the pleasant countenance she had had for her hostess. 'We have met, Lady George, briefly, in India.' She lowered her head, the merest bow.

Hervey was grateful for no more formal a greeting (it

would have placed them back in the Calcutta drawing room). Sir Ivo's widow looked very much as he remembered her, but in a dress of dark blue watered silk instead of widow's lace. She was a woman of considerable, if aloof, beauty, and marked self-possession. He bowed by return. 'I am very glad to be reacquainted, ma'am.'

Lady George laid a hand to Lady Lankester's arm. 'My dear, I would know your name, if you please,' she said, in an even more maternal fashion.

Lady Lankester smiled, not full, but appreciative nevertheless. 'It is Kezia, ma'am.'

'Oh, how delightful! And unusual. Is it family?'

'The Bible, Lady George.'

'Major Hervey would be able to say precisely where,' Lord George suggested.

'Indeed, Major Hervey?'

Hervey smiled, almost apologetic. 'I have sat beneath my father's pulpit these many years, ma'am.'

'And do you know precisely where is this singular name to be found?'

He glanced at its bearer. 'I believe . . . in the Book of Job.'

'Is he correct, my dear?' asked Lady George, reflecting Hervey's smile.

'He is.' Lady Lankester smiled, although not with her eyes.

Hervey supposed she was not completely out of mourning, despite the blue silk. How *could* she be, indeed?

He observed that she had attended to her appearance carefully, nevertheless. Her skin was fair, she had applied a blushing rouge, and her lips, though thinner than Kat's, shone in the way that hers did. Her hair did not look as full as Kat's, either, but he thought it might just appear so on account of its colour, which was as fair as he had seen in many a year (in Calcutta her hair had been concealed under a mourning cap).

Lady George's interrogation was halted by the arrival of two members of parliament and their ladies, then the general officer commanding the London District and his lady, the Bishop of Oxford, the dowager Lady — (Hervey did not catch her name) and her niece, a plain-looking girl, and diffident, whom Hervey supposed he would have to sit next to at dinner. Then finally, at ten minutes past eight, came Major Benedict Strickland, acting commanding officer of the 6th Light Dragoons.

'I am most fearfully sorry, Colonel,' he began. 'And *Lady* George. I was not let go from Windsor until past five. We fairly had to gallop for it, and there was a deuce of a fog.'

'I am sorry the regiment's officers are detained in the afternoon,' replied Lord George. 'Even on such matters.' He turned to the general officer commanding the London District. 'Is the date now fixed?'

'It is: the twentieth.'

He turned back to Strickland. 'And what duties shall the regiment have?'

'All dismounted, Colonel, standing duty for the Guards.'

Lord George shook his head as he looked at the two members of parliament. 'It astonishes me how rapidly that great machine we had at Waterloo has been dismantled!'

The sentiment was shared by all the males present. The dowager Lady — complained that soon there would be too few soldiers to keep the Catholics from her door (by which Hervey understood she had estate in Ireland), and now that the Duke of York was dead there would be 'no one to gainsay the wretched Emancipators'.

Hervey said nothing, and prayed he would not be seated next to her, either.

In fact, Hervey was very agreeably placed at dinner. On his right was the wife of the Honourable and Gallant Member for North Elmham, a constituency in not too great need of reform, and she was an easy interlocutor, principally upon the subject of Greek independence, of which she seemed to know a good deal. Their conversation was without interruption until the entrées, when convention required that Hervey turn to the place on his left.

In the best part of twenty minutes, he had been unable to think how he might adequately begin. 'Lady Lankester, may I enquire of your situation?'

He cursed himself for the ambiguity. But Lady Lankester was an intelligent woman and, as he had observed on first acquaintance, as well as again this evening, remarkably self-possessed for someone ten years his junior (as he understood from the Calcutta drawing rooms).

'Both my daughter and I are well, Major Hervey. And for the moment we are living in Hertfordshire.'

The Lankester estate he knew to be in that county. 'My congratulations, ma'am, on the birth of your daughter. When was it, may I enquire?' In truth he had no interest whatsoever in the answer, but he fancied it was a safe line – except, he now realized, her condition being what it had been in Calcutta, she could not have sailed for home at once without some peril.

'June.'

She said it with some finality, so that Hervey found himself without a sequential question or remark, and much to his dismay. However, she appeared then to make a decided effort, even turning a little towards him.

'June: I never thought anything so hot as then, the air so heavy. And then the monsoon – such a great relief when it came. I confess I was very afraid of the fever and all the other pestilences. Not so much for myself as . . . I suppose you became used to it, Major Hervey?'

They were speaking of the weather, he observed, but she did so easily, and he enjoyed her apparent engagement. 'I suppose we did, though the time *before* the monsoon tried us sorely too. The horses bore it surprisingly well. When did you return?'

'We sailed in July, towards the middle. The sea air was most wonderfully welcome.'

Passage to and from the Indies was a subject on which Hervey felt assured. 'You did not encounter too many storms, I trust? The worst, I think, would have passed by then.'

'Only once, off Madagascar. For the rest we had pleasant sailing, even in the Atlantic, and very fair winds. We made a fast time, only a little over sixteen weeks.'

'*Very* fast, I should say. Ours was twenty-two! But that was rather earlier in the year.'

Lady Lankester picked up her wineglass and turned from him to take a sip. 'But I understand that *you* have a daughter, Major Hervey?'

He was surprised by her knowing. 'I do, Lady Lankester, though I own she has never taken so long a cruise.'

'She has a governess, I presume. Does she then not live with you?'

Hervey felt the merest challenge. He answered cautiously. 'My sister is guardian, and so far, I have not thought my postings suitable for them to accompany me.' As he said it, he realized that it might imply disapproval of her own intrepidity – the very furthest from his mind. Indeed, he had always admired the willingness of Sir Ivo's bride to risk herself in the Indies. And he had admired her husband equally in this regard, for a man of his means and station frequently sold out of a regiment on posting abroad and paid twice the sum to take up the same appointment in one on the home establishment.

But he need not have feared. Lady Lankester took no offence. 'Perhaps, when she is a little older, your postings may be more conducive. How old is she now, Major Hervey?'

'Nine . . . *rising* nine.'

'What a delight she must be to you.'

Lady Lankester did not smile, her remark almost mechanical; but Hervey did not notice. Speaking of Georgiana he never found easy – the feelings of guilt and regret, and great sadness still. Instead he was concentrating hard on his responses. 'Oh, yes, indeed, ma'am.' He took a sip of his wine by way of reprieve. 'May I ask what brings you to London?'

'I was about to ask you the same, Major Hervey,' she replied, this time with a warming smile.

'I, ma'am? I am just returned from Portugal. I had business with the Horse Guards. I return to the regiment in a week or so. They are at Hounslow, as you may know.'

'No, I did not know. I thought them somewhere in Sussex.'

'That was where we formed a depot for India. And you are in London . . . ?'

'My father was to have attended a levee, and I accompanied him. My mother is presently in Devon visiting my grandmother.'

'And shall you remain long . . . now that the court is in mourning, I mean?'

She smiled again. 'Two or three weeks, perhaps. My father was glad of respite: his birds have not obliged him much this season!'

Hervey was intrigued by the change in his table companion in the space of an hour. When they had been introduced he had observed a stiffness, a remoteness, as if she were of a world very distant from his own. Henrietta had never been stiff or remote, even during the years of waiting, when he fancied she thought him but a dull country son without the refinements of high society. Henrietta had teased him with mock haughtiness, and when they had met again, after an absence of seven years, she had teased him greater still, until he had been man enough to defy her and declare his passion. Then she had returned it, and it had grown ever stronger during the brief span of their marriage. But Kezia Lankester he did not imagine was of the same fire. Perhaps it was her situation as widow and mother; perhaps it was her position (the county gentry frequently had a more elevated view of it than did the Whiggish nobles). Perhaps it was nothing at all. Perhaps he himself had been absent from English society for too long. Was not Lady Lankester smiling easily now, and making jokes at her father's expense? He *had* been away too long: Kezia Lankester was a fine woman. She had enchanted Sir Ivo Lankester, and that was recommendation enough.

When the ladies had withdrawn, there was a quarter of an hour's conversation – mainly on the Corn Law bill and who would be next commander-in-chief – and then, when the gentlemen in their turn withdrew, Strickland took Hervey to one side, the first opportunity of the evening.

'It is very good to see you, Hervey. What a trial it must all have been. I am grateful for your communicating with my sister; she writes that you managed to visit twice.'

'I wish it had been more, I assure you. Your sister was the most engaging of company, and the convent a pleasant place. I'm sorry not to have been able to carry back any correspondence, but my last days in Lisbon were . . . shall I say, *constrained*.'

'Quite. Think nothing of it. Now see here, when do you return to Hounslow? I should be much obliged for your support.'

Hervey shook his head. 'My dear Strickland, I should return tomorrow were it my decision. Lord George has told me to take leave for one week. He wishes the business of the court martial to be settled. Settled publicly, as it were.'

Strickland nodded. 'I can see his reasoning, though I think it not necessary. However, if I may count on your coming in a week's time then I am content. The Duke of York's funeral will be over, and there's much to do before the season's drills.'

'You may count on it.'

Strickland drained his glass and looked left and right before beginning again, his voice lowered. 'I tell you, I shall be deuced glad when this funeral is done. There isn't a moment's peace between the castle and the Horse Guards. I didn't think I would be able to attend in time this evening. I shan't stay long, forgive me. The weather's damnable.'

'I have a short walk only, I'm glad to say.'

Strickland took a glass of brandy and seltzer from a footman's tray, and lowered his voice another degree. 'What did you make of the widow Lankester?'

Hervey glanced at the door. 'I was thinking how very different things were since the meeting in Calcutta. Had you seen her before this evening?'

'Yes, a month ago. I took some of Lankester's effects come up from the depot to her in Hertfordshire. I thought her one of the coldest women I'd ever met – in Calcutta, and the same in Hertfordshire. I'd thought to invite her to dine at Hounslow, but it would be the sorest trial.'

Hervey frowned. Strickland was not given to quick judgement, but . . . 'My dear fellow, considering what she had just learned when we met her in Calcutta it's hardly surprising. And she could not have been long returned when you went to Hertfordshire. I confess I found her agreeable enough. *Very* agreeable.'

'I could understand it, perhaps, if she were my senior, but she's a full ten years younger!'

Hervey smiled. 'I confess I found that fact rather appealing! She warmed very markedly during dinner. Perhaps she is shy. Did you meet her people?'

'Yes, and they were agreeable enough. It took half an hour to drive through their park, and the house was as big as

Blenheim – well, perhaps a little smaller. Sir Delaval Rumsey is of some consequence in that county. But I was not greatly at my ease, I tell you.'

Hervey smiled again. 'Perhaps they smelled the papist!'

Strickland's eyes widened. 'Do not joke of it, Hervey: Emancipation's flushing out Tory bigots faster than a spaniel springs partridges!'

'You will admit, I suppose, she is a very handsome woman?'

'If you like that cold sort of countenance.'

Hervey placed a hand on his old friend's shoulder, his smile turning wry. 'Strickland, I am wondering if you protest too much. You have not been rebuffed, have you?'

Strickland would not take the bait. 'Hervey, mark my words; that is all. And now I think we should attend on our hostess.'

Hervey left Berkeley Square at eleven with Strickland, who was posting back to Hounslow and who took him in his chaise to the United Service Club en route. It was a cold, foggy night, and they both agreed that, whatever the vexations, Calcutta was infinitely to be preferred to London in a month such as this. When Hervey alighted, Strickland was already swaddled in travelling blankets and fortifying himself with brandy. 'One week, Hervey, and then I shall have your best support!'

'You may depend upon it, Strickland,' he replied, raising his hat and smiling at what he saw. 'One week! I bid you goodnight, then!'

Strickland raised his flask, Hervey closed the door, and the chaise pulled away.

Hervey felt strangely invigorated, despite the damp night air. He knew he had drunk too much coffee, but as a rule that was little but a hindrance to sleep. He fancied he had found the company of Lady Lankester really quite agreeable. Despite being ten years his junior she had given every suggestion of being his equal. Sir Ivo must have fancied the same, for he had been his age too, and Hervey did not suppose that such composure as he had seen this evening was acquired in the space of eighteen months – not even with motherhood and widowhood. As he entered the United Service he was turning over in his mind what occasion there might be for further acquaintance.

'A message for you, Major Hervey, sir,' said the hall porter, more than usually sombre in his black-buttoned mourning coat, handing him an envelope.

Hervey recognized the handwriting at once. His stomach churned. 'Thank you, Charles. Is there brandy?'

'The Coffee Room waiter is still there, sir.'

Hervey found a chair between two good oil lamps in the corner of the Coffee Room, ordered his brandy, and opened the letter.

> *Holland-park,*
> *14th January*

My dearest Matthew,

I heard from Lord Palmerston this very day that you are returned and in great good spirits. I am myself returned these several weeks past, for Madeira was not so agreeable as I had supposed, and there is so much to be done here. I have dined with the Duke on three occasions alone, and even with the Duke of Cambridge, though the Court's mourning has moderated such parties of late somewhat. We all wonder who shall be the new Commander in Chief, though it surely must be the Duke, think you not? I greatly hope so, for I have always found his company the most vigorous, and I fancy he is of the same mind as mine. I long to see you

and to hear your news, though I believe I know it in
great part already from Lord P and the Duke. Please
call on me without delay. If you are dining this evening
please come on to Holland-park afterwards, for there is
music and cards until late.

Your ever affectionate Kat

He read the letter a second time. He could only marvel a
Kat's art. In the space of a few lines she had reminded hin
of her intimate connection with the Secretary at War (the
acting commander-in-chief), the Master General of the
Ordnance (the commander-in-chief apparent), and the roya
duke, the only rival to Wellington for the appointment
Could there be any more complete prospectus? And ther
there was the music and cards – the perfect, decorous
invitation to arrive late. Except that Holland Park was no
around the corner, and on a night like this it might be long
past midnight before he arrived – even if he could engage a
carriage.

He rose and went back into the hall. 'Charles, do you
know how may be had one of these hackney cabs?'

'Certainly, sir. At this hour there will be a line of them
just around the corner in Regent's Street. Shall I send for
one, sir?'

Hervey thought deep. 'No, Charles, I . . . I will engage
one myself if need be.'

CHAPTER TWENTY-EIGHT

A NEW ORDER

Next day

Hervey returned to the United Service Club late in the afternoon. The hall porter looked relieved to see him. 'Major Hervey, sir, there is a most urgent letter for you. It came an hour ago. I told the messenger I did not know where you were or at what hour you would return, sir.'

Hervey took it, anxious. If it was not an express it could not be bad news from Wiltshire, but rats were scrambling in his stomach again, and he was certain it must be a reverse in the matter of the court martial. He withdrew from the porter's lodge to the middle of the hall and, expecting little less than the worst, opened the envelope:

> *Berkeley-square*
> *3.30 p.m.*

My dear Hervey,

I should be obliged if you came at once, on a matter of very real urgency.

Geo Irvine.

The rats in his stomach were now racing: the letter was so peremptory. He had been ready for a summons to the Horse Guards, and *that* he could have borne defiantly; but to his colonel, whose judgement in matters of the regimental good was infallible . . .

His head began to swim. Last night things had been so promising. A week's 'quarantine' and he would be back with his troop and all the family of men who bore the numerals 'VI' on their appointments, a family of saints and sinners just as any other, but a place a man could always redeem himself.

He ought to change his clothes before presenting himself to his colonel. But did so imperative a summons allow him the time? He approached the porter's lodge again.

'Charles, I am going to Berkeley Square, to General Irvine's, should any further messages arrive. I will return directly, but I am engaged this evening.'

'Very good, sir. Did you find a cab last night as I indicated, sir?'

'What? Oh . . . yes, I did. Thank you, Charles.'

'Very good, those hackney cabs, all the members say, sir.'

Hervey buttoned his coat and replaced his hat. 'Indeed, yes; quick about the place, very.' He smiled, dutifully, then stepped into the darkening street again.

It took him ten minutes to reach Berkeley Square. It would have taken less at the brisk pace he set, but he had to walk a good way along Regent's Street to find a clean crossing. The door opened almost the instant he rang, and a footman showed him into the library, where the colonel of the 6th Light Dragoons was reading the *London Gazette*.

'Hervey, I am sore relieved you are come,' said Lord George, and sounding every bit as if he meant it. 'I thought perhaps you had gone to Wiltshire.'

Hervey was at once partially relieved – it was perfectly

evident that he was not to suffer summary punishment – yet equally dismayed by Lord George's uncharacteristic discomposure. 'No, Colonel, I have been abroad in London all day, and received your letter but a quarter of an hour ago.'

'Then of course you have not heard?'

He had heard nothing other than from Lady Katherine Greville, and nothing of that would have occasioned his colonel's present state. 'No, sir?'

'Strickland was killed last night.'

Hervey's mouth fell open. '*Killed?*'

'On the King's New Road, not a mile from the Piccadilly bar. It seems his chaise ran full tilt into the Oxford Mail. He was brought to St George's infirmary, which was nearest, I suppose, but by then he was dead.'

Hervey could hardly speak. *Strickland*, who had been through the Peninsula, and Waterloo, and Bhurtpore – dead in a carriage smash on the best road in the country! The haphazard of it all was never so shocking. 'Colonel, I barely know what to say. What would you have me do? Take the news to his people?'

Lord George nodded. 'I have written the letter. I thought to send an express, but it's a damnable way to learn such news. An officer deserves better than that. And you will know his people, I imagine.'

'I could try to catch tonight's Ipswich Mail, but—'

'No, I would that you post with my chariot. I shall delay my return north until after the Duke of York's funeral. If you set out at six in the morning you can be back the evening following.'

'I am certain of it, Colonel.'

Lord George fixed him keenly. 'And then I would have you go at once to Hounslow and take command. I told you yesterday: it will be three months at least before there's a new lieutenant-colonel. And frankly, Hervey, with things the way they are here and abroad, a very great deal of trouble there may be during that time.'

Hervey stood silent. Only days ago he faced court martial; now he was to take command of his regiment. The fortunes of soldiering were ever changing, and rarely predictable – but never so surprising.

A very great deal of trouble there may be during that time: he knew it as well as did Lord George. As a Christian man he would pray for peace in the months ahead, but as an officer with ambition he might hope otherwise.

THE END

The adventures of Matthew Hervey continue in

COMPANY OF SPEARS

now available from Bantam Press

HISTORICAL AFTERNOTE

Lieutenant-General Sir William Clinton's intervention force, which began landing at Lisbon on Christmas Day 1826, comprised four squadrons of cavalry, four companies of artillery, two battalions of Guards, seven battalions of Foot, a company of the Royal Staff Corps (engineers), and a detachment of the Royal Waggon Train – around five thousand men in all – with a naval squadron under command of Nelson's famous flag captain, Rear-Admiral Sir Thomas Masterman Hardy. Meanwhile, the Miguelites had mounted another invasion of the northern provinces of Minho and Tras os Montes, and so in the middle of January 1827 Clinton marched north to the Mondego river – as the Duke of Wellington had almost twenty years before – and with this strong force to underwrite their counter-offensive, loyal Portuguese troops were able to eject the invaders. Then at the end of April, sixteen hundred of the two-thousand-strong garrison at Elvas mutinied, subverted by Miguelites at Badajoz and encouraged by a whole corps of the Spanish army mustered menacingly at the frontier. The mutiny was put down smartly, however, by the fortress commander, the admirable General Caula, and the country began to quieten once more. Clinton was able to withdraw to the area of the old Lines of Torres Vedras, although the fortifications were in a very poor state, and there his force remained until the late summer, when they moved into quarters in Lisbon, Belem and Mafra – all without firing a single shot.

On 20 January 1827, the Duke of York's funeral took place at Windsor. The day was so bitter chill, and the proceedings so prolonged, that several of the mourners succumbed: at least two bishops are said to have died on their way home. The Foreign Secretary, Mr Canning, caught a severe cold which turned to inflammation of the lungs and liver. When in April therefore, after Lord Liverpool died of a stroke, he became Prime Minister, Canning was already a sick man. He lasted only until August, when he too died. Viscount Goderich succeeded him. Goderich, however, could not hold his cabinet together, and resigned the following January, whereupon the Duke of Wellington became Prime Minister. The duke, never having been much of a believer in the Portuguese intervention, and as former commander-in-chief knowing the strain which it placed on the army, soon recalled General Clinton's five thousand. The Miguelites seized power not long after, Dom Pedro brought an army from Brazil, and there began the protracted – but in truth remarkably unbloody – 'War of the Two Brothers'.

The British intervention was testament to the efficacy of a bold and timely foreign policy, but also to the ultimate futility of intervention without the military means to sustain it. Then, as now, the British army simply did not have enough soldiers.

THE GREEK ACROSTIC

Here is a brief explanation of the Greek acrostic used by Matthew Hervey to communicate the password 'Napoleon' to Colonel Laming. Taking the Greek transliteration of Napoleon and removing the initial letter for each subsequent word, the sentence is formed: 'Napoleon, the destroyer of whole cities, was the lion of his people.'

ΝΑΠΟΛΕΩΝ ΑΠΟΛΕΩΝ ΠΟΛΕΩΝ ΟΛΕΩΝ ΛΕΩΝ ΕΩΝ ΩΝ

Written in lower case, with full accents and breathings:

Ναπολέων ἀπολέων πόλεων ὀλέων λέων ἑῶν ὤν

Ναπολέων	transliteration of *Napoleon*, accented on the analogy of Τιμολέων.
ἀπολέων	strictly speaking the future participle of ἀπόλλυμι – *I destroy*, hence *about to destroy*. But future participles are sometimes used with no real future sense; as a participle it ought to be followed by an accusative, but the genitive could be justified on the grounds that the participle has effectively become a noun – *destroyer* (of).
πόλεων	genitive plural of πόλις – *city*.
ὀλέων	a fudge: it should really be ὅλων (feminine genitive plural of ὅλος – *whole*). The ending

395

including an epsilon might be possible as a dialect form, but the word is readily recognizable, and it would be easy to parallel the general phenomenon of variant endings or the assimilation of an ending to that of an adjacent word.

λέων   nominative singular – *lion*.

ἑῶν   masculine genitive plural of ἑός – *his own* (as in Latin, supplying *people* is a very common idiom).

ὤν   present participle of εἰμί – *I am*, hence *being*, but very common as idiom for *is/was*.

I am grateful for the erudition of Dr John Taylor, head of classics at Tonbridge, author of *Greek to GCSE* (Bristol Classical Press/Duckworth) and *New Testament Greek: A Reader* (Cambridge University Press).

Allan Mallinson spent thirty-five years in the British Army, and commanded one of its oldest cavalry regiments. He is the author of *Light Dragoons*, a history of four regiments of British Cavalry, and a regular reviewer for *The Times* and the *Spectator*.

Allan Mallinson's six previous novels featuring Matthew Hervey, *A Close Run Thing*, *The Nizam's Daughters*, *A Regimental Affair*, *A Call to Arms*, *The Sabre's Edge* and *Rumours of War*, are all available in Bantam paperback. *The Sabre's Edge* and *Rumours of War* were *Sunday Times* bestsellers.

He now lives in the Scottish Highlands.

RUMOURS OF WAR
By Allan Mallinson

THE SIXTH GRIPPING MATTHEW HERVEY ADVENTURE

1826: Bonaparte is dead and there is peace in Europe. But in Portugal, the rumour is of civil war following the death of King John VI. With Spain, and perhaps even France, threatening to take sides, England's historic treaty with Portugal is set to be invoked.

Newly returned from India, Matthew Hervey joins a mission sent to assess the situation and lend support to the Portuguese agent. But the Peninsula is redolent with memories. It was there, nearly twenty years earlier, that the young cornet Hervey had his first taste of action when the 6th Light Dragoons played their part in Sir John Moore's defiant stand at Corunna. And as he prepares for battle once more, Hervey finds himself confronting ghosts from his pasts . . .

'I enjoyed the adventure immensely . . . Mallinson's descriptions of what it's like to be on campaign are as compelling, vivid and plausible as in any war novel I've ever read. What gives them the edge is his own experiences as a serving cavalry officer. Inevitably he has a better understanding than most of how it might feel to ride a horse into battle, of military discipline, and of the nature of command'
James Delingpole, *Daily Telegraph*

0 553 81352 8

BANTAM BOOKS

THE SABRE'S EDGE
By Allan Mallinson

MATTHEW HERVEY'S ENTHRALLING ADVENTURE . . .

The year is 1824; the 6th Light Dragoons are still stationed in India and the talk is of war. For the Burmese are becoming ever more bold in their cross-border raids while in Rajputana the rightful claimant to the throne has been usurped by cruel warmonger Durjan Sal. With conflict now looming on two fronts, British troops must intervene.

It seems Durjan Sal has taken refuge in the infamous and purportedly impregnable fortress of Bhurtpore and the trial ahead will test Captain Matthew Hervey and his newly blooded troop to their very limits, their fortunes to be decided by the sabre's edge . . .

'What a hero! What an author! What a book! A joy for the lover of adventure and military buff alike'
Lyn MacDonald, *The Times*

'Splendid . . . the tale is as historically stimulating as it is stirringly exciting'
Andrew Roberts, *Sunday Telegraph*

0 553 81351 X

BANTAM BOOKS

AND NOW READ ALLAN MALLINSON'S THRILLING NEW MATTHEW HERVEY ADVENTURE

COMPANY OF SPEARS

AVAILABLE FROM BANTAM PRESS

All looks set for Major Matthew Hervey: news of a handsome legacy should allow him to purchase command of his beloved regiment, the 6th Light Dragoons. He is resolved to marry, and, rather to his surprise, the object of his affections – the widow of the late Sir Ivo Lankester – has readily consented. But he has reckoned without the opportunism of a fellow officer with ready cash to hand; and before too long, Hervey is on the look-out for a new posting.

Hervey has always been well served by old and loyal friends, however, and Eyre Somervile comes to his aid with the means of promotion: there is need of a man to help reorganise the local forces at the Cape Colony, and in particular to form a new body of horse.

At the Cape, Hervey is at once thrown into frontier skirmishes with the Xhosa and Bushmen, but it is Eyre Somervile's instruction to range deep across the frontier, into the territory of the Zulus, that is his greatest test. Accompanied by the charming, cultured, but dissipated Edward Fairbrother, a black captain from the disbanded Royal African Corps and bastard son of a Jamaican planter, he makes contact with the legendary King Shaka, and thereafter warns Somervile of the danger that the expanding Zulu nation poses to the Cape Colony.

The climax of the novel is the battle of Umtata River (August 1828), in which Hervey has to fight as he has never fought before, and in so doing saves the life of the nephew of one of the Duke of Wellington's closest friends.

0 593 05341 9

BANTAM BOOKS